MAY All your love be of — Hugs,

Cat

Journey

Part I of III

'Tis not so much

the path we take that counts,

What counts,

is how we choose

to travel that path

For more information about Journey, to order bulk
copies, or have comments directed to the author, send
an email to:
catlansamuels@gmail.com

For more information about our books, visit:
www.treborarthurpublishing.com

ISBN: 978-0-9884957-1-5

Covers by David Schoeffler
Edited by Suzanne
Website by Deaf Girl Amy

The Journey series is available on the web, search on:

Journey Catlan Samuels

Part I of III – The Love Story of the Century

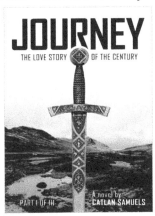

Part II of III – Continuing the Love Story of the Century

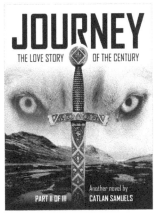

Part III of III

Catlan is amongst the trees
writing the conclusion

For my sons

Brian and Kevin

Follow your dreams and your world will be complete.

You taught me that…and you were right!

But remember – the devil lurks in the details…

Forward

This is about a number of people whose stories come together as one— probably a little like your life. And, as in life, we come across all sorts of people; some we love, others we endure. Hopefully not often with the theatrics suffered here, but sometimes it does feel that way.

Often I am asked, "Where does this take place, what year is it?" It is hard to be exact. Because the place is where you put it, the time is what you need it to be (needless to say, it was a very, very long time ago). There are more clues later on.

Now that may seem like a flip or callous answer, but the movie that runs in your mind is the most powerful one that ever existed; so let go, and be part of the story. Permission granted. But take careful caution, as with any long journey, pay attention to even the most mundane of details, events and people and of all that is around you - it may be important later. Don't say I didn't warn you.

Thanks to the many who encouraged me to continue the quest of our main characters (not mentioned here—it would spoil the fun!). Your input, excitement and critical observations were not only welcome, but vital. The twisted trails they followed have twisted more over time.

And thanks to you, treasured reader, for stopping by. May *your* journey be interesting—one of adventurous travel and destination! This book is a window to my soul—I sincerely hope the window to yours gets opened.

And, if you want to know how all this got started, read the Afterword.

Finished late, one cold and blustery winter night,

Catlan Samuels

'Only in imagination, does every truth find an effective and undeniable existence. Imagination, not invention, is the supreme master of art, as of life.'
Joseph Conrad, 1857-1924, Polish Novelist and Short Story Writer

Acknowledgements

Without the encouragement, advice, prodding and gentle editing of friends, this journey would not have lived to find its twisty bumpy path.

To Pat for your eternal inspiration. You helped me believe, I hope you believe, you have much to believe in!

Allison, you were just perfect. Just very perfect!

Marilyn, my walking partner. When you got excited about the story, it kept me going. Thanks for all the little yellow marks and your continuous effervescence.

Debbie, my horse expert, helped me understand how to make their pain real and the relationships healthy.

Sue, the sunshine in your face is reflected in a few places. Sorry, can't tell you where, at least not here.

Beth, thanks, he made it, and it's a better place now and she thanks you (especially for those few critical words that make so much of a difference).

Paolo, you inspired me, you helped keep me on track and added some important sanity.

Joan, your sincere interest brought smiles to me when I needed them. To you I send a long distance kiss and hug.

To the lady who started it all because you broke my heart, we knew there was a reason we met; hope you are well.

Mr. Schultz, please excuse the liberty I took, but you continue to be an inspiration.

Suzanne, you came, you edited, and you delivered wisdom to the folk of Journey. To you I owe the debt of your magic, your patience and your ability to do honor to our heroes.

Amy, your guidance and patience were just right, well timed and gracious.

Dave, the cover ideas hit home so well, they brought tears to my eyes.

Peg, the 2nd edition edits add so much grace and just a bit of spice in the right places.

To you, treasured reader. Without you this journey is but a wisp of a dream. With you, it is alive and part of the real journey.

To my family, who got to hear all about it, time and again. You know what you are getting for Christmas. Thanks for the understanding.

Some Choice Words

The language you will find as you make your way through Journey is an eclectic mix of (very) old and new. In addition to the highly distinct local vernaculars and dialects you will encounter, many of the more interesting words come from ancient Gaelic and Celtic cultures as well as some highly colorful, yet old-fashioned street slang. Some of the more obscure words are listed below (there are a few that I just made up to fit the story, because it seemed right at the time):

Word	Description
blowdown	An area in the forest where a strong wind pushes down many large trees. It makes for a wide open space, full of logs that over time lose their bark and turn bright white to the elements. It's a great place for animals to find sunshine and play. Any hiker knows of such things. They are places both full of beauty and vivid reminders of nature's ability to be wildly destructive.
chac	Shit. Used a fair amount by folks as an angry slang term.
chinking	Material that goes between logs of a cabin to keep the wind, snow, rain and small animals from getting inside. Most often just clay, but historians have found evidence of crude concrete and mortar in ancient dwellings.
chippering and twerping	Words of my own creation. When you have a woods full of animals, they make noise. This was the noise I could hear. Consider it the music of nature.
dubisary	A thing-a-ma-gig. Just a "watcha call it." No particular meaning other than a reference to something different.

flens	Dick-cheese, a really gross substance that smells bad.
galla	Gaelic street slang term for bitch.
knarfing	Not really a word, it's made up. When I went to see Katie's horse one day, I listened carefully to him chew because I needed to describe horse chewing in part of the story (to honor Samoot who eats like I wish I could). The sound was amazing, and the best way to describe it was with the word "knarfing." I drive my editor nuts sometimes ☺
Knull, knullare	Gaelic slang for non-romantic intercourse (as in just doing it, but not rape), or a nasty (almost savage) and demeaning insult.
kuk, crann	Penis
plucsh	After having spent years in the woods listening to the leaves fall in autumn, this is the best word I could come up with to describe the sound of millions of them landing all around.
snarfling	The sound wolves make when talking quietly amongst themselves (yes, I made it up).
snow snogs	Snow shoes. Bent braches tied with rawhide strips.
tiadhan	Gaelic term for a man's testicle. Not sure or bothered by whether it's plural or not, since the times to use such a word are usually painful or filled with negative emotion.

Some Framing & Characters

For early readers of Part I manuscripts, a character synopsis was added and they loved it; so here is a quick overview of each of our friends (the order of the introductions is on purpose, since each of the characters builds on the other). The order of the characters is simply to show the genealogy from a timeline perspective. You may want to read the descriptions now, or wait until you run into each person, and then read up on them. It's your choice.

The Time and the Land...

The story of Journey begins, as Part I states, *"a long time ago; before the mountains were fully tall and the seas very salty."* The place is actually a northern hemisphere environment with a very ancient Celtic/Gaelic flavor to it, probably not too far from the Arctic Circle. The time? Well, it will become more evident as you read; just suffice to say it was an extremely long time ago (before mathematics, before writing, before clocks, before lots of things...).

This tale is built on what is currently a commonly held truth, or could be myth (but the author feels after considerable research and conjecture, the story is of probable reality). It is a story of such vast proportions and long term dire consequences that the very roots of civilization as we know it would change if it became common knowledge.

As it is told, a great civilization grew up in the north of what we now know as Europe; one that built and held dear, many centuries before, the kind of culture and freedoms we enjoy today. The people lived and protected the same ideologies as modern society and had the same passion for what is right in the due course of what we see as the natural right to the pursuit of happiness.

Their story however, ends on a sad note. As it is told today, the story states that these smart and advanced people did everything right except develop the written word. So in the end, they could never spread their ideas, save their history and share their ideology. They are, as is the common thought amongst historians on much of a worldwide basis, "lost." Their whole way of thinking was lost with the demise of their society when they were conquered sometime during the dark ages.

Well maybe that's true, and maybe, just maybe, they had some other way to spread their political theories and version of truth? There are some who say their ideas and way of life was crushed and lost, there are others who feel differently. You may find the truth lies here in this marvelous tale of love and deceit.

And it may cause you to rethink history as we know it. Most definitely, you should rethink the future.

Now the characters...

Valterra & Kaitlyn

They built Journey a very long time ago. What Harold and Karina did not know was that Valterra and Kaitlyn were special in their own land. A land that was unfortunately brutally conquered and they had to escape. If their true powers had been discovered, they most surely would have been forced to use them to hurt others.

You see, Valterra and Kaitlyn were of the city of Troy. Their flaming power was the secret weapon that kept the Greeks at bay for ten long years of war. Not until the Greeks used the Trojan Horse to sneak into the city was anyone in real danger. So when the great city was overrun, Valterra and Kaitlyn escaped via a water tunnel to a ship they had standing by, and sailed north with as many of their fellow Trojans as possible. The story is told that the Trojans were not only mostly blond and redheaded, but were by nature extremely fierce warriors, great engineers and a people of deep passion for justice. So, as the legend goes, they predated the Vikings (and very likely were their predecessors) and built that adventuresome if somewhat brutal culture, so many years ago.

You will meet both Valterra and Kaitlyn and how they got started at Journey. Maybe they were a different sort of Viking?

Harold and Karina

Harold and Karina, are the second set of caretakers at the Journey Inn. Harold and Karina are truly a perfect match for each other. They have been the proprietors of Journey for very many, many winters. Harold is a kind, hard working honest and caring man. Karina runs the kitchen and keeps all who are about the place fed and in order (when necessary).

Normadia

A quiet hardworking lass who has been Karina's ever faithful assistant for oh, so many a winter in the bustling kitchen of the Journey Inn.

Dessa

A true princess, she is the daughter of King Tarmon and Queen Gersemi. Dessa is a tall young woman in her late teens with flowing waves of sturdy red hair, deep blue eyes and a dead on shot with a bow and arrow (even atop a moving horse!). She is smart, nimble and bold (sometimes too bold).

King Tarmon and Queen Gersemi

A wise man, King Tarmon is the father of Dessa. Tarmon inherited the throne from his father, Keegan. Tarmon's wife Queen Gersemi was killed by a pack of wolves early in Tarmon's rein. He was devastated by his loss, but through the urging and understanding of Gale and Sanura, he recovered to lead his people through a time of peace and relative prosperity.

Sanura

Personal maid to Dessa. Sanura is a wise woman from a distant land; she is actually of Greek descent and is part of the family of the Greek hero Odysseus who is purported to have developed the idea of the Trojan Horse.

Quillan (note - his full name is Quillan GianFrachesco)

A big man with red flaming hair. Quiet and steely deep down. Although Quillan seems to be wise, he is actually wise beyond his years for reasons you will have to discover. Probably in his early 20's although seems older.

Torrin

Torrin the prince, the eldest son of King Trebor and Ethelda. As a vibrant and growing young man in his mid teens, he is kind, but a little headstrong (imagine that of a teenage boy?).

King Trebor and Queen Ethelda

Torrin's mother and father. Living high in the hills, this small kingdom is still a bit of a mystery to Journey readers. However, it is Torrin's home. He longs to return. Even though Torrin is the oldest son, for some reason he is not heir to the throne, his sister Gretatia is heir. Torrin would like to find out the real story behind this strange twist from normal royal tradition; it haunts him. Torrin's short stories of his home intrigue us, and the people there seem content and friendly.

Rebecca and Bartoly

These two are intensely in love and make for a picture perfect romantic and creative couple. They live in a well crafted bungalow deep in the woods, hidden from most other living creatures. Bartoly is a smithy and a very good one at that. Rebecca is a very artistic and accomplished potter.

Gaerwn

If you had to define evil with one word, it would be Gaerwn. He is the father of the twins Darius and Haphethus as well as Chadus.
He is a troubled man.

Scraddius

The right hand man and most senior advisor to king Gaerwn. He is an incredibly smart and cunning scoundrel. Scraddius has something in mind for Gaerwn; however, what it is, is not quiet yet clear. Something to remember though, Scraddius is not the kind of person you would want to turn your back on.

The various colorful inhabitants of the Journey Inn...

We periodically get to interact with the mostly transient and interesting folk who make the Journey Inn their home. Some will come and bring with them interesting stories (all true we are told) or deeds of both wisdom and folly. Some will go and we are sorry to see them leave, some we usher out, some we, well, we play with, because they need to be played with (not always in nice ways you see...).

There are some children about, some of the others are old, some young, some with various sorts of ailments or issues. But mostly a vigorous and happy lot of folk.

Ol' Dogger (Dog-er) is the oldest; he has but one good eye and one that wanders (makes for great fun for everyone about half way through a barrel of strong brew, including him!) that makes himself and everybody laugh. No one knows how long he has been at Journey, or what he is up to, but nevertheless, he is a fixture of the place.

Others will come and go within the story...

Just pay attention to the details...

You have been warned...

Enjoy the ride!

Journey

Part I of III

A little background...

As the story goes, in about 1200 BC, the Greeks invaded Troy, and after a long hard battle of many years, the Trojans lost when the Greeks used the Trojan horse to gain entrance to the heavily fortified city.

Many of the Trojan people fled far to the north to start life anew. They were a fierce group of survivors who diligently embedded a strong sense of community and patriotism to their new land.

Alas, these people died off without a trace, leaving behind what historians now consider, through putting the small traces of their world together, to be one of the most advanced civilizations of all time...

Legend has it they were advanced in tool use, building, civic culture, organization and a democratic form of government. Their biggest mistake, according to historians: not recording their history to pass it on to others.

Well, maybe they did...just in a different way...

1.
Beginning

This journey begins a time long ago. So very, very long ago. Before the first Christmas even.

Days where summers are filled with hot, clear sunshine. Winter nights, ghastly cold and stormy. A time before the mountains were fully formed, before the seas were truly salty.

Not many people, as we know them now, (people like you and me) inhabited the earth. You might say the population was considerably sparse. The majority you will meet though are sturdy, caring and happy to be part of this wonderful adventure called life. Some, as you might expect however, are downright nasty, evil people.

The funny thing overall, life seemed somewhat new. Everyone to a degree understood that, although not exactly sure how the pieces all fit together. Even the stories exhorted repeatedly by hearty, smiling, foot weary travelers had a short past. They were good stories. Stories about people whose future could be wonderful.

But that wonderful future would take some work.

This journey starts in two places, or in three, depending on your view. You, careful reader may decide later.

As in any grand, long and wonderful journey of any significance, you may not really know how you got started. It's not like a vacation. It's a journey...

...and now it's your journey!

2.
Trapped

Our prince surely thought that death should feel different. He had always imagined a cool breeze, light music and endless sky. This was somehow wrong. When he opened what he thought should be his eyes, he did not see. But he could feel?

He felt, more than saw, the deep black humid air that enveloped him. He would have been more concerned about not seeing with his eyes fully opened if it was not for the terrible rotting stench and warm soupy mess that enclosed him. It was surrounding him in wet, disgusting, fetid ways. The soup clung like sap to all his body parts, it felt like hot grease soaking and burning into his skin.

Deciding that trying to look around was not a practical thing to do, he closed his eyes tightly. This allowed him to turn his attention to his inner soul to make an attempt to remember who he was and how he might have gotten into what seemed to be a very terrible mess. Whatever this terrible mess was.

Now memory is sometimes a strange and wonderful friend. Friends are want to play tricks on you, because that is what friends sometimes do. And, at this time, our prince and his mind were at odds.

He remembered walking down the wide path from his father's grand castle in the warm, morning air. The contrast from the blustery cold stark night was always interesting and often severe. The sun, shining against his face, had filtered through the thick green leaves of the trees in the always changing patterns of nature's kaleidoscope. The wild animals of the forest had skittered fast away at his approach, searching for the safety of their comfortable and private places. Dust had blown gently from his boots as he trod the familiar path of the forest that surrounded his home.

His memory traced the glad picture of that morning. He had been in search of adventure. In search of life. His carefree quest was for his future, the untold story of today that could bring so much promise.

It came back to him now, the carefree feeling of the search. It had been a wondrous search for the calamity of his creation in the unfolding of life's journey. It had been a marvelous walk, a marvelous morning.

As he relaxed, he felt the rigid tension of his body evaporate. A gentle smile came across his face and he opened his eyes.

Reality came rushing back, like a boulder crashing down the mountain, tearing unsuspecting trees from their place of life. Crushing everything in its path, destroying the serenity and peace of nature to shreds. This hot, rotting black cave made no sense. No sense at all. His mind gave him no clues, no history, no possibilities. He was trapped, he was a prisoner. He felt doomed.

Then the cave started to move. The rotting retched mass that surrounded his body sloshed to each side. The acid air burned his eyes as the inky blackness began to take shape.

He had often experienced the wonder of seeing dim shapes and outlines that formed muted colors when he had walked into the dark after relaxing inside around the warm fire. Now the black around the prince began to turn a dark, ghastly green. Not the friendly natural green of the forest, but a hazy, swampy, greenish mass, like a boiling green fog.

With nothing to hold onto, our prince was helpless. As the green hazy cave moved, he rolled and bounced like a puppet out of control. As if the strings of the puppeteer were playing harsh, brutal games with his limbs. This seemed like a terrible way to die, or even worse, a most horrible way to live.

He began to feel he was faced with a certain wretched, all be it short, future. Or worse—a long one? And with no explanation for his current situation; his very skin starting to burn in a way that felt like demons tearing at his flesh, our prince did the only thing that made sense.

He closed his eyes tight, blocked out his evil surroundings and actually started to think.

Taking stock, his mind began to race. There must be a way to break out. The sides of this rotting, stinking tomb seemed soft. If only he had a tool?

Now, the prince was your standard issue prince and he remembered that he carried his trusty blade. This had been a present from his grandfather; a wise, patient and not unkind man who taught of high standards and pride. A man whom the prince admired, yet was baffled by in certain ways. However, those musings he decided must wait for later.

Reaching down in his hot cramped quarters, our prince grasped the carefully wound hilt of the long blade. Although slippery and almost burning to the touch, there was a comfort in the hard, familiar rippled surface. It was something solid he could hold onto. Finally, there was something he could control in this terrible out-of-control situation that would soon drive him crazy!

Heaving up with both hands, the hilt of the sword smashed against the room of his prison and a loud roar ensued. He sensed rather than felt his world tilt, pick up speed and thunder forward on a steep path to unknown terror. This chamber of horrors that trapped his body seemed to steam up all around him.

With a mighty heave, he plunged the blade upward in a frantic, superhuman slice. The scream that came from his body pulsed in his ears as the world above him opened up and the afternoon sun blinded him completely.

What had been a wildly uncontrollable and maddeningly, frightened world, now stood still.

Slowly, he opened his eyes. Blinking back the bright sunshine, he rolled to one side and shakily got to his knees. What lay before him was startling, astonishing, and now made at least some sense to his jangled, frayed nerves and mostly startled mind.

A huge monster of a dragon, thick and furry, lay dead at his shaking, stinging knees. Four times him in length, twice as wide, and smiling gruesomely in death. The dragon's vacant gaze gnawed at his shaken soul. Rotting chunks of meat spilled out of the wide, gaping gash he had created, and floated upon the cool water of the stream on whose black, sandy bank our prince now kneeled.

He rightly concluded that King Trebor, his father, was not going to believe this.

Dragons were a myth; this could not be happening! Nevertheless, as he continued to take stock the prince noticed a large amount of steam gurgling out of the now deceased head of his captor. This explained the heat! It explained the fumy interior. But it did not explain the large bump on his head.

Fighting a wave of pure nausea, our prince rolled into the clear water and began to frantically clean himself. Only then did he realize the pain in his leg. Just at the top of his thick, leather boot he saw blood fairly squirting out in a red stream mingling harshly with the clear, brisk water.

With great effort, and his teeth firmly clenched, our prince hauled his tortured body to the warm, black sand in the noonday sun. The thought of removing his boot to attend to the spurting gash sent a surge of sheer terror up his spine. But he knew what needed to be done.

Actually, it didn't hurt so much until the boot was off. The gash in his leg was to the bone. The view of the jagged edges of his very own muscle, fat and skin became surreal. Acid from the dragon's innards surreptitiously dripped in the wound, burning him to his very soul. With a powerful leap, he pushed himself deeper into the cleansing cold water.

Stripping naked in the stream, he used the black sand as a pumice to grind off the scourge that had surrounded him, burned him and clung to his every shred of being.

He firmly tied his scarf around his wounded leg. The cold wet fabric felt snug and secure. The throbbing of his head he could deal with. However, standing wet, naked, cold and bleeding in the stream, he felt very vulnerable.

It took a while, but our prince was finally washed - very wet, somewhat cold, but clean. He walked slowly back to the corpse. Having no memory of what had gotten him into such a state, he just stared for a moment, dressed himself in his soggy clothes, and painfully started walking downstream.

He was mindful of the water, mindful of his steps and paying close attention. There might be others, he mused. But he promised himself there would be no more surprises.

He was wrong.

3.
Destination

Walking along, with the pain in his leg ebbing and flowing, the shadows of the day began to grow long. Our prince knew he needed to find shelter and warmth from the oncoming brutally cold night that lay ahead, for it was early spring, and night still harbored winter. He shivered at the thought of the cold wind blowing the nightly snow around him. Every part of his being; clothes, skin, hair and boots were deeply drenched. After escaping the terror of a monster and terror of bleeding to death, the terror of freezing to death loomed real and treacherous.

Educated in the ways of the world, our prince was taught to walk downstream when lost. Eventually you find places where people use the water. That theory now meant the difference between life and a certain cold, shivering, icy death.

As with most mountain streams, as the day wears on, the cold of the surrounding hills rise up icily to take over from the heat of the day. The mountain exhales its frosty breath and the cold rumbles down the hills in silent chaos.

Misty tendrils of cold whispered through the trees and around the thick plants that heartily survived these brutal evenings. Our prince had just about decided to build a hasty lean-to when he heard, at just the top of his ears, a change in the very essence of the sounds of the forest around him. It was subtle, but nonetheless, it was music!

He ran as well as his crucified leg would allow, his wounded head pounding the steps in time with his feet. He ran for all he was worth, knowing it could be far, it could be close, or it could be his tired mind playing cruel tricks. Each step jarred him, the pain shooting up his leg.

The running warmed him. The very nature of the work gave him hope. It made a sharp contrast against the pain and fear that kept gnawing at his soul. It reminded him that there was no success in wanting, only doing. The end was not the goal; it is the battle of the journey that mattered.

He pressed on.

Bursting into a clearing, he encountered a sturdy, monstrously big, rough log building. Thick black smoke rose majestically into the oncoming frigid night from a well-built chimney. Large cut stones gave support to huge timbers of rough sawn logs. Heavy chinking between the logs was neat and smooth with a wide variety of colors showing where someone had carefully repaired it over the years. No windows faced this side except on the upper levels. Thick rippled glass shined in the waning sun, with heavy curtains for warmth. All signs pointed to a well planned, cared for and successful establishment.

It suddenly occurred to our prince he had no idea where he was.

Carefully making his way to the front, and starting to shiver, he looked for the entrance. Steam poured off his soaked clothes, wicking up into the gathering cold. His boots squished when he walked and small clumps of what had been warm black sand ground his now wrinkled wet feet. A wide door stood solidly closed at the middle of the building. Above the door, a hand painted walking stick adorned with feathers was the only indication there was purpose to the place.

The prince pulled opened the door and limped into the warm dimness of a great room. As if on some unseen cue, music from the corner halted mid-note. Tables filled with hearty revelers stopped as one. The entire place seemed to come to a total, complete and utter standstill in the space of a heartbeat.

It was a large room, full of what looked to be a vagabond sort of traveling lot. Numerous eclectic common folk sat at a variety of large sturdy tables on long wooden benches. Food was about, drink was about, and pipe smoke filled the high ceiling.

It was a kindly looking place, but most of all, it was warm and felt secure. There was a friendly attitude about the big room. The majority of the residents seemed to be smiling, or at least comfortably enjoying themselves. One got the sense that they either knew each other, or did not take each other too seriously. They took each other for whom they were - well, at least most of them.

A kindly looking woman, with a large tray of hot food easily balanced on one sturdy hand, looked at our prince and said, "Welcome to the Journey Inn! It's about time; we 'ave been waitin' on you. Close that door, get by the fire and take them clothes off aefore you catch your death of cold. My, that is a nasty gash on your leg!"

She turned toward a back door and boldly shouted, "Harold, bring out hot wine, he's here!"

4.
Princess

A number of years before our prince found himself in his unsavory predicament; the gods determined the land needed a beautiful, enchanting princess. They delicately scooped hot clay from volcanoes to build her skin. It would be forever soft and clean, light in complexion, with a few freckles sprinkled in for joy.

Large perfect mountain almonds served as outlines for her eyes, and the gods gently washed them in the deep blue sea during a fierce, raging and tumultuous storm. The colors of her eyes would morph with a certain wildness, yet stay warm and moist with a tenderness that comes only with the mountain almond. Her hair was spun from the work of a million tropical silkworms. They burnt it a deep golden red with the sacred fire of the sun. It was thick and forever wavy, but softer than the clouds, and angels warmly slept there.

To form her mind, they mixed sunshine, lightning and arctic snow; it was active, fast and sincere as creation itself. Finally, from a far away galaxy, they mixed light from a thousand giant stars to light her smile.

She was perfect. She was radiant. She was human. They bestowed upon her the name of "Dessa." She lived at the other end of the land from where our prince grew up. She is free spirited, a wanderer, a compassionate explorer and has the blessing of a critical eye.

In the end, all she needed was a prince.

Or so she thought.

As her days passed, she journeyed to the far reaches of the land. Her quest for truth, life and the mysteries of the world, she felt, would never let her down. She sensed more than knew that this spinning world would hold her safe and warm. Still the prince, the right prince, was elusive. Her father, King Tarmon, was a kind, benevolent and righteous ruler. He continued to mourn the tragic and violent death of his dear sweet wife, Queen Gersemi. Although some time had passed since her death, he was wise and knew that not all in nature was fair or wonderful.

He bestowed upon Dessa all the love and caring a father could have for a child—without spoiling her. He knew nothing was quite as wretched as a spoiled brat princess. He was wise in the ways of children, and understood that a busy mind might keep her from straying as a headstrong girl might.

He was close to right. It would give him some peace in eternity for trying, when the time came. And trying Dessa was. But he never gave up.

Dessa learned to spin heavy woolen yarn, sheared with great effort from the thick backs of the kingdom's sheep. This task never seemed to end. Sanura, Dessa's long time personal attendant, made sure of that. Sanura's experience told her the oils of the wool would keep Dessa's skin soft and supple. The forceful pulling of the tough natural fibers would strengthen her fingers. Deep down Sanura knew Dessa would need to be strong if she were to survive. Because Gillespie was still alive.

Once when younger, yet almost of age, Dessa tired of spinning yarn. She screamed that a princess should not have to do such work. That evening Sanura stripped Dessa to her final thin and almost transparent layer of fine silk and had her thrown into the snow. The great gate of the castle thundered shut behind Dessa as the snow pummeled her almost naked and shivering body. With the wind whipping her hair about her face she screamed into the night that she would have Sanura beaten.

Finally, as the cold overcame her, she fell weeping at the gate. The tears of her beautiful eyes froze to her face. Her gown, stiff with frost, her hair rigid with ice.

Eventually, the gate opened and Sanura picked up the frozen girl. Roughly she carried her to the stable, stripped her naked and left her in the bed of the spare room. A bright fire burned, and the blankets scratched roughly on her tender skin. Dessa was wet, cold and very alone.

She had not seen the guards who had been just beyond the forest line, smartly file in after Sanura.

When morning came, Dessa had stopped shivering under the pile of rough wool blankets. Her hair was still damp, she was naked, she was mad, she was hungry, and she was also very scared.

Sanura arrived with a bowl of warm porridge. Not the type of breakfast Dessa was used to eating.

Sanura glared strongly at the young girl. Dessa was suddenly beside herself with fear. Sanura had never looked at her in this sort of menacing and threatening way

Dessa asked, in a quiet, almost desperate, but pleading voice, "Why?"

Sanura sternly replied with respect, but rather matter-of-factly, "You have finally experienced what it would be like to live without the love of your father and the care that this kingdom gives you. Nature is furious around us. All we have in this world is what we make, what we grow, what we hunt and most importantly each other. We count on each other for our very survival. You sleep each and every frigid night with soft covers around you. While most people in this kingdom are warm at night, they sleep with rough woolen blankets."

Dessa thought carefully; she sensed that in all her years this was an important lesson. However, she also felt mistreated. Dessa asked, finding her inner strength again, the anger of the lesson beginning to boil in her blood, her eyes blazing, "Does my father know what you did to me?"

Sanura calmly looked down at the disheveled young girl. She was growing into a beautiful, strong-willed woman; so much promise was before her, yet so much energy. Would they be able to tame and form all that energy for the future? Could Dessa be the great queen the kingdom would need for the coming tests?

She said quietly, "Does your father know? Why my dear, he ordered it."

5.
Introductions

In a different part of the world, not extremely far away by today's standards, but within a winter or two of that same cold evening Dessa spent shivering in the cold, Harold brought out the largest mug of wine our prince had ever seen. The heat coming through the thick handcrafted mug from the boiled dark liquid instantly warmed his cold, damp hands. He was shivering by the fire and had all too quickly consumed every drop. The heat coated his stomach and he could feel the warmth fairly glow at his ears. It felt wonderful.

Harold, with a keen eye asked, "Hungry?" Our prince nodded, but looked down sullenly and muttered "But I have no way to pay you for any food or hospitality." He was keenly aware that he was for some reason far from home and not in a place where his status of prince was going to get him his customary meal.

Harold replied in a fatherly tone, "Yes, we know. We wouldn't expect you to have a way to pay. You have the gift, which is all that matters. And, by the looks of it, you don't even know you have the gift. Do you?"

Torrin looked at the older man with his mouth open. This was not the way he was used to being treated, nor was he understanding what was going on. Even though the wine and room were warm and the atmosphere friendly, it was all very confusing. He searched his mind of any story at all of a large place in the woods where people gathered. There was none. The only gathering he was used to was in the castle.

Harold, on his way back to the kitchen, with the empty monster wine mug in hand stopped, turned and asked the wet young man the obvious question, "Oh, by what name are you called?"

Our prince looked up and smiled, which caused the bump on his head to throb. Much warmer now, the wine heating him on his insides and the fire sizzling behind him, he felt cozy and safe. He stood up as tall as his mangled leg would allow, and replied, "I am Prince Torrin McKenna the Third, son of King Trebor, Royal Knight of the Winter Bastian, and Scholar of the Royal Liege."

"Oh," replied Harold, somewhat startled. "OK, we'll call you Torrin", he said as he turned back toward the kitchen. "Take those boots and wet clothes off as Karina told ya. I'll bring ye some food, clean bandage and some more wine. You and I have much to discuss an I'hl bet ye be'en hungray too. We'll take care of that in good order after yer dried out some and warmed up."

Torrin frowned, he was used to people standing at attention when he spoke. Something was different here. Very different!

Outside it began to snow. Big thick, heavy flakes that stick to the trees and give the forest a surreal look. Later that night as it always does, the cold and biting wind would pick up and push the snow off the trees, and the world would prepare itself for another day. Fortunately, spring was quickly arriving a little more with each day. It was a welcome change. But tonight, all living creatures needed to be inside a warm shelter.

6.

Dessa Glows

Gale, the head stable hand, old looking, frail but with strength of character that defied his age, supervised Dessa's riding lessons. As early as she could remember, Dessa was astride the great steeds of her father's stable. The riding started with simple forays to the woods. Pleasant trails, flat and well worn.

As Dessa grew, she desired to see and explore more of her wonderful land. In addition to the riding lessons, she was also tutored, under Gale's orders, by the best hunters the kingdom had to offer. Dessa grew strong and lethal with a bow and arrow. She was so accurate, she could sit calmly astride a large black steed of the kingdom and guide an arrow true to its mark.

With her fondness for riding, hunting and adventure, her respect and admiration for the horses she rode was as natural as the flowers that grew on the sunny side of the trails. Dessa loved spending time with the farrier, and soon she became quite good at shoeing a horse. She did not even shy away from working with the foundered horses. Dessa would work until exhausted to keep the stately beasts healthy. Caring for the animals gave her a peace that she could not describe; it mattered deeply to her heart and soul.

In turn, these horses grew to respect and admire Dessa. They never threw her off, always obeyed her commands and protected her from the natural dangers of the deep forest. There was, however, a playfulness to the relationship.

Dessa would sometimes tease her favorite mount, Uta. She'd start to eat an apple just out of his reach. Uta would play along and whinny for some morsel from his favorite rider. And Dessa would always end up sharing. However, Dessa often found herself wet on a warm day when Uta would, on his own, ford a deep creek. Or when she was not looking while walking through the barns, Uta's long tail would wrap around Dessa's face. Dessa would always give a startled shout when she got a playful nip in the rear end. It was all good fun, with both learning to love each other on equal and sincere terms.

Dessa mused that she hoped to find as genuine a love with a man, as she found with the residents of the castle's stable. Especially Uta.

A time came when Dessa asked her father if she could stay out with the hunters overnight. Tears welled on his old friendly and very bearded face. He simply said, "No. And, my sweet daughter, do not ask again." By this time Dessa was wise enough to understand that there are some questions you do not repeat. Yet she pondered why.

When she asked Sanura about the puzzling response from her father, all she got was a quiet, "In time my child."

*   *   *

With the arrival of early spring when our story begins, Dessa was of that age when it seems to be a wonderful time for love. And a Prince had arrived heeding King Tarmon's widespread call. King Tarmon had been soliciting for an appropriate suitor for Dessa since the last summer. All in splendor, the prince's carriage was spectacular, his presence infectious. She did not notice that all who surrounded him were conscript.

His name, as they called him, was Darius. He was wealthy beyond compare. But it was not wealth that he or his family had earned. High taxes, cruel slave labor and piracy were the sources of his riches. Darius's father was King Gaerwn, the most powerful and feared ruler ever. Dessa had no idea Tarmon had been given bad information. However, for now Darius was strong, virulent and tall with a radiant smile.

In all her imagination, Dessa had never conjured a pungent aroma so strong. The aroma of her wanton desire, her need to be fulfilled. Darius made her quiver, yet she did not quite understand why—yet.

Dark curly hair spread thickly to his shoulders. His face was sturdy, supported by a firm chiseled chin. He rode a horse in a tall, regal manner.

For a week, Darius and Dessa rode together, hunted together and ate side by side in the great hall of the castle. It was a fast courtship, but for Dessa it was a dreamy time of her fantasy being fulfilled.

When Darius had arrived, Dessa was already of age. For what seemed many summers, she had gazed upon the men of the kingdom wanting to know more - but knowing that her father would kill any man who touched her. Her desires went unmet. The stories she heard in the kitchens and from the maids made her skin tingle and caused heat to rise from her fair skin.

The marriage ceremony was a spectacular event. The entire kingdom put the hard work of life on hold to celebrate with their beloved and wonderful king and princess. The feasting, the dancing, the music, the revelry, lasted for days.

Darius and Dessa danced with wild abandon. She lost herself in the almost harsh twirling among the happy, sweating throng of people. Food and joy were piled high upon the best silver the kingdom had to offer. The maids and butlers scurried about, keeping all the guests well-fed and plied with drink. By the second evening, they too had joined in the revelry. King Tarmon knew that all his people should celebrate this happy occasion.

On the wedding night Dessa was starry eyed and completely in love with her new prince. She was bathed from head to toe in rosewater for a long and most glorious final time by Sanura. Her hair was brushed a thousand times and the thick red waves shown silky smooth in the flickering candlelight of the wedding chamber. Dessa's thin white silk gown clung gently to her soft tender flesh. The golden threads outlining the collar reflected the red from her hair and danced as stars upon her neck. As she entered the room she felt a hardening of her nipples and a warm flush rose up from the nether regions of her body that startled and seemed to bewitch her at the same time. Her skin and her very being ached for the touch of the man she loved. A warm stirring between her legs told her that this would be far different from any other night.

Yes, Sanura had explained to her all of the mechanics of becoming a woman on the wedding night. All this information brought Dessa to a higher state of excitement and anticipation. Anticipation of the hot, passionate love that she would soon feel from her prince deep inside her body made her strong and weak all at one time. She tingled with the thoughts of finally knowing the real joy the maids talked of when their men bedded them on cold winter evenings. She longed for his arms to hold her safe and firm after their lovemaking. A firm welcome of safety that would assure her she would be happy forever.

Upon the marriage bed, she laid her warm, virgin body. Deep soft blankets surrounded her in the large well built mattress lending a sense of safety warmth and comfort. Down feather pillows held her head gently, and her silken hair spread across the satin eyelet cases. She closed her eyes and drank in the heavy perfume of the splendid future that awaited her.

The large door opened solidly and Darius strode across the threshold. He had arrived in his marriage chamber.

It was like nothing she had ever expected, experienced or ever wanted to experience again. He was drunk and dirty, he was rough, nasty and by no means well endowed. In five minutes he was asleep, snoring like a moldy stable hand.

Dessa laid back on the bed, hot tears of anguish stung as they slid down her cheeks, scratched red and raw by the stubble of his wretched face. The longing between her legs was not only completely unsatisfied, it was as though her body was now of two worlds. The void between her legs was nothing compared to the flaming, anguished vacuum that tore within her heart. Her quivering sobs gasped loudly and competed with a hurtful smashing of her heart against her ribs.

How long she lay there until sleep finally rescued her she did not know, or care. When she awoke, he was still snoring, drooling and stinking up not only her bed, but now it seemed, also her life.

She still desired the peace and true joy of a real prince. A true love. Love that would hold her, protect her, keep her warm and respect her. For she knew that forever only lives in the heart of true, tender, honest love.

The second night, much to her chagrin and disappointment proved to be more of the same.

Dessa went to speak with Sanura and gather guidance. Trembling, frightened, yet more angry than anything, she pleaded with Sanura, her blue eyes on fire with rage, "You promised me the bed would be wonderful after the first night. It is horrid. He stinks, he is disgusting and I feel nothing yet a longing for his death. All he does is fall on top of me, have his way and then rolls over into a drunken stupor." Tears stung her face as the volume of her lament increased. "How could I have been so stupid? What do I do?"

Sanura was a kind and gentle woman. However with her experience, she was of the world. She too had once been full of grief and pain. And she had let her painful existence go on too long before she had taken control of her life and moved on to the life she now had. Through a series of strange events, she had come twice to Tarmon's kingdom many years before. He accepted her without question. At the time, Tarmon knew the pain he could see in her eyes was real, yet knew the fire in her heart was just and pure.

After Lady Gersemi was killed one night on the fall hunt by a pack of wolves, she had cradled Tarmon's grieving head in her arms. She endured his rage at nature and listened to him cry himself to sleep for many nights. She soon helped him understand his people needed a strong and benevolent king. They looked up to him for guidance, trust and strength. Gersemi would want him to stand strong, to help the people see courage and strength and to be the compassionate king that would fulfill his density.

Sanura looked at Dessa. Many summers before, tears would have come rolling down her warm, generally smiling face. Today, she knew that her life experiences were the most important teacher and she must share that wisdom carefully. It was wisdom Dessa needed, not sympathy, not even cuddling and caressing. This was real, and it was real trouble.

"My dear," she whispered into Dessa's ear, an ear that was on fire with detest. "Sometimes men settle in, sometimes they don't. However, with time, patience and faith all will dwell well. Give me some rest, let me think."

Dessa looked up at the strong woman who had been as much a mother to her as anyone. Swallowing hard, she nodded. Tears filled her eyes. Her sense of betrayal made her knees weak. Her depth of fury had no boundaries. She was mad beyond belief, at mostly herself for being such a blind fool. And an anger like this does not often have much patience.

At that, the ravaging, beautiful young princess turned smartly on her heel as she said to Sanura, "I shall not wait long before I take matters into my own hands."

7.
A Quiet Little Room

Torrin ate steadily of the tasty and well-roasted meat and bread Harold brought on a large, beautifully carved wooden platter. Now that he was warm, full and mostly dry, sitting next to a roaring fire settling into a large warm blanket draped about his frame, Torrin asked carefully, "What is it we need to talk about?"

Harold was not a terribly big man. However, he was calm, sturdy and wise. His bushy blond eyebrows scrunched as he contemplated Torrin.

"Young lad," he said, "Do ye even have any clue as to where ye are?" Those eyebrows lifted quizzically. He paused, leaned forward, "Do ye even know why ye are here?"

Torrin knew exactly where he was and why he was here. "Harold," he almost shouted. "You are a funny man. Of course, I know where I am. I am in the valley below the castle! As to why? Well, I came in here so I did not freeze to death out there," Torrin's hand pointed at the large door he had come through. "And I must say," he added thoughtfully, seeing the puzzled look on Harold's weathered face, "I am very impressed by what I see here. This is a magnificent building. Well put together!"

Now Harold had been waiting a long time for this moment, but this was not going as he had expected. He scratched the back of his large, furry neck and said with a slight nod of his head and a quizzical look in his eye, "Excuse me fer a while. An, while ye waitn', put these on." He handed Torrin a bundle of coarse wool clothes. Harold promptly got up and walked back to the kitchen. It was a place where Harold and Karina could talk in peace.

"Karina," Harold said, starting to sputter, "Are you sure this is the one? He is clueless. He is a mere lad." Harold began talking faster, "We'll have to train him or he will not survive. What if it happens too soon? What if he is not ready?"

Karina loved Harold. They had been first loves, and when she met him, there was no turning back. He was a good man. He worked hard, protected her, was faithful and kind. She never once regretted her decision to be his wife. Even now, when he got so very excited about things.

"Harold," she said firmly but with the conviction, caring and sincerity as only true love can hold. "My dear, relax. Everything takes some time- anything worth time and effort is not easy. So settle down. Tonight, just tell Himself in there," nodding toward the great room, "where he is. He is not going to like it. Just let him work through it."

With that, Karina took Harold's bushy face in her hands. She drew him close and they both kissed each other, not her to him, or him to her. It was both. And not just any old kiss. Not a regular kiss. Not even a kiss that you might expect of people who have been together for a very long time. It was more a deep, strong joining of their souls. Each clinging to a passion and the profound understanding for each other they shared. A passion and caring they learned never to take for granted, since they knew how rare their relationship was in the close order of the universe. As Harold's big hand found the small of her back and pressed her close to him, you could almost taste the fire in the air as the room heated up. It was something like a hot summer day, after a massive lightning storm, where the air is crinkly clean, the cleansing heat making it all somehow different.

Presently, the reality of having to attend to their guests and establishment took hold again, and the two parted. Looking refreshed, happy and sincerely in love, they went back to the tasks that beckoned.

"Here, take another wine with you, it always takes the edge off." And then, almost as an afterthought she said, "Remember though, this is a time to celebrate. There will be much work, as there always is." But with a sly wink she said, "Celebration is important. Now go on. But don't plan on staying down here too late." And with that she gave him a solid wink and a sly grin.

Harold blushed, but he blushed with a big smile. As he turned to leave, she gave his firm bum a good squeeze.

8.
Dessa Fights Back

On the third night of their marriage, Darius arrived again, drunk and reeking. Dessa sat upon her mother's softly padded embroidered bench. She was combing her soft wavy silken hair. Her white gown shimmered in the candlelight.

Darius bellowed, "Get into the bed my tawdry little wife. I will again make you the happiest woman the land has ever seen."

Dessa did not move from her bench.

Setting down his large tankard and grumbling mightily, Darius stripped off his clothes, dropped them by the bed, and turned his attention to Dessa. He brutishly picked her up and threw her onto the soft mattress leaving harsh fingerprints on her arms and ankles where he had grabbed her.

Tonight though, Dessa was ready. Her strong foot came swiftly up between his hairy legs. She kicked with all her might, her target clear in her mind. Her eyes blazed hot and almost red with a furious, mad rage that seemed to possess her very being.

He was impressed with her strength. Unfortunately for Dessa, his experience told him what was going to happen. He simply grabbed her leg, twisted sharply, and flipped her around on her stomach. He reached down and tore her gown from her body. He put one hand firmly on her head, pressing down so hard that she could feel the hair pulling from her scalp. His other hand grabbed her wrist and twisted her arm at a wretched angle behind her back, almost breaking her elbow. He took her, promptly, harshly and with meaningless abandon.

When he was done, he said to her, "You are my wife. You do as I say, and if you ever try to strike me again I will whip you, naked and in public, for your nasty insolence. Do you understand or shall I break your dainty little arm right now?"

Dessa knew she was in no position to fight. She felt beaten, betrayed. Worst of all, she felt helpless and completely alone. She simply nodded her head, as well as she could, and with a resigned and weary "Yeth," that struggled out from the blankets pounded into her mouth she told him he had conquered her.

He got off the bed and drank of the tankard he had brought with him. As was his custom in their short marriage, he did not offer any to Dessa. He just glared at her and fell onto the bed. Darius rolled to his back. In a few moments, he was snoring loudly. Yet tonight, he did not sleep peacefully. Too many evenings of drinking, eating and bad living were catching up with him. It did not take long and he rolled off the bed onto the cold stone floor. His drunkenness keeping him firmly, if not loudly, asleep.

Dessa waited quietly for a short while, thinking he would get up and get back into bed. After a while, the hot tears had stopped flowing down her cheeks. When his snoring and sputtering quieted she relaxed and fell into a deep slumber. She relished the peace of being away from him.

*   *   *

When the light of the new day woke her, she quietly got up, careful not to disturb the menace next to the bed. Her feet lightly dropped to the floor. The last thing she remembered was taking a single step toward the door.

9.
Where Am I?

Torrin could feel Harold's uneasiness and it bothered him. There were too many questions without answers. Nothing felt familiar. Now that he was no longer cold, even the language sounded strange to his royal ears. The ill fitting clothes scratched at him like when as a young lad his mother used to scrub him after he had enjoyed the outdoors all day, and it was bothersome. The steaming mug of wine in Harold's large hand almost looked menacing. His leg ached; he seemed to see some things a little blurrily. His head hurt.

What the devil was going on?

"Torrin," Harold began, "Have ye ever been on a long journey?"

"Of course," replied Torrin, putting down the fresh mug of wine. "Why do you ask?"

"Well my son," Harold said with a deep sigh, "long journeys are sometimes fraught with unknown things. Aye, people get lost and things get broken and sometimes the world is just not what you expected when you get there."

"What do you mean?" asked a wary Torrin, annoyed somewhat by this circular talk, but mindful not to be harsh to the people who were giving him comfort and a warm place to stay.

"Suppose you started on a journey, with no particular end in mind, just went to go and see where you got; sort of taken?" Harold asked.

Torrin replied coldly, "That seems somewhat dumb."

Now Harold put his face in his big hand and slowly shook his head. When he looked up, he was smiling. "Suppose your plans got changed and it was a long time before you really knew what the change was and how it was going to affect your journey?" he asked hopefully.

Before Torrin could reply, one of the Journey's patrons stepped over and reminded Harold that it was getting just a bit cold in here. Harold asked Torrin to come help fetch some wood for the fire.

Torrin got up and stretched long and hard. His muscles were stiff from the effort of killing the beastly dragon and his fast trek through the woods. As much as it hurt, it felt good to move the leg a little. It felt good to move all his joints. He limped after Harold, finally starting to pay attention to the inside of this place in the woods called "Journey."

What he began to realize was that just as the outside was sturdy, the inside was built like a fortress. The timbers were massive, the planking thick. A number of mysterious looking birds and animals adorned the walls, doubtless from hunting expeditions. But they were like none Torrin had ever seen. There was no freshness or newness about, of anything, anywhere. Everything looked as old as ever. The wood was very dry, the chinking inside, as on the outside, had been repaired a number of times. Actually, many different times. More than Torrin could really count. He suspected that the cold, blustery nights were very severe here. Left to his own devices, he would have used stone, he mused. Maybe start covering the outside with stone. It did not look like the wood was going to last many more winters.

Torrin walked into what was obviously the woodshed. Logs of all shapes and sizes were stacked neatly from floor to ceiling. There was an enormous amount of firewood here. More than could be burned in a very long time.

Torrin asked, "Why so much wood?"

Harold turned to look at the young man. He then returned to the pile of logs he was stacking on a small wooden sled. "One o' the rules at Journey is, each morn, evryon' who stays 'ere goes out to chop, cut and gather wood." Many a fierce storm has come up and we are forced ta stay in here for days. Nice an cozy an warm."

Very strange, thought Torrin. In all his seasons, he never once remembered a storm that lasted more than one day. Things still did not make sense here; every turn provided more mystery.

"Ye get yur turn in the morn," Harold said. "Now help me push this load to the fireplace so our guests can stay toasty warm tonight. It looks like a fierce one out there, ye are lucky ye made it in, or ye would be a chew toy for the wolves in te mornin." Harold threw Torrin a smile that told Torrin to relax and take everything for face value. At least for now.

They stacked the logs in silence next to the big stone hearth. Torrin had never seen such a large fireplace. He ran his hand across the large, round smooth stones, carefully layered together. The whole thing was quite huge. The stones, he noticed, went up through the ceiling. The burning area was quite big enough to stand in. Pegs, like those that held his hanging clothes, were all around the blazing furnace. Maybe people get regularly wet around here, Torrin quizzically thought. Harold piled a goodly amount of wood in the fireplace too. Soon the fire was raging again, beating back the cold seeping through the heavy walls.

"I need to help Karina for a while," nodded Harold. "Why don't you go chat with Quillan? He seems to have traveled much, even being as young as he is."

Harold nodded toward a rather largely built young man across the room. His back was against the wall, one foot propped up on a stool. An air of odd familiarity whirled around him, yet he sat alone for now.

Torrin limped over to the table and Quillan warmly gestured to him to sit down. Torrin was beginning to feel tired. His leg had stopped bleeding, but the ache was pounding. He put his leg up on the bench, put his head in his hands and peered out through the slits between his fingers at this new stranger called Quillan.

"Eh boy," Quillan said through lips that were clenched around a heavy, hand carved pipe, a Gaelic lilt emerging. "Whatcha don' in this 'ere part o' the world?"

"First of all," answered Torrin, raising his head, a little color seeping into what had been pale cheeks, "I am not a boy! And secondly, I'm beginning to wonder what the galla I'm doing here!" Then with a heavy sigh he said, "And finally, just where is here?"

The lines on Quillan's face foretold a man either of many winters or wide ranging tough outdoor experiences. The wrinkles made him look much older than he really was but you could not really guess his age by looking at him. The chipped and yellow teeth lent an eerie mystery to his broad smile. You might have guessed that not too long ago, he was a handsome devil. His hair, eyebrows and just about all of him were a deep crimson red. Fair skin, with a healthy smattering of freckles, had endured much sun, rain and wind. His long velvety eyelashes would have worked well on a tall woman's face, but Torrin was sure no one had survived telling Quillan that kind of detail. But for Quillan those lashes added a level of what seemed to be intense caring when he relaxed and focused on you with aqua green eyes that had the look of a hawk.

He was obviously of kind heart, yet being a well-seasoned traveler - even for his youth - he was of sturdy composition. Torrin regarded this large and meaty frame sitting before him as one that would have worked well as a member of his father's guards. A large broadsword hung on a wooden hook within reach of Quillan's hand. The hilt was woven with thinly cut leather. Two small bracelet-like adornments hung from the end of the grip. A rounded flap of fur hung off each of the pommels. Green jewels adorned the heavy and rather wide sheath. Fine tooling was evident on the sheath, but many deep gashes, dents and scrapes sent a message of use, abuse and long, dangerous experience. Torrin guessed that this brutal, menacing weapon was probably not the only one within a quick reach of Quillan's large hands.

"So yer not a boy, eh?" queried Quillan with a sidewise grin. "So then, tell me about you. Torrin. Mr. Torrin the man!" The last part was delivered with a throaty, deep and sarcastically low growl.

Quillan settled back onto the heavy planking that supported him. He raised a large tankard to his lips and with his eyes gently closed; he took genuine delight in drinking whatever was captured inside. As he settled the tankard back on the exact damp spot that seemed to be its official resting place, he cocked his head toward Torrin and waited.

It did not seem to be a patient kind of wait.

Torrin thought this a strange place, some things moved so slowly you could not tell they were moving, and others wanted things fast.

He bit the inside of his lip to help him think.

10.
Storm...

Large storm clouds had formed and the close thunder was decidedly chilling in its magnificence. Thick, ragged lightning bolts split the sky with blazing heat that seared branches nearby and split large unsuspecting trees into piles of worthless smoldering kindling. Hot rain tore at the night as the mighty storm lashed its fury upon the entire land. All at once, the rain became soft and quiet. Cool water gently, peacefully ran down her cheeks and quenched the fire burning in the back of her head.

As Dessa's eyes opened, the harsh lightning dissolved into muted daylight in an anteroom where the curtains were pulled across the windows, letting in, wispy, subtle rays of friendly sunshine.

Sanura was quietly bathing Dessa's flushed and swollen head, the back of which felt like it had been beaten with a club. Dessa moved to sit up. A wave of nausea overcame her as her eyes folded inward, dizzy and distorted.

"Shhh, rest my child," murmured Sanura in a soft voice. "You took a nasty bump on the head when you slipped on the wet floor."

Dessa's arm moved up over her swollen and tired eyes, the light, warm pressure giving her stability and calm.

"Why was the floor wet?" she asked.

"The answer for that better comes from your father, not me," warily replied the older woman. "I am not allowed to say anything."

Sanura stood up and went to the door. "You stay right there, young lady. Do not try to get up yet. I will fetch your father. Now be still."

Dessa heard Sanura quietly say to someone, "She is awake now."

Dessa closed her eyes. The dizziness stopped after a time, but the pounding on the back of her head was incessant.

Soon the muffled and slow shuffling of many feet told her that there were a number of people in the room. Dessa slowly opened her eyes to look up into the worried face of her father.

"Father, what happened?" she asked in quiet desperation, sensing his unease. "What is going on here?"

"What did Sanura tell you?" he asked gently.

"She said I should ask you," replied Dessa. "She would not tell me anything other than I hit my head on the wet floor. Why was the floor wet? Please tell me what is going on here?" Some anger and fear were beginning to creep into Dessa's voice.

King Tarmon asked, "What happened between you and Darius last night?"

Dessa flashed angry hurt eyes at her father. "He is a brutish oaf. I wish he was dead." She did not see her father recoil or sense the rapid intact of breath from the others in the room. "Just as the last two nights, he came in, drunk and stinking, and he forced me to oblige him in the most unsatisfactory and demeaning ways. It has been horrid. I was so wrong about him. He is a fraud." Dessa began to sob; low deep weeping that emerged from the very core of her body.

"Dessa," began her father, "I know this is hard, painful and very tiring for you. But it is vital, very vital, that you tell us exactly what happened last night."

Dessa told them what had transpired. "He came into the room; I was combing my hair. He was drunk, dirty and reeking. He threw me onto the bed. I tried to kick him between his stinking hairy legs. I was so angry. I so wanted to love him. Wanted him to love me. He just wanted, I don't know what." She turned her head, sobs choking her, tears stinging her flushed and swollen face. "He grabbed my foot, twisted me over, tore off my gown and had his way with me." The collective room gasped. "Then he drank more from his mug." She spat out the word 'mug,' as if it was a bitter food. "He then went to sleep. After a time, he was so drunk he fell off the bed. This morning I woke up, got out of bed and then woke up here, with Sanura wiping my head. What has happened here, what has happened to me? Why are you looking at me so?"

In a soft, yet stable voice, with obvious effort King Tarmon spoke, "Dessa, you slipped in the blood of Darius. He died last night of a wound in his leg. When we found him this morning, the knife was still buried in his leg. He was so drunk I doubt he even felt the pain." Tarmon cocked his head, looking at Dessa to see her reaction.

Dessa's whole body seemed to go slack. At half speed she closed her eyes and exhaled a long pain-filled breath. A swarm of thoughts leapt into her brain. She was married a few days, now a widow. She was no longer pure. She was angry for Darius dying on anything other than her terms. She did not know what to think.

Tarmon interrupted her thoughts. "It is the opinion of the council that you murdered Darius." He spoke in what sounded like a rehearsed voice. Your trial begins in a fortnight. Until then, do not leave the castle. When you exit your rooms, you will be followed by a guard. Unfortunately, Darius's father will not be pleased, and he is not a kind man."

Tarmon, and all who had quietly stood around, left the room, leaving Dessa alone, hurt, frightened and angry.

As Sanura re-entered, Dessa remembered the punishment for murder in Tarmon's kingdom. Since the time of Keegan's rule, decided when Tarmon was but a young man, guilty meant being burned alive at the stake. No one was above the law.

Great waves of nausea wracked her tired body as visions of Kael's last moments swept through her head. He had been her dear, sweet younger brother. So young to die in a cabin fire. The stories she overheard from the kitchen's helpers caused her to run to her room crying on many an afternoon.

It all seemed so unfair.

11.
Night

As Torrin gathered his thoughts, Quillan keenly regarded the young man sitting in front of him. Not really too much younger than himself, maybe ten winters. The idea made him feel a little old.

He thought him not bad looking, a little scraggly about his black curly hair. Of course, that could be the result of his hectic deliverance, mused Quillan. He has hardly been shaving very long he thought. Broad hands, dark inquisitive eyes, good teeth, fairly strong, but still a boy in many ways. Goodness, he was young. That might make the training harder. Or, of course easier since the work would not be so tiring. Quillan soon gave up on his quiet fortune telling and returned his attention to the question at present.

"Go on," declared a slightly irritated Quillan. "Tell me about you."

"I am Prince Torrin McKenna the Third, son of King Trebor, royal…" Quillan put up a beefy hand and smartly exclaimed "Ya, I heerd all that rubble before, when ye did yer royal proclumation. Tell me about Torrin the man. Who in bloody blazes are ye? Why should I not take my dagger and gut ye here? What makes ye worth anything?"

This was the sort of question Torrin had not contemplated, nor had ever really prepared an answer for—or at least one that would seem to make sense to this red ogre sitting across the table.

Torrin shifted his wounded leg uneasily. He noticed his sword across the room hanging near his steaming, drying clothes. Too far away to be any good here. His knife had been lost in the dragon experience. Seeing no tools with which to defend himself, Torrin decided to just be himself. It was all he had at the time, hopefully it was good enough.

"My positions at the castle are vital to our survival," declared Torrin. "I am in charge of rampart repair. That all by itself would keep even the smartest man busy full time."

Quillan arched one furry eyebrow.

"The ramparts are the walls," said Torrin, instantaneously wishing he had not said it. "We have to be able to repel attack, keep from being undermined and provide safety to our people." At this Quillan looked at least somewhat interested; Torrin felt relieved.

He continued, "I also keep track of the kingdom's herds for the King. To survive we must keep a good supply of cattle, goats, horses, chickens and other livestock." He rapidly finished with, "And I can hunt the smallest and the biggest of the animals; brought down a bear that took four of us to carry last winter!"

Quillan smiled a surreptitious, yet gentle smile. He said, "So ye know stonework and ye can keep track of things. And ye say ye can hunt. Hmmm. Do ye have a wife or a woman to keep ye warm?"

"No," declared Torrin quietly.

"Oh, I sense ye never been wi a woman" said the rust colored human, in a not unkindly or menacing tone. "Relax, I won't tell the boys. Too bad there are no wily steamed up misses here tonight, we could get ye started!" Quillan let out a mighty roar of a laugh.

Torrin suddenly felt tired. Very tired. The events of the day had caught up with him. His leg ached, his head ached, his belly full, too much hot wine. It was time for sleep. It was also evident that no one would really tell him where he was. So better to sleep and then be off early in the morning. He would hike up the stream, then find the path back to the castle. It could not be too far.

And, since he had not known about this place before, did they pay their taxes? He would have to check on that. In the meantime, he needed a place to lay his weary bones.

"Where do people sleep here?" asked Torrin of Quillan.

"There are some rooms upstairs with beds," replied the big man.

"Where is Harold?" asked Torrin. "I would like a room."

"Why?" replied Quillan as he threw a couple of large wool blankets, one side lined with fur, on the table. "Ye aren't sleeping tonight, ye wer the last on' in for t evening. Save ol' Dogger there the trouble." Quillan looked at an older man, completely grey about the head and beard. He was already dozing on a bench. "Ye need to attend to the fire so we all doan freeze to death."

Torrin's fist pounded on the table as he reached for the other man. He froze when he felt the sharp point of a knife on his throat. Quillan was smiling like a cat, his deep green eyes had a hunger in them that froze Torrin's blood.

Behind him, he heard Karina loudly proclaim, "You kill him and you watch the fire tonight you old bag of dust. Did you tell him where he was?"

Quillan looked sheepish and slid the sharp shiny dagger back into his sleeve. "No, not yet."

Karina snorted, "Men." Shrugging her shoulders she sighed, "We'll take care of it tomorrow. Everybody get some sleep. Torrin, you are in charge of the fire. Let it go out, I'll gut you myself. Of course it won't matter, we'll all be frozen. Goodnight." With that, she tossed him a bundle of blankets and then covered up the sleeping Dogger with a pile of old, worn looking skins. She seemed to tuck him in nice and warm.

Outside, the wind howled through the trees so violently it almost sounded like thunder. Journey fairly shook under the onslaught of snow that attacked in a blizzard of proportions Torrin had not ever encountered.

Inside, to Torrin, what seemed like a transient group, tonight were the residents of Journey. Each found a table, or put two benches together as a bed. Everyone seemed well supplied with a variety of blankets and skins and began what appeared to be the regular routine for a normal night's sleep for them. Torrin was surprised there was no discussion about the building being shaken by the mighty storm. They seemed to be used to it!

"Quillan?" Torrin said gently, "Is the night always like this? It sounds rather fierce out there!"

"Ah my lad," Quillan sighed as he pulled what looked like a huge bear around him, "'Tis winter in here parts. Things will freshen up presently. The change is always amazn' to me, I mean how fast it happens and how wonderful it is. Guess ye not used to this, eh?" Quillan smiled gently, and as he laid his furry large head down and said, "Are ye begun to see yer not near ye 'ome? Don't sleep on the floor, the frost'll blacken yer toes."

He was asleep before Torrin could respond.

12.
Dessa and Valdemar

Trapped, alone and desperate, Dessa was beside herself. Her father would not speak to her. Sanura told her he was too grief stricken to see her. It was not a good time.

The room felt cold, dark and damp. One more night; one night closer to the end.

Within one more moon, Dessa knew the warmer days would be coming. She was certain she would not experience the delight of another spring. She shivered, thinking of her dead burned body nailed to the stake in the cold, snowy night. There would be no heaven for her, just pure hell.

The thought of asking her father for pardon had crossed her mind more times than was possible. But she knew he was bound by the law. A law that kept the kingdom relatively quiet and without harmful mischief.

The history of this law was known to all who lived within the walls of the great castle. They knew of the murderous riot almost costing the entire kingdom its life. One night, people, drinking more than they should after a spat with Gillespie and a small dog, as the story had been told to her, had met to debate in the market square. No one knows for sure what happened. However, anger ensued and in the morning, almost all in the fight were dead or dying of a variety of wounds. Whether it was fighting over ideas, drink or opinion did not matter. Children were without parents, and ultimately more than half of the residents were eventually dead. Caring for the wounded took much effort, and was generally futile from the rapid and massive infections.

As winter approached, there were barely enough people to bring in the crops, execute a decent hunt for meat and care for the animals. That winter was brutal. The king had many folk move into the great hall for safety, warmth and comfort. As with any winter, many died. More so this year from lack of nutrition, and some just from loneliness. The scar on the people was real and deep.

That spring, as the snow and cold slowly melted into the streams and sunshine, the king made a proclamation. "Any person who kills another in this kingdom, for any reason, will be burned at the stake, in public, within one moon's time. Anyone who cannot live under this rule is free to leave before winter."

No one left.

Dessa's musings were interrupted by the deep thud of her heavy door closing behind her.

Dessa turned to see Valdemar, chief of the council approaching. Never before had she been in his presence alone. Ever since she was a little girl, scurrying around the castle, the man had made her skin crawl.

Tarmon explained to Dessa, when she told him her feelings concerning Valdemar, "He is very smart, he is honest, he gives me good advice. I am not fond of him, but I need him to help keep the kingdom safe, secure and running smoothly." She remembered his heavy sigh as he laid his warm hand on her head, "Sometimes you must work with people who are so very different. They help balance your consciousness, they bring a different perspective, a perspective I sometimes find perplexing. It is the weight of leadership to have to work with differing opinions. But it is my duty to honor their gifts of insight and see the world from many points of view. I must listen and respond. In time you will understand." He smiled the wonderful deep fatherly smile she always loved. "Trust me now, understand me later," he said. And she always did. That saying always worked.

Until now.

Now she felt helpless. Out of control and the cold, painful fire in her stomach ached not only for her, but also for her beloved father.

Valdemar spoke in a slow, deep voice. "My child, you look so distraught." His small red eyes, they seemed too close together, fairly burned into her soul. A shudder crept through her, from the soles of her feet to the back of her neck. Her heavy red hair was not thick enough to protect her from the chill that gave her goose bumps of trepidation and loathing.

He continued, "You need peace. You need what many in this kingdom call the devil in white. I have come to give you what you dream of. To make you the woman you want to be. To make you whole before you leave us."

Warnings of fear and horror surged from her inner self. But a small voice told her to wait. "Stop and think. Thinking will save you; you can only save yourself one day at a time. However, save yourself you must. Breathe. Breathe deep and slow."

The words from her father came to her, "Listen and respond."

She listened.

Valdemar never even blinked as he talked. He stared solidly at her, not at her eyes, not at her face, but at her whole being, all at once, but not at all. Surreal, deep and with shocking cold brutality.

His thin and frail shoulders pushed back, and his deep colored robes dropped gracefully to the floor. He stood before her, completely and totally naked. His entire body hairless. His thin, almost transparent skin was colorless. Age spots pulsed contrast in the light of the oil lamps and candles. His thin legs and arms were of no muscle, and she wondered how he moved.

However, he stood before her with the most massive and ghastly large male member she had ever witnessed or heard of, and he was quite erect. His hairlessness seemed to accentuate the size. The rest of him hung low, large and seemed to be swollen in great anticipation. A small spot of moisture showed itself at the end.

Her sharp intake of breath seemed to excite him.

"I see you are impressed. Young ladies always are." He said in a knotty, almost sneering tone.

Dessa's eyes moved back to his face. She slowly moved toward Valdemar. Swallowing hard, her right hand playing with the ties of her nightshirt, the corners of her mouth turning up into a slight smile, she slowly ran her tongue over dry lips.

"Valdemar," Dessa softly purred, "I had heard rumors. I listened to the tales of the maids. I had thought it not to be true, not possible. I guess I was wrong."

Her hand left the ties of her nightshirt, slowly descending between her breasts, down to her stomach. She reached across and wrapped her hand, as well as she could, around his largess. Her other hand gently grasped him from below. His guttural sigh told her she was doing this right. The very explicit thoughts racing through her head brought her to an even higher stage of exhilaration.

Small beads of perspiration materialized on her face. A soft twinge began in her stomach and raced through her body. Her stress began to abate. A strong desire began to take hold of her.

Dessa moved closer. He could see the excitement of her nipples through the fabric of her gown. He ached for his time with her. Her deep and uneven breathing, along with her perfect grip, told him he had found a willing, able and most wonderful morsel.

With a deep intake of air and a soft moan of desire, Dessa dropped to her knees. Both hands working magic and wonder on him in a deep and glorious massage. He groaned with thick pleasure.

Suddenly his world exploded.

She savagely twisted his crann to an angle that would have brought him to his knees; but he instinctively knew it would only be worse if he went down. Her nails dug deeply into his very fragile and swollen scrotum. With lightening speed she stood before him.

She seemed taller, menacing. Harsh.

Dessa glowered into his face, "My father trusted you. This kingdom trusted you. You stupid and vile slime." She twisted harder, her nails dug deeper, her grip tightened. His knees began to buckle.

Her one hand left the lower parts of his now pain wracked body and harshly grabbed his thin colorless, lifeless hair; it was so dry it felt dusty in her hand. Thrusting her hand back caused his gnarly chin to thrust up. Spittle clung raggedly to the sides of his thin lips; his hot, harsh breath was uneven and shallow. Now, not only did the pain begin to own him, but the powerlessness and unexpected depravity he had intended for her, not for himself, clung fearfully to his sore lack of true manhood.

She said, "Leave now you miserable, worthless scum, and know this well; I will tell all the ladies you were wilted like a rose after the frost and not worth one minute of my time."

She pushed him backward with a savage thrust. His pale body sprawled twisted on the floor. His hollow chest heaved with stress and bewilderment. Quickly he grabbed his robes and ran to the door. "I will light the fire myself!" he spat towards her.

Something strange happened to Dessa just then.

She smiled.

Not exactly sure as to why, but nonetheless she smiled.

13.
Morning

It hurt, but in a pleasant sort of way. When he opened his eyes, the harsh sun blinded him. It was warm and freshening. The brightness added life.

Torrin moved to stretch long and bold. His leg reminded him of reality. And the sharp pain stopped him in mid stretch; his head felt better, the bump going down. All around, the residents of Journey were rolling, folding or somehow stuffing their sleeping tools away for another day.

Suddenly Torrin remembered the fire. He looked up; the ashes in the hearth were piled high. The stones fairly glowed, but now their warmth competed with the heat of the sun glowering through the thick glass.

"Eh boy," Quillan said slowly, as he rammed his bear into a large sack, "Ye must o' got up enough times to wood the fire and keep us all alive. Good job. Now mind ye, don' be the last one in tanite, or ye geet to do it agin." He grinned warmly at Torrin, as his father did sometimes.

Torrin got to his feet. The cut in his leg felt like crusty fire. The rag was brittle and tight. He bent down and untied it. Soft ooze ran around the cut.

Karina quietly arrived and knelt beside him. She looked refreshed, younger and radiant. Her hair was combed, her face washed and she smelled of flowers. "Looks good," she genuinely said. "I was afraid it might be all hot and festering by now. Thought we might have to boil yer leg this morning. But ye did a good job cleanin' it right away. Best thing for a gash, get it clean."

She produced a jar with yellowish, sticky looking contents. "Now this may hurt a little, just for a minute though." She applied the yellow ointment to his wound and then proceeded to tie a clean fresh cloth around it. "Don' be stretching your leg today. Let that heal; you will be good as new before you know it."

His gaze would have left her cold if she had looked at him. But she was busy packing her supplies.

Torrin muttered a real "Thank you." He pondered that it might be nice to get to know this woman better. She was by far the smartest he had met so far. However, home called. His heart was beckoning to the familiar.

Harold emerged from the kitchen. Both hands full with large heavy platters of steaming eggs, sausage, bacon and a myriad of brightly colored vegetables Torrin had never seen before. "Ey ye ragged rabble, eat it while it's hot or I'll give it to the goat," Harold said playfully.

The residents of Journey all had bowls of a sort and set upon the platters with desperate sincerity, however with a certain polite order. Karina emerged with tankards of drink and the lute player from last night started a gentle strumming from the far corner. Journey seemed at the moment for most, a destination. In fact a very happy destination!

Torrin limped over to Harold who was heaping strange looking green leafy things into his bowl and said, "I am sorry but I don't have..." as Harold produced a bowl and placed it into Torrin's hand.

"Relax son, just learn to relax and sometimes enjoy right now. Sometimes ye have to have faith tha' the future will provide," Harold threw back his head and laughed heartily, "and if it does not, you'll be dead anyway. So eat and have a good morn. It is a glorious day!"

Torrin ate. He ate well. Even tried the strange green things. They were acceptable; a little stringy, but acceptable.

He sat back and looked around as he ate his food. As always, things look different the next day. Torrin still felt like a chicken in a wolf house though. His mind started to plan.

"Come with me." Quillan said after a short time. It did not sound like an option. "Everyone helps at Journey."

Torrin countered, "I understand, but I must speak with Harold and Karina for a moment." He hurried toward the kitchen, his stiff leg suffering him.

Bursting through the door he found Harold and Karina in a warm embrace. Harold's bushy face was pressed against Karina warm soft skin, lips locked, her hand wound through the long thick hair on the back of his head.

They parted, not at all embarrassed, not at all annoyed.

Karina smiled and said "Yes dear, you are leaving. Here is some food; it's all I have for now." She held out a large package, wrapped in a thin oilskin. There is also a blanket for you to sleep with tonight.

"How?" remarked Torrin, surprise clouding his face.

"Never mind." declared Karina.

"I will send the highest ranking members of the liege back to pay my debts as soon as possible; you have been most kind and I thank you," declared Torrin. "You will be rewarded well. And, I will not need the blanket."

"Take the blanket, please, you can return it later," Karina said in a kind yet strange way. "And thank you."

Torrin turned toward the door, food in hand. As he pushed it open Harold said, "Just remember, you can come back in any time you like."

Torrin turned to Harold, smiled and walked out.

As he left, Torrin had a strange feeling. Journey was empty. Everyone had gone to do their deed for the day, payment for the ensuing and oncoming night.

He quickly donned his princely clothes. Now dry. They felt good, warm and secure.

14.
Trial

Dessa sat in the chair for the accused. Its hard surface would have been intolerable if it had not been for Sanura adding a soft, small blanket under Dessa's skirts.

She had waited for days as preparations for the trial and debate had gone on, and it had been agonizing. At least now, sitting here, things were moving forward.

Each morning she arose, dressed and watched the kingdom arise around her. The market became alive. The stables became alive. Even her beloved Uta set out on hunting trips, now without her.

The arguments droned on. Her father had accessed the smartest debaters of the kingdom. But she knew it was of no use.

Darius' father, Gaerwn was a hateful and powerful tyrant. He would require revenge, more so than justice, but justice was the most that Tarmon would allow. Even if it was a most tragic and unjust justice. He was sworn to protect his people.

Tarmon's mountain people, though hardy and strong, were no match to Gaerwn's army. It seemed that the very survival of the kingdom rested in the event of Dessa being harshly tied to a rough log and roasted to death in a hot searing fire.

She wept. The kingdom wept.

After the third day of the trial she summoned King Tarmon to her room, which by now felt like a prison.

"Father!" Dessa spouted as he entered the room. Both hugged each other ferociously.

"My child, my life." said Tarmon, "I am so sorry. My heart is breaking. Please forgive me."

"You are bound by the law. You are bound to protect your people. And as you said, sometimes things are out of our control."

Dessa turned her face to the window. Squaring her shoulders, she recited tersely what she had practiced, "Father, we must end this. There is no hope. End the trial and set the date. The waiting is worse than the end. I am sorry, I know this hurts, but you must know. This is what I ask of you."

Tarmon looked long and hard at his daughter. The sadness in his eyes dripped down onto his face. A weariness had set upon him that sagged his shoulders.

"Dessa," he began, "I love you with all my soul. Just as I loved your brother, and still love the memory of your mother. This situation may be the end of me. However, I understand your pain, I understand that the waiting is the worst part. How long do you want?"

She had not expected this question.

"When is the best time for you?" she asked softly.

"Three days after the new moon gives us time to send word to Gaerwn," Tarmon replied, tears streaming down his cheeks.

"So be it," replied Dessa firmly.

Overall, it would have been twenty-one days.

The window in her room seemed very small.

15.

Upstream

The warm sun filled Torrin with hope. His happy whistling kept him company as he trod along. The grade of the stream was not harsh, and the banks wide since the spring rains had been light this year.

With the sun high in the sky, he came upon the carcass of the dead dragon. The animals of the forest had made quick work of the kill. The area was decimated with broken and matted vegetation. Arguments over the larger chunks of meat, mused Torrin. It seemed different here though. Like he had been here, but it was new. The whole thing did not make sense.

Looking around, he spotted the object of his desire. Glimmering brightly in the streambed was his trusty and most favorite knife. Picking it up, he shuddered at the thought of having to use it on something as beastly as a dragon. He did not linger long.

By the time the sun was two-thirds of the way through the sky, Torrin began to wonder how far the dragon had taken him. Nothing looked familiar. The hunting paths did not appear, the trails he and the guards used were not in sight. In fact, the vegetation still looked oddly strange, heavier, thicker than he remembered.

Majestic mountains rose up all around him. The peaks were covered with thick snow and ice. The tree line was visible where the air became so thin; nothing survived. Torrin remembered one expedition up a mountain. They had all wanted to see why the trees stopped growing. What caused it?

By the time he and his party had reached the place where the trees stopped, the pain in their chests was powerful and overwhelming.

Gasping harshly, it dawned on Torrin that this must be where the world ends. The air was gone.

Quickly descending, he made note to stay low. The helpless feeling of no air had left him strangely educated.

Torrin now felt the twinge of fear, not so much at being low, but enduring the outside for a treacherous night. He had never experienced a storm like the one last night. The very world seems at odds with itself.

But today was warm and sunny; a fresh breeze gently blew. The dichotomy was fascinating, yet made no sense. But it was very real.

Having gone too far to turn back, Torrin looked for a place to spend the night.

At the edge of a clearing stood thick green pines, their long heavy needles reaching to the ground. He carefully entered the pine forest, cautious not to disturb the natural windbreak the intertwined branches provided.

Moving deep into the forested area, the scent of pine was overwhelming. The sun fairly boiled the sap and sent heavy, almost noxious fumes over him. Finding a sheltered and protected locale, he set out to scooping a cavernous impression in the thick needles that covered the ground.

As the wind began to increase and the temperature dropped, Torrin covered himself with the blanket from Karina, and then the pine needles.

As he lay shivering in his hole for the night, his mind raced for answers. It was obvious he needed more information. Still nothing made much sense.

Finally, sleep relieved him of the cold and he dreamt warmly of Karina's soft friendly eyes, the fresh aromas wafting from the kitchen. He dreamt that Quillan was laughing heartily.

When morning came, he packed up his few meager supplies and began walking back downstream. Home seemed far away. Home, he thought, seemed not to exist.

Home? He wondered where it was and if he would ever see it again.

Little did he know.

16.
Pounding

The thunderous pounding of brawny, well-shod hooves was only slightly muffled by the thin layer of snow wafting across the well-worn path. Geysers of thick steam raged out Dalmonda's snout as she sailed through the night. Her large eyes intent, her strong mind completely in charge of a muscular body. She was on a mission. A mission she knew was vital. Her rider was firm and strong, and she could feel the stoic determination through the familiar legs that gripped her sides.

Every third day for the last twenty-one, Dalmonda had made this journey. Always at night, always at a dead run. Somehow, this time was different. This time it was final. This time it mattered.

The cold air had dried the tears on Dessa's face. Her fear replaced first by hope, and then by the natural vicious desire for survival. The wind blew through the thick wool cape that surrounded her. The breeches she wore felt strong, snug, secure and strange. Heat from Dalmonda's back rose up warmly to keep her from freezing. The blanket under her was just thick enough to keep the big horse's bones from jarring her to death. However, none of the discomforts mattered; she was free.

Dessa was amazed at the power, speed and determination of the horse. Twas not like a race; was more like lightning that would not stop.

At one point wolves pursued them; there must have been a pack of twelve or more, Dessa had not bothered to try and count. Her sword had dispatched three or four. However, Dalmonda had not missed one stride. She thundered through the night, a number of the wolves meeting their end under her machete-like hooves. Even her beloved Uta would look fearful at the sound of wolves.

It was as if Dalmonda was possessed.

The only time they stopped was at the edge of a stream. Dalmonda came to a fast and determined halt. She drank heavily for just a moment, and then like an arrow let free from a well-tuned bow, she turned and continued, full stride.

Dessa knew they headed toward the hunting lodge. Dalmonda knew it too. Dessa relaxed and let the horse take the lead.

As her world sped past, the full moon lit the trail and Dessa's mind turned to the fast paced events of only a short time ago that changed everything.

* * *

The knock on the door to her chamber had startled her. Even though she knew it was imminent, the reality of it stopped her heart cold.

She had not eaten much of the wonderful meal Sanura left for her. The hours in the church that morning had done nothing to calm her. It only left her more frightened and feeling alone.

Valdemar walked into the chamber in front of Tarmon. His leering grin preceded him into the cold damp room, adding to the gloom. His long, dark blue velvet robes lent an unnatural elegance to what she knew was a despicable man.

Tarmon closed the door firmly. He turned toward Dessa. He looked strange, different. Odd? She was at once concerned, more now than before.

He did not look at Dessa. Instead, he was focused on the back of Valdemar's robes. With lightning speed that belied his years, he brought a thick, long leather strap over Valdemar, down quickly around his torso to the level of his wrists and bound him tightly. Even before Valdemar could react or shout, Tarmon had pushed Valdemar to the floor face first, and buried his head in the thick carpet.

Sanura fairly leapt into the room from Dessa's private entrance, carrying all sorts of odd things. Dropping her bundle, she too, with lightning speed attacked Valdemar. Sanura had a shorter strap that went over Valdemar's head and over his mouth.

When the two attackers were done they flipped Valdemar over, and tied his feet to a rope. The rope went over one of the heavy wooden beams that supported the roof.

By this time, Dessa's mind had begun to function. She did not know what exactly was going on, but she believed it to be good.

The three of them hauled Valdemar up, feet first. By now, Valdemar was struggling and making all sorts of grunting and spewing noises. However, not loud enough to be heard outside the chamber.

Valdemar's robes fell to the level of his hands revealing his pale naked body. Fortunately, the fallen robes now covered his head. Tarmon looked at Dessa and smiled.

"Dessa, you must do exactly what we tell you, no questions, or we all die. Agreed?"

Dessa nodded, still reeling and not quite able to comprehend what was happening.

Sanura set a stool down in front of Dessa. "Sit," she commanded.

Dessa sat.

Sanura, then using a sharp knife began to cut Dessa's hair just below the ears. Taking each clump of the long red tresses in her hand, Sanura laid them neatly side-by-side. From her bundle she produced a thin leather strap, coated with beeswax. Carefully, she pressed the hair into the wax, forming a very crude wig.

Sanura handed Dessa a set of men's clothes—breeches, heavy shirt, thick boots and a belt. "Quickly, get dressed," she ordered. Dessa slipped out of her robes and began dressing. All modesty quickly forgotten. Two daggers and a light, yet firm sword finished the set.

Valdemar had stopped twitching and squirming and now hung quite unconscious above the room. Surprisingly, Sanura began to quickly drop her clothes to the floor. Despite being quite amazed at the drama unfolding all around her, Dessa was impressed with the strength and litheness of the older woman. Sanura was long, and not so much muscular as sinewy. With the air of authority she carried, her body fit her well. You could tell she respected herself and had not let herself get heavy like so many of the castle's servants.

Tarmon released the large belt from Valdemar and stripped the unconscious man of his robes. He handed these to Sanura who quickly put them on. Tarmon then let Valdemar down to the floor. With the help of the two women, they dressed Valdemar in Dessa's robes. They then affixed the wig to his head, added a large woven bag that covered his head and then re-applied the straps. He was now trussed tightly, hand, foot and mouth.

Tarmon approached Dessa. She seemed taller in short hair, wearing breeches and boots, somehow older. "My dear and precious daughter," he began, with tears welling in his eyes. "I love you more than anything on this earth. All I ask is you do what you can to live your life well and fully. I will miss you, but I cannot bear to see you hurt. Please try to send word that you are well after two summers. I can then die in peace for my time comes soon." Dessa started to speak, but Tarmon put his fingers to her lips. "Shhh, before you speak, here is what you must do. Go to my bedroom. There is a rope at the window. After you see the fire lit, throw it down, and follow it to the ground. Sanura will arrive on Dalmonda. Ride her to the hunting lodge tonight. Dalmonda knows the way. I know you do too. Trust me."

"Oh father," Dessa gasped, arms encircling his neck. Hot tears stung her eyes. She could not speak; her face told him all he needed to know.

Dessa turned to Sanura. "I am blessed," was all that she could choke from her swollen throat.

"Yes my child, and so are we. Ride safe, more is waiting for you." Sanura turned and said to Tarmon, "Let us finish this ruse."

Tarmon picked up the now partially conscious Valdemar and roughly threw him over his shoulder, the long red hair swinging about. Sanura pulled a thin black bag over her head and then with her hands together in seemingly earnest prayer, followed Tarmon out the door.

Dessa looked about the room for what she knew would be the last time. Hastily snatching up her mother's comb, she stuffed it under her shirt and then left through the door Sanura used. Carefully she made her way to her father's room. No one was about; all were at the castle's center to watch the burning.

Cautiously she watched from her father's window. Sanura sat astride Dalmonda, holding two large torches. Tarmon hung the struggling and writhing body on a nail on a large pole. He placed both hands on the head and gave the forehead a large kiss. He then said something; turned, bowed his head, and walked away.

Sanura threw a torch to either side of the twisting figure. The black oil pitch coating the dry wood flamed instantly. Dessa stood transfixed at the sight until Sanura rode Dalmonda rapidly out the main gate.

Dessa flew as though possessed. The rope at the window was tied tight to a heavy beam. She heard it hit the ground with a dull swish. Before she could even think, she was out the window and walking down the wall. As she set foot on the ground, Dalmonda and Sanura arrived. Sanura leapt off the horse. After one fast and last embrace, Dessa mounted Dalmonda and the steed took to the trail like the wind. When Dessa looked back, Sanura was already half way up the wall. Dessa wondered where she found the strength.

She would soon find out it was the strength of love.

17.
Gale

For many a day now, Gale had been tending to completely well horses. He was at the kingdom's main hunting lodge under the pretense that the grand steeds were in need of tending because they were very sick. Ever since he had finished all the preparations, he had become bored. Not just a regular boredom, but one that eats at you when you are forced to wait for something very important to happen. Boredom he never wanted to repeat, but one he knew was important to a very special person in his life.

The lodge had been securely built for the harshly cold winters and oppressively hot summers. It had actually been built twice for some practical reasons. The first effort created the inner structure. Living quarters at one end, stables and tanning room for dressing the bounty of the hunt at the other. The inside walls consisted of fairly thin logs closely fitted together to form a smooth surface. Then the outer walls had been built—larger heavy logs, carefully laid, heavily chinked with thick grey clay.

The width of a thick boot separated the two walls and this area had been packed with solid mud. The result was a lodge that could withstand the fiercest of storms, hold heat and keep all unwanted animals outside. One large fireplace heated the living quarters and the stables. The lodge was quiet and secure, and the inside sometimes felt like a wooden prison—when you spent a few days there during a blizzard. But it was safe and worked well for the kingdom's hunters.

Anyway, Gale had been counting the days for the event. He and King Tarmon had counted out the same number of stones each to keep track; Gale at the lodge, Tarmon at the castle. Upon rising each day Gale would take one stone away from the small leather bag that hung near the door. It seemed to take many days before he removed the last stone. Tonight, he was ready.

A splendid fire warmed the stones in the fireplace to a warm glow sending soothing warm waves of heat throughout the structure, keeping the chilly night at bay. The finest venison Gale could find boiled at a gentle simmering pace in a thick and tasty stew accompanied by delicate onions, potatoes, a few light roots and even seasoned with some precious salt. A plate of dried fruit, covered carefully by white muslin, sat waiting on the table. Bold red wine stood ready in a green glass bottle by the door, where it would stay cool, ready to escape into large, chilly crystal tankards.

The king's bed, fluffed pillows lightly stacked, clean blankets neatly folded at the foot awaited a weary traveler. And, best of all, Uta and Calandra were prepared, and they seemed almost expectant. Their special and carefully organized loads were wrapped and ready nearby.

Gale sat by the one and only window, staring into the dark night. His mind raced over a million memories. He practiced his speeches, he checked off the mental list that was so vital. He shivered at the thought of it all.

It was as if he had been practicing for this night and this event all his life. Yet, he had never dreamed it would all end this way. Or maybe it was a beginning? This was not a time for romantic dreams and fantasy! Romance, or the thought, maybe the desire for romance, had forced this play. That and the need for too much power and control.

He sighed deeply.

Gale had removed the inner frame of the window so he could rest his long and tired arms on the sill. Try as he might, he could not escape the sleep that overtook him.

A very deep sleep.

18.
One Question Answered

For Torrin, the first part of the morning was pure hell. Fresh snow from the night before that covered the ground made every rock slippery, and getting around was nasty work; his leg was as stiff as a monk in a whorehouse.

After a while, the sun took care of the ice; exercise took care of the stiffness in his leg. Unfortunately, Torrin had taken care of all the food yesterday, thinking he was close to his castle. By midday, he felt like his throat had been cut, and eating was only a memory. He stopped to take a long drink from the stream, which helped for a while, but only for a cursed short while.

At one point, he stopped to sit on a large rock to rest. This stone was in the sun sitting silently by the swift waters of the creek. It was warm, it was smooth, and after sitting down to rest, the warm stone became a place for a nice nap.

Strange as it seemed, he felt powerless to move, maybe frozen from fright, as the huge dragon, its hairy face smiling in victory, swallowed his good leg first, and then the other, cooking the flesh and then the muscle with his internal fire as he gnawed and swallowed. His hands could not find his sword. Blackbirds overhead mocked him with their frenetic caw caws. This time, the huge teeth were gnashing at his entire body, not just his leg, broiling him and tearing him to shreds. The pain was not so bad, but the sight was ghastly terrifying.

He awoke with a frantic jump. The chipmunk that had been exploring his leg scampered away with a squeaky yelp. As he looked around, the nightmare faded, yet it dawned on him that it very well could have been real.

Again!

It was time to start to think and take action unless he wanted to become a victim again. He felt foolish. He finally became acutely aware that being foolish in this land could be fatal. He had escaped once; he did not want to count on his luck holding out.

Eventually he arrived back at Journey. No more a blessed sight had he ever encountered. Since it was late afternoon, all sorts of animals were about. They were enjoying the sun and rough winter grasses that were giving over to the thin tender spring blades with the warming of each day. Cows grazed contently, sheep and goats moved about with carefree abandon. A number of chickens scurried through the dark brown grass looking for bits of food. It was a serene setting.

A group of Journey residents, carrying firewood into the service door around the far end of the big building, nodded to him. Torrin felt more than thought that he was going to somehow pay for not working yesterday. He would find that later he was right.

A big hand roughly clasped his shoulder and he heard the loud happy bellowing of Quillan. "Back sa soon ye wimpy lil' colt?" he proclaimed. "One ni in the wds and yer back hr scrounging for a free meal ugain? Ifn' ye ah axed nice I wooda tol ye that the castle is no more thn a month's fast iken, in warm summer weather!"

"Thas right, go head and glare at me ye tempestuous little wart." Quillan shot back at Torrin's leering look, "Slow down boy, oh, excusssse me. Sir!" Quillan mocked a little, "and wll hep ya out." Quillan picked up the biggest buck Torrin had ever seen and without what seemed any effort at all, carried it into Journey. He could hear Karina's yelp of joy from inside.

Torrin quietly wondered to himself if she would be as happy to see him as the carcass Quillan had just deposited in the kitchen.

She was.

19.
Family Tree

The gentle hand that squeezed Gale's shoulder woke him. He had figured that staying awake was futile, so he was not surprised by her intrusion on his dreams. His arms and head were cold. The outer window frame where he had been sleeping was not very tight, but to this, he paid little heed.

"Dessa, sweet Dessa! I am so happy to see your beautiful face," he joyously exclaimed. Gale was somewhat surprised at her serious expression. However, after all, he mused, she had in a short time endured so much. Just half a night ago, she was expecting to burn at the stake. Now she was here. Poor girl must be a little fanatical by now? He had seen her angry before and had heard about her little episode with Valdemar. He hoped she was of good humor now or at least tolerable. He knew some sleep would help her disposition.

He reached toward her to give her a big hug and she fainted dead away into a mass of wet clothes and sweat onto the floor.

*   *   *

When Dessa awoke, she took stock of herself and her surroundings. No, this must not be heaven; there was the sweet homey aroma of food cooking. Yes, she must be, she was alive! It had not been a long bad dream!

Dessa tried to swing her feet out of the familiar bed and noted with some embarrassment that all she was wearing was a thin shift. Her legs ached from her ankles to her stomach. It was an aching dark hurt, like she had been whipped. Pulling up the shift she took careful view of herself and what felt like nasty injuries. Her clear pink skin was still smooth and unharmed, but rubbed raw. The muscles in her thighs, butt and stomach were all bunched and a little swollen. Then it hit her; riding bareback, or just on a blanket half the night was not something she ever wanted to do again. Especially if she HAD to do it again. The circumstances of the last few weeks were something she truly hoped would never repeat.

All her strange new clothes from last night hung on pegs near the fire, quite dry. And what a glorious fire it was. The room seemed to radiate warmth. Bright sunshine poured in through the side window. Gale, bless his heart, lay sleeping soundly, quietly snoring on one of the small beds.

She was sore, but she was alive. She had learned that lesson in thankfulness from dear Gale on the many adventures she had encountered growing up around him. Now she stretched all she could. Pointing her toes toward her head to keep the leg cramps away, she twisted and pushed in every direction, enjoying the slow freedom of taking the harsh clenching out. Only after stirring the lot of her body did she venture to stand up. Still tender, she pushed her hands, fingers tightly intertwined, over her head and stood up tall. Her lithe body responded wonderfully, everything either tight or protruding out in just the right places and size, or at least in a manner with which she was content. She thought about some of the other girls in the kingdom, already pudgy, starting to sag and losing their youth, far too early. Of course, most of them had already given birth or were regularly sleeping with at least one man (and if the stories were true, they were sleep deprived from their late night romps) on a regular basis.

Part of Dessa was jealous, another part of her glad to be free. She knew she wanted to wait for the right man—the right time, the right everything. Until then (and after, she had resolved), she would take care of herself, so when the time came, she would be able to give him what he needed, and she would be able to enjoy him in the deepest possible ways. She let out a little sigh, and then turned her attention back to reality.

As she sat down with a handful of dried fruit on a stool in front of the fire, the warm glow of the stones radiated luxuriously into her skin through the thin fabric. Dessa ran the events of the previous night through her mind. They seemed chilling. Yet, they seemed rather well thought out. Who, she wondered, had put it all together?

"I see you are back among the living," quietly exclaimed Gale, breaking her reverie. "I really cannot keep up these horrible hours at my age," he said, stretching his long frame.

"Oh Gale," she exclaimed. "Who came up with such a wicked and wonderful plan?"

"Well, that would be your grandfather," Gale said as he added a few logs, probably the last for the day, and stirred the big pot of stew. Steamy tendrils floated off the top adding the spicy and satisfying aroma that only well tended stew can add to a chilly evening.

"Grandfather?" inquired Dessa with what looked like a scowl on what was still a very dirty face hidden beneath a matted mass of tangled, all be it shorter, red hair. "He died before I could walk. Gale, such jokes are in bad taste."

Gale stood at the fire, attending to the stew. He watched the flames slowly find their way around the wood he had just added. He shuddered quietly, thinking of the horror and pain it must have been for Valdemar. Evil as he was, it seemed awful, yet justifying at the same time. Gale just shook his head.

It is said, as Gale had heard, that a person's legs go numb from the heat, yet their insides frantically try to stay alive. The amount of sweat produced actually steams them alive inside their clothes. Once the body gets hot enough, their blood starts to boil and then the internal organs explode upon each other. The last great event of being burned alive is when the brain heats up and either the head explodes with the sound of a pumpkin hitting the ground as if tossed from the top of the wall, or the eyes shoot out like corks from a shaken beer keg. All in all, it is a painful and wretched way to go.

Although Gale was basically a peaceful man who spent his time tending to animals and enjoying nature, he reckoned that in the end Valdemar got what he deserved and ultimately the satire in the story was that the evil man saved Dessa and was a painful reminder to all who lived in the kingdom that violence was not an answer that would be tolerated. If it was not so hateful, all of it, Gale would have laughed at the wicked irony. He turned his attention to Dessa.

"Put some warm water in a bowl and wash up lass. You look a fright. Get cleaned up and we shall eat. You must be on your way by midday, for you have a very long ride of ahead of you."

After Dessa had washed up, brushed her hair and gotten dressed, they sat down at the big hunting table to eat. It was a feast fit for a king and queen. The stew had simmered all night. The potatoes, onions, various roots and greens were tender and tasty with the fragrant meat. The dried fruits added a gentle sweetness and the water Gale fetched from the nearby creek was fresh and almost bubbled with the morning air. He had declared it was too early in the day for wine. Dessa had reminded him in a gentle teasing way that he must be getting old.

"It is time for you to hear the story my dear," began Gale after they felt stuffed and satisfied. "I would guess there is no time like the present for you to hear the family secrets and about the skeletons in the closet." His big blue, clear eyes stared out the window for a moment, and then he softly began.

"Your grandmother Saoirse was a wise and prudent woman. She very much loved Keegan, her husband, who became a good and benevolent king. That was not what Saoirse's mother and father had figured would be the case. "But," he said waving his hand, "Keegan turned out to be a good man, once he settled down some. The only problem, Saoirse was without child for many seasons. Not until she was much older, did baby Tarmon appear. Giving birth almost killed her for her age. I do not think she would have cared if she died, if it gave life to her son. She loved Tarmon so."

"You see, Keegan is not Tarmon's father." Sighing heavily, and now pouring two glasses of wine, Gale continued. "I am not sure what criteria she used to make her choice. Height, hair, features, build? Who knows? But Saoirse one day decided to find a man to do the job Keegan seemed to lack. She didn't know which one of them, herself or the man she loved, was responsible for no babe arriving, but she figured it was worth a venture. Better to leave an heir than let the council determine who shall rule."

Gale's blue eyes seemed misty and far away. "It was fall, time for the hunt that would feed the kingdom through the onslaught of the brutal winter. The evenings were getting nasty cold as they do every year. Those bright warm days were so wonderful." Gale sighed, slumping down onto the seat, his eyes watery with memory. It was evident that his throat had failed him and the choke caught there would require a few moments to abate.

Dessa stood slowly, the heavy tankard of wine unseen and unfelt in her hand. "You?" She said breathlessly. "You are my grandfather? All these years, I thought you were just a very nice man! The head of the stables, the …," she blubbered.

"Yes, I am your grandfather," he quietly replied. "You have held a special place in my heart since you were born."

"Does father know?" asked the startled and somewhat dazed Dessa. She felt like a little girl again. So many memories of wonderful times with Gale began flooding her mind.

"Yes. Saoirse told him just before she died. I was afraid he would have me burned. Instead, he came, alone, one night to my place in the stables. I remember it well. He knelt in front of me, kissed my hand and thanked me for making his mother so happy and giving him life."

After taking a long drink from the tankard, Gale continued, "We very seldom had a chance to speak alone. Sometimes on the hunt, sometimes in the stable. Kings are often surrounded by people trying to gain favor. To tell you the truth, it drives him a little mad."

"At times, when I was first teaching you to ride…" pausing, he smiled, "thank goodness you liked horses!" Continuing, "Tarmon would send for me. Oh, it was a great time! I would approach his throne, hat in hand, all bowing and bending and he would proclaim 'come forward Stable Master' in that kingly voice he loves to use. And then we would exit the throne room, much to the chagrin of all the court, and together we would walk around the castle, talking of you, his mother, his father, the kingdom. So many things. You my dear," Gale looked lovingly at Dessa, "your childhood mischievousness gave us much to discuss, and many times for sharing our thoughts and stories. Thank you."

"Your father loves you so. He would never see you harmed. No matter what the law said. So after Valdemar put on his little show in your chamber, it all came together. That low life idiot provided the critical element. You see, we needed a body. Before he pulled his little stunt, we were going to use a recently deceased person. A live person, trying to escape was much better, don't you think? Sanura and I planned the events. My part was to teach Dalmonda the way here at night and make sure you were provisioned for your trip."

Dessa interrupted, "How do we explain Valdemar's disappearing?"

"Easy and already done." Gale stretched, "After I had laid you down, Dalmonda received a new saddle blanket. One side was torn so that it looked as if it had been attacked, and covered with blood from the stag in the stew. Dalmonda will walk into the castle courtyard, riderless. Any prudent person will conclude that he rode out, distressed at killing the lovely Dessa, and was attacked and eaten by wolves."

"Remind me never to make you angry with me," Dessa mumbled. "Gale, I mean grandfather, oh dear," Dessa sat down. "So much, so fast. What's next, I cannot live here!" she exclaimed, much of the news and the story sinking in.

Gale looked up into her now wild, violet blue eyes; his heart breaking. "My dear, you will leave here and head mostly south. You must travel for a good part of the summer to a place where you will be welcome. An inn named Journey. You leave this afternoon. Your half brother is there."

"Oh god!" cried Dessa. "I have a half brother! What else don't I know?"

"Well, this," replied Gale with a steeled face. "When you arrive there, you must find him, but you cannot ask for him outright. There are things he can tell you, which I cannot. He is in danger and will not reveal himself easily. I am sure you will find each other. But take care, be cautious and move slowly."

20.
Home

Torrin entered Journey and noticed something different. Many of the tables were pushed to one side. A large area in the middle was open for some kind of activity. Energy was in the air; he could almost taste it.

He heard a shout from the kitchen. Karina ran over and threw her arms around him. "I'm so happy to see you back so soon my lad! Come in and have a nice meal."

Quillan groaned from the far end of the room. He had already assumed his perch upon the stout bench, one foot resting up on the table, tankard in hand.

"Oh shush up you big lummox, you eat pretty well here. Don't you worry, his day will come," scolded Karina.

Once in the kitchen, Karina turned toward Torrin, a stern look on her face. "Do you have anything to say young man?"

Torrin, taken aback, looked down at the well-swept floor. "Yes. Thank you for the food and I am sorry I left in such a hurry. I guess I really don't know what is going on. Can you explain it to me?" His eyes were pleading with her. All of a sudden, he felt tired and suddenly hungry. The smells from the kitchen, usually wonderful, were overpowering and he noticed a lot was cooking all around him.

Karina relaxed a little as she handed him a large slice of bread covered with well seasoned, still warm meat. "I can tell you this for now. We have been waiting for you for a long while. It is foretold; a prince shall arrive at the right time and carry on." She stopped, cocked her head and looked quizzically at him before continuing.

"It is the right time. You are a prince. The rest; that I shall leave up to Harold to explain. Just suffice to say, be patient waiting for the explanation, he has much to show you first. You have to prove you can do this." Torrin had hardly tasted the food he had wolfed down while she was talking, but he felt better already, although the questions he had that were not even clear were spinning in his head.

"Now go and clean that buck Quillan brought to us. It will go well with tonight's party. Mind you, we use everything." She turned to the cooking that surrounded her.

"One last question if I may?" Torrin said with a wet glimmer in his eyes, "Will I ever go home?"

Karina looked at the young man standing in front of her, her face serious and caring, yet stern. "Eventually, yes, you'll understand when the time is right and you are ready. Now get to work."

Torrin was glad he had found his knife. The buck was big, but did not look very old. Not much fat, since it was just the end of winter, but it would feed many. His mind wandered to all the unanswered questions. Maybe once summer came, he could earn a horse and go home. Oh well, he mused. At least it sounds like a party for tonight. He could use some entertainment and fun after all he had been through.

He traveled back and forth from the butchering area to the kitchen, helping Karina hang, chop and prepare all the meat, some of which went on drying racks. Karina explained that they always used a portion of all successful hunts to prepare and be safe for next winter.

As he wiped the last of the deer off his hands, he heard loud female giggling from the great room. When he walked out to investigate, he stopped short. There were six or so stunningly beautiful women surrounding the dance floor, all their attention turned to Quillan. Quillan, in a show of his youth, power and more than not proof of his vitality (or show of virility thought Torrin), was swinging a tall lithe strawberry blond girl around his middle, as if she was no more than a small child's toy. The rest of the girls were watching, clapping and giggling. Especially the happy young lady being tossed about.

Well, thought Torrin, it is a good night for a party and the mood seems right. Might do me good!

21.
New Beginning

There were three horses in the stable. It was quite evident they were well taken care of; their coats had a buttery sheen. Brushed well, fed well, exercised and loved. They were the most gallant steeds of the kingdom. Unfortunately, two of them were going to experience a nasty and violent death.

At least that was the story that would be told over and over for many a winter to come.

Gale would be contending that the wolves were becoming a menace. Not just two gallant and important steeds but Valdemar too! These fanatic, destructive menaces need to be hunted and exterminated. If the wolves were left to their devices, who knows what would happen? Maybe small children would start to disappear? His reasoning was, give people something to worry about, something to do. They would soon forget about Valdemar, they would mourn Dessa, but they would fight to protect their horses and children. They would turn their attention to the threat at hand and miss the sleight of hand played on them.

At least he hoped they would.

Dessa walked a little awkwardly into the stable room. Her thighs still warm and scratchy, her bottom sore and her hands stiff from last night's hellish ride. But all the pain was forgotten when Uta came into view. Both horse and girl had a very happy and emotional reunion. It bothered Dessa to cry outwardly. And if others had been around, you would not have seen the emotions. However, she was safe with her feelings around Gale.

Throwing her arms around Uta's big neck, she hugged him mightily. He gave a wet snort and long whinny of delight at being reunited with his favorite rider, caretaker and friend. Out here at the lodge, Uta had felt secure since he knew Gale was a good man. But for many days now, ever since things had seemed to become tense, he had missed the delicate feel of Dessa's body on his back as she would post as naturally as water runs down a clear creek. She fit like no one else. She was commanding, but never mean. They were meant for each other.

When a horse finds a person who truly fits with him, something strange occurs between both. A bond that is hard to explain. It is like love, but is more a natural earthly connection, cemented in a deep honor that grows to commitment. The human is expected to respect and care for the horse. The horse will do everything feasible for the human, including die. The rest of the relationship is impossible to describe, but if you ever experience it, you will know it. Both Uta and Dessa knew they had a special bond. It was one that would come in very handy later in the strangest of ways.

Dessa was standing with her head resting on Uta's long snout when she felt a tug at her shoulder.

"Yes Gale," she said softly. Her eyes were closed, her mind resting in the company of her most dear friend. Her shoulder tugged again. She turned to tell Gale to be patient, she had been through a lot, but she looked straight into the big brown eyes of Calandra. "Oh Calandra, I am so sorry, I didn't mean to ignore you. You are a dear friend. I love you too!" Dessa hugged the big mare. Calandra did not share the same level of connection with Dessa that Uta did. But she respected the young lady and was glad Uta, her brother, was content. He was such a big strong brut. Dessa calmed him, kept him at bay, soothing what could be a very bad and dangerous temper.

Calandra went back to chewing the soft grasses Gale had provided. Calandra thought it strange how humans talked so much. She did not understand but a few words. Mostly, just the commands they gave. All the rest of communication, the broad bulk of it was through emotion. The hug and the genuine joy on Dessa's face was what told Calandra what she wanted to know. She wanted to know Dessa cared, that Calandra was part of the family, the group, the order of things in Dessa's life. She gave a long wet flap of her large lips. Oh, this grass was good. Where did Gale find it during this wretched season?

Unhem was Gale's horse. He stood quietly chewing and thinking in his stall. "Hello Unhem," Dessa said as she passed. Unhem gave a snort and went back to his chewing. He pondered, "Maybe we can go home soon."

He was right.

Gale tossed a thick saddle blanket to Dessa. "Get Uta ready. We have to move fast if you are to make camp before dark. And it looks like a nasty spring storm is brewing."

"Gale," Dessa protested. "Why can't I stay here tonight? Who would know?"

Gale looked at Dessa sternly. "Dessa, if by chance anyone decided to come by, all would be lost. Think of it. Your father would be disgraced and probably burned at the stake. Sanura would at best be whipped. I would be forever without work, the steeds would be cared for by some fool."

Dessa glanced worriedly at the horses. They seemed to be suddenly tense. She quickly walked over to Uta and tossed the blanket over his strong broad back. "Relax you old worry wart," she said playfully. "I guess we are going somewhere. My legs are just tingling at the thought!"

Dessa and Gale saddled Uta and securely strapped a large pack on Calandra's sturdy back. Gale handed Dessa a variety of clothes and accessories to wear. Three daggers of various lengths were attached to her person in different and secretive places by a variety of methods. The most interesting contraption being a long heavy thread that ran inside her coat from the middle of her right sleeve to the fingers of Dessa's left hand. Inside the right sleeve, her father's favorite silver dagger was positioned so that when Dessa pulled the thread with her left hand, it untied a slipknot and the golden hilt, adorned with her family's coat of arms, descended silently into her right palm. Gale made her practice deploying the special weapon and resetting it until she was comfortable with the whole operation.

One of the daggers looked familiar; black, almost evil in its heft. Gale looked at Dessa and said, "It was the one that took Darius's life. Your father thought it might continue to protect you." Dessa slid it into her boot.

A long, sharp blade hung from the side of the well-polished saddle. Dessa's favorite bow tied in front and a quiver of thirty or so very sharp, straight arrows rode on her back over the thick leather coat she tied down the front. A large thick hat with fur lining and ear coverings fit her head nicely when needed and bounced with comforting familiarity on her back as she walked, secured with a strap. Leather mittens with warm rabbit lining to cover her slender hands were tied to each sleeve of the coat.

All of a sudden it seemed, all of them were outside in the stiff chilly breeze. The sun was over the tops of the trees and dark clouds bumped each other across the expansive sky. Uta and Calandra were ready to go. Dessa knew she had no choice. She felt like the fate of so many, maybe even the future of the kingdom, rested on her successful escape. Even the sad fact of finding her body would bode badly for all the people she loved so dearly, for then the ruse would begin to show. She owed Sanura, her father and Gale the ultimate debt. A debt she intended to repay, at least by doing her part, and more if she ever got the chance.

Big tears welled up in Gale's eyes. They rolled down his face like large balls of fear and trepidation. He sniffed loudly. "Oh, how many times over the past few days have I practiced this speech? I told myself to be strong and worthy. Now look at me. I'm just a sniveling old sod!"

Dessa held both his shoulders and looked at him with warmth, caring and a pleasant sternness. "Gale, I love you, I love my father, and I love Sanura, with all my heart. You have not only shown me that you love me, you have put yourself in grave danger. You have given me a debt I cannot repay, but I shall live. I shall thrive. That is about all I can give you."

Gale took a long, deep breath and expended it across his thinning lips in a slow cleansing manner. He finally smiled a strange smile, one of peace mixed with resignment. He then slowly, but deliberately, started to speak.

"Dessa, please listen carefully. You must ride to the outer most hunting lodge; it is prepared for you. Spend two nights there. If the weather is bad, spend three, but no more than three. I know I can hold off a hunting party for a little while, but not long. With summer approaching, some of these people are hungry for fresh meat."

"Always ride straight into the direction that the sun rises. You want to camp in protected areas." She looked at him sternly. "Yes, I know you are new to overnight camping in the woods, but when Gersemi was viciously maimed and murdered by that pack of wolves, your father forbade you to spend even one night in the wilderness. I don't blame him." He looked deep into her eyes, "You should not blame him either. Never hold a parent wrongly for trying to keep their child safe." Her nod told him she understood, although he felt that words might escape her for now. He worried about her lack of experience, but that was something he could not change right now.

Continuing on he carefully delivered the instructions that would send his granddaughter to her future. "After about three or so days of travel, you will find yourself at a huge, high and broad set of cliffs. At the bottom of this cliff is a body of water, so large you cannot see across it. Its beauty and majesty will astound you; it is the sea, the ocean, the edge of the earth. Be very careful there. The earth mysteriously and without warning moves and shifts. It trembles! Sometimes cracks appear in the ground itself."

"Is it haunted by demons?" asked a now cautious Dessa.

"No," replied Gale, "As I understand it, it has something to do with huge ice flows from long ago and the ground still trembles in fear. Do not fret, the ice is long gone. Except it seems like it tries to come back in the winter," he said with a smirk.

Travel south along the cliffs to a place of training operated by a man named Tallon. Depending on where you find the coast, his place may be many days of riding. He will teach you how to use your swords, daggers and to protect yourself against the sometimes nasty and belligerent people you are sure to encounter. He is a strange man and teaches in very different, sometimes slightly dangerous ways. However, his place is where we send the castle guards. Tell him you are my granddaughter and that his horse is ugly. He and I have a pact. If you ever showed up, he would know what to do." Dessa quizzically looked at Gale. "Don't ask me why we made that pact," he said with a mysterious look and whimsical smile. Gale then whispered to her a secret. She looked puzzled. He just nodded his head and then seemed to move on. He was done with that part of the conversation.

Gale needed to pause for a minute, gathering his thoughts. "There are thirty pieces of gold sewn into your coat lining. That is why it is so heavy. Give Tallon ten of them. He will ask for more. Just tell him that he will get more when he truly starts to know how to teach. He will guffaw and smother about when you say this, but do not worry. It's all an act. He really is a pussycat deep down. Unless you get him really mad. If he truly becomes mad, his face goes beet red. Just stay out of the way."

"Please send word back to the kingdom after two summers. Let us know you are safe. I do not think it wise to ever return," Dessa's shoulders slumped, "But that does not mean we cannot arrange a meeting somewhere," Gale said with a sly grin.

Dessa looked at the frail old man. A man whom she had loved since her memory began. She suddenly understood why her grandmother, Saoirse, had decided upon Gale. Not only handsome, he was honest to a fault, yet smart in ways some could only hope for, and then creative, always. Using his experience to build a better and more hopeful tomorrow for all he loved and cared for, in this world and for others far away. His honor and true love for life and people stretched far beyond his own self.

"You have my word, you have my honor and you have my heart," said Dessa softly. Her long arms embraced him in a thick hug. She kissed both his cheeks. The salt of his tears stung her lips. She squared her shoulders and walked resolutely to Uta. As she swung up, she wondered if she would ever see this place, Gale, Sanura or her father again.

"Thank you Gale," Dessa said with a sudden fervor. "For everything, for everything through all these years! Tell them I love them. Tell them we will see each other again, if it is the last thing I do." She turned Uta towards the trail, the bright glorious sun warming her back; it was now streaming through the trees. The clouds were menacing, but not so thick.

Before she and the grand steeds took to their heels, she asked, "How do I find Journey?"

"Ask Tallon," shouted Gale. "I have no idea."

Dessa shook her head. This was going to be interesting!

The last sight Dessa had of Gale was him waving his big hand over his head. The tears that were running down his smiling face were glistening in the shadows the sunshine cast on his kind features.

After a short cantor to warm the horses, she launched into a bold determined gallop. Then, as they gained their pace and rhythm, the three of them fairly flew down the path. None of them wanted to spend the night outside.

There soon would be enough of that. The next stop was the outer lodge.

Well, maybe.

22.
Encounter

"Torrin," Karina shouted from the kitchen, disturbing his fun at watching Quillan toss the girls, "Go upstairs, second room on the right. There is a basin of water, soap and some toweling. Go make yourself presentable for tonight."

As Torrin ascended the stairs wincing at the stiffness of his leg, he noticed the steps of heavy timber were well worn. Smooth indentations ran up the center with small scratches scattered about where a boot or some heavy object had marred the surface. It was as though these steps had been in use for many, many summers and winters. Torrin made a mental note to ask Harold about the Journey Inn. What was it like before he and Karina took over? Who owned it? How long had they been here? Did they have children? The questions tumbled through his mind as he sought out the room.

Turning into the small room he found the water and toiletries as promised, neatly laid out. A tall ceramic pitcher, splendid in blue with colorful designs carefully adorning its outer layer, was full of steaming water. The table that held them was quite unique. Three legs made a tripod upon which a most wonderful tabletop lay. About as thick as his thumb and cut from a log, the surface's round rings showing many years of warm, dry and wet seasons by their alternating thicknesses. The symmetry was beautiful though, and the top was incredibly smooth. Torrin considered that someone had spent considerable careful time with a stone leveling the surface of the now deceased tree. It was not just a table; it was a work of art.

One open window provided light. The heavy and well-puttied glass stood clean in a carefully built frame set against the wall on the floor. That certainly gets put back before night, shuddered Torrin. A large low bed stood along one wall. Its mattress though was substantial. Heavy thick wool and puffy down blankets neatly folded at the foot stood ready to serve the night's resident. A small oil lamp sat upon a rough shelf in one corner.

Stripping off jacket, shirt, breeches, hat and everything else he wore, he set to the task of cleaning up. He poured a generous amount of the hot water into a large bowl. The small triangular patty of soap smelled of cloves and honey. Its texture seemed somewhat rough. A very strange combination, thought Torrin. He was more used to the tender scents of flowers pressed into the soaps at the castle. However, it did not matter; it felt wonderful to gently abrade the layers that had built up over the past two days. The soap, combined with the soft woven threads of a dark red washcloth drenched in hot water, did what the waters of the creek could not do. It got him clean and helped restore his soul.

The smells of roasting meat and all that Karina had cooking in the kitchen wafted through the open window. The moving fresh breezes gently cooled Torrin's wet skin and raised healthy goose bumps that caused the slender hairs of his arms to stand at attention. Torrin reflected that this place was truly wonderful. Very mysterious, but wonderful.

He wet his hair and lathered it with the curious soap. The water ran in skittish droplets down his back as he rinsed and the big soft towel chafed pleasantly on his skin as he finished drying. After brushing his dark curls, he used a short leather thong to tie his hair back into what he felt was a smart ponytail. As he turned to put his breeches on, he was startled to find the tall, strawberry blonde he had last seen being swung about by Quillan, quietly watching him from the doorway.

Giving a muffled and startled gasp, he almost tripped backward trying to cover himself up with his breeches and knocked his arm clumsily on the tall ceramic pitcher. It tipped toward the girl, who, with the speed of a cat came to its rescue. She now stood only what seemed a breath away from his somewhat damp, but now very warm body.

Smiling genuinely, she gracefully put the pitcher back to its rightful place on the table. Her slender fingers releasing the heavy, hot cylinder as you would carefully release an egg to keep it from breaking. Her eyes were deep sparkling blue. Not just any blue, as if that were common anyway, but sharply clear with a penetrating deep color. Almost cutting, but mostly with a look born of the wild. Graceful white teeth, framed by clear, clean skin and lips of the softest pink made her look as if she might be vulnerable. But, on closer inspection, she was hard as gemstone, with a mischievous devil about her.

Her hair shone in its colorful softness; she had been twirling it wonderfully around her slender fingers. Was it anticipation, was it shyness, or was it deep thought? It did not matter; it just added additional spicy mystery to Torrin's own already overheated thoughts.

"My humble apologies sir," she said with a gentleness that belied a lie. "I was looking for a place to fix my dress, as it has become quite a wreck from Mr. Quillan's fun. I did not mean to intrude."

She glanced surreptitiously down at his hand that held his clumped breeches and softly smiled. With that, she turned and left the room, silently in soft-soled boots. A long sigh escaped Torrin's pursed lips. He was amazed at the instant physical reaction these quick few moments had created. Quickly crossing the room, he securely shut, and this time latched the door, with the sturdy wooden peg. Sitting down on the bed, he let his simmering mind and body parts relax.

After dumping the used water out the window, Torrin made sure the room was neat before descending the stairs. He had figured out by now what rules Karina worked under, and there was no sense in creating any anger in the cook. Especially with the wonderfully fierce aromas rising from the kitchen and his stomach agreeing with his thoughts.

"Well, don't you look splendid and handsome," declared Karina accepting the tall blue pitcher. A long wisp of dark blond hair hanging in front of her perspiration covered ever smiling face. "You seem flushed though, feeling ok?"

Torrin replied that he felt extensively better, refreshed but mad with hunger. Smiling she handed him a buttery looking scone-like morsel. "Here, sit down and eat this. Then I need your help setting the food out. It is almost time for the feast. The players are here and there is no need to wait!" Torrin sat on a stool and watched in amazement as this lady, of unknown age, plied the kitchen like a sorceress. Meat sizzled, pots bubbled, and bread lay cooling on large smooth racks woven of clear thin oak branches. What seemed to be a huge bread pudding lay chopped in a pan with sweet creamy sauce melting into the baked delight.

A number of ladies took orders from Karina, swiftly and expertly moving things around. Two of them stood at a large window scraping pans and cleaning them as fast as they were dirty. The detritus fed a number of goats and birds below the large opening. The window was open from the bottom, a large hinge holding it secure at the top. Stout rope tied to the bottom had been threaded through a large hammered "U" bolt nailed into an overhead stud. Torrin mused that this allowed anyone to open or close the window, since the frame would be heavy. Whoever designed it was very smart. Smart and creative indeed.

Torrin's thoughts were interrupted with a command by Karina. "OK, as we put the feasting's delectables," the last word she said with a smiling flourish, "on this table, take them out to Harold. He will show you where they go. Tell Quillan to get his big body in here to help too. Now get going, I want to dance!" Without missing a beat Karina commanded, "Normadia, get that hot water upstairs so we can all wash up. I am not going out there covered in grease!" A stout girl with a long, plain brown dress began scooping hot water into the blue pitcher. Her long blond hair was tied in a knot. Her bright green eyes were all business. Torrin was certainly glad he brought the pitcher back in one piece.

He turned his attention to the table and marveled at the number of trays, bowls and racks of food appearing. Carefully lifting a large tray of what looked like turkey legs, breasts and assorted meats, he pushed through the door to the great room. Harold quickly stood, and striding forward, pointed to a long table. Large candles lined up all along the center. A pile of deep wooden bowls sat at the middle. "Here," declared Harold putting his large rough hand on a point about middle of the first half of the table. "Meat goes here, vegetables down there," pointing to the other half, "sweets acrost from the meats. Keep it comn' now."

Torrin glanced toward Quillan. A pretty girl on his lap, twirling her fingers in his rust colored hair. He had a deep smile on his face. His big hand was on her neck, covering her white skin, gently kneading her muscles.

"Doan be telln me ma work boy!" he said before Torrin had his mouth completely open. Then, with a large happy voice. "Ye tell missus Karina I'll be ri theer."

It did not take long. The table was set and people appeared from all corners and doors of Journey. As seemed to be the custom, the musicians filled their bowls first.

Torrin sat near Quillan, who in a seemingly unnatural gesture of gallantry introduced him to the young women attached to the big man. Torrin found that Gwendolyn was the name of his upstairs observer. When she spoke, Torrin noticed some color high on her cheeks. She explained to her friends that she had briefly met Torrin in the hall up the stairs and looked forward to dancing with him after the meal. Her long blond lashes fluttered demurely in the room's muted light.

Gwendolyn's dress had certainly been fixed and put to right. The top of her ample soft bosom rose naughtily above the lace-trimmed décolletage. The dark green material accented her blue eyes and he noticed that unlike the other ladies, she wore no cap. Her hair fell down her back to her waist and was clean and brushed. A few light flowers had been pinned to her hair and added an accent of color to her womanly brightness that blinded Torrin.

The conversation turned to the oncoming spring. Torrin was not sure if he heard much while he ate and tried not to stare.

23.
Rest

At least they were finally closing in on the lodge, but Dessa was sore beyond explanation. Her bum was ablaze. Even the well-tailored breeches she wore could no longer protect her bruised and battered skin from the serious chaffing. Her thigh muscles kept bunching and cramping. Her shoulders were sore across her back. Her nipples, nay her entire chest, were rubbed raw from the steady and incessant bouncing.

The warm sunshine had diminished to a dark silvery grey that sent cold shivers up her aching and tired spine. It was not so cold as it was the thought of entering a cold dark lodge with two horses to care for. And that she knew she had to do; her life fairly depended upon it out here in the deep wood.

The ride had been difficult.

Pounding all day along the trail, the horses had worked well together. They never faltered or misbehaved. Dessa knew they were working hard. Traveling along, the monotony of the day started to lull her into a sense of wakeful unconsciousness that almost got her thrown.

As they had rounded a curve in the trail Uta came up short and almost reared. It took Dessa completely by surprise! Fortunately, the big horse had not gone too high, or Dessa might have ended up bruised and battered on the rocky trail.

Ahead and just to the right, a lone wolf stood on a large outcropping of granite. His old grey fur was almost the same color as the huge stone. Dessa could more feel than see the steely grey eyes sizing her up. He cocked his head to the left and then the right. Maybe, she thought, he wants to see if there are more riders behind me?

Without making any sudden moves, Dessa extracted a long tapered arrow from the quiver that had been bouncing on her back all day. She was now glad she had resisted the urge to tie it to Calandra's pack.

With the other hand, she smoothly picked up the bow, never losing eye contact with her new and menacing predator. Nocking the arrow, she gauged distance, wind, fall and target. Her soreness all but forgotten, her arms feeling strong with the rush of adrenaline, she slowly pulled the arrow back to its farthest position, her knuckles against her cheek felt reassuring and natural.

In a flash, the target disappeared. Dessa slowly released the bow and then sent the arrow back snugly in the quiver. Her heart racing, she looked around. Nothing. Nothing but the deep forest and gathering darkness. Was there really a wolf there? Was she so tired she was seeing things? She did not wait around to see.

"OK Uta and Calandra, it's not far, let's make this quick!" With a might yelp, the three of them shot down the trail in a blur of dust. Dessa had her sword out, ready to take on the fiercest of predators. Fortunately, none appeared.

In a short while, the lodge appeared in the gathering gloom. Dessa dismounted and stiffly hobbled to the large stable door. Swinging it open, both Uta and Calandra knew what to do. They walked in and entered the safety of their well-worn and familiar stalls. You could feel them both relax.

"You can graze tomorrow. I will get you some water and hay in a minute," she said as she removed the saddle and pack. Dessa thought that talking to the horses might be an interesting pastime for the foreseeable future, as she lifted two large ceramic urns and carried them to the well.

Many years before when the lodge had been built, this site was chosen for two reasons. First, a steady and plentiful artesian well. The second, a large cliff protected the lodge from the fiercest of winds. It really was a glorious place. Except it was pretty forlorn being here alone.

Dessa filled both urns and returned to the lodge. Setting them down near the fireplace, she quickly checked the door, window and stable entrance. All were securely locked and barred. Although feeling a little trapped, she felt safe.

Something was unnatural though. Something did not smell right. Looking around, Dessa noticed a large oil lamp on the big table where the hunting parties ate, shared stories, arm-wrestled and did all the things hunting parties do. Walking over, she looked down at the lamp.

An ever so low flame burned softly in the base of the mantle. "Oh Gale," Dessa cried softly. "You are such a kind and wonderful friend, well, er, grandpa." She turned the flame up to its normal cheery height and the gloominess around her disappeared. Her worries about starting a fire abated and her spirits lifted. She marveled at how a simple act of kindness could make such a difference.

Carrying an urn of water to the stable, Dessa watered the horses, gave them a cursory brushing—promising more in the morning—checked their hay and left them to slumber, however horses slumber.

The big pack from Calandra she set on the table and Dessa, after turning down the lamp, lay down on one of the bunks. Every bone, muscle and part of her body ached. One of the big quilts she pulled up snug under her chin. She decided to start a fire. It would be getting cold tonight. Nevertheless, before she even finished the thought, she was fast asleep.

Quite fast asleep.

*   *   *

Outside, high on the hill, in a deep shelter, he listened intently, head cocked, eyes closed.

Early for a hunting party he pondered. But from the sounds, it did not seem like a large one. Maybe this would work out after all, he thought with some excitement! He put his head back down. He was warm and snug and settled in for the evening. There was no sense in venturing out now, it could wait until morning.

Then the fun would begin!

24.
A Dragon

As Torrin carried his overflowing bowl to the crowded table, he heard the strangest of sounds. A high pitched, melodic whistling. As it came closer he recognized it as some sort of flute.

Suddenly the big heavy door to Journey burst open and a tall smiling man playing a flute, fairly floated into the big room. Behind, twenty or so little children, laughing, singing and giggling loudly, bounded in to become part of the crowd.

It was the strangest scene of happiness Torrin had ever witnessed. Many of the adults stood and twirled about the floor with the youngsters. Smiling, dancing and laughing. The rest of the crowd stomped their feet, clapped their hands and shouted something that sounded like "hi hi hi." The joy was infectious and Torrin, who suddenly realized he had been feeling a bit "old and cantankerous" joined in with the wonderful raucous. His dinner food momentarily forgotten, his spirits lifting.

The revelry lasted the space of 20 heartbeats and then the children stopped dancing and raced toward the food, grabbing a bowl and expertly filling each one with their favorite delight. Much ohhing and ahhing could clearly be heard. Their smiles told of untainted glee and the delicate charm that comes only from the pure heart of a child.

"That was something I have never experienced or heard of before," commented Torrin to the group now happily seated and eating at the table.

"Well Mr. Torrin," replied Quillan. "These chilln ave 'nuf to worry about with the weather killn der parents. When we ken gev 'em som fun, we do et right. Dey are the future."

The food was wonderful. Tasty, hot, well cooked and there was plenty for all. Torrin noticed though that there was very little left over after all had eaten their fill. Wasting was not part of Journey. Torrin wondered how Karina would know what amounts to cook? Must be experience he reflected, as the last scoop of creamy bread pudding exited his bowl into his mouth.

Without warning the children were sitting on the floor all around Harold, their small hands folded neatly on their laps, their happy faces looking up at the joy filled man. One little girl came up, boldly climbed onto Harold's lap and said, "Uncle Harold, please tell us the story about the dragon before we must be off to bed?"

Harold smiled. He feigned a stretch and a big yawn and said, "Well, I dunno Miss Salandra, I is awful tired after wrkn all day. I was thinkn o goin to bed meself just right now!"

The children all groaned and moaned and loudly complained, with big smiles on their faces. This being a normal and obvious ploy by Harold.

Salandra countered, evidently being chosen as the children's spokesperson by her determined, but polite, demeanor, "Now Uncle

Harold, we know ye is old, but we did not think ye was dead yet. This is a party, not yer wake!" Everyone, including Harold laughed.

"OK," said the smiling man. Salandra took her place among the children. A gentle hush fell over the big room and the entire place became genuinely quiet, except for Quillan who was, without being asked, adding some wood to the fire. He finished and gracefully sat down, putting his leg up on the bench between two of the girls; slowly melting his big back against the wall. Arms folded, his head turned expectantly toward Harold with almost the look of a child smeared across his weathered face.

Quietly, Harold began. "Twas spring, the flowers, they was bloomin all around! Soft grasses for the animals had burst from their grey brown winter death that seems to kill them every fall." This Harold had said with much theatrics, putting raw emphasis on the word "kill." The children had gasped, the adults nodded in agreement.

"About this time, a knight, his name was Valterra, arrived on a huge white steed. Eighteen hand tall was this gallant and brave steed." An "ohhh" emerged from the crowd. They knew a large horse was fifteen hand; eighteen was a monster, of sorts.

"Now, the name Valterra itself means 'man strong of the earth,' and he was a big strong man. Why Mr. Quillan hiself would only have come up to Valterra's elbow." Quillan smiled and waved as two of the smaller boys jumped up on the table, tousled his hair and lay down on his big stomach. Quillan's big arms held these two boys like they were golden goose down. So gentle, but never would you have been able to break them free, because they would not have left.

"Valterra was hunting the last of the fire breathn' dragons. This last dragon was so big an powerful that it has melted all the glaciers. But so mean, that it was eating all the people who had built farms here an tried to start families." The crowd responded with hisses and negative growls at the mention of the evil dragon.

"While Valterra stretched, and his trusty steed Coronado grazed, the dragon suddenly bounded into the clearing." Harold delivered this with a flourish. "Valterra, always prepared, ran and hid behind a large tree. As the dragon approached Coronado, Valterra told Coronado to be still." Harold said with a strained hush voice. "As nervous as the horse was, he trusted his partner and pretended to eat more of the sweet spring grass. But ready to leap (the word leap was delivered with startling presence and caused everyone in the room to jump a little) if he needed to."

"Valterra circled around to the back of the big scaly, smelly beast; you see, dragons hardly ever take a bath, they don' listen to theer parents." The children eehhhd and giggled. "Valterra ran, quick as lightn' and fairly flew like the fastest bird up onto the dragon's back. He sat on the dragon's head, forcing his big snout down and made the dragon burn his fire onto the ground for over half a day." Most of the children covered their mouths in their own terror, imagining what a fiery fright this must have been for Valterra.

"The beastly fire was so blasted blistering, it scorched the earth and made the rocks far below forever hot, almost melting. That is why Valterra built the fireplace for Journey right where the dragon delivered his final burning breath. That is why the fireplace at Journey is always warm!" A few children ran over to the hearth feeling the big smooth round stones. And yes, they were warm! They turned to the other children and nodded big "Yesses" so they all knew; the rocks were still warm, verifying Harold's words as truth.

"Finally, the dragon ran out of fire. Valterra slew him quickly with his silver sword and the dragon's meat fed everyone for the entire summer. Valterra liked it so much here, he decided to stay and build Journey. And here we are!"

All the children erupted into wild applause. Each gave Harold a genuine kiss of love and a sturdy hug before heading toward the stairs. The adults were clearing things up and the musicians seemed to be coming to life one string at a time.

*   *   *

Torrin danced and drank until he thought he would collapse. Actually, all of Journey did on this night, celebrating the coming of another spring.

Four lute players seemed to compete for the crowd's attention. Each had brought a number of well-crafted instruments. Some double strung, some single. Some large, some small. The variety was curious, the craftsmanship beautiful, bordering on wondrous. As the wine flowed and the merriment continued, the music grew louder and more raucous.

Presently Quillan produced a most curious looking instrument. He called it a nyckelharpa—a cross between a violin, lute and guitar. Quillan generated quite a bit of foot stomping loud music for a goodly while. Torrin was very impressed with his creative and masterful ability. Quillan's fingers quickly but gently pushed the keys up and down as he bowed the strings with the short white bow.

"Is there anything the man cannot do?" Torrin breathlessly asked Karina after one wild and noisy dance.

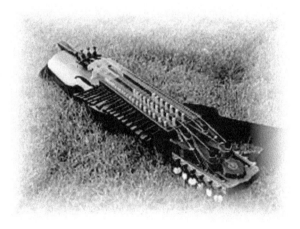

"I do not think so," replied a happy and somewhat tipsy Karina. "But what's it matter anyhow?" she almost sang. Off she went in search of Harold.

Gwendolyn skipped over to Torrin and sat down next to him. He suddenly felt like his tongue had swollen and someone had removed his ability to speak. She put her arm around his and leaned her head on his shoulder. She was warm from the dancing; her hair was soft and fairly glowed in the light of the many flickering candles.

After a moment, she turned toward him, the side of her splendid green gown tight against her long body, showing Torrin all her wonderful curves and displaying a generous cleavage. Gwendolyn asked, in a way that somewhat denied any answer other than firm agreement, "Would you like to dance Mr. Torrin?"

"Of course," he squeaked as well as he was able.

She led him to an open area of the floor. The music by this time had settled down. Many of the dancers had either left or were asleep on the table of their choice. It all felt somewhat calm, but detached to Torrin. He was now focused on this girl who took his breath away.

As she put her hand on the small of his back, she looked up at him. Her head, tilted to one side, a small smile spread determinedly across her pretty face. He noticed that the soft high color that had blessed her cheeks during the introductions had returned. His entire body felt warm, but his hands were icy cold.

As they danced gently and slowly together, he could feel her melting into him. She laid her head, with her shimmering sunset colored hair upon his chest. He deeply breathed the perfume of her body. A strange mix of womanly perspiration, light smoke from the fire and good wine. It was a foreign mix of scents that sent his mind to wander to places he had only dreamed of before. He sighed softly, deeply, and with authentic happiness.

Presently, the musicians ended their noisy revelry. Gwendolyn gazed up at Torrin, met his eyes and seemed to be waiting. He was not sure what to say. He felt out of step.

Wordlessly, her soft hand took his, her head seemed to glide, oh so slightly to the side. Her body turned, his followed. As they walked through Journey, folks were sound asleep, having found sweet escape from the evening's wild gyrations.

As if walking on air, they arrived at the steps leading to the second floor rooms.

Gwendolyn paused, turned toward Torrin and ran a finger down his shoulder to his hand. Her delicate nail leaving a trail of fire deep inside of him.

"Well", began Torrin, clearing his throat, wishing his voice would come back in from the cold and join him. "It was wonderful meeting you and dancing with you tonight. I hope we can do it agai…" Gwendolyn interrupted him by placing that same sweet finger that had just inflamed his arm over his lips, turning her nail to the side and pressing its sharp edge against his fragile and tender skin, and without a word took full control of the situation.

She uttered a low "shhh," her lips puffed out seductively as the sound escaped from deep within her. Then grabbing his hand and moving with the speed of a cat, she ascended the stairs. Torrin in tow.

He never looked back.

But he should have.

25.
A Day to Relax

A loud whinny woke Dessa. Warm sunshine trailed in through the window lighting hundreds of tiny dust specks in the air, like emerald stars lost in daylight. Uta and Calandra were hungry, thirsty and ready to stretch their legs. So was Dessa.

Climbing out of the bunk she realized she was still fully dressed. This new way of living was not to her particular liking; but she thought, "I am going to have to get used to many different things." Pulling off her heavy outer coat, she laid it on a stool. The hidden dagger in the right sleeve came loose and clattered to the stone floor. Picking it up, she mused that such things should probably stay close. Tucking it safely under the drawstring of her heavy breeches, she departed the main room toward the expectant horses. It's chilly in here she thought; that has to change.

Both Uta and Calandra were happy to see they were not really alone here in the lodge. They had both decided she was lost; what with the sun up and all and no sign of her for a good part of the morning.

Dessa decided to devote some much-deserved attention to these wonderful steeds. They had pretty much saved her life yesterday, and she felt she owed them the consideration.

Opening the big stable door, the bright day flowed in. The air was cool, but the sun foretold of a glorious afternoon. Thick grasses around the lodge beckoned the hungry beasts and they set contentedly about consuming their fair share.

After pouring water into the big drinking bucket for the horses, Dessa filled the large metal cauldron that hung in the fireplace. Later, she planned to take a wonderful bath. Just the thought of getting clean with hot steamy water made her tingle.

The lantern dear Gale had left for her still burned low. It made getting a fire going a fast activity. Dessa piled in some thick heavy logs that would burn good and long. She wanted the water hot and the stones in front of the big hearth warm.

Spreading out the pack Calandra had carried, Dessa decided that it would be very smart to explore the contents Gale had so lovingly packed after taking care of the horses. Putting some venison jerky between her teeth, she began to contently and slowly chew. It felt good to eat; it felt good to be doing things.

Dessa claimed her horse brush and set about the intimate task of attending to both horses. While brushing, Dessa talked calmly and gently to both of them. Telling them how wonderful they were, how beautiful their coats shone in the sun and giving them a good massage accomplished many tasks. Not the least of which was the warming and stretching of Dessa's tight muscles.

Uta and Calandra, she convinced herself, felt assured and relaxed. They knew they were on an adventure. They would be trusting Dessa as much as Dessa trusted them.

With their coats clean, they looked beautiful in the bright sun and light breeze. Dessa looked around and drank in the beauty of the surrounding deep forest. The buds on the trees were bursting forth for a new summer, the grass growing steadily. And as she hushed herself, she could hear the buzzing of the woods, alive with small animals. It was time to explore the pack Gale had put together.

The first thing that struck her was how neatly everything had been arranged. Tightly rolled and strapped with either twine or leather thongs, everything seemed to fit well together. The sides and top of the pack were made of thick leather. The large top was overly big so rain would not penetrate to the contents below.

Two wool blankets were tightly wrapped in an oilskin. Dessa remembered that you put the skin down, put the blankets down on one half, get between them and then pull the oilskin over to keep out bugs and rain. She figured that her big hat, hung quietly for now on the chair would cover her head day and night! Well, at least it was protection.

Two stout arm scabbards were within the belongings. Dessa tried them on, lacing them up snuggly. They fit just fine, but she wondered for her need of them. Other items included fire starting tools, small hatchet, an iron pan, an extra shirt, some odds and ends and essential toiletries; and then two of the most glorious things ever. Dessa held up her soft silk shift and her favorite dark blue velvet dress. The shift was most wonderful for sleeping in, and she had often dreamt of it lying next to her as she made love to her prince. Many still yet to be created memories lay in its soft fabric. She still held dear to the future that might be.

The sleeping shift was dark green. Not thin like her wedding night outfit (one that was short and you could almost see through; she shuddered at the thought), but sturdy, silky and warm. Very soft. She laid it carefully on the bunk, noting that tonight it would be wonderful for sleeping in. But, she wondered how often she would get to use it?

Her mother, on the other hand, had made the dress for her. Puffy shoulders, slender and tapered wrists added to her tallness as the sides narrowed toward her waist. They narrowed toward her back though, the white threads that created the pleats carefully coming closer together and tighter as they descended, adding tightness to the look of her waist. The front neckline plunged to a dangerous level and brought a little shiver as she looked at it. Her mother knew how to fish for a man and show off her daughter.

Dessa wondered, as she rolled the dress back up in its cover if there might be more to finding the right man. Inside she knew there was an answer, and she hoped finding it would this time be a pleasant experience. Not like before.

Suddenly, the horses started to raise a mighty fuss. Dessa grabbed the blade she had hung by the door and ran outside. Both of the big steeds were on their hind legs and making a major racket, completely at a high level of distress. Dessa looked about, expecting to see something, someone, some threat. But there was nothing. The three of them stood expectantly for a short time, letting their hearts slow down.

Dessa slowly started toward the brother and sister, talking soothingly as she walked. Both horses were still somewhat spooked, but quieting down. Grabbing the reins, Dessa escorted the pair back to the stable. They willingly obliged. For them, it was time for a nap. For Dessa, it was time for chores.

Food and firewood were on Dessa's list. The roots planted last year had kept well in the ground during the winter. She dug up two of the brown delicacies. They felt cold and heavy in her hand. She carefully filled in the holes left behind and covered them with brown grass.

Walking over to the artesian well, she washed the roots. The cold water running over her fingers felt soothing. Although cold, it reminded her of the touch she longed for, for the deep passion she desired.

Almost before she realized it, a slow chill descended on her. Keeping her wits about her, she unhurriedly raised her head and looked around. The little hairs on the back of her neck were all in a stir, her heart beating strongly in her chest.

Standing up, with a deliberate slowness, she turned around, the roots in one hand, the other reaching back for the sharp safety of the dagger held tight in her waistband.

She carefully and deliberately scanned the area in a long slow circle. Her senses taut, her ears tuned to any sound that might betray an intruder.

Nothing. Nothing at all.

Well, this must be how the horses get spooked, she pondered. Taking a deep breath, she deliberately put one booted foot in front of the other. Her head moving slowly left to right, scanning the grass, woods and forest beyond. Watching for some telltale sign that the fearful intuition she had flaming about her was right.

Again and still, she saw nothing.

After putting the roots on to boil, Dessa set about pulling in an enormous amount of firewood. Stopping only to eat and check in on Uta and Calandra, it took the best part of the afternoon. The pile she accomplished impressed her. She had what she wanted; it was time to make her little dream a reality.

Darkness was descending upon her little haven. The air outside was cold and windy, but not as beastly miserable as the winter nights she had endured for the past few moons. Little did it matter. She had bed the horses, securely locked and barred the stable door, double-checked the window, and the lodge's main door was as sturdily fixed as the walls themselves.

Into the big hearth, Dessa added wood to the low fire that had been warming the rocks all day. The fire now blazed throwing off huge waves of heat. As the water boiled in the big cauldron, Dessa began to undress. First she removed her dusty boots. Her toes met the warm air, almost with a sigh. She decided that having her little pink toes trapped in the boots for two days in a row might not be smart.

Next came the breeches. Yes, they felt secure to wear, but they were confining and cumbersome when it came to using the loo. She hung these on a peg near the fire, making sure they would be nice and dry by morning.

After unlacing and peeling off her shirt, she stood stark naked in the warm and somewhat intense firelight. Looking down, the curve of her breasts seemed almost foreign after wearing a shirt for two days. Her waist felt like it had escaped from a prison. Breeches were not for a woman she decided. She stretched like a cat, from toe to fingernail. Enjoying the freedom and willing all her muscles to relax.

Dipping hot water from the big pot, she poured it into a waiting basin on the floor. Into the basin went a small soft towel. After that, Dessa took a large scoop of hot water and poured it right over her head. She did this three times. The very luxury of the water flowing over her body brought her to both a state of excitement and relaxation. The irony of feeling both was not lost on her soul.

Using the small towel and a piece of ginger scented soap Gale had packed, Dessa scrubbed herself clean. Feet, legs, tummy, arms, breasts and face all got a good scrubbing. Gently she cleaned between her sore legs and attended to her backside. As the fire roared, the water steamed off the very stones where her feet trod. It felt so good to bathe with warm feet and the sounds and smells of the fire. It was a luxury she was afraid might elude her for a long time.

Presently, she scooped again to rinse. And then standing in the waning light of the fire, she used a large cloth to dry. Her hair dried fairly quickly she marveled, it was so much shorter now. And it did not seem to knot up so bitterly.

Walking over to the bunk, she luxuriously slid the silken shift over her damp warm head. The homey natural peace it gave her almost brought tears to her eyes. But she squared her shoulders and cleaned up the room. With towels on pegs, soap in its case, water left to its own devices, she sat down for the final important step. Taking her mother's comb, she set about combing her now shorter hair. The tines of the well-carved tool slid smoothly along her moist scalp. She completely understood why the horses appreciated the firm brushing they got. It soothed her mind, gave peace to her soul. Not only the feel of the comb, but the very nature of taking care of herself.

Dessa's mother would comb her hair at the end of the day. Sometimes Gersemi would softly sing to the rhythm of the combing. Other times, poetry, or at least it sounded that way, accompanied this graceful act of love and compassion. Whatever it may have been, the quiet special times that mother and daughter shared were deeply imbedded in Dessa's clear, quick mind. And when Dessa slowly combed her hair, now by herself, an unhurried smile crossed her face. Her eyes were closed, her memories replayed, as they should.

Finally, absolutely at peace, Dessa collapsed into the bunk for a long, restful sleep. She knew it would be the last for a while and she was going to make the most of it.

As the firelight flickered to an end, and she watched the glowing logs slowly fall into the ash pile, she relished the warmth on her face. Memories of her dear Sanura, her father and Gale flooded her mind. People so precious, people who mattered. She felt herself like the burning log. Its heat slowly dying, pieces falling off into the ash pile. She mused that she must be tired, must be relaxed, must be melancholy. She did not have thoughts like these often. But when she did, she felt much better the next day. These kinds of thoughts did not as much as drive her, as they did pester her from time to time. Maybe they were necessary. Whatever it was, her thoughts were now her company for many a night. Her memories her stories; her wishes her driver.

        *   *   *

He had sat on the big stone, back from the window watching her bathe. It was intriguing that such an easy thing should be so much work. Too bad the place was like a fortress tonight. He had ventured close to the horses. They were very astute to changes in the wood. When he sat and watched her clean the roots at the well, she had sensed something. This was not going to be any ordinary hunt. These victims were aware. They were ready.

He sighed heavily as he slowly padded back to the warm bed that awaited. The vision of her naked body, steaming in the firelight burned into his brain, a vision that he could not shake. A vision he would have to act upon. This winter had been a long one. Ahh, what a wonderful way to start the warm season.

26.
Deepest Sleep

If you asked Torrin today, he would deny it. He did not remember walking up those steps behind Gwendolyn. He does, however, remember everything that happened upstairs though with a pointed vivid clarity that would stay with him—forever.

Torrin and Gwendolyn entered the same room Torrin had used for his bath earlier that afternoon. The small lamp now glowed low and cast warm dancing shadows along the walls. The window had been securely replaced and the room was actually warm and cozy. Torrin would later learn that all the upstairs rooms had one wall on the huge fireplace. The hearthstones added warmth to the rooms.

Gwendolyn quietly closed the door and turned her attention to the waiting and slightly petrified Torrin. She came up close to him, put one lithe hand behind his head, tilted her lips up to his and kissed him.

Now, mind you, Torrin certainly had been kissed before. When playing tag with the girls of the kingdom, over the past couple of summers, kissing someone to "tag" them had become pretty much a silly, regular routine. Torrin remembered Tacy. A tall girl, long brown hair, beautiful eyes, and for a girl, (as far as he was concerned) a very accomplished runner. Tacy had caught Torrin at tag. She told him if he kissed her back, he could be 'un-it." Torrin had obliged. Their kiss had lasted no more than a three count. Tacy's thin lips seemed cold; they had remained taut and closed. Her eyes wide open, her hands open at her side, her face red with the exertion of the game (or the thrill of kissing the kingdom's only (and very attractive and available) prince— he would never know). Since then, Torrin had determined kissing was highly overrated. In the space of just a few warm breaths, he was about to find out he was pleasantly wrong.

Gwendolyn's eyes were lightly closed, long lashes lay gracefully on her lightly flushed, clear cheeks. With her head tilted to one side, Torrin could feel the warm exhalations from her slender nose grace his cheek; it was a feeling he had never experienced before. In his head he all of a sudden wanted everything to slow down, yet move ahead faster. He was in the quixotic place of not wanting anything to stop, yet not wanting anything to happen too fast—it felt wonderful!

In fact, it all felt exotically hot and wonderful at the same time. Her one hand behind his head gently massaged his neck and played with his hair that was damp from dancing. Her other palm rested firmly on his chest, covering the place where his shirt hid his hard excited nipple. He felt her palm slowly flexing like a cat flexes its paw in an erotic massage that seemed to spread all over his body.

Gwendolyn's full moist lips were soft—so different from Tacy's. They slowly, almost imperceptibly parted and he felt her delicate tongue begin to carefully explore his teeth. The trail of which, formed no less a fire than had been assaulting his arm only a short time earlier.

She gently took his upper lip between her teeth and sucked him into her warm mouth, her tongue gracefully dancing over the happily captive lip. This kiss, so completely unlike before, made his heart thunder and his body engender a heated desire that coursed through his very existence. He did remember later feeling excited and vulnerable all at the same time.

Without warning, the girl backed away. Eying him with a sultry look and with measured movement, reached back and released the tie on her gown. Torrin could see the tension in the fabric release and then the entire assemblage dropped to the floor. Gwendolyn's delicate, warm, naked body stood before an evermore excited Torrin.

Only in his dreams had Torrin imagined such a wonderful sight. Her hair partially hid one of her breasts, adding to the erotic moment. The tangle of brush between her legs matched the color of her strawberry golden locks. Her skin was a pale white, but even pale, she radiated intense erotic heat. He was frozen in place and on fire staring at her naked form.

"Allow me," Gwendolyn said as Torrin had almost involuntarily started to work at the ties of his breeches. Gwendolyn got to her knees in one fluid and graceful move. Using the soft cloth of her gown as a kneeling pad, she expertly untied the lines of Torrin's breeches. Then working them down to his knees, she commanded him to sit. Quickly his boots and breeches became residents of the floor with Gwendolyn's dress. Torrin's shirt speedily joined that group of tangled and tumbled clothes on the floor.

When Gwendolyn looked up, she let out a long, wet, sigh. A large smile crossed her face as she became aware of his proportions. Taking him into one slender hand she firmly stroked him in decidedly commanding pumps which made him weak in the knees. Then, standing up, she suddenly seemed to take a higher level of command and there was a strong urgency about her.

"Lie down," a breathless Gwendolyn told the now rather firm Torrin.

He excitedly followed her commands, although somewhat distressed at the thought of moving, as he was afraid he might burst. As she pressed one very firm sweet nipple in his waiting mouth, he sensed her movements to position herself over his very swollen and ready crann. As her weight increased on his prone body, Torrin groaned a long sweet groan of pent up delight and anticipation.

As his hips rose to meet her waiting wanting, the most amazing thing happened. She became light as a feather, actually lighter than air. As she rose into the air, her nipple extracted from Torrin's mouth with a loud slurp. And he heard "her" say in a low gruff voice, "On no ye don' ye sodden lil whore."

Torrin's eyes flashed open in strangled disbelief. There above him, Gwendolyn hung in the air, kicking and struggling. She was being held quite firmly by a not too happy Quillan who was, it seemed, madder than a branded horse.

"Let me down you stinking meddling pig," screamed the now beet red and thrashing mad naked girl. "He is mine. He was ready to have me."

"No, my dear," said a soft voice from the doorway. Karina stood decisively in a thick nightshirt, with her arms folded across her chest. She looked a little perturbed, actually a cross between mad and loathing. "I told you he was off limits. You could have ruined everything. Put your dress on and go sleep downstairs." Turning her attention firmly at Torrin, she stated, "Get some sleep."

As they all left the room, Torrin pondered. How did they know? Why did they care? This all made even less sense now. Moreover, it was quite frustrating! As he lay in the now dark room, listening to the wind rattle around the big building, his mind became a ravenous cauldron of unanswered questions and pent up desire.

His felt as if his face were on fire, along with his mind and other parts of his body. The memory of her soft lips burned on his own. The scent of her hair, soft washed in heather, lingered in his nose. The vision of her naked, almost shimmering body, intensely forged in his mind, he was sure, forever.

Pulling the thick down blanket up around his neck and feeling very frustrated, he eventually fell to a deep and emotionally exhausted sleep. His last thoughts focused on getting some answers—tomorrow.

He might get more than he bargained for…

27.
Departure

Dessa was up as the first light of day broke the darkness of the lodge. Her skin felt reborn. What had been raw sensitive skin between her thighs was now back to a normal pink. She mused that today's ride would be a normal one; steady, not rushed.

She looked forward to it.

The weather was with her too. Bright sunshine pelted through the trees. The leaves growing thicker with each passing day as winter loosened its terrible grip. Dessa made a mental note of the sun's position; the direction they should travel. She would have to go around the hill before heading east. She figured by midday she would be in territory that very few people from Tarmon's kingdom had ever seen, let alone visited. She looked forward to the upcoming adventure.

Uta and Calandra went out to graze as Dessa carefully repacked her gear. After the large pack was ready, she hefted it onto Calandra. Once secure, she returned to gather her personal items: sword, arrows and trusty bow. She filled a skin with water. These were securely attached to Uta's saddle.

After tidying up the lodge, she made sure the lantern was out and put in its rightful spot. The water jugs were empty, the fire out and the stable door secure. The blankets hung over the rafters so the mice would find no home in them. Finally, she looked around, one last time. Breathed a heavy sigh and walked outside.

Once the door was shut tight and the latch secure, she turned toward Uta; the sun was almost blinding. As she walked forward, she pushed her big hat up on her head, shading her eyes from the magnificent brightness.

Without warning, her hat took flight and the thin rawhide chinstrap with the finely jeweled slide sliced up her neck and sharply cut her under her chin. This cut she did not notice for now; what she did marvel at, in that instant, was how the big black hat had suddenly turned brown and was flying. It seemed very confusing and all of a sudden, nothing made sense.

Then her brain caught on. She reacted, Uta reacted, and Calandra let out what Dessa would remember later sounded like a terrible scream as they both thundered away.

The biggest cougar she had ever seen rolled over twice in the grass with her hat compressed flat in its massive jaws. His front legs holding its "victim" in a crushing embrace. Long sharp claws, deadly white at the tips, fully extended, intent on making a sure and quick kill.

The cougar seemed almost as surprised as Dessa. As he stood, he looked up at the red haired girl and then down at his catch. It was not what he had expected—not at all. The hat stubbornly stuck to one long yellow tooth, he shook his head and the hat landed face down on the ground.

By this time, Dessa had dropped the golden hilt of the silver knife into her right palm and had extracted a long and menacing blade from her left boot. She could feel her family crest, almost soft against her palm; she wondered if she would die with her father's knife in her hand. Down now on one knee, she waited. Her jaw firmly set, her normally deep blue eyes changing to a roiling dark turquoise, locked on her target; she did not blink.

He looked at her with a savage strength. Shaking off the hat, he slowly crouched, like pushing down a spring, adding tension. Tension designed to be deadly and honed with experience.

As the two stared at each other with an intensity that would melt granite, a strange occurrence happened. The big cat slowly uncoiled, and then, with unexpected calmness sat down on his two overly long back legs. His strong muscular shoulders relaxed and he brought up one furry brown paw, giving it a long lick. His tongue was rough, but mostly pink. You could see a few ragged scars on its broad surface, the whole thing rather dainty on such a ferocious beast. As he preened his paw, he kept one eye on Dessa; she could almost hear him thinking.

With a heavy sigh, he turned his brawny body and trotted off toward the forest. At the edge of the clearing, he turned to look at Dessa once more. She felt that he wanted to say something. Wordlessly, with a flip of his tail his long sinewy mass disappeared into the wood, nary a sound emerging.

Dessa finally remembered to breathe. Dropping both knives, she slowly put her hands on the cool grass to steady herself. Gasping now for air, she could not believe what had just happened. Was she that menacing?

Retrieving the knives, Dessa went to the very rock the cougar had utilized to watch her bathing the night before. She peeled off a now sticky warm, sweat soaked coat. So much for bathing, she pondered. Before retying the silver knife, she let out a long loud whistle. Looking around she contemplated that the horses sure were going to go fast in a bad time. "Lots of help they are," she said to herself, almost aloud. Giving one longer whistle, she set about retying the knife.

Presently both horses came down into the clearing, eyes wide and wondering. Dessa gave them both a good rubbing on the nose. Assuring them they were too big to be eaten by one cat, and that anyway, they were old and tough. Not a tasty morsel such as herself. She did shudder at the thought. Her finger fit through the hole on the side of her hat. Well, she decided, tonight we do a little sewing.

Dessa mounted Uta. Without looking back, they made their way for the base of the big hill that sheltered the lodge. Moving quickly through the tall trees they made good time. The old forest was high. Ground cover was sparse and made for easy passage.

Dessa was on her way.

28.
The Deal

"Harold, it's time for some straight answers," exclaimed a somewhat still frustrated and indignant Torrin. "Where am I? What is this god-forsaken 'gift' you keep alluding to and what training do I need? And finally, I want to go home!"

It was morning at Journey. A morning after a big party. Everyone, including Harold, was moving a little slower than usual.

Harold was sitting firmly at a table, head in hand, massaging his temples. He slowly looked up at the energetic lad, his eyes slightly bloodshot and said, "Oh, just shut up for a lil while will you? My ead is poundn' and I feel like I been chopn wood all day, what wit Ms Karina slashn me about the dance floor all ni."

Torrin suddenly felt a little foolish at his outburst and sat down. He mumbled a sincere, "Sorry, I am just getting very frustrated. I want to go home." The last word sort of whined out of Torrin, Harold noticed. Hmm, homesick he is, Harold thought; he needs more to do.

"Torrin," Harold began, still rubbing his head. "Quillan tells me ye kilt a big bear on the hunt las year? Right?"

"Yes," came the reply. There was an undertone of quizzicalness to it though.

"And wasn that the first hunt ye been on?" Harold quietly asked.

"No, of course not," Torrin looked at Harold, wondering where this was going.

"Well, see, there is that thing called experience. You gotta learn some things so that other things make sense. If I tol ye everythin now, you'd prenny much jus laugh at me. So ya need some experience." Harold was feeling alive now, he got on a tear. "As to ye gon' home. Go ahead. I don' have a horse or guide to give ye. Quillan says it's a month's ride to get there. Nothin's holdin ya back, go ahead."

The stern and menacing look on Torrin's face slowly clouded to one of puzzlement and bewilderment. He was seething inside. Hot with lonely anger and worst of all, he felt suddenly and completely powerless. His shoulders slumped, he put his head in his arms and you could see the pressure release as the true nature of his circumstances began to take hold. His young face looked up at Harold. A serious expression formed and he seemed to be making up his mind.

"Well," came out, as an exasperated sigh from his troubled face. "I seem to be in this place, for some particular reason." His arms swept the whole of Journey. Continuing, he said, "The reason is not clear to me, but seems to be clear to you," and steeling his eyes on Harold he finished with, "And I do not have a way to go home, for now, and there seems to be a rule that says I cannot touch any woman here." With that, he topped off his little diatribe with a hearty, "Cach!"

Harold, in what he hoped was his most unassuming and gentle manner said, "Now Torrin, ye seems to have come to sm sornta grips with ye present condition. Smtimes we don' like wha we gotta deal wi, but this is wha we got." The older man paused, waiting for some sort of response. Presently, Torrin nodded his head that he understood. It was a slow, sort of resigned nod, but, it at least it was a nod of recognition.

"Verra well," said Harold. "I'll make ye a deal." Torrin's head slowly rose up, he looked at Harold with one eye throwing a harsh cynical look and waited. Harold seized his chance and took it, "You pay attentn, do as I say, no questns asked, for the next turn o the moon, and then ye will know why ye are here, whether or not ye want what's in stor for ye, and ye will have the ability to head home afor winter sets in."

Now this was a moment for Torrin, when he came to understand later with time, experience and age that there are times in your life when you must make decisions you would rather not make. There are times when you want more information. There are times when you really wish things would change, because right now, it's just wrong. These are the times you want to think. To ponder. To ease the pit of fire burning in your stomach. To make things more sure, to be more set in what you need and want and knowing what you will get.

Torrin wished he had more time. More information. Some past experience to call on. The lack of all this was frustrating and almost exhausting. So he did the only sane thing he thought he could do.

Torrin simply said, "Deal."

*   *   *

Karina and one of the kitchen helpers appeared with a platter of eggs, ham and fresh bread. Well, thought Torrin, things look better already.

It's always better to at least know the devil you are dealing with, vs. the devil that catches you by surprise.

Karina said somewhat firmly, "Torrin, see me in the kitchen after you are done eating." With that, she turned and purposefully walked away.

Torrin sighed.

29.
Making Time

If you had to be in the woods riding a horse, the day could not have been better. With a high canopy, the going easy, cool air and gentle sunshine, Dessa actually found herself surprisingly happy and content to be on this wild unplanned (well really forced, she had to admit to herself), adventure.

This forest had grown tall very quickly. The trunks of the trees were not thick. They were, however, tall. She thought the earth here must be very rich. The intertwining branches at the top of this wonderful world formed a green flickering mosaic of needles and sunshine.

As she was moving, she noticed that up ahead, the forest formed itself into a green wall. The fir trees suddenly grew their branches all the way to the ground. As far as Dessa could see, the wall of thick, heavy prickly foliage stopped her path. Dismounting she walked up and surveyed the phenomenon. For most of the day, the travel had been good. This was new.

Tying the horses to a nearby tree whose lower branches had died long ago, (as the top of the tree competed with the others for sunshine and starved the lower branches) she pushed her way forward on foot. After just a short distance and enduring a number of needles finding their way into her shirt and boots, she emerged into a bright hot sun. The air was dizzy with humidity; insects buzzed. The cool shade of the deep forest suddenly gone. When her eyes could again focus, what she saw astounded her. As she looked, it was not so much a sharp intake of air, but a long, glorious, warm deep breath that showed her surprise.

Spread out before was an enormous valley. Its proportions that of a mountain, yet upside down. Billowing clouds framed tall trees that seemed an endless distance away on the hill forming the casing on the other side. Dessa relished the idea of riding, maybe walking in the sun. Its warmth took her soul to a happy smile and let her mind relax.

Entering back into the forest, she felt a brief chill. This environment was her home, yet now it seemed somewhat dark. The coolness of the pine needles on the ground gave almost a damp feel to the whole forest. "Let's get out of here," she thought. "However, how do I get these huge horses through this wall of branches? It is like a fortress!"

Thick sheaths of intertwined limbs grew bulky and strong all ahead of her and her two great steeds that she so desperately needed. Dessa could almost feel the heat of the sun awaiting her, beckoning her to come forward. The sun teasing her in its potential brightness.

Rummaging through the pack on Calandra, she found the sturdy hatchet. Its long blade sharp and carefully covered by a strong leather sheath. The head of the tool was build like a hammer. Besides being useful, she thought, the hammerhead gives it some weight for chopping.

Climbing up on Uta's back, she maneuvered the big horse to within her arm's reach of the branches on a tall, thick pine. Bringing the sharp hatchet down on the branch with all her strength produced nothing but a bone quivering bounce. Pine branches are very flexible when healthy, she discovered. A far cry from the dead, dry sticks that littered the forest in every direction.

Jumping down and stowing the hatchet, her arm still shaky from the bouncing, Dessa retrieved a long thick stick from the ground. The stout log would provide life in its long quiet death and rest on the floor of this magnificent forest. Or at least it would provide a means of escape!

Maneuvering to the edge of the wall, Dessa planted one end of the stick into the ground, as far under the branches as she could reach. Levering up, she pushed in the same direction as the base of the stick. With pushing and heaving, sweat boiling out of her, she managed to open up a hole. Whistling to the horses, and with some prodding, she got them through. When she let go of the stick, though, it snapped back and pounded her lower lip with the force of a hammer.

Getting up off the ground and tasting blood, Dessa wasted no time in getting to her horses. Even though the valley was new and wonderful, she did not want to leave them alone. And, she thought, the big lugs might go walking. This was not a good time to lose them.

The vast open space was foreign to her. She loved it. It was freeing. The horses seemed unfazed. Of course, they were relishing the grass that grew in the sunshine. She almost hated to interrupt their happy grazing, but they needed to press on.

Again climbing aboard Uta, she continued on, in the now familiar easterly direction. She began to survey the seemingly immeasurable valley. Its long vastness stretched before her and turned to the right after what looked like at least an entire morning's ride. Wild flowers of all shapes, sizes and colors poked up steadily with their natural purpose from the ground. They assumed with quiet determination their rightful place in a beautiful setting after having endured another cold dark winter. Once again, they were a striking and essential element of the earth's surface, adding color and fragrance. The reds, purples, pinks and general mass of wild colors were breathtaking. As the horses walked amongst the spring foliage, the gentle breezes carried the heady scents of the fauna up and assaulted her nose. It was an assault, because these kinds of flowery experiences were so few and far between for her.

When she had lived in the castle, although it was generally clean, it was a huge pile of stone, dirt, bricks and logs. The alternating cold, general darkness and damp were perfect for forming heavy green moss in many places. Built for protection, most of the rooms had small windows, and these were only open in the warm, humid, short summers. With the dark, thick forest that surrounded the monstrous structure, very little wind moved through its inner halls to freshen the air. It was musty most of the year.

Therefore, Dessa not only breathed in the fresh untarnished air, she soaked in the vast expanse of beauty, freedom and unsullied nature caressing her face. A low and gentle smile raised the corners of her mouth as she watched and became aware of all that was here, all that was beautiful, all that was so immense around her!

Birds sailed through the air in large flocks that almost looked like swarms, so great were their number. They moved with such a fluid motion and then darted left, right, up, down, almost as one. Who decides she thought? Who decides when to turn, where to go? Who is the leader?

Far below and straight ahead stood a pond of sorts. Rushes growing around its banks to one side indicated a moving stream on the other. A quantity of birds, large, small, brown and colorful frolicked in the water. High above this peaceful natural sanctuary and playground near the edge of the forest, stood a gathering of large grey and black-flecked boulders. Carved into large and distinct shapes they reached out to the valley, hugged the sides of the hill and rested their weight in the warm dirt. They seemed to have been tossed there by some giant hand and then their sides hacked in crazy angles by some giant knife. Strewn about, yet somehow acquainted. Like a number of different sized and shaped people lounging about on a warm sunny day. All with the same intent of relaxing, enjoying themselves, visiting, eating or taking a brief escape from life. All with some related and similar purpose, yet not together.

She decided the rocks would be home and hearth tonight. They provided cover from rain, protection from intrusion via the rear, and the evening sun would have warmed them.

As she passed through the base of the valley, a small stream moved between the plants heading toward the pond. She noticed, over her right shoulder, that the valley started in this area. It ended in a curved bowl at the forest edge. The stream would grow in size and strength. She was happy to avoid a major crossing for now. The thought of getting wet did not sit well with her, nor did she want to spend an evening trying to dry her clothes by a fire.

However, a nice fire she decided would be welcome. Unknown to her, this would be the last of her quiet evenings for some time. Dismounting at the rocks, Dessa set up a comfortable camp. Dried leaves and pine needles, blown into the covered outcropping from last fall, protected from winter moisture by the boulders, provided a somewhat soft, although crinkly bedding. Smaller rocks provided a natural hearth for the fire. The horses were able to graze within her sight and firewood was not only plentiful, it was easy to gather. Dessa climbed into the forest on her forays for firewood that would bring cheer to her night through a natural entrance the boulders provided. Their huge mass breaking the tree line, interrupting the thick wall of green.

As the light began to fade, the sun carefully ended its work for the day by slowly sliding over the treetops and disappearing behind the seemingly impenetrable forest. Other than the warmth from the rocks, the air almost instantly harbored a chill. The swarms of insects feasting on and exploring the spring's new growth made a hasty retreat to their homes. It was a magical time of the year in the valley. The peace that settled in was serene and deep. The crickets were not yet ready for their usual evening festivities. The larger bugs had not yet hatched. The grasses, flowers and assorted growth were still close to the ground. It was almost as if you were part of nature in the process of being born.

She was happy for the fire starting tools Gale had packed: flint, steel and some finely spun cotton. Cotton was quite the rare commodity, coming in the late summer by horseback from the traders that made it their habit to trade at Tarmon's castle. They were a hearty lot. Fun, full of interesting stories, hard drinkers, better gamblers. They somehow did not fit in long with the somewhat graceful culture of Tarmon's kingdom. After a few days, they would leave with coins or the barter from their dealings. Tarmon's was the last stop they said. The next stop would be south to start again.

According to the traders, no one of any consequence lived any further north. Dessa figured no one with any money or items worth trading at least. She felt somewhat guilty using the rare cotton to start her fire, but she was also very happy to have it. Might as well use it while it was dry. It lit instantly; the small twigs she fed the small flames caught quickly. In a few minutes she had a good blaze. Its warmth spreading, its light comforting.

With the thought about dry wood for future fires still in her head, she ascended the hill to get more firewood and gather the tiny, dry pine twigs that were helpful in starting fires. These she added to the small bag of cotton and carefully wrapped the whole package in waterproof oilskin.

The horses needed water, so did she—her mouth was dry and the swollen lip was in need of a bath. She led them down to the pond, to the side where the water ran clear and smooth. It was not a rapid rushing stream. It was more of a slow brook. Moving enough to stay fresh, but making nary a sound. Silent water, so smooth, so refreshing. She thought about water; how it can be so calm yet so violent.

Splashing her face was calming—although the initial sting on her lip was startling, she felt wonderfully better. Filling her water skin and taking a remarkably large drink herself, she thought it best to start drinking more. Probably unhealthy, she reflected, to get too dry. Away from the fire, with the sun now almost put to bed, she looked up. The heavens were unfolding for her as the darkness enveloped her earth. A bright moon did show itself as a flickering orb just below the treetops, its light playing tricks with the oncoming darkness. Dessa wondered what path it would take across the slumbering sky of this quiet peaceful place. One by one, stars began to amuse themselves and flicker to life in their part of the evening's show.

She remembered the cool summer nights as a little girl, snugly wrapped in a warm blanket watching the stars with Gale. He would arrive after she was ready for bed with his little candle lantern, all glowing, a genuine smile painted across his face. "Ready to watch the show, my little friend?" he would ask her. And of course, she was always ready with willing feet after she gave him a big hug. Her small hand would feel safe and comforted in his large leathery grip as they climbed the many steps to the top of the battlement. There, they would hide the candle lamp in a place where you could not see it from the platform. Gale explained that you did not want any other light around for star watching. The stars were like some people and might become afraid that their light was not as pretty and they might hide themselves. Just like some people, the stars worry too.

The horses were satisfied with their happy lapping of the fresh water. She filled her small iron pot with water and topped off the skin. Both of her friends climbed the short hill with her. They seemed to find a nice place to stay. She decided to let them stay loose. If anything

attacked, they could run. If they decided to take off on an adventure, they would return soon. She knew that for their huge size and willingness to fight for her, alone they were as vicious as kittens. Of course, unless they were cornered.

As she lay down in her blanket, watching the millions of stars pushing their beauty down upon her, she wondered if she was looking at the same sky Gale and her father were watching. A flickering thought passed through her mind that she was being watched.

It did not last.

And, as it were, Gale and Tarmon were toasting to her health and safety at the same special place Dessa and Gale had stood to watch the stars, high atop the castle. They were both a little drunk, but they decided they had done the best they could do and were celebrating the ruse and rescue of the century.

*   *   *

Later, when Tarmon slid his old, tired frame into the large feather bed, he moaned softly. Maybe it was a sigh. We'll never know, and anyway, it does not matter. Because ever so slowly, with the practice of years, the patience of love, and the tenderness of caring, Sanura kissed his kind face, and they fell contently and warmly asleep in each other's arms.

*   *   *

And, far down the valley, half a day's journey from where Dessa slumbered, Bartol told his father it looked like they might have company tomorrow night.

Good, thought the old man, we might need the help since the latest threat seemed to be so much stronger than before.

30.
The First Lesson

Torrin entered Journey's kitchen from the main room by pushing through the big oak door and stepping carefully inside. He was not sure what he was going to face. Karina was busy at the big fireplace used for cooking, putting together a light meal for midday. No one else was around.

"Sit down," she said without turning around.

Torrin wondered if she had eyes in the back of her head? How did she even know he was there? With all the racket coming from the boiling pots and fire, she could not have heard him come in.

He sat.

"Let me explain something," the older woman began. "I'm sure you are not very fond of me just right now, having interrupted you last night—but this is important. You are destined to meet a very beautiful and special woman. It is the way this works."

"Excuse me, but Gwendolyn is about as beautiful a woman I have ever seen or expect ever to meet," piped in Torrin. He was somewhat peeved at this time, not imaging any woman could be more beautiful.

At this point, Karina wished there was a deep snow pile she could roll a very naked and hot Torrin in, to cool him off. But alas, words were all she had to make this a safe lesson and hope he would listen. Lives were at stake.

"Yes I know," she replied steadily. "I know you don't think a more beautiful or exotic woman could appear here for you. After all, there is nothing quite so exciting for a man," she used the word "man" carefully, knowing Torrin was at that tender and exciting stage of turning from boy to man, "than to be pursued by a tall shapely woman who wants to share her hot ready body with you. But there is more to this than you understand."

"You will have to excuse me," replied a now slightly irritated and excited Torrin, having had the vision of Gwendolyn's naked body reappear in his mind, "but whom I choose to be with is my doing. Please do not interfere again. As much as I appreciate what you have done for me, you crossed a line last night. Do not cross it again."

With that, Torrin exited the now overly hot kitchen. He found Harold moving tables and asked him what he needed to do today. Harold sent him out to help Quillan cut and haul wood. Tomorrow the entire assemblage around Journey would be up early to plow the large field, high on the hill for the summer crops. Today was wood.

Torrin did not see or hear Karina weeping.

*   *   *

Torrin traveled just a short distance, which was a good thing, since his leg was mostly stable, but not yet fully healed. Tromping into the thick forest just two hundred paces towards a heavy pounding sound, he found Quillan heaving an axe on the top half of a mighty oak tree, which was oddly impaled firmly in the ground. This old and stately member of nature had met its demise from a massive lightning strike the previous summer. The bottom half still struggled to survive. Actually not a difficult thing to do, considering it took almost fifty paces to walk around its massive trunk (typical of many trees in this old growth forest). Strange mangled branches grew in twisted ways between the split and ragged top, left naked and raw by the lightning. Jagged limbs, some large, some long and slender, hung in the upper branches. These dead and dry branches, now orphaned, had been caught by the mighty oak's neighbors of the forest. In doing so, they saved those having been murdered by the lightning from a certain and violent inferno within Journey's massive hearth.

Logs, large chunky woodchips and broken sticks lay all about. It looked as if a mortal rampage had taken place. Quillan was soaked in sweat, despite a steady breeze, his thick sinewy muscles taut and alive with the work. He seemed possessed, intent on taking the already dead tree's wood to its next level of eternity.

"Weel, it's about time sombady came heer to gyv me a hynd," he said breathlessly. "Start stackn the wood on th' sled."

Torrin stripped off his shirt. He relished the warm air on his bare skin; even the stiff breeze felt refreshingly warm. The clean air gave him an exhilaration he had not felt for a while. Forgetting about his leg, he began stacking the wood on the sled he and Harold had used to transfer logs from the woodshed to the fireplace's massive hearth. The two worked in a cautious silence. Torrin thinking deeply about asking Quillan why he had deprived him of his satisfaction with Gwendolyn the night before. Quillan careful not to make eye contact, lest Torrin start asking questions.

Presently, after some heavy lifting and stacking, the sled was full. Torrin strapped the wood tight with a stout leather sheath. The two men, working together, pushed and pulled the load back to Journey. The morning of sweaty work pretty much replaced the wood used the previous night for the party. It was a job well done.

Throughout the work, Torrin had taken some time to think. Gwendolyn was not only beautiful, but she made his heart pound. His eyes were out of focus around her. He felt comfortable with her. An "at ease" kind of comfort he had never experienced before. She was as gentle as she was exotic. She was a good dancer, she was, well, "Perfect!" As far as he could tell.

This was all very frustrating. He felt awkward here with Quillan, but only about this girl. There was something about Quillan that was exciting and yet, almost dangerous. Torrin knew he could trust the man, it's just that this was so frustrating. Torrin did not know how to even begin to talk to Quillan about what was on his mind.

Anyway, it was not the right time to bring it up.

"Go back an get yer shirt and the axe," Quillan told an entirely sweaty and somewhat scratched Torrin. "Thanx fer yer elp."

Torrin gave Quillan a thin smile that said "my pleasure" and sauntered back to the tree that had sacrificed itself for the warmth of Journey and all its inhabitants. He retrieved his shirt and the sharp axe that Quillan had firmly imbedded in a large log. As he turned to leave, a very naked and trembling Gwendolyn stood before him, her pretty feet standing soft upon her dress as a warm escape from the chilly damp ground. She stood in the small patch of golden sun that broke through the treetops, courtesy of the lightning strike. The golden rays danced lightly upon her hair. She looked angelic.

"They shall not deny us now," she said quietly, holding out a long slender arm, beckoning him to her side. "We shall be together forever, my sweet and wonderful man." These exultations were delivered to Torrin in low sultry tones that excited him as quickly as a match lights a warm candle's wick.

From wanting him, her skin continued to shimmer in the sunlight. Small tight circles of luminescence danced across her fair skin as the golden rays were broken by the swaying branches above. Her face was alight with anxious lust. As one hand beckoned him, the other ran slowly from the inside of her smooth thigh to the soft, lightly colored tousle between her legs. From there her graceful and slender fingers followed a trail up to the ardent space between her breasts, then her index finger and thumb did things to her nipple that Torrin breathlessly wanted to practice with his own hand.

With carefree abandon, Torrin approached the young lass, his excitement already evident. He wrapped his arms around her cool naked skin and they shared a long, deep wet kiss. She smelled of heather, the memory of the scent making his head hurt with lust. Her hair was intertwined in his hand, and as it slid through his fingers, he felt its gilded softness soothe his trembling skin. Her mouth gently, but firmly sucked his tongue thickly into herself, making sure he knew how deep, profound and hot went her desire.

He lay her down on the large "blanket" her dress provided. She emitted small purring moans as his mouth explored her fair skin. Cool breezes swirled about the two lovers, but did nothing to assuage their ardor. Her skin felt free and unsullied under his lips. Cool in many places, others warm. Some wet. He lost himself in finding the pleasure they had craved last night, lost and now shared. Somehow, Torrin knew his time had come; he was ready.

As she had the night before, Gwendolyn untied his breeches and slid them off. She revealed the manifestation of his pent up longing. A small moan escaped from her lips and she used them to tease and explore the heat of the man she wanted. Her tongue tasted his saltiness, mixed with the sweet spicy ale of lust and want.

Gwendolyn laid herself down in front of Torrin. As she opened herself to him, he sat back tall on his feet to take in the deep beauty of the woman who would be his first. Gently grasping both her ankles, he ran his hands up her calves, over her knees and to the inside of her trembling thighs. He gently explored her, tantalized her, relished her.

Gwendolyn was almost in tears desiring him. She let out a small moan and said just one word, "Please!" This was followed by a long slow intake of the fresh forest air. Her genuine smile of pleasure and deep seated mounting desire was in need of quenching; she was not only ready, she was quivering with anticipation.

Still making ready, not wanting to rush, he turned his head to kiss her knee. He could feel the fire of her flesh on his lips. As he looked at her warm flushed face, he felt a small stirring. In the space of a heartbeat, the stirring became a thunderbolt as one of the orphaned logs, tall as a horse and hefty as a large man's leg, loosed by the stiff breeze, shot down like a missile. Its sharp and jagged end, in a blink, impaling itself firmly, completely and savagely all the way through Gwendolyn's soft chest, spiking the girl securely to the ground.

Torrin could only stare. Gwendolyn's arms were still reaching toward him. The look of sheer desire still painted on her face. But then, in a savage and terrible twinkle, her arms dropped to the ground, blood gushed from her soft pink lips, and she fell completely and forever dead.

Quillan arrived. He had come to fetch Torrin and his axe, wondering what had been keeping them in the woods. With a steady eye and with a surprising lack of shock, he surveyed the gruesome scene that lay before him. The beautiful and young Gwendolyn, completely naked, with legs spread wide, a massive log imbedded in her chest. She was firmly affixed to the ground, obviously violently dead. Torrin covered with her exploded gore, a look on his face of complete and utter agony, or, more like sheer terror.

He hardly flinched and quietly said, "Ye should ave' listened to Karina."

31.
Magic

It took Dessa a little time and the luxurious effort of stretching to work the kinks out of stiff long muscles, but she felt rested and at peace with her world. She looked around at the boulders that had provided a safe haven for the night and counted her blessings. The horses were in good humor, the sun was shining and the birds of the earth sang in mad harmony, providing a wonderful, if not cacophonic cadence of sound.

As the last of her hardtack ran out and with the venison jerky getting low, she decided today would be a hunting day. They might not make as much time, but getting to Tallon's place seemed like it need not be such a hurry. Just as well to enjoy the serenity of this peaceful valley for a while? It would seem a waste to leave too soon.

As she sat on her rock, urging the last of the previous night's fire to respond and help chase the morning chill, three ducks hurried their way down the valley and splashed noisily upon a wet landing in the little pond. Two mallards seemed to be arguing with a great ferocity of quacking, ruffling of feathers and beak bashing over the hen. Who, by the way, calmly swam around, feeding and enjoying a morning swim in the sunny, mostly quiet water.

Presently, one of the mallards decided the hen was not worth the fuss and he flew off with a few well placed quacks. The two who were now left, and obviously happy about it, flew to the upper reaches of the valley. Soon Dessa could hear a raucous quacking and witnessed much thrashing about in the growing grass. She sighed quietly and grinned. "At least the ducks are good to go!" ran through her mind.

She walked slowly down to the little pond, absorbing the abundance of nature's creation all around her. As the sun warmed the air, the flowers that had closed for protection against the chilly night air opened, and once again renewed their relationship with the bees. Water bugs skittered merrily across the surface of the pond where the water stood still. A frog "riveted" along the bank.

Dessa knelt in the soft grass that created the edge of the little sanctuary. The water felt cool and bracing as she splashed her face. She ran her fingers through her hair. As the ripples settled down, she caught her reflection on the water's crisp surface. A memory of this vision, one that included a deep love for her father crept up from the depths of her mind and her shoulders dropped with a little moan as she reminisced.

When Dessa was but a little thing, the two of them would go to the castle's pond and "visit" with the secret people who "lived under the water." Only she, with her father, together, could see these two special folks living in a smiling peace, there just under the surface, always looking up at them, enjoying the visit. Tarmon explained that truly beautiful people: kind, friendly and with a good heart lived there, under the water. She should cherish them and always look after them. It was not until Dessa's celebration of eleven winters that she finally deduced the secret people under the water were but their own reflections. She remembered being saddened at discovering the truth behind the story. It was a loss of innocence, a decided part of growing up, she supposed.

Before the wedding to that pathetic leech Darius, she had taken her father to the pond for one last visit to the "secret people under the water."

They had stood together, close, in the bright sunshine. Tears ran down their respective faces as she thanked him for the treasure of seeing herself in his kind face on the steely surface of the old pond. She thanked him for the wonderful blessing she had come to know that was her luck, at having a kind, benevolent and caring parent.

She remembered asking him, "Why do the secret people under the water go away when we get older?"

Tarmon had looked down at his beautiful daughter. It was a time of great joy for him; she getting married and so in love. Moreover, at the same time a world of sadness and loss. He did not want to give her up, but knew it was the right time, the right place and for now, he seemed to be the right man.

His strong arm had reassuringly encircled her shoulder. His big burly hand barely holding on, almost quivering in its gentleness. In a quiet voice, just above a whisper, but with the low resonating baritone that was his trademark, he said, "My dear, you see, as a child, you take things as they seem to be, as you see them or taste them. You do not question, because every day, every moment is new and wonderful. As a child, every day, every discovery, is magic for you. As we grow, we try to figure things out; we try and unravel the mystery of the magic. We want to know how things work. But alas, in that curiosity, in that new knowing, it carries the magic away." Pausing, he cautiously and slowly said, "But if you look carefully, and you keep your heart open to the magic, you may see something special."

Dessa had looked down at the clear water, its surface joyfully glistening in the sun. She saw it then. It made sense, just as it did now.

Tarmon continued, "You see, our secret people under the water are still there. Yes, now you know it is only a reflection. But those faces are no less there, nor are they any less special than they were when we discovered them many springs ago. There are some things that have magic in them, if you believe it. If or when you do not believe, then the magic disappears. For some, it never comes back. For others, as we grow older, the magic comes back and then grows stronger. It is difficult and not easy to explain so that it makes sense, but sometimes, when the magic comes back, it is more real than before. Because it is real in our hearts and we understand the magic, which is actually true love. It is as true as the reality that surrounds us."

Her reflection today was of a very different girl she decided. Was the magic gone, or was this excursion to who knows where, a search for the lost magic?

Whatever the reason, she decided to let the magic stay in her heart. She would explore this world and not let herself, her father, or Gale down. She deserved that much and so did they.

Rising with a steely resolution, she turned and ascended the hill to her granite sanctuary. She put out the last remnants of the fire, packed her things and called the horses.

She and her stately entourage headed down the valley. Her silent hope was that the turn up ahead would be sharp enough to let her stay here and travel in the valley, toward the rising sun. The exhilaration of the warm sun in her face was deep and cleansing. The heat seemed to burn the mold of the past from her soul. As they marched on, and rounded the turn, the size of the valley unfolding before her was immense and almost beyond understanding. Green, lush and full of white moving dots? Hmmm, sheep she decided. Suddenly it occurred to her that she probably was not alone. Sheep needed tending.

Her guard went up, and the magic of the day was stored away quickly as she knew she must now face reality again.

32.
Listening

Torrin was in an angry sort of depression. Agony beyond description racked his brain and seemed to tear gaping wounds in his body. All his young life he had felt in control. As long as he could remember, most anything he had wanted or asked for in his kingdom became reality. It was just delivered to him.

Life here was so different. This all seemed unfair, it seemed unjust.

He felt his heart was shattered. Lacerated into useless fragments. He felt black. Empty. Defeated.

That final image of Gwendolyn, her arms outstretched was burned into his mind. It would not go away.

* * *

The two tired looking and to Torrin, ancient people, who came to retrieve Gwendolyn's body were stooped and gray. They were obviously sad, yet seemed to shed few tears. Torrin wondered where they came from. It could not have been far, since they had arrived in the course of the afternoon. It was not even close to dinner yet. Even with the grueling work of the day, he did not feel hungry, except maybe for a few large tankards of wine. His heart was heavy; his head hurt, his leg ached.

Quillan had helped Torrin dress the dead girl and together they carried her back to Journey. Laying her gently on soft pine needles and in the shade of a tall blue pine that stood sentry at the edge of Journey's clearing, she looked peaceful. They had cleaned her face and carefully wrapped her in a rough white muslin sheet, tying her up as you would tie a bundle of goods from a traveling merchant. It just seemed so improper.

Quillan, Harold and the old man were off to the side, sitting on an old bench, talking in muted quiet tones. The old man, parked between the two, looked numb. His head was often in his hands, his threadbare coat providing little in protection against his obvious agony.

The woman, whom Torrin assumed was the man's wife, sat on the ground next to Gwendolyn's still form. By now, some time had passed. Torrin could hear soft sobs coming from the woman's tear streaked face. A number of other women, some he recognized from the party, some new, murmured soothing and quiet support to the mourning old woman.

Karina sat next to Torrin on the rock he had occupied for a long while that horrible afternoon. Whenever he went to rise, she sat him down. When it looked like he was going to speak, she carefully, but with a stern look, quieted him.

Presently, the old man rose and walked somewhat unsteadily and slowly over to where Torrin and Karina sat. His grim features set, a look of despair and loss filling his face.

Torrin slowly rose. He trembled at the thought of what to say. His mind was spinning harshly, pounding, and his eyes were almost losing focus. His mind struggled with how to explain the accident. How to tell this man the feelings he had felt for his beautiful, wonderful daughter? How to begin? But his lips were locked and would not move.

The man stretched out a long thin arm. His hand was very large, scarred and wrinkled, from what must have been a lifetime of harsh and unrelenting work. Torrin looked at his own hand, probably not yet fully grown, tanned, yet without lines and scars. He felt small, foolish and completely out of control. His knees shook.

"I is told yer name is Torrin," the man said slowly. He was missing a number of teeth, but the rest that remained were white and strong. "My name is Camelo Gregor and that is my wife Sata," he pointed the other long arm across the clearing. "I want to thank ye for takn' care of my daughter's body after the accident. She loved to be part of the forest and lay in the warm sun. We neva thought the forest would go an kill her though." He sighed heavily. "Gwendolyn was our youngest. Last of twelve lil chiln. Only got four left now. They is older, seems safe enough, I hope. This worl is a dangerous place for chiln. She was a dreamer though," his eyes misted over. "She always said she would find a prince to take her to a better place, if it was the last thing she did."

He turned to look at his wife and the white muslin that held his youngest daughter. "I guess, by you carrying her out of there, and laying her here, you brought her to her better place. So you are her prince. Thank you for your kindness."

He turned and trudged slowly to the group. They parted to let him be near his wife. He held out his arms and Sata stood with a grace that Torrin could feel across the distance. Their embrace was supportive, enduring and true. He could feel their love across the clearing. Something born of a force he may have seen before, but never sensed.

Something small snapped in the back of his head and he was now forever changed. He knew it, but did not really know it—all at the same time. Whatever it was, something was different.

Two young men picked up Gwendolyn's still wrapped form and carried her gently, following behind the grieving parents. The rest of the group dispersed, heads shaking, fingers pointing up to the tops of the massive trees that surrounded this beautiful, yet at the same time, horrible place.

Torrin had to remind himself to breathe. He sat back down on the rock and started to shake. His mind now numb and stalled. His mouth dry, his hands unable to grip. He was in a state of shock and fear that he had never experienced before.

Harold walked up to the shivering young man and put a hand on his sagging shoulder. 'Ye see me lad," he began in a low, steady but benevolent voice, "ther is afoot in yer worl now, forces that ye canna toy wi. Ye are destined for somthn others wi kill fer, but ye got to respect it. When either Karina or meself tell ye somthin, ye got ta believe us."

Torrin looked up at Harold's kind yet worried face. Harold finished with, "Does ye believe us now?"

33.
Short White Lie

Dessa rode in a still, yet thoughtfully deep silence for a time. She carefully surveyed the hills, the valley below and the lushness ahead.

As she rode, she decided to camp early in the afternoon at the edge of the woods to hunt (assuming the sheep were not tended). The water would be better lower in the valley and would attract more game. There would also be more wood for a fire. The fire last night, although warm, was small.

But for now, sunshine, glorious sunshine warmed her face. After a while, she pulled the big hat down to shade her face, remembering Sanura's warnings about sun and wrinkles on fair skin. Later on though, the heavy black riding gloves came off; they were just too hot.

By the time the sun was directly overhead, the valley was in full glorious bloom all around her. Alive with bees, birds and a wide assortment of buzzing busy animals, attending to the warm work of the day. They too were glad of the arrival of spring and the sunshine!

The sheep had now come into a much closer and clearer view. It was a large flock with at least three smart looking collies trotting around keeping all close at hand and reminding the sheep to attend to the important business of eating. The options, so it seemed, were to go forward and take her chances with the shepherd, if one was about, or head into the forest and avoid all contact.

She went straight ahead. That she would find, was a grave and severe decision.

Walking the two horses carefully up to the flock, she looked around. There seemed to be no one about. The collies paid her little heed, except for a glance or two to make sure she was not a threat to their charges. Thick baaing was prevalent; small lambs, a special part of the spring, walked carefully beside their mother ewes. A couple of goats trotted in and out of the herd, the collies barking a sharp warning lest they get too frisky with the sheep. The rams just grazed, their work done earlier in the winter.

Dessa was almost saddened by the lack of company. She was not one for large crowds, but being alone the last nights had led her to realize the value of good discussion and of sharing a meal.

"You're new here," came a man's sweet sounding deep voice from just behind her left shoulder. She almost leapt from the saddle in shock. Her left hand firmly on the cord, ready to loosen the silver dagger. Dessa turned to see a tall, thin man, smiling broadly, a long staff in one hand, thick brown cloak covering slender shoulders looking up at her. His large floppy hat in the other hand. He looked unarmed.

"Yes," she replied, trying to smooth the fright from her voice.

"Welcome to Uddhaven valley. I am called Phlial the shepherd. If you would like, please join my sons and me for our afternoon supper, and if you are not in a hurry, please stay for dinner. We do not have many visitors here; it would be our pleasure." Phlial bowed and swept his broad hat gracefully out in a regal gesture of welcome.

Well, thought Dessa. I have found civilization amongst the sheep.

"It would be my pleasure," she replied.

Phlial looked up, startled, "You are a girl!" came his surprised comment, his eyes wide with wonder.

"Yes, that would seem to be the case, have been for a while now," replied a wondering Dessa. After she said it, it occurred to her that a woman, alas a young woman, riding alone would be something unheard of and just not done. "I am at your service," she said, sounding as tough and grown up as possible.

"Please follow me," said Phlial. He began to trod his long frame toward the right side of the valley, away from the flock. His long legs taking him quickly toward an unseen destination. He displayed an interesting gait she noticed. Tall limbs moving purposefully in an almost artfully loping stride. Dessa watched and deduced he did not bend much at the knees. His shoulders swung broadly to and fro, long sweeping fawns of swinging hair and robes. His staff ostensibly keeping him upright. There was a peace about him, yet purpose. He did not only walk; he traveled, he journeyed.

She was instantly concerned. Not so much about Phlial, but about the place, the whole chapter that surrounded her. Something was speaking to her. She could not discern it.

Dessa and the steeds followed.

Presently, they began to climb the side of the valley. The thick dense forest loomed above. Stately, majestic, the trees were very much in charge of the property that Phlial called home, or was it just his pasture? She did not know a great deal yet. She told herself to relax. He seemed like a good sort. Of course, him sneaking up on her like that did give her a scare. How could such a tall, loping creature move through the valley and be upon her so fast, so quiet, and without even the horses knowing? That would have to be a discussion and understanding for later.

Phlial headed straight for a large sweeping pine. Its thick branches hiding the ground, with a preponderance of old pine needles stacked at the lower edge, looking like a roll of rough canvas ready to peel down the hill in wild escape from the dark sentry overhead. Shifting his lanky frame to the right, he disappeared. Dessa stopped and stared. He was just—gone.

Uta sensed her discomfort and let out a wet, deep exclamation from his large lips. He even took a few steps back, not knowing which way to go. It was not a typical moment for the two of them. They were usually tight to each other's needs and travel. Uta knew sometimes before Dessa could tell him which way to go. Dessa knew which way Uta would travel. It was a synergy that couples strive for and few achieve. But at this moment, it was broken. They both felt off kilter. Calandra conveyed her discomfort with the painful feelings by stomping around and making wet snorting noises for anyone who would listen.

As with most people who face something new, unknown and possibly dangerous, Dessa had three choices. Stay and fight the obscure threat that might present itself, wait in frozen anticipation until the issue passed, or turn and discharge herself and the horses from the unseen danger as fast as they could run. Warily, she chose the first. Her mind told her that if she started running, she would always be running. Freezing in place and hoping things would get better was not her style.

Now she pulled the cord in her left sleeve. The cool metal of the knife felt comfortable and calm in her hand. Control returned to her brain in a warm washing of stillness and peace. With the brain calm, her body followed. Then Uta settled down. All this happened in the space of three heartbeats. Later she would marvel at how many thoughts she had experienced and relied upon in such a short time. There could be power in learning how to capture and control that process. She would learn how true that was in a scant time, and how very difficult it could be at the most unexpected moment.

The sweat that had appeared on her forehead started to cool in the breeze. Her eyes narrowed as her now rational brain began to take control. Where could he have gone?

Phlial appeared from behind the tree, staff in hand, none the worse for wear. "I am so sorry," he exclaimed with a sincere look of regret on his face. "I forget how easily we disappear when we have company about."

"We?" thought Dessa, he had spoken of sons, how many?

"Just lead your horses up and around the left side of the tree. You will find a path," instructed the happy and welcoming man.

Dessa dismounted, now feeling somewhat foolish having a shiny silver dagger in her hand.

He did not seem to notice.

The forest was instantly cool compared to the warm humid valley. From the outside, this wood looked completely black. Once inside though, shimmers of sunlight danced in narrow slivers on the ground. A mysterious lack of shadows though was somewhat disorienting. The giant trees ruled the earth and sky here. As she looked around and began to take in all this new information, she began to notice the myriad of details surrounding this interesting, yet dimly lit place.

A cabin, of sorts, sat long ways upon the slope of the hill. It was long, built of stout logs with what she assumed was a large stone fireplace running up the middle. Two windows faced this side of the building. They were covered with what looked to be sheepskin. That, she accepted, made sense. The cabin was long, and on this side ran a long sturdy, low fence. Probably the place where the sheep spend their evenings was her correct guess.

Phlial was leading them toward a low hut. As it turned out, it was a barn. With part of its size dug out of the ground, the inside was large and roomy, if not somewhat rickety. Two mules sat quietly chewing as Dessa led Uta and Calandra into the somewhat improvised structure. She fastened them to a post on the wall and started their rubdown. Phlial sat and watched in amusement for a few moments and then said, "I must attend back to the sheering; please come over to the other side of the house when you are done." Quietly he left. His feet seemed to make no sound when he walked.

When the horses were attended to and content with their rest, Dessa decided it was time to get to know this place. And anyway, a lunch, or supper as Phlial had named, it sounded wonderful.

Rounding the cabin's wall, she was treated to an interesting sight. The tall lanky man was single handedly sheering sheep. Their loud baaing could have ignited the dead. With the sheep firmly strapped to a post, he worked great shears around the frightened animal. Floods of sweat poured off his body as he steadily attended to his duties. When he was done, the entire coat of the now much thinner animal was in one piece. First he helped the very scared animal up and gave her head a good rub. Looking at Dessa he said, "If we don't stand them up, they die from the gas in their belly, they get so nervous," he smiled and let out a small chuckle. Hefting the heavy ball of wool over to a table that had a number of long slats in it, he gracefully laid out his cuttings. Carefully, but quickly, he picked out anything that wasn't wool, separated some of the end and bottom parts and then with a skill made of many years, folded the lot in thirds and stuffed it in a large burlap bag. The sheep, much lighter, was finished and now seemed blissfully happier. Losing the warm winter coat, with warmer weather here was obviously a freeing experience for an animal. "Come, let's return her to the flock and then rouse the boys for supper. They have slept enough," he said to her without really looking.

A large pile of wool bags lay against the cabin. It was taller than Dessa and each looked quite heavy. He must be very strong she surmised. Tall, fast and strong; a good combination that could also be dangerous.

They walked the ewe across the valley. Phlial let his wandering thoughts spill from his mouth. "Yes, came here fifteen winters ago. Probably before you were born missy," he said in a polite and non-demeaning way. "Helped out old gray-beard, never knew his real name. Poor man attached himself to a cough that winter and died up so fast we didn't know what happened. Poor old sot. At least he didn't suffer. He was one funny old man. Could tell a story that would make your sides split. Me and the misses, we would sit around the fire at night and laugh our hearts out." Phlial let out a heavy sigh that was followed by a smile of remembrance. "We'd planned to stay just one winter. Were tired of traveling with the caravan. Our parents were traders and tin smithies. So we stayed."

They had reached the flock and Phlial pushed the ewe forward, while one of the collies came up and nudged her ahead. She got the picture and joined the rest of the flock. Happy to be home.

The collie sat and looked at Phlial with his head cocked to one side. "Yes, you are a good dog, smart too, now get to work," he said in happy tones. The collie ran off to watch his charges. "They just like to know they are doing well," said the tall man. "Come on, I could eat the south end of a northbound caribou about now," he grinned at Dessa. She smiled and followed the man back toward the woods. Wonder where he went to school she thought, his speech is impeccable.

The inside of the cabin was neat as a pin. Warmly decorated with curtains, lace, trim and keepsakes all around. A pair of large wooden rockers sat in front of the big wide fireplace. Off to one end stood a large bed with upper berths built above. Two long dark-haired people slept in these berths. Immensely thick wool blankets rolled up at their feet. The entire place was warm, cozy and friendly.

Phlial roused the sleepers. They turned out to be two young men. Not much older than Dessa. You could tell they were related to the older man. Not only did they look like him, but their movements were a mirror image.

"Look sharp now, we have company," Phlial spoke with the tone of a proud father showing off his own. The boys stood up and stretched. Even thought still sleep ridden, they showed their manners by coming over and bowing wonderfully to Dessa. She learned their names were Bartol and Rancy. Just one winter apart in age, they could have been twins. They both washed and they all sat down at a large wooden table in front a broad heavy pot of stew and pan of bread Phlial had extracted from the low fire.

As they began to eat, Phlial asked, "So may I inquire as to your name young lady?" Dessa blushed a deep crimson. It had not occurred to her to introduce herself. In all her years, everyone introduced themselves to her. She was the princess of the castle, it was always one-way. This was so very different though.

Her mind raced. If she told them her name, she was sure it would get out to someone passing through. They must sell the wool, and word could get back to the castle. All would be lost. She searched for a suitable stage name. Finally, she succumbed to the silence and said, "Saoirse."

"Hmm," replied a thoughtful Phlial. "The old queen's name; I thought King Tarmon forbade anyone from using his mother's name out of respect for the old lady." He grinned at her, cocking his head, waiting for her to figure out how to get out of this obvious fictitious trap that she had sprung on herself.

By this time, Dessa's brain had caught up and she calmly replied, "My given name is Gale. Nevertheless, my mother was so in love with the queen, she secretly named me after her. I don't get to use that sweet name much. I just love the sound so." She looked up steadily at her host. Her eyes bright, her mouth set sturdily. She hoped the look on her face hid her pounding heart.

Phlial was obviously satisfied with the lie. Either the content or the way it was delivered. Whichever it was, he seemed to relax, chew a little on some bread and then ask, "So where are you headed?"

"I am off to visit with a man named Tallon," she replied, figuring there was no harm in the truth there. I am told he can teach anyone how to defend themselves, and I intend to learn." She finished the statement of intent with a purposefulness that she hoped was believable.

Now Phlial raised a bushy eyebrow and looked at Dessa through the corner of his pleasant face. "Why for the love of earth would a nice girl like you go see a beast like Tallon?" he asked with genuine wonder to his words. "The man is a prig at best. If he does not kill you, at the very least you will come away maimed. Taught, probably, but at the very least maimed."

Now it was Dessa's turn to wonder. What had Gale done? Was Tallon really so bad?

Her thoughts were interrupted by Phlial who calmly told the boys to get to the shearing. He expected twenty more sheep today and no cuts or nicks. The entire flock had to be done before it rained again you could not shear wet sheep she learned.

The boys left in a graceful silence. Dessa stayed to help clean up from the supper, which had been delicious. They chatted about everything and nothing. Dessa told her story of the cougar, Phlial spoke of his beloved wife who had died of the cough two winters before. Dessa inquired as to his educated manner of speech, and found that while traveling as a merchant boy, his mother had carefully schooled him in manners and speech. She did not want him disdained by others as just another lowly gypsy seller.

Without warning he climbed into bed and told Dessa she should get some rest too.

"But it is just after mid-day," she replied, somewhat confused.

"Yes, but we will be up most of the night," he told her with a sad face. "We have been having great trouble with wolves."

34.
Planting

Torrin bent over the heavy metal hoe and turned the packed dirt as a continuous stream of sweat dripped down and spent most of its time stinging his eyes. Behind him, a small army of planters meticulously drove fertilizer and seeds into the ground in neat, even rows. After the seed was firmly packed into the earth, another group was busy trekking water from the nearby creek, decanting their loads on the newly planted furrows. It was a short growing season and the people of the valley had to grow as much as they could if they were to survive the harsh winters.

Everyone was pleasant enough to him, although the state of affairs seemed somewhat strained. He rightly guessed it was only natural. No one could fault him for what happened to Gwendolyn, but he knew they harbored a sense of something for him.

Maybe it was guilt. Guilt from having not stopped her?

Him?

Maybe it was a hatred that he was here? Whatever it was, he knew somehow that now the sequence of things was out of his hands. In many respects he knew he must pay careful attention to what was going on around him. He did not want any more situations to occur like the one in the forest. Forces beyond his control had clearly told him to wake up.

"Stop yer daydreamn and get plown'," groused an equally sweaty Harold. Torrin stooped back to his task. The harsh work felt good. It let him work through his feelings, in a physical way. And, as the day wore on, he felt mentally better, even if he was terribly sore.

During the lunch break, he was able to find out more about the people he had been meeting and working with these past few days. It seemed that Journey was the closest thing to a castle in these parts. There was certainly no need or desire for a king. The valley was certainly cut off from the rest of the world by steep hills, thick forest and some treacherous gullies. And unless you knew about the place, you more than likely would never find it unless you were very lost, lucky or looking to hide. Therefore, invasion was not an issue that developed very often. Anyway, the people here were equipped to do battle; Torrin noticed that even the women arrived at the field with a sword or hammer. They were friendly, but cautious folk, and watching them work, he rightly guessed they were a strong lot. They lived deeply and quietly in the woods. He had passed a few homes on the trek up here. Sturdy, large, all had huge firewood piles. The winters were cold, and the snow was sometimes so deep you could not walk about. Therefore, you had to be ready. Being always at this level of 'ready' was new to Torrin.

The people talked of their children, their lives, their homes. They talked of each other. There was an easiness about them that shone through in their smiles, their caring and what seemed to be their unquestionable integrity. They did not complain about working here today. They seemed to relish the challenge. They were a team. Something forged a relationship as hardy as thick rock. Yet nothing was central to them.

Or was there?

Something struck Torrin about these people that told him they were different, but he could not put his finger on it. There was a nagging kernel of a substantial departure from his current culture and thinking in the back of his head. These thoughts would not go away, but it was clear to him that there was more to this story than he saw. What troubled him were the deeper questions, "What is my role in this? Why am I here?" What did occur to him, as the mass of workers began to disperse from the day's project, that whatever he had gotten himself into, was bigger than he.

As the day drew to a close, Harold and Torrin stood at the bottom of the freshly furrowed field with all its neat rows, and they surveyed the planting.

"Whatcha think lad?" asked a sweaty and dirt streaked Harold.

"I have never been so sore in my life," replied the parched and sunburned young man. "I am also thinking there is something different about these people here. You too, Harold. What is it? What am I doing here?"

"No, I mean the field. Whatcha ya think o' the field?" sighed the older man.

"I guess it's OK," replied a slightly bemused Torrin. What else could he say, he wondered. He had forgotten about his other question.

"Any predictions about the crop?" prodded Harold.

"Well, I see a good crop of yams, but the sun will bake dry the green beans unless we water them. Also, the corner of the field, up there," he pointed, "will wash out during any heavy thunderstorms. We should ditch it or put up a wall of sorts to protect it."

"Ye do ave an eye for things," smiled Harold. "Good. Tomorrow we build a wall. Now, as to yer other thoughts." Harold seemed to ponder a deep thought, "It's good yer been thinkn. What is ere is important, almos as important as whas not ere. Your job, ifn ye wan it, is to understand it, an then, ye will own it. Yer comn' along. But is not nothn ye can be tol, that makes it a lil difficult to see it or understand it. Ye gots to make it yer own. Own it in yer heart and brains. But once ye ave it, yel neva be the same. An wi the gift, it changes not only yer own self, but it makes yer soul different like ye canna believe." Harold's eyes took a glassy sheen, he slumped forward some, a low smile lit his face, his head shook slowly left and right; a sort of "yes", that he meant only for his own self. Finally he said, "Let's go ave a nice dina."

       *   *   *

The days for Torrin, passed in busy workings on and around the Journey Inn. It was an occupying task for Torrin to mend the great roof. Using slabs of oak and thick pine tar they had boiled in a huge kettle at the edge of the clearing, it was hot but satisfying work. Until he looked down at the ground. He got a new appreciation for keeping his feet in the right places those days. Harold was quick to remind him that roof work was something you did very slowly. For two reasons, the first being, one quick step and you were fast dead. The second was, do the job well. Coming up here in the winter to fix a hole was not something he liked to do. They worked very slowly for these few days that it took. Torrin liked the teamwork. He did not like the day in and day out routine of the roof though. After what seemed forever (but was really only about fifteen days), Harold declared the roof fixed and good for another chunk of winters.

Chinking the walls was a messy and laborious task too. Removing the old dried and dusty material was not so difficult physically except the majority of it landed in Torrin's hair and eyes. It took time, patience and much trial and error before he could run a smooth bead between the large old logs. But one section at a time, and for many days he toiled. But he also learned the value of the work.

Covered with dust and mud from the experience, he ended up bathing in the creek most days, sword nearby least some unforeseen danger wander into his life.

Where Torrin bathed in the rushing natural waters, it seemed almost a magical place. A waterfall, higher than himself, rushed foamy bubbles over silky unwrinkled stones. The chilly flow crashed smoothly in a milky white mist. A never ending cascade of powerful grace. He marveled at the might of the dashing water and how the pool at the bottom, beaten, smashed and pummeled constantly, was rather a source of peace. Just a few paces, seemingly planned, from the fury of the descension was a rather calm smooth pool. Flowers grew at the edge. Large polished rocks bordered the languid tranquility.

His feet walked gracefully over the well worn gravel at the bottom of the pool, now made smooth by the rushing rapids over the years.

Little clouds of muddied dust sprang from his footsteps under the water as he walked. The power of the torrent soon cleared the cloudiness, and brought the magical sparkle back to the water.

Something tugged at his heart. This was not a place where one should be alone. This was a place for sharing. It reminded him of the wonderful nights, not so many years before, when he would be scrubbed clean in a warm bath by his mother, Queen Ethelda. She would scrub his hair in a vigorous but gentle fashion. She was a kind lady, secure in her values, yet soft in her ways.

As he had grown, his mother reminded him often to go on living life to the fullest. Make everyday your best. He was born into leadership; people watched and wondered and would take his lead. He was royalty. He should always think about his actions. This would be his gift to her spirit.

The waterfall and pool of peaceful water left him melancholy for a moment. His thoughts and memories of the first and only woman he really loved or trusted, warm in his heart. But only for a moment, because he was true to her request. Live life to its fullest. Ethelda had no idea what she had set in motion in her son.

*   *   *

Late one afternoon Torrin was mucking the large stalls that served the horses of Journey's guests. He had developed a keen appreciation for the groomsmen and stable boys who had tended the stalls at the castle. On warm days, the stench could be unbearable, and the flies seemed to multiply as if on a mission to cover the entire world.

Torrin had not been paying attention to the smell, the heat or the flies.

He was thinking.

Pondering the questions that had been nagging him. Thinking about his role, when a strange thing happened to him for the first time. A deep heat started in his shoulder and pushed its way up into his head. Gooseflesh rose on his neck, his head throbbed.

Then just as a summer thunderstorm sneaks up on you when you are picnicking, an air of excitement suddenly charged the sticky humid day all around him.

Presently, a new face appeared. He was on a large horse that he rode well. Tall man, dark curly hair that fell to his shoulders, well dressed, carried himself in a regal manner. His chin seemed to be chiseled from stone. Torrin felt immediately disturbed, almost angry. He did not understand why the hairs on his neck stood up, why his fists clenched. Something was astir.

Dismounting, with a mean-spirited look firmly written upon his face, the stranger looked around and seemed to scowl in rampant disapproval at the domain around Journey. Some women were bargaining with a traveling oil lamp seller. Others were gossiping about the latest affairs. It was a natural scene. He seemed tense, as if he was obscuring something.

Walking with an air about him that belied any humility, he sauntered up to a gaping and wondering Torrin, handed him the reins to his horse and said, "Take care of him, he worked harder than you today. I certainly hope this piteous outpost has some decent food; you people look like you could use help. Where the hell am I?"

Without really waiting for a reply, he turned and walked toward the main room of Journey. Torrin stood with the reins in his hand, a scowl on his face, his stomach aching for no reason and his mind wondering what was going on.

* * *

That night, with Journey's regulars present, and the usual itinerate crowd in attendance, Torrin sat quietly, his thoughts in turmoil, his sense of danger high. He listened as the man who had handed him the horse's reigns treated the room to all sorts of fascinating stories. Great hunts, long trips and voyages to distant lands. Tales that rambled of large cities where hundreds of people lived together in huge buildings with many rooms. Great ships that sailed on massive ponds, so big you could not see the other side of the water.

It was not the stories that bothered Torrin. It was the manner in which it was told. These chronicles, although fascinating, all seemed to center around how important and smart the man with the dark curls was to the future of the very earth itself.

Torrin, helping Karina, carried an armful of plates to the kitchen.

"Karina," began a tentative Torrin. "Do you sense something wrong with that man out there? When I am near him, my head hurts, my arms ache, the world seems out of balance."

Karina turned to look at Torrin and smiled, "Sure, he is a fraud and blowhard. Does not matter, his money is good. He'll be gone tomorrow. Don't let it bother you."

Torrin smiled at her reassurance. But inside, his mind was racing.

As Torrin returned to the room, he did not see the concerned look on Karina's face.

Most of Journey had turned in, but Quillan and the traveler were conversing in low tones. Torrin sat down and waited for a lull in the conversation.

"Kind sir, your horse is settled for the night, and my name is Torrin; I am at your service," he said, holding out his hand in a friendly gesture (as one does to prove they are not holding a weapon). "May I ask your name and where you, with that wonderful steed of yours are headed?"

The man did not extend his hand. He looked at the young man and grinned. "Ye seem pretty well bred for a stable boy." Torrin bristled, but held his temper in check.

"My name is Haphethus." Stretching his long arms and leaning back against the wall he continued, obviously pleased with himself, "I am on a long trek to visit my twin brother Darius. It is told he married some hot wench princess up north in Tarmon's kingdom," he said with what Torrin saw as a sadistic smile. "Figure he and his new wife can keep me in good food and snuggled with the warm kitchen help for the winter." His boisterous laughter was not infectious for the men around the table. "I have been riding now for two months. Seem to have gotten lost," he said looking around. "How do you people survive without a castle? This place is sturdy, but certainly not made of stone."

Harold started to say something. Torrin noticed his hands were clenched and there was an odd look on his face. However, Quillan firmly interrupted with a look that said, "I'll take care of this, relax!"

"We seem not ta get bothered much here. Not much ta pillage, and most of the people live so deep in the wood ya wo' na fine 'em." Quillan continued, "Sides, most o the women ha the itch. A traveler brung it er a few winters back. Dey make bad slaves when dey ga de itch."

Looking around the room, Haphethus took in the people making Journey their evening center of entertainment. A wide variety of men and women constituted the crowd that made Journey its normal happy place. Many were talking, laughing with some serious flirting taking place in the shadows of the dark corners.

Haphethus looked at Quillan with a questioning eye. Quillan, without missing a beat, calmly, and almost offhandedly finished his little tarradiddle, "Sure, but once ye get it, even wi the awful terrible burn'n, the smelly pus when ye piss, the screaming agony when a wild woman finishes ye off, ya wanna use it before it falls off an ye go mad burn'n looney!" Quillan's eyes were just a bit wide, a spittle of drink hanging at the edge of his very pink mouth, and his free hand was scratching himself with a vengeance, below the table.

Wearing a poker face that was a little too well rehearsed, Haphethus eyed Quillan. He then drained his tankard, at which he seemed very adept, and put the empty vessel down in front of Torrin. "Be a good boy and fill it up," he enjoined sneeringly. It was not a question or a request, it was an order.

Quillan gave Torrin an odd look that said, 'He'll be gone tomorrow. Just make do.'

Torrin filled the tankard. He mulled over dropping just a little rancid meat from the swill bucket in the bottom; the man had drunk enough, he would not notice. A good case of the runs might help him be civil. However, he thought the better of it. If this louse got sick, he might stay around.

Torrin excused himself, saying he was tired. Haphethus bid him a good night, commenting that, "After all, growing boys need their sleep."

Torrin left the room; his head felt like it was in flames, the banging at the base of his neck would not go away.

*   *   *

When Haphethus came for his horse in the late morning, he said nothing to Torrin. He just rolled himself into the stable, full of attitude, saddled the broad back of his gnarly steed and rode off fast and hard.

Torrin just shook his head and thought, "if I must learn patience that was a good lesson." As the nasty man retreated into the distance, the banging in Torrin's head diminished.

After mucking the stalls, he decided he needed one of Karina's warm treats that emerged from her almost magic ovens. He planned to spend the rest of the morning furthering the construction of the stonewall he had been building on the north side of Journey.

The great room was empty. The fireplace eerily cool. It was an unusual silence for what was usually a busy, clamorous and hectic theater of life. Torrin looked around, thinking that the few days left in his "deal" with Harold could not pass fast enough. He was ready to go home.

Or, something said quietly in his head, "they might pass too fast." There was a comfort here, a sense of belonging that was substantial; it felt strange, but nice. He was not sure what to make of it. Life at the castle was fun, but he was treated differently here. This seemed more genuine, more sincere. The castle folk at home were always pleasant, but not as down to earth as Quillan, Harold, Karina and the others.

Then a deep thought suddenly seemed to strike him. No one was officially in charge here. There was no king, no queen, no ruling council.

No guards?

Yet everyone worked together. And they not only worked hard, they worked well. That was why Haphethus was so out of place. In addition to the ignoramus air about him, he did not fit because he was lazy. He was a fraud, disingenuous. And, Torrin sensed, he was evil at his core. That really bothered the young man. He had never felt that way, nor experienced such deep disregard about someone before. Never had he felt such a need to be away from a person. Putting space between himself and Haphethus was important.

He was wondering when more of this would make sense though. Why did so many of his feelings smack so differently against his brain? Where were these thoughts coming from? The loss of his normal sense of himself was disquieting.

As he pushed through the big door to the kitchen, he could smell the warm pungent scent of the big sweet rolls Karina loved to bake. Except they smelled burnt? And Karina lay on the floor in a pool of dark red blood.

35.
Night

Dessa awoke to the touch of a warm and gentle hand on her shoulder. Blinking in the low light of a few candles, she slowly got her bearings. Phlial handed her a steaming mug of tea, which she gratefully accepted. Its strong aroma waking her further, erasing the cobwebs that are always present when being roused from a deep sleep during the night.

She became aware of movement. Not so much strong movement, but a lot of it. Soon it became apparent that the sheep were now next to the cabin in the fenced area. They were not settling down for the night; they were nervous.

"How long have you had wolf problems?" she asked Phlial. He was busy strapping two long knives to his chest. He already had one strapped to each leg.

"Last few days. Never seen anything like it," he replied. "We tried scaring them off, but that didn't work. Now we try to knife 'em if we can. Got two last night. But they just keep coming," he shrugged his shoulders and sighed. "If word gets out, the buyers won't want to stop here for fear their horses or young ones will get attacked."

"Well, let's show 'em whose boss," she said and walked out the door.

In the barn, she retrieved her sword and quiver, checked the bow to make sure it was tight and ready for use. Satisfied, she slung the weapon over her shoulder; the taught bow line felt snug. As she made ready to leave, she remembered the two stout arm scabbards. On they went, and their stiffness too felt snug and secure. Uta and Calandra stood quietly sleeping, as well as horses sleep. She made sure the door was tightly secure, before returning to the cabin.

Phlial had put out a plate of dried mutton. He and the boys were quietly chewing. They looked like warriors ready to do battle; deep in thought, sincere, and when you looked behind their fierce exterior, a little scared.

Bartol, the oldest, looked at Dessa's bow and chuckled. "Excuse me, but they are too fast and it's dark out there. That bow will be useless."

Dessa looked at him and smiled. "We'll see," she said with raised eyebrows.

Suddenly her eyes hurt. Her ears rang, she was short of breath. It was eerie; she knew she had felt like this before, but not this strongly. This was different.

Sitting down heavily on a chair, she looked up at the three men who were staring at her, in quite a concerned manner and said, "The wolves, they are coming and they are not coming for the sheep. They are coming for us tonight."

Suddenly the feeling in the room changed from one of a defensive posture to offensive. You could almost taste it in the air.

As they walked outside and secured the door to the cabin, Dessa could see silvery clouds playing hide and seek with a long white moon. It was quiet and the entire valley around them seemed to be in a silent sleep. Frankly, it was hard to tell. The woods here were very thick and seemed days away from the warm beauty of the sunny valley, even though it was only a few paces away.

The peacefulness belied the death that was to come.

The father and sons had prepared well. They spread out and climbed up into trees, sitting on a stout limb. Apiece, they all had a good number of large stones stacked on a platform within easy reach. It made for a deadly arsenal. Dessa found refuge on the roof of the big cabin next to the stone chimney. She felt like she could get a clear shot from here; it gave her room to maneuver.

When the wolves came, they did not come in a stealthy way. There must have been twenty or more. Their harsh barking, snapping of jaws, snorting and the rough grating of their claws at the trunks of the trees as they sought the shepherds was harrowing.

Dessa could not believe the ferocity of the attack. The wolves looked possessed, as dark spit flew from their frothy mouths. Their incessant yelping and ruthless staccato barking hurt her ears it was so loud. They had seemed to team up for the assault. No one wolf worked alone. It was a coordinated effort. Even as a large stone would crush the life out of an attacker, another would take its spot. She was certainly glad the three had been wise enough to go high in the big trees.

Stones, small boulders and knives rained down with deadly accuracy. But even with a broken leg a wolf would continue its driven assault. They seemed possessed.

At first Bartol was right. She missed two shots. The wolves were fast; they never stopped for a moment. Leading the next target, she speared it through the shoulder just as it was about to attack a terrified baby lamb. The mangy creature tried to snap at the foreign object in its shoulder before running back toward the deep of the wood. The next target was not so lucky. Dessa could hear the arrow enter its skull. Dropping dead instantly, it no longer threatened anyone. Some in the pack took a look at their fallen comrade, unsure of what to make of this new weapon they had never seen before, and then kept up their own attack.

Not having any luck with their intended targets, the wolves soon turned to the sheep. The three collies were in a frenzy. Even though the wolves were tough, the collies were smart. They were also fast, strong and well fed. They made quick work of a wolf once they got their long teeth into its scrawny neck. Between the three collies, the wretched souls of eight wolves left the earth that horrific night. Dessa added six more before the pack, what was left of it, turned and maneuvered back to the safety of the deep woods.

Suddenly, the only sounds were the sheep, panting dogs and the pounding of each of their hearts in their ears. Dessa sat down to catch her breath. The battle had only lasted a few moments, but it had seemed like an eternity. She could not believe how winded she was. She was shaking from the frenzy of it all.

The scene below spread out in a ghastly image. Dead and maimed sheep, lifeless broken wolves' tongues already black in death, lay still on the dust. Heads split open, shattered bodies littering the forest's ground. Blood pooled as it waited to be absorbed back into the earth.

It was a scene that she felt should be reserved only for the worst of nightmares. The kind you wake from very tired and wishing you had not gone to bed let alone asleep. The kind of nightmare where you're subconscious negotiates with the unconscious, giving into whatever hateful scene or thought must be delivered to allow for balance to return. Begging to wake up and end the hell that runs amok.

Then the burn that had started in her eyes that seemed to have abated arose again. Blinking hard and slow, she tried to quench the fire that seemed to cook her vision. Radiating into her shoulders, the heat caused the sweat to pour off her skin. Crashing waves of turbid dissonance mucked through her ears. It sounded like a million voices raised in the screaming agony of imposed doom. This feeling, although much more subtle, had been with her for days she would later recall. She had just not paid it heed. Until this time, she knew now it was a warning.

Standing slowly, she twisted to look behind her. She could feel the source of the evil at her back. Sitting at the top of the roof's peak the old gray wolf admired her form. His eyes stared not so much at her, but through her. As though she was in his way, yet he was obviously there for one reason, and only one reason. Dessa uttered a loud, deep throaty, "Why?" as he leapt for her. His fangs glistened in a raging dripping foam of hate. There was no regard for the danger he was putting himself in—he was surely going to go off the roof. Something was driving him. Some mad need to see her dead.

This was something beyond rabies, for it was too early on the earth for such a terrible disease. That dreaded disease would not surface for over a thousand years. This was a drive to defeat her. To stop her. To destroy her. Something evil needed to do her harm.

Dessa was catapulted off the roof and felt a hot wet burning sensation on the left side of her head. Part of his massive jaw caught on the thick leather scabbard Dessa wore, the rest of the teeth were working their way into her head. She had raised her hand to instinctively defend her face. The two landed hard in the sheep's gated area, her fall broken only by straw and the natural soft earth you find in the forest.

Try as she might, Dessa could not break the tight grasp the sharp jaws had on her head. Even pounding the wolf's face with the other hard scabbard did not deter it from its dreadful, hateful mission. On her knees, she could not stand, she could not lie down, she could not move. The skin of her scalp tore as the wolf tried to shake his prey, an instinct that usually broke its victim's neck, but she was too heavy and strong to shake. His hot breath blew like wet thunder in her ear. The stink of rotting meat, caught between its teeth was nauseating.

Where were the collies? The men were climbing down from the trees, but she would be long dead before they reached her. She felt dizzy with pain and fear, her heart was racing, it was surreal; a dreamlike fantasy nightmare she could not control. Time began to slow down. The ragged curdled gasps of air that heaved in and out of the wolf seemed close up and distant at the same time. The sound drummed in a fast cadenced echo in slow motion in her ears and in one furtive twist one of her eyes locked with one of the wolf's eyes—for a heartbeat they stared into each other's souls.

Instinctively she twisted her arm and left the scabbard in the wolf's mouth, freeing her right hand, and then reached in and pulled the cord in the left sleeve. The silver dagger slid into her hand. As in slow motion, she reversed the blessed tool so the blade pointed out, and with a calmness that surprised even herself, slit the wolf from its anus to the bottom of its ribcage. She reached inside the hot heaving chest cavity, grabbed its small rapidly beating, adrenaline drugged heart, and with savage strength, fed with her own need for survival, twisted and yanked. The racing organ pumped twice in her hand before going silent.

The now very dead wolf did not move. He just stood there in a shocked state of bewildered demise, death now dark in his eye, his jaws tight on her head. However, the mounting pressure of his teeth had abated. She did not make a motion for fear her face would tear off.

What seemed like hours passed. It was only a few moments. Rancy, the first to hit the ground, carefully pried the dead predator's teeth off her face. He tossed the dead animal aside and helped Dessa to lie down. She heard him say in breathless wonderment, "Praise God woman, you are either the luckiest or most dangerous girl I have ever met." She sensed Phlial running by, into the cabin. Bartol started removing dead animals and calming the dogs.

Dessa whispered something. Rancy put his ear to her mouth so he could hear, as she said gaspingly, "The arrows, save my arrows, they are special." The arrows were a connection to Gale; she did not want to lose a one, and her subconscious mind was taking over. Her conscious mind was frozen.

Phlial came to her with cool water and soft clothes. After washing her face, he happily proclaimed that the wounds were not life threatening. She would require a number of stitches, but considering what had happened, was more lucky than he had words for.

With some help, Dessa stood to go inside. She looked down at the empty carcass. Something in her leapt as she recognized the wolf. It was the large grey leader that had stood on the rock, looking at her on the way to the outer hunting lodge. Things stirred in her brain; they made no sense. She limped wearily into the cabin.

Inside it felt warm and safe. Phlial brought her a mug of strong drink, it smelled of juniper berries. He instructed her to drink it; it would take the edge off the pain.

He was as gentle as a mother with a baby as he stitched her face. She lay very still deciding in the recesses of her mind that he must have done this before. Most of the cuts were on her head, but one, high on her cheek would show on her face for all her days. Bartol said, "It shall make you look rugged."

Good, she thought, nothing like a "rugged looking" redheaded widow. She let out a little sigh. Her eyes were teary, her nose ran; it was not pleasant and it had started to hurt like the devil. She felt grimy, she felt violated, she felt happy though to be alive.

As Phlial laid her tired and sweat soaked body on a soft mattress, he said, "We owe you a great debt. We could not have survived without you tonight." He smiled at her, "As a father first, then a shepherd, I thank you." He laid a thick wool blanket over the girl who had helped save not only himself, but his children and his livelihood.

Dessa was shivering, the shock settling in. However, she was ready to sleep. She looked up at the kind face and muttered a soft, if not raspy, "You are most welcome my friend."

Before her fatigue finally overtook her whole being and drifting off to a deep sleep, her final thoughts were, "Yes, but if I had been here alone tonight, camping in the woods, it would all be over. He had been following me. Hunting me. Actually kind man, we needed each other, maybe me more than you."

36.
Justice

Torrin looked at Karina laying on the floor in disbelief. He knelt cautiously beside the still form of the older woman, unsure of what to do. She was still breathing, but he sensed she was struggling for air. Raspy breaths, shallow and wet came from lips that were swollen and red.

Without thinking, and actually without knowing what to do, he did what most people feeling pretty helpless would do—he frantically ran for help.

He came flying out the stable door at a dead on run, yelling at the top of his lungs. Many faces turned to look, not quite sure of what was happening, but not a few people thought the young Torrin had finally popped and had gone loony.

Harold and Quillan were just coming off the path, with a plentiful cache of wine and spirits strapped snuggly on the bed of a large cart. They had been up to Dunwidy's place, Torrin figured, shopping on behalf of Journey's residents. But that was for later.

Torrin's shocked and ravage soul told more of the story than his words. The shear fright in his eyes brought both men to a prompt run in an instant; somehow they seemed to know something was wrong inside. Ladies who were about, tending to their daily grocery, picked up their skirts and started toward the massive building; either to help, or partake of the excitement. You could never tell with some folks.

When Torrin finally arrived back to the kitchen and wormed his way through the crowd to the front, Harold had Karina sitting up with her back against the wall. Her face was a frightful sight. In addition to the swollen lips Torrin had seen, the right side of her face was black and purple. Her left arm was red and bloody. A long gash ran across her fair skin. She held something in her right hand, which Harold carefully pried away from her grip and gave to Quillan. It was a large white tooth. Quillan quickly washed it and handed it back to Harold. He then did the strangest thing, opening her mouth with his hand, he inserted the lost part back in and told her to "bite down hard and don't talk" (a pretty tall order for Karina, thought Torrin, as he struggled to catch his breath and take in the scene that was playing out in front of him).

Torrin scratched his head. Never in his life had he neither heard nor seen such a thing with a tooth.

Harold quietly said to Karina, "It's worked before, it might still work, we'll see."

Harold looked firmly at Torrin, "Get these people out of here!" It was clearly not an option and Torrin reckoned he had never heard that tone of voice before coming from Harold.

Torrin turned to shoo the crowd away, but they had already gotten the message. Muttering to each other about how evil must be lurking about, they dispersed.

Harold then looked up at Quillan and said in a slow measured voice that was even more measured and forceful, one again that Torrin had never heard before, "It was him. He wanted her, he would not leave graciously, denied his pleasure, so he cut her."

Quillan nodded to Harold and then turned to Torrin and put his arm around Torrin's shoulder saying, "Let us go, we have work to do."

"But she needs…," Torrin sputtered.

Quillan quickly pointed out in a stern voice, "She needs to be with Harold. Come, we have work to do."

Leaving with Quillan, Torrin purposefully set his direction toward the stables. Quickly he started saddling two of the biggest and fastest horses Harold had in the lot. In just a few moments, he had both horses in the sunshine, ready to go. With not a movement to spare, he retrieved his sword and knife from the upstairs room.

He met a very serious and determined looking Quillan outside sitting on the wooden bench.

"OK, let's go," said the excited and somewhat out of breath Torrin.

Quillan gave Torrin a look that would melt stone, "Go where?" he quietly asked, head cocked to one side. It was not a mocking look, but it was not one of kindness.

"Why to get that scum Haphethus," Torrin said straightaway. He was hopping mad to get on his way, on the hunt.

"Go 'head yasef," replied the calm and steady man. "Let me know how ye make out."

Torrin could only stare, slack jawed and amazed. "We have to catch that man! Did you see what he did to Karina? He must pay. We must have justice!"

"Torrin," Quillan softly began. "Frst off, he has a qurtr day ahd o' us, an we don' know his way of travel. And, we canno prove ifn he done it—sides, he ain't gonna admit it anyway if we do catch 'im. Also, he is a nasty brut. Ye think yer gonna take 'em?" Quillan ran his big hand through his bright hair. Sweat covered his palm.

Torrin stood and stared. He seethed a fire that would melt iron on the inside. How could Quillan be so cavalier? Justice must be meted out. This was Karina they were talking about!

"Go ask Harold if ye want," Quillan firmly said, standing up, looking down at the young man. "She ain' gonna die, an mostly a man like that get 'is due in time. Anyways, the games start on ta morrow an yel be busy."

Torrin was only half listening. His sense of values had been violated. Only worthless scum would attack a lady like that. He must pay. Torrin swore to himself, if he ever could, he would make sure that Haphethus would pay and pay dearly.

Then his brain caught up with his emotions and he knew Quillan was right. They had no proof, did not know what direction Haphethus had taken and then there were the—games?

"What games?" he asked of the tall sweaty man who was sauntering away toward the cart still piled high with casks of beverages destined for happier times.

"The planting celebration, ye dit," came Quillan's gentle, yet somewhat devilish reply.

"I didn't know about any games," said Torrin. "Where, when, how do I sign up?" He was suddenly full of questions. How come he never knew of these things?

"Well," said Quillan slowly. "They start reight here, on the morrow. Ever on 'ell be arrivn ere. Is great fun!" He swung his big hands in an arc, indicating the clear area in front of Journey. "Ther'll be girls here," he said with a sideways smirk.

"Oh no you don't," replied the suddenly cautious Torrin. "I learned my lesson. I have to wait for someone, hope I just know when she shows up!"

"Don' ye be worryn yerself," smiled Quillan. "I am sure yel miss er' an I'll ave ta elp ye. Now elp me unload this cart. After the caber, ther is lots o' drinkn ta do an I want this scotch cooln' in the' cellar."

37.
Tallon

Dessa slept for the better part of two days. Phlial swabbed alcohol, distilled from the spirits he kept for winter on her wounds while she slept. It did nothing but help and caused a few mumbles to emerge from the obvious stinging. Her body was bathed in sweat. Not any sweat. But the thick heavy sweat a mortal body creates as part of the healing process after major trauma. A steady cleansing stream of evils and poisons that seem to emerge through the pores.

When she finally awoke, she felt disoriented.

Lost.

Bewildered.

But after a fairly short while, sanity crept back, as it does. Maybe a little more clearly from the experience? Presently, she began to feel better. Actually she began to feel oddly spectacular. Sleeping for two days had revived her. She felt, besides the pain in her face and other bruised body parts, wonderful.

As she started to sit up, reality came strumming back. A dull throb met the right side of her face and then seemed to pinch. It was dull and sharp all at the same time and it was deep. There was no escaping it and a dizzy sort of vertigo engulfed her.

Slowly and carefully, making sure that the tender parts did not touch anything, she lay back down. The dizzy sensation abated as she closed her eyes. The soft pillow gently caught her head in an almost mystical way that allowed her to relax.

The rest of her body was waking up now outside of the bruises. Small tremors of feeling began to emerge from her long sleeping muscles. The wonderful ache of being alive slowly walked through her body, as her parts became known again and reconnected to her brain.

She began to take inventory. First the right hand, flexing her fingers, slowly, she felt stiffness, but no severe cuts and all the fingers were there and responding. Then the left side. There was a painful throb here that hurt as she flexed and turned her left arm. Since the wolf had settled his teeth into the right side of her, she correctly figured that her left side had taken the brunt of the landing. However, everything seemed to work OK, even if it was a little tender.

Her legs were stiff, but responded to requests for movement as she patiently stretched them back and forth. Then she put her hand to her face and ever so slowly moved her fingers around. Like a blind person "looking" at her face. Her thick curly hair was matted and stiff. She could feel the cuts under her hair. The slash on her face was clean, except for the stitching. It seemed to itch.

All her teeth were intact. Her eyes worked, and as she again sat up, this time very slowly, there were no great pains in her chest or back. Although she figured correctly, the bruises were going to take some time to abate.

Her memory however, was badly marred. The vivid flashbacks of the wolf. The black burning hatred, the blackness of his eyes. How her eyes had felt like they were on fire before he attacked. How her shoulders ached. The screaming doom in her ears. The warnings she had not heeded.

There were so many questions. What would an old wolf want with me? Why had he been hunting me? Why would I sense his dark hate? Was it just fear? She figured it must be something more.

She was right. And as she would find later, he was not alone.

* * *

Dessa's eyes fluttered open once again. No one was about the cabin. It was light outside, but she had no idea of the time of day. However, one thing was for certain, she was clearly and completely hungry.

As her body and brain worked together again, and her whole being came alive, she realized she was famished. And incredibly thirsty. Not just any thirst, her throat was parched and her eyes dusty dry. The veins on her arms stood out, as they do on a dehydrated person. She felt a little dizzy.

Moving slowly this time, she succeeded in sitting up in the bed. More rolling than sliding to the right, she got her feet to the floor. It felt good to be moving, even if it did seem to exhaust her.

The wool covered skin on the floor felt cool and soft at first under her feet. Sitting quietly, she caught her breath, gained her bearing and stood. Holding the post of the bed, swaying slightly, she relished the achievement. Standing up told her she was back in charge of her adventure. The journey could continue.

It then dawned on her that all she was wearing was a long, softy spun, very white, lady's shift. It came to just below her knees. A delicate green ribbon kept the front closed (which did seem quite optional), however long slits on either side of her thighs made the garment the most revealing and rather exotic clothing she had worn since her fateful wedding night. Looking around, she found her clothes neatly folded on a seat. Picking them up, she smelled soap and lanolin. Sweet smells and a softness she had not expected. Some kind soul had washed out the mess from the battle.

Loosening the shift's ribbon, she dropped it to the floor and proceeded to slowly and carefully get dressed. Her undershirt was almost bright in its cleanliness. It covered her snugly, a feeling of security and snugness that she relished. She thought if somehow humorous familiar clothes and the implements of life brought joy and security when we felt bad.

The outer shirt, breeches and stockings were all fresh and smelled of sunshine and fresh air. Her boots had been brushed and oiled; they firmly held her feet.

Dressing exhausted her. Sitting down, she noticed a large pitcher of water and a mug on the stand next to the bed.

"Thank you!" she said aloud to no one in particular. Drinking the cool liquid made her gain not only strength but also appreciation for the sincere graciousness of her hosts. Even if they had stripped her naked and put her to bed!

Anyway, it was a small price to pay for their care. Without them, she would have been a wolf's main meal for an evening. She shuddered at the thought.

Rising, she slowly made her way to the door and stepped out into a glorious day. Warm, dry, a soft breeze blowing through the trees; you would never have guessed the high level of violent and tortuous death and destruction here just a short while before.

Walking unhurriedly to the edge of the dark green forest she gazed out at the serenity that lay before her. The sheep calmly ate at the lush grass, the collies playfully working at keeping order. The shepherds sat on a log just a few paces to her right, enjoying the sun. Even Uta and Calandra contently stood and enjoyed the warm sun and thick green vegetation, munching away on the pasture's bounty. It was very serene.

Phlial was instantly on his feet, lankily running over to her. The boys sat quietly stunned. Sensing adolescent embarrassment, she blushed.

In a most warm way Phlial boomed, "Welcome back! It has been a few days since you went to sleep. We were beginning to wonder about your fate. It is good to see you up and about." He seemed to stammer some and then added, "Please excuse me washing your clothes. You were covered in sheep cache, blood and dead wolf entrails. I assumed you would not mind. I attended to you myself; the boys had no part in it, the shift was my wife's. If I have offended you, my deepest apologies."

The man was so sincere and good, Dessa was almost in tears. "Well," she began slowly. "I guess it would not have been my first choice, but waking up covered in that mess would have been horrible. Thank you for your kindness." She looked up at him and smiled.

Relieved, the tall man extended his arm to her. "Come, you must be hungry."

*   *   *

She ate slowly. The stew was wonderful. Phlial would only serve her small portions. He said it was too easy to overeat and get sick.

The wine he poured had a burnt oak musk to it. The bread was fresh and warm. She could feel herself gaining strength, and at the same time growing tired and in need of rest.

A thought crossed her mind of staying here. It was peaceful. The people good. There would be plenty of work. Before long she could go home, or make arrangements for a meeting.

As the outside light grew dim, she could hear the flock coming home for the evening. She looked up at Phlial. Her eyes told she had a question.

He beat her to it.

"Your horses are well tended to," he began. "In a few days you leave?"

The look on her face must have startled him. He came over to the table and sat down with a delicate altricity that told her he was serious.

"You are a young, beautiful woman," he began slowly. "Well bred, well fed, well mannered. I sense you are of royalty."

Her look and lack of answer told him he was right.

Continuing, "You are on a mission. For some reason, one that I cannot fathom, you are on your way to see that brute Tallon. If this is true, your reason must be severe. Forces greater than I have set you on this course. I must not interfere, you must not waver. As much as it would be good to have you here, I fear that something more powerful than a wolf would intervene." Phlial was stern, but friendly. He was most of all, as he always was, sincere.

"So you see, you must go," he added quickly. "But you are always welcome to visit. Let's just hope you don't experience quite the same type of visitors next time."

Dessa smiled. She knew she must go; the thought of staying was she guessed fleeting. It would have been the safe and secure thing to do. But, she mused, this place was too close to home to be safe. I would be too easy to be found out here. So even asking the question about staying was not in the cards for now.

As she stood, with a questioning smile across her soft face, her reply was a sincere form of thanks. "You and your sons have been most wonderful. I owe you a debt of my life." And with all the strength she could muster, she embraced the awkwardly tall man and hugged him until the tears in her eyes dried.

*   *   *

Upon cresting the next rise Dessa broke into a small flat area, clear of trees and tall vegetation, and at the far edge an incredibly expansive valley spread before her, almost beyond imagination. Shear rock cliffs,

dazzlingly steep and high ringed the colorful edges. Rock faces carved from eons of natural lashings and studded with green splotches of vegetation painted a working mosaic with the sunshine. Rocks lay strewn about the floor as if flung about by the giant hands of monsters at play. Great green swaths of long tall trees lent shade to bright areas. Incredibly tall and powerful waterfalls fell from unseen streams high in the hills with great piles of water crashing onto the valley floor, where wispy tendrils of mist rose tall in response to the long tumble of the cascade, their power hidden by the trees.

For a time Dessa sat tall upon Uta and gazed out over yet another magical wonder of nature that this journey had thrust upon her. And then soon she began to consider the immenseness of the beauty spread before her. Never before had she experienced such splendor and her mind clamored to take it all in. Whereas, slowly, piece by piece and stone by stone her brain absorbed the breathtaking view.

And it was by the contrasts she could discern how the parts fell into place.

At first, she marveled at the unbelievable amounts of water crashing down from the waterfalls. These vast towering giants were ten times what she had ever before experienced. Yet then in the sound of her own breath, her breath. And, she pondered, with this much water all I should hear is water. Yet an overwhelming silence fell upon her startled ears. So, she mused, these long ribbons of mighty water are truly farther away than I first thought.

And then, as she focused her listening, the sounds of the living valley began to emerge. Whippoorwills called to each other, frogs croaked, branches rustled with unseen small creatures scurrying about. And far off now, the thunder of the giant falls crept into the sounds that filled the valley. Their might but a whisper in the grand scene.

Spurring Uta on, she moved toward the bottom of the valley. No trail existed, no marks from other humans having passed this way.

The valley was so vast that it was not until noonday that she reached the waterfall. Dismounting, she walked to the edge of the pool where the water finished its long drop and felt the cool mist of the cascade beat back the midday heat. Once she was satisfied that the water was fresh and clean, she unbridled and unburdened both horses and let them enjoy the misty coolness.

After some time, with all her fresh water containers well washed and full, the little party mounted up and continued their trek down the valley, following the stream created by the majestic waterfall.

As did happen on many afternoons when the sun would heat the air, intermittent thunderstorms popped up and delivered not only a spectacular show of lightning, but also of sound and artistic virtue. Black lines of rain swept like great brushes across the sky making all it touched glisten like fine porcelain once the bright sun rendered its glow upon the now wet landscape.

As evening approached Dessa found a sheltered place among the huge boulders and made her evening camp. The boulder was as big as a large cottage with an overhanging shelf that offered overhead protection for the night and was large enough for her and the horses. Wood for a brisk fire was plentiful from the trees that had tumbled for many seasons from the edge of the canyon. A plentiful pile of logs soon appeared as long as her arm with broken and shredded wood at each end attesting to the violence that attended their demise and probable rapid bouncing descent down the steep walls.

After a restful meal of dried venison, a warm fire that removed the chill from her bones and enough heat to dry her clothes, Dessa nighted the fire and fell fast asleep to the long mellow echoes of deep rumbling thunder that slowly rolled up the valley.

                    *   *   *

Cool misty fog greeted her eyes upon wakening. She lay warmly ensconced in her bedroll for a while, knowing that she would soon have the fire blazing again (Gale had taught her on numerous outings how to add three layers of damp wood to the fire before retiring so that upon arising, a core of hot coals would be ready for the dry tinder that she wrapped in oilcloth and taken to her bed). She just wanted to lie there for some time to listen to the valley, hear its heart and feel its soul.

Small creatures scurried about. Gentle breezes atop the cliff sent hollow, long low whistles to the ground. And then curiously, every few heartbeats, the light sound of distant thunder met her ears.

Something was strange though. She heard thunder but did not see rain nor did the air feel right for rain. It was as if the thunder was of some other source. She was not frightened, but she was cautious and as she thought it, she smiled sincerely to herself; she was as usual, curious.

All morning she and the horses worked their way down the valley, just as Gale had instructed. The thunder growled louder and more ominous with each few steps. She did notice too that the sounds seemed to last longer and the notes of the sound had risen. She was worried that she might be walking into the den of a dragon.

Suddenly bright light shown in a white glare through the thick trees. She retreated back a number of paces and secured the horses (who seemed completely calm for all the noises that were about). Cautiously she crept from tree trunk to tree trunk, seeing nothing past the glare of the light. Finally she leapt boldly from behind the last few pines that had sheltered her, her favorite knife grasped in her leather gloved hand.

She promptly lost her footing and slid down a steep incline, stopping with her butt firmly planted in a great expanse of salt, bordered by the largest body of water she had ever seen.

She sat with mouth agape. Large soft blue waves gathered up, seemingly in order, and as they approached the edge of the vast pond, surely destined to crush all in its path, they gracefully folded over as if bowing to the shore. Their tops churned in frothy disarray until they heaved their massive might upon the white salt sending sounds of thunder skyward.

You see, for Dessa, she had never seen an ocean or a beach before. Nothing she knew compared to this; it was all so utterly foreign, but most of all enchanting and exhilarating and exciting!

Dessa knelt down and felt of the fine white crystalline salt. Each direction along the shore, all she could see was, in her mind "salt." Immediately she cursed the traders who brought salt each spring to the kingdom to sell. They commanded such a high price, yet here was more than all the kingdoms of the world would ever need! Just come here and scoop it up.

With these thoughts racing through her mind she stuffed her gloves in the waist of her breeches and brought a pinch of the fantastic stuff to her tongue. As a girl she had done this only once and the memory of the scolding that burned her ears still seemed fresh. For the cook's assistant had caught her in her innocent desire to explore her world when she dared taste a pinch in the kitchen. For it was worth its weight in more than gold.

No? What?

It was not salt! Just grit. Quickly removing her boots and breeches she walked to the water to wash the sand now gritting her teeth and discovered, almost painfully that the water was salty!

Almost beside herself with confusion she ran to her water jug to wash out the grit and salt that had invaded her mouth. After she had finally swished clean, and since there was really no one to talk to, she said to Uta, "We have discovered a place that is backward and strange. The salt tastes like dirt, the water tastes of salt and this pond has no other side."

As Dessa returned her water gourd to the saddle she could have sworn she heard, "You have a lot to learn my dear, and in such a short while."

Dessa looked at Uta, who was now rolling a fresh wet grass ball all around in her mouth, with her teeth grinding what they could, and she shook her head.

As they travelled, low rumbles periodically shook the very ground. The ocean she discovered, made her feel very small. The endless water, the huge pounding surf. Its magnificence made her shudder.

Little did she know it would play a large part in her life later.

Picking her way along the coast, the air was clean. The forest sandy and windswept in places. She rightly assumed that winters here were violent and harsh. Anyone who lives along here must be a very sturdy sort she thought.

The nights she spent camping in the forest along the coast were quiet and peaceful. She hunted when she needed to, rode when she could. The warm summer sun was out for many days, although she did endure what seemed a long stretch of cool grey days. When the blue sky greeted her, she welcomed it and the sunshine with open arms.

Presently she came to a high wall of sheer rock. The only path led to the right. Coming out at the top of the wall after a steep climb, a broad plateau spread before her. At the far end, inside the dark forest smoke trailed to the sky.

As she approached the setting, something seemed amiss. The cabin was black. The horses in the fenced area by the black outbuilding were black. Sheep grazing nearby were black.

As she dismounted a large man, dressed in black descended through the front door. He carried a black sword. He had black hair and a scraggy black beard. He was dirty. He was not fat, but he was big.

All this darkness was numbing.

With a rather deep voice the dark man sounded out to Dessa, "You have no business here. Go away."

"I am looking for Tallon," replied Dessa in as strong a voice as she could muster.

"He is gone," came the gruff reply. "Go away and leave us alone." He turned and started back into the dreary black cabin.

This was not the news or reception she wanted to hear. After all these days of traveling, almost being murdered by a wolf, fending for herself and having strange feelings with animals around, her nerves were on edge. She was not in a patient mood.

"Well, where the knull is the lazy, scurvy bastard?" came her firm reply.

The dark man stopped and turned. He looked down at her with disdain. She could tell he was clearly taken off balance by being addressed in this manner, and most of all, by a girl.

"Gale sent me." She was able to say with some authority. She hoped he could not hear her heart pounding in her chest.

Since she was gaining an audience, she continued, "He said that Tallon might be afraid of trying to train me, but I should tell him he will be paid well."

His dark beady eyes did not show a knit of emotion. He set the black point of the heavy sword down on the wooden step and leaned heavily upon the hilt. She noticed that he seemed very strong. When he leaned, he did not sag. He mostly rippled.

"That is a load of chicken cach," came a strange reply. "Gale would not send a woman, let alone a girl here. Cach, half the boys he sends beg for mercy or kill themselves outright. They cannot stand the program."

Feeling her oats, and knowing she must pass muster if she had any chance of acceptance, she pressed on, "Well tell the old broken down sod I have a message for him from Gale."

"And what be that?" came the slow and steady reply.

"That message is for Tallon," she said and started walking toward the outbuilding.

Picking her way along, she suddenly and savagely found herself face first, pressed down in the wet, mostly slimy ground. Her arm twisted behind her back and the cold feel of sharp steel pressed against her neck.

"If yer gonna be here lady and learn, the first thing ye learn is never turn your back on someone ye don't know. Now what did Gale say?"

This was an interesting turn of events. All the days of travel, the wolf and her whole predicament seemed to well up in her. And, having a man hold her down from the back did not help either. Evil memories arose. It was a savage anger that took over her.

Savage as she was though, he was stronger, bigger and had the advantage.

Sputtering through the leaves and pine needles stuck in her mouth, she said, "I am Gale's granddaughter. And he said to tell you your horse is ugly."

Just as suddenly, she found herself standing back up again, lifted like she was a leaf. As she spit the foliage out of her mouth he said to her, "You sleep behind the barn," indicating the large black building. "Training starts at sunrise. Be ready; wait for me to come out."

With that he walked away.

Dessa began to made camp and it started to rain in cold nasty drops.

38.
The Games

For Torrin, the games were more than a wonder; they would become five days that created a personal emergence from within him— not an easy one mind you.

That next morning the area around Journey was completely transformed and this continued throughout the day. Not just into a field for competition, but a field of frenzy, sport and spirited camaraderie. This was truly a festival of celebration and excitement!

Men, woman and children emerged from within the forest, coming in all manner of transport from all directions. Horseback, mule, wagon, walking, pulling carts—the only thing consistent was there was no consistency. They were all different, unique and happy to be there. Many made camp in the woods. Some stayed inside Journey.

Day one of the games, Torrin had found was basically exactly what Quillan had said, "arrival." People who had known each other for many winters, and families that had known each other for generations became reacquainted.

The Kellons showed up, proud with new twins. Both boys, dark haired and wailing almighty until their happy, albeit somewhat tired mother, gave them each a swollen nipple.

Swagerts had two new horses. Great brown beasts with diamond shaped white emblems upon their large heads. It was a proud time for Mr. Swagert. He seemed to have arrived. No more plown' the field by hand for him.

The Celsys'(pronounced kel-sis as Torrin found) entered this field of companionship with their fair-haired twin girls dressed in all their finery. They had come of age, and there was no finer place to find a man than this fest of fun and muscle. The girls kept scampering around, all atwitter and whispering to each other at every turn. Torrin paid no heed.

And there was more. Much more.

To Torrin, the smiles, the energy and the fresh clear happiness that surrounded the entire carnival atmosphere was intoxicating. Mind you, he had his hands full. The stables were full, the upstairs rooms full and, Harold informed him, Journey's great room would be toe to toe tonight. With all the drunkenness, they better light some lamps (keeping them high upon the walls, up and away from the revelers) so nobody got walked on.

The most amazing thing of all to Torrin was Karina. Her recovery had been magnificent. Her face was clear, her arm seemed not to bother her, and she smiled mightily. How she had recovered with such great speed was something Torrin vowed to investigate. But right now, he was running wild. And, Quillan had convinced him to enter the hammer competition. His main hope at this point was that he did not kill either himself or some innocent bystander.

That first night, a series of large bonfires kept the biting bugs at bay, the moths busy dying and the entire boisterous crowd toasty warm. The night air was cool and damp, but that did nothing to diminish the party that everyone had been looking forward to for what seemed a long cold winter.

Quillan's scotch from Dunwidy had sufficiently cooled for tasting. And taste they did. Torrin had never tried the amber beverage, but tonight he was getting an education in good scotch drinking.

You see, once you have a recipe and a cooking system that worked, you keep doing it the same way winter after winter. That is the law of scotch creation. Over the next few thousand years, the shape of the kettles would be maintained. Even to the point where, when a kettle wore out, the new one would match the old one, dent for dent, least you change the taste of the brew from your still. And, you don't tell anyone the key secrets to building your own unique taste. Those secrets become closely guarded family treasures. Now of course, there was always the bragging about who is the best still master or blender in the crowd. But no secrets would be told, no matter how blasted drunk ye might be.

Since peat, a key ingredient in true scotch, was in short supply here, you could almost not call it scotch. But the people had improvised and used any number of items for drying the malt. The end product was sometimes a whiskey that had overtones of black walnut trees or poplar. All in all, it was not bad.

But it was potent! Very potent!!

And as the tastings continued, the stories and pride grew. There was a public pride that each man had for the two or three barrels of drink he had hauled to the festivities. And wherever you were, you were going to hear about which cask or recipe or method was superior. And of course you had to try each one.

Quillan had tried to temper Torrin by telling him not to mix the different drinks. "It'll give ye a blastn eadache so bad ye'll wann remove yer brains if ye mix," the large man had told him. Torrin had stuck to the whiskeys.

So for the night, along with a number of large spits cooking meat, there was the fun of a long awaited and wonderful party taking place. Along with the scotch, there was mead, wine and foamy beer. The alcohol contributed to the party's raucousness, as did the music, the dancing and the hearty jokes.

Torrin awoke early the next morning, sorely in need of water. He did not remember going to bed. He must have made it alive somehow. His boots were still on, but he was in one piece. His head felt somewhat numb, but all in all, not bad. He did remember watching a number of men and woman head off to the woods to retch their stomachs out. They had been trying some of everything. He decided to remind himself to thank Quillan for sound advice.

Even with the hangovers, the games began in earnest that morning. First came the musicians, loudly proclaiming the festival. Then Harold got up and made a rousing speech about the wonder of the valley, the people and the peace they shared. That this was a year of great change and growth as they added babies, old folks passed on and life marched along its mortal path.

Torrin watched and listened in amazement. He was experiencing a different side of Harold. There was immense pride in the man. Such an orator Torrin had never witnessed. All the people had stood around and listened intently. In the end, a huge cheer went up. It all felt good.

At one end of the field, the girls danced to see who was best. At the other end, the men gathered to see who was strongest.

First came the throw of the Stone. A round river stone of about sixteen pounds was tossed from the height of the neck as far as possible. The younger boys threw about thirty paces. The larger, older men about forty-five.

The games continued throughout the day. There was the toss of the weights for distance (forty-two and twenty-eight pounds), and the toss of the weight for height (forty-two pounds). Since there was only one stone and one weight of each kind, the progression of the events went rather slowly. But no one was here to work. This was for relaxing, visiting and showing off.

Anyway, a fair time after midday, the fires were started, and pigs, chickens and deer were trusted up and hung for spit cooking. As the shadows began to grow longer and the sunlight played games with the trees, the mood began to grow somber for a time. It was a mutual relaxation. A kind of convergence of a group communion born of the knowledge of their mutual and shared existence.

In short, it was time to cook, eat, drink and either create or share more stories.

The events had been fun if not mostly uneventful. Sorkasas Dumont caught a finger in the throw for height. He did not lose the finger, but it was very broken. Karina had soaked him internally in as much distilled mead as he could take (distilled mead being a very potent drink) and then lined his finger back up before wrapping it snugly. Bets were made that Sorkasas would end up with a long finger. At this point, he did not care; he was sound asleep.

Swagert had won the toss for distance proving that he did not buy the horses because he needed them. He wanted them. Relishing his victory, he was passing out as much of his home brew as possible. As the evening wore on, he would become very successful, at least in his own mind.

The highlight of the day was actually a different event, not really planned at all. Mrs. Panoleney had given birth to a new baby boy, upstairs in Journey. All were doing fine, including husband Jadwal Panoleney, except he was clueless on how to cook dinner for the five children they had in tow. His oldest daughter, only seven winters old was directing him around as if he was a dumb plow horse. Torrin figured they would eat just fine, and Mr., Panoleney would sleep just fine too; he really was in good hands.

The second night was like the first, except somewhat more subdued. The music was lighter, the conversation a bit more in earnest than boast, and the drinking moderately more in line with what you might call "civilized."

Torrin noticed the Celsys twins talking to a couple of tall blond boys. The girls were giggling and laughing and having a wonderful time. The boys seemed not to know what to say. And to make things rough, the girls kept dancing around, so once you knew their names, they would switch. Torrin decided that they should all live together; eventually you would be able to tell them apart.

Karina had been tied up most of the day with the Panoleney birth and had informed the folks staying at Journey dinner would be outside tonight, "Fend for yourself," she had announced. There was a point where you just had to be reasonable, she told Harold. Of course, a variety of breads and desserts still emerged for all to share. Torrin marveled at her organization.

Quillan had taken Torrin to the throwing field during the midday lunch break to show him the fine art of the hammer throw. It was a beastly looking instrument, and in a time of crisis would certainly do in a foe if necessary. A heavy metal ball (sixteen pounds) was securely fastened to a stout, yet flexible handle, the length about half again as long as Torrin's arm. The handle had been soaked in water to keep it flexible. The point was to hold the hammer in one or both hands, spin yourself around no more than three times and toss. The goal was, as Torrin realized, to gain as much bend in the handle as possible. This bend launched the entire lot forward. Also, you had to stay in the circle of stones or you fouled out. Your best throw of three was your score.

Now, mind you, it was heavy, you are nervous, your hands are sweaty. So, if you let go at the wrong time, some bystander might get a hammer in the face.

Quillan sensed Torrin's discomfort. "Torrin, ye jus need ta focus on yer throw," he said. "Jus put yer mind on the spot where ye wan it ta go and do it. Got ta believe in yerself boy!"

Torrin made a couple of tosses. They went about half as far as Quillan's. Torrin felt demoralized. Gift or no, whatever the hell it was anyway, this certainly was not it.

"Yel do jus fine," remarked a happy and smiling Quillan. "Les eat, I'm starvn!"

Torrin could not wait for the laughter he knew would come with his effort on the morrow. He felt haunted.

* * *

Sleep would come easily to Torrin that night, even though he was concerned about making a mad and complete fool of himself. It had been another long day. But a good day. He met more people, experienced more joy and camaraderie than he had in all his youth at the castle. It was so different here. So much more relaxed.

Well, most of the time.

Words had been exchanged when Talus Malooney had told Walls Gregeret that using damp smoldering sawdust for drying malt made whiskey fit only for children and women.

Quillan convinced the men to settle the dispute with a throw of the stone. They both conceded, since their respective wives told them if they got injured in a fight, they were sleeping alone tonight.

It was comic relief by the time they both got to the throwing circle. Come to find, Talus had thought the idea good. He was just jealous that someone else had thought of it first. Walls had been upset, thinking that Talus took him for a fool. Entering the arena, arm in arm, toasting to each other's health told of a friendly duel.

However, men being the creatures they are, they had to do the throw and see who was better. With the toss of a coin, Talus was to throw first. Standing in the circle, a little unsteady on his legs, he made a valiant effort. With a loud scream, he launched the stone; it sailed farther than anyone had thrown today. Everyone stood in shocked amazement. Talus beamed.

Walls approached the circle and made a great show of stretching his muscles, eyeing up the arena and mustering all about. When he finally took the stone, he slumped a little and told Talus, "This is foolish. Talus, you are the better man and there is no sense in going forward."

But a bet is a bet, a wager a wager and a duel a duel. Walls was convinced he must complete his throw and that he would do, if it killed him or his foolish pride.

A great hush fell over the crowd as Walls crouched down and began the throw of his life. Throwing under such scrutiny and with this much social pressure is difficult and you could hear the creaking of his bones and almost feel his breathing as he started up. Basically, with determined effort he flew his body two times around the ring and then let the stone sail.

Now, if you have ever thrown an object like this, you know that much of your success is dependent on form. Strength is vitally important, but when you achieve good form, you can lengthen your throw by a considerable margin. Walls would later recollect, and tell the story for the rest of his days, about achieving form for that throw. It was perfect. He had uncoiled himself at just the right time. Breathed just right and heaved just right. You can feel it in your bones. It makes you light headed when you catch good form.

But as luck and timing would have it, his right toe caught on the front marker rock, possibly due to something he drank (what a surprise), and as the stone sailed away, so did Walls. He continued forward with the inertia of the stone and fell flat on his face with a dull thud. Arms outstretched, legs straight back, and even his hair, straight forward from his head—so straight was his throw.

The judge called foul. The stone though, landed in the exact same indentation made by Talus. Something no one has ever seen before nor expected to see again (and mind you, since no one seemed to be really hurt, it was decided by the crowd that the whole thing was amusing).

Talus walked up to his fallen competitor, helped him stand up, shook his hand and happily called the duel a tie. A loud clapping and cheering rose from the crowd and if you looked closely, you could see that Walls' eyes were wet (of course, him being a strong man and all, we would guess it being from the effort he put into the gallant throw). It was a great way to kick off the festivities.

It was a friendly start to a wonderful evening. An evening that for Torrin, finally wore him out. As he slept, he dreamt of swinging the hammer. It went around and around and around. He could not let go. It would not stop. Finally, he sailed up into the air with the hammer and landed on the top of a mountain.

When he awoke the next day, he was nervous. He had been clutching his boot in his sleep.

39.
Setting the Stage

It had been a dark and stormy night, but nevertheless Dessa woke early. The oilskin had kept her dry; the blankets kept her warm. It was still mostly dark, the sun just starting to lighten the morning sky. Rolling up the bedroll in the grey dampness of the morning, she moved to the outside back corner of the building. This gave her a view of the cabin. This way that monster Tallon could not sneak up on her from either direction.

Sitting on a large log, she ate the dried mutton from Phlial. It was heady in its flavor, but it gave her strength. She had eaten many wild berries the last two days and now she missed them. She also missed taking a bath and finding fresh water. Dessa supposed that once she reached Journey, she might find civilization. There did not seem to be much here. She tended to these thoughts while keeping a steady eye on the cabin.

The sun sailed silently above the trees, casting its rays all about, trying its best to add life to all the blackness that seemed to hem her in. The humidity rose as the heat extracted the evening's rain from the surrounding foliage. Chickens pecked their way about the clearing around the cabin. She sensed rather than saw horses in the building that created the back for her perch. But nothing from the cabin.

In time, she attended to her horses. Removing the pack from Calandra, she set it down on a couple of branches so it was not wicking up moisture from damp earth. Both the horses got a good brushing. She turned them so she could watch the cabin.

Down the hill just a way from the clearing was a small spring. Dessa washed her face, filled her water skin and then watered the horses. She was constantly watching over her shoulder.

Still, silence.

She began to wonder if Tallon might have passed on (to hell she was certain) during the night. Surely he must have remembered telling her to be ready at sunrise. Maybe he needed her help. Maybe he was playing games? Maybe she should just walk up to the door and knock?

Remembering the previous experience with the man, she decided that if he had passed, he could just rot for a while. She was not up to dealing with him just right now.

Exploring Tallon's place was about as exciting as watching a pool of rainwater evaporate. She carefully walked around the buildings and clearings.

There were two horses in the outbuilding. They had plenty of hay and seemed content to stand in their stalls. An archery range occupied a small rise just a short walk from the cabin. Two piles of hay, tied into the form of a man stood at one end.

Dessa mused that she had never loosed an arrow at another human being. Well, this might be a good thing to do—here. Get a feel for that kind of target. She shuddered at the thought. Nevertheless, it was a reality of her life.

One area, about thirty paces by thirty paces looked odd. It was trampled and worn. The ground was all sand. It was out of place with all the lushness about.

Her thoughts were interrupted by the sound of a closing door. Turning around, she walked back to the cabin. Tallon was sitting on the front step. A cooked chicken leg in one hand, a goblet in the other. He looked at Dessa and smiled.

"So, how did you like your first lesson?" he asked her in a patronizing sort of way.

She gave him an incredulous look. "I would guess you are a lazy lout," she replied, head cocked, one eye looking at him in question, the other seeming on guard. She stood back far enough so he could not easily reach her. Her left hand firmly grasping the cord in her coat, ready to go. "If this was a lesson in fighting and combat, then I would say Gale has been a fool all these winters, thinking you a great and wonderful trainer of the defenses."

He just sat there, all among himself. Seeming quite content. He did not even glance her way. He did not reply, nor even show he had heard her talk. He nosily chewed the chicken leg, working off all the meat and disgustingly consuming just about everything but the big bone itself.

After a while he stopped the eating and looked at the bone. It was all but bleached, she thought. He tossed it to one side. Picking up the tankard, he seemed to drain it in one long confluence of noise, Adam's apple movement and of course a long satisfying belch.

Wiping a long hairy arm across his dripping mouth, he sighed and finally looked at her. He looked at her with that severe look a teacher gives a pupil who is either too stupid to understand or too thick to get it. He seemed after it all, just a little bored.

"What's your name, little girl?" he asked in a surprisingly polite manner.

"My name is Dessa," she said a little slowly. "But no one must know I am alive. It would mean death to Gale and ..."

He held up a large hand. "No," he said. "All I asked you for was your name. I don't need the rest. Maybe you can tell me later, if you don't bore me to death."

She stood quietly, waiting. It was a good thing she did.

"Tell me Dessa," he started, in an inquisitive and kind voice. "After I thumped you down last night, told you to be ready at sunrise, were you?"

"Yes, but..." she started.

And again came the hand. "Just answer the question." This statement came out one word at a time. He sighed, "That will be your last warning. If you don't start to think about what you are saying, this will not work!" He was getting a little annoyed. Some color rising in his face.

Dessa shifted to one leg and said stoutly, "Yes."

"When you got up this morning and were prattering about, were you thinking about me and what would happen today?" This question he asked firmly.

"Yes," was her simple and direct answer.

He had a satisfied look upon his hairy face for once. "Proper method of response! Finally. Thought I would have to send you packing before lunch." Standing, he continued, "and your focus was on me, because you did not know what would happen. Because for you I am unpredictable. Because I decided to control your thoughts, your energy and your actions."

She looked at him a little quizzically.

He continued the lecture, knowing it was time to make his point. "I am unpredictable and just enough of a threat to put you in a state of unease. I kept your focus on me. I controlled your thoughts. I got you up early, whereas I slept in. You, if I kept this up for a few days, would grow weary, edgy, nervous, unready for a real fight. I am in control." He looked steadily at her.

"May I ask a question?" Dessa said.

"Yes," he replied, eyeing her to see if she was going to ask something of worth or just trivial bother.

"So you played your mind game, and I fell into your tepid trap. What should I have done?" Dessa asked, hoping to sound at least almost only half as lost as she was.

"Well now, you had lots of options. Can you think of one and more importantly, why you have options?" came the instant reply.

She decided he had done this before. He was ready. He actually, maybe, knew what he was doing. That thought somewhat chilled her, for now she knew that paying attention might be a good idea. A very good idea.

Breathing deeply for a minute, she stammered to think. "I guess I could have ridden off and just not bothered with you," she said.

"Right," came a bold and exuberant reply. "But you chose not to. Why?"

"Gale told me to stop here. He told me I would need training to take care of myself," she replied, stating the obvious.

"Yes, but if I was really just a crackpot you could have carried on just fine without staying. What was the real reason you stayed?" He eyed her with piercing black eyes.

Dessa thought long and hard. There were actually a number of good reasons for staying. Not the least of which, was getting directions to Journey, but she was not ready to divulge that need. "I want to know if I have the right skills. I have never killed anyone," came her answer. "Yet," she added, looking at him with what she hoped was a steady eye.

Tallon grinned up at her. "At least you are telling some truth."

Dessa grinned. How does he know? she wondered.

"OK," he said "Tell me what you have learned."

"Keep the enemy off balance. Don't be predictable. Figure they want something. Leave if need be, if you are able." She hoped he was satisfied with this answer.

"Well, leave if you are willing and able to do so," he countered. "If you are not able, then you have fewer choices. Then you have been caught in a corner. That means you are in trouble."

"Now," he said slowly, what is one key thing YOU don't know?"

She hated this style of questioning. Since he was predictably unpredictable, it was annoying, and she felt, patronizing.

"I am stumped, great teacher," she said.

"Don't patronize me. What you learn here, it is not a game. What you learn here is designed to kill your enemy or beat him senseless, and keep you alive." His eyes glared at her.

Roughly he said, "You don't know why I let you stay, or let you live. Not everyone does. In addition, I don't give a wit about Gale. Since you are on the run, he will never know if you got here, left here or are buried here."

"So, why?" she asked, her anger slowly rising.

"Well, I've never taught a girl before. And, I want the money. It's been a while since I have felt a good challenge. I dare say, you will be more of a challenge of head than strength. And," he continued, "I always get caught when I do something bad, so Gale would stop sending the castle troops for training and I would be out of work. Don't ask me how he would know; the old coot seems to have eyes in the trees." Tallon gestured to the vast forest that surrounded them.

"Fine, you condescending, evil dark bastard. Let's see if you are up to it." She stood firmly in her place, jaw set, ready.

"First archery," and he pointed up the hill. He stifled a yawn. "Go get yer bow and arrows. We'll see if ye can shoot at all."

As Dessa walked away, righteous as ever, determined to prove Gale right, herself deserving and that Tallon was nothing more than a genuine blowhard, she noticed her hands were clenched. She was seething.

He watched her walk away. She had so easily fallen back into his trap. He wondered how long it would take to train her so she might have a chance at living in this dangerous world. Goodness knows, he thought to himself, she acts so tough, but has probably lived a sheltered life.

When Dessa returned she noticed he had returned to the cabin and was walking out carrying a large black bullwhip.

40.
Hammer Down

Torrin attended to his duties that morning with a heavy heart. The Sheaf Toss would take the morning, the Hammer event that afternoon followed by the Tug O War. All his mind could see was to him the obvious. The men in the games were burly, incredibly strong and they were all confident and experienced. What was he doing here? Why had he said "Yes"?

As he watched the Sheaf Toss (tossing a twenty pound sack of hay using a pitchfork, over a high bar without touching the bar) he noticed that some of the smaller men were able to gain some amazing height.

His interest piqued, Torrin sauntered over to one of the more successful contestants at lunchtime and figured he would ask some questions. He found Larenzque Mackinaw sitting quietly on a large log, idly sewing a tear in a dark brown leather shirt. No one else was about; it was quiet. A peaceful setting for someone who had maybe just won a major event.

Stretching out his hand, Torrin said, "Hello, I am Torrin McKenna; I was quite impressed with your Sheaf Toss. May I ask you a few questions?"

Now Larenzque was a smallish man. He stood a full head and a half shorter than Torrin. He was not of superior build, but he was no slouch either. He seemed a quiet sort. One who thinks for a while before speaking. The kind of person who when they tell you something, you get the impression they have really thought things through.

Larenzque nodded to a space and went back to his sewing. "Would ye care for a drink?" He asked in a voice so quiet Torrin was not quite sure Larenzque had even spoken.

"Thank you, yes" replied a now quizzical and slightly uncomfortable prince. He was not sure if he was intruding, or even belonged here. He could not put his finger on it. Larenzque was quiet, not unfriendly. The pace around the man seemed slower. It was as if the day moved at a different tempo. The man nodded toward a small barrel and simply said, "My own honey and heather mead. Have all ye want. I've got plenty."

Larenzque sewed away. Torrin felt like he did not exist for the other man. However, after just a short while, and as Torrin reflected later, only after two rather wonderful mouthfuls of the mead, Larenzque set his sewing down, completed in a neat and skillful manner, and looked intently at Torrin.

Two eyes bore into Torrin's face. They seemed quizzical, but there were no words to explain the questions that seemed to lurk behind the quiz.

So Torrin spoke. You see, he was somewhat uncomfortable with silence. Especially, with a seemingly long silence. And this seemed perishably long. So, because he was a mite uncomfortable he spoke rather haltingly at first, and not knowing what to say, he just said what seemed to come to his mind.

"First off, your mead is wonderful!" Larenzque smiled. "As I had mentioned, I wanted to ask…" Torrin stopped. How do you tell someone you're just a small guy, how do you toss that heavy sheaf so far? "Well, how does someone who is not, not, well not…"

Larenzque interrupted with a sly smile, "How does a little cach like me rip off a Sheaf Toss that pisses off the big boys?"

Torrin stared at Larenzque like he had two heads and one was on the ground, his mouth agape, eyes wide. "Yes," was all he could muster.

"It's hard to describe," the smaller man said, with an earnestness that Torrin could feel. "Before I go onto the field, I tell myself I can do it. You see, not too many winters ago, I was just a short man who was also very fat. So, I have learned to tell myself that I can do it. Because I know I can." Larenzque stretched his arms high above his head. Knuckles snapped and popped; Torrin could see sinews in his arms ripple.

Torrin looked incredulously at the man. "That is it? Just tell yourself you can do it?"

Larenzque continued, "Now it's easy to tell yourself that, but if you don't truly believe it, then you know you are just telling yourself a lie, and," he paused, a firm look settling on his kind face, "you won't do it. Maybe it comes from finally really believing in yourself. Because if you don't, no one else will."

"How do you do it?" replied a very interested, suddenly becoming ex-boy, and turning the corner to becoming a man asked. "I mean, are there certain steps you follow?"

"Let me think for a minute," replied Larenzque.

His eyes looked down. You could more feel than see him withdraw into himself. A serene look of intensity filled his face. His hands opened, closed, opened. For Torrin, it was entirely eerie. He had never seen anyone stop to really think like this. Larenzque was there, but completely shut out the world during his concentration. Torrin was used to hearing people think out loud, all boisterous and verbose.

When Larenzque "returned" he had an answer. Actually, step by step. All the details.

"To begin, I determine if I want to win or put in a good show. Once I decide that, then it is all or nothing. These games here, I decided that the Sheaf Toss would be a win for me. A lot of people think I am too small to give them a run for their money. I made up my mind I would prove them wrong." Larenzque stopped to take a long swallow of mead. He ended the drink with a genuine smile.

"Then, I see myself winning." Larenzque noticed Torrin's scrunched and questioning eyes. "It's not so much getting the highest score. Winning to me becomes personal. Winning means performing at my best. Nothing less! If I do that, then I have won for me. If my score is better than any other sod, I win even more. I am competing with myself. Because that is all that matters."

"Finally." As Larenzque continued, this seemed to Torrin so orderly, just step by step. "As I get up to do my bit, I focus on my goal. To do it, I pick up the sheaf or weight, tell my body how heavy it is and then I decide on a goal. I pick a spot in the field, or a height for a toss and I fix it in my mind. At that point I run the event through my head. All the weights, the breathing, the movements, even the sheaf landing on the right spot. That becomes all I see and know for the time until it's over. That goal, that movement, becomes all I think about. At that point, the noise, the crowd, everything else disappears. Nothing gets in the way or distracts me from making that goal." He looked steadily at Torrin, "Nothing, nothing at all. Someone could burst into flames and I would not notice."

Larenzque seemed finished. There was no more coming from him.

Torrin tried to understand what Larenzque had told him. Maybe it was true. Maybe not. At any rate, it worked for Larenzque. Maybe it could work for Torrin.

Finishing his mead, Torrin thanked Larenzque and left. The midday sun was warm. White fluffy clouds danced across the sky. All around, a jovial party continued along its merry way. Win, lose or draw, Torrin felt he at least had the chance to not get laughed off the field. He was not sure about believing in himself quite this much. That would take some deep thinking. But, he only had until a short time to get his mind ready.

Finding a secluded place under a quiet shade tree, he sat down. His head lay comfortably against the cool bark. His feet stretched out before him. He ran through his mind the sequence of events for throwing the hammer. Well, at least the easy parts.

It was frustrating. This was his first time in front of all these people. Larenzque had obviously been doing this for a long time. Torrin decided he would do what he could at this event, and if he were ever back here for the games again, it would get easier. This thought seemed to calm him.

As Torrin arose and walked toward the field, he saw Larenzque standing with Quillan. They were laughing at something. Stopping to see what the fun was about, he heard about the Celsys twins and how they had come back from the waterfall with their hair wet and their clothes very dry. Mr. Celsys was looking for two boys who had some questions to answer about skinny dipping. Quillan thought it somewhat queer that Celsys was so very nervous. This was just the "natural course of events."

A large group had formed around the Haradin family. Their son had decided to stay at the farm and plans were now in motion to build a second cabin. Corny Haradin was a good looking young man, hard working and full of life's adventure. You could see a number of the young girls looking at him differently now. Now that he had stated his intentions.

It was all very good.

Torrin excused himself, knowing he had to show up and check in. Quillan wished him well and Larenzque sent him on his way with, "Keep your head on square and ye'll do fine. I know how ye feel; this is just my second time."

*   *   *

Torrin walked up to the head judge and told him his name. The judge, a generally jovial sort, seemed ruthlessly angry. He was just taking his job somewhat seriously today. The seriousness of the man put Torrin on edge. What Torrin found out was that he was the last entry, and would throw last. The game was the best of three throws.

Well, thought Torrin, we end with comic relief.

The field was clear of obstacles. Two hammers lay in shallow pans of clear water, keeping the handles flexible. The ten contestants lined up to throw.

Erin Svensne was first. He was a tall lanky fellow who seemed to spend a lot of time stretching and waving to his tall blond wife. She had her tits trussed up in a blue dress, to a point where they were almost a shelf in front of the woman. Torrin wondered how they managed to keep it all supported. But Erin looked like a happy man and she looked contented too. So, maybe their little games worked.

Erin had a respectable throw, although it was not going to win the day. However, the marker judge firmly walked out, placed the white stone in the indentation and handed the hammer to the runner boy who, huffing and puffing, brought it back and laid it in the soaking pan.

All the men did an honorable job. The crowd roared its approval for each contestant. No one was near the record, off by a good stone or so, but it was honorable.

Torrin came up to the circle. A boy handed him the hammer he would throw. The head judge, in a loud, proclaiming and distinctively official voice announced him to the crowd. Just in the way he had announced the others, "Torrin McKenna, first year, first throw."

The gallery went wild. A good lunch had everyone feeling better. And, as was custom, drinking of alcohol did not start until after lunch. It had started.

Bowing politely to the crowd, Torrin looked down the field and set his mind on a spot a few paces beyond the best throw of this round. The bagpipes, playing for the dance contest across the field, lighted a melody in the back of his mind. He felt at peace.

Picking up the hammer, he felt its heft. The shaft felt almost loose in its wetness. But it was right. Finding his starting spot in the circle, he took three deep breaths and began his windup. The crowd roared. His muscles shook with the effort and in a wild maze of sweat, breath as hot as a dragon and muscle burning effort, Torrin threw the hammer in his first ever event.

The heavy object sailed up into the air, its steel ball leading the way. Without so much as a whimper, it thunked down, a good two paces short of the best previous throw.

The marker judge ran out. With all the respect and aplomb due the games, he made a hand gesture that indicated "no position." The head judge resolutely called out, "Torrin McKenna, first throw, no position!"

Bartoly Swanquer was credited with the longest throw. This was his seventh attempt at a championship.

Round two was generally a repeat of round one. Except Walls Gregeret lost his grip and the hammer sailed just a little close to the gallery. No one was hurt and Walls was fouled out.

Torrin stepped up, determined to better his first throw. He carefully tried to put his mind on the objective. The very indentation marked by the white stone.

Pausing to try and clear his mind, he heard the crowd chanting for his throw. Smiling up at the noisy throng, Torrin hefted, hauled and swung for all he was worth.

When the hammer left his hands, he felt like his arms were going to sail forth with the heavy object. The burning in his shoulders told him he had spent all the energy he had in this throw. It was for all he was worth. He felt marvelous.

The hammer landed a good four paces short of his first throw. The crowd clapped politely and Torrin felt small.

Sitting on a log, Torrin had his face in his hand. The sweat poured off him like rain. He felt like crying, but he was too physically exhausted to even try. His whole body shook. His arms felt like they had been stomped on and his ego was bruised. His throat burned from his short raspy breaths.

Larenzque strode up and sat cross legged in the grass in front of Torrin. "So ye think it's muscles that win this game?" the little man said. And, Torrin noticed, he said it kindly. Without jest, without dishonor.

"Guess I just don't have the muscle to compete," declared the dejected prince of late. "It's not my game."

"When ye went up there," continued Larenzque, not seeming to hear the whiny lament, "I saw ye look at the goal. I saw ye do everything right, except one thing."

Torrin was in no mood for existential jokes or riddles. "If you are trying to tell me something, I am not hearing it. Just leave me alone."

Larenzque said, "Get up there, and don't just look at the goal and want it. More than wanting it, make it yours. In your head and your heart. Not just in your eyes. Let your whole being be part of the quest. Nothing else matters at that time. Nothing."

Torrin just shook his head.

Finally, the small man said, "It's up to you. And that is all. But, you see, I know you can do it. Quillan knows you can do it. Why don't you know you can do it?"

With that, Larenzque got up, brushed the loose grass off his breeches and sauntered off. It was a happy, light saunter.

* * *

It was all about experiencing "flow," and it's an experience one does not forget.

Torrin stood in the ring. One hand on the handle of the big hammer, the head resting on the ground in the mashed up dirt of the throwing circle. The sun beat down on his back. The large crowd milled and talked, laughed and drank, waiting for him to make his move.

Suddenly, but actually, in a smooth progression of thoughts and a blending of experience, something started to take hold. It was bigger, faster, stronger and wilder than nature itself. Or maybe, it was nature?

Torrin remembered that wild wintry day he had beat the odds. He had limped miles on a cut leg to survive when many would have given up. He remembered the peace that overcame him as he finally started to "think" when he was caught inside that fiery dragon. It was more brains than brawn.

The white stone beckoned his gaze. Little chips had flaked off its shimmering coat as it had gotten tossed about in the field. He could clearly see every speck. The clarity of what he was looking at, even though it was over forty paces away startled him. The clarity also excited him.

All around him, people carried on in the life and custom of the grand party. As Torrin contemplated, not the goal, not the stone, but his very own desire for success, the crowd melted away.

The noise disappeared.

The people actually disappeared from his sight.

And, for right now, the only objects on or near this field were Torrin, the hammer and the little white stone.

A flush came over him. He turned a bright red. People in the gallery began to hush and whisper. "What if he exploded into fire?" they asked.

Torrin hefted the big heavy hammer. It felt both as light as a feather and as heavy as a horse. It did not matter. The weight was not part of the issue. There was a gap in space and time, and Torrin, for just right now, owned it.

In the world of art, sport, competitive battle and combat, it is called "flow."

So Torrin, for the first time in his young life, was experiencing "flow." It is existential for the folks who believe in such stuff. It is totally heady for the "now" crowd. It is, to a degree, for the rest of us, a linking to a higher level of existence. A level of existence that we "know" exists, we just don't get to connect to it often enough.

For Torrin, right now, nothing else existed. Nothing of this life or universe was part of him, except the hammer, the stone and the throw he was about to make.

Keeping his eye on the goal as he turned, Torrin slowly began his spin. And, you could tell, he was in flow. Something about him was different. Very different.

What had been a grunting, sweaty push on the previous throws now came as a graceful swinging arc. Torrin had become one with the hammer. He was one with the effort he must expend, the distance and even the air between him and his goal.

He spun once, twice and suddenly, as Torrin entered the third and final spin, the crowd was on its feet.

Crowds get excited when they see someone in flow. It's that mental state that allows a person to do whatever they want. A crowd wants to be part of that. When a person is in flow, everything else disappears. All of it. Nothing else matters. It is a state of mind not often achieved. People want to experience it—even once in a lifetime is more than many will ever experience.

Torrin reached the peak of his flow.

As the crowd had stood to cheer, they could not see the determination or the internal pressures of the man. Nor did Mrs. Devon see the bumblebee that her son Shimkus pissed off rather savagely.

Her son of six winters was, without warning and declaration, stung by this large bee right on the nose (the bee feeling this was just due for being swatted at). Being six, and in a great deal of pain, little Shimkus ran screaming from the front of his mother's skirts. He was swatting at the attacked nose trying to scare the intense pain away.

So, as the story would be told for many generations; Torrin McKenna had achieved a level of flow never before experienced by the people of the valley, and little Shimkus dammed it up. Actually, Shimkus helped that flow take flight.

As Torrin came around on his third and final turn, he more felt than saw the little boy coming across the throwing circle, nose in hand. The acid shrieking that Shimkus was effectively delivering to high heaven was not part of the picture. Torrin could hear nothing. But the fact that Shimkus was about to have his young little head either caved in or loped off, did occur to Torrin. We might call it instinct.

Fortunately for Shimkus, it was quite to his advantage that the human brain is able to process a few million data points in the matter of just a few milliseconds.

To save the young lad from either death or maiming, Torrin did the best he could, and about all he could at the moment.

He took flight.

Springing skyward with a mighty heave of his legs, he swung up and he swung hard. The heavy ball grazed Shimkus' ear which stopped the screaming, since Shimkus now looked with eyes boiled wide as potatoes at a steel death he had just escaped.

But for Torrin, it was over. Torrin's body was carried out of the circle. He landed only half as far as the hammer did. The hammer, he would be told later, achieved super human height. But it, and Torrin only made it about half way to the little white stone, even if you added their distances together. Which of course the judges would not do. Not that it mattered anyway.

The target judge ran out and called, "Foul, game over."

As Torrin carefully fished the grass, sand and small pebbles from his mouth, the head judge was declaring the winners. All were to meet after the tug-o-war at this very spot to accept their accolades. Torrin noticed blood on his hand from a very scraped and bleeding nose.

Larenzque and Quillan were on the judge in a moment's time. A great debate began. "Torrin did the right thing," they lamented. "Shimkus would be dead or deformed now if Torrin had not realigned the throw."

The judge looked at both Larenzque and Quillan and told them, "You know the rules." And calmly walked away.

*   *   *

Torrin sat with his back on the cool grass. A large tankard of Larenzque's mead sat comfortably on his stomach. His feet were propped up on a log and the warm sun tickled his face.

All around him the severe debate went on about the failed attempt.

"He should be allowed to throw again!"

"No! Others might try the same route if they think they are losing. It would not be fair."

"If a child is involved the rules should be flexible."

"Give Torrin a break, it's his first year…!"

Torrin heard all of this chatter and deliberation as only a moderate buzzing. His eyes were closed. His heart at peace. The throw did not matter. What mattered was he had experienced the state Larenzque had told him about. It was indescribable. He was deliriously happy.

Giving a heavy sigh, he stood up. The scrape on his nose burned a little in the sun, but it was of no great consequence.

Standing on the log where his feet had been resting, he raised his tankard up and said in as loud and commanding voice a young man can muster, "Let's go to the tug-o-war!"

And with that, he sprang down to the ground. With a light heart he set off for the place where a few families would end up covered with mud this sunny afternoon. Quillan thought he heard whistling.

*   *   *

After the tug-o-war, all met at the field for the awards. Bartoly Swanquer was the winner with forty-six paces. Davis Knight was second by three hands and Fornel Fesn' third by just another hand.

Three stumps of different heights had been placed in the field. The judge called out the winners' names and they came forward. The men stood in front of their respective and rightful places on the pillars as the head judge recited their feats and granted public acknowledgement to their strength. The stoic resignation of men receiving more acknowledgement than they wanted covered their faces.

All in the crowd cheered.

As the judge came forward with the winners' ribbons, he beckoned them to stand upon their rightful elevation of victory.

They refused.

Bartoly spoke. "As a team, we have decided we will not accept these awards in light of what happened to our faithful competitor Torrin. Rules are rules, and decisions are decisions, but what is right will always be right." Bartoly heaved a large sigh and continued. He made sure he had the eyes and ears of the entire valley. "The three of us," Davis and Fornel moved up next to Bartoly, "will not only not accept or acknowledge these awards, but unless Torrin is given another chance, we will never participate in these games again. Our honor as competitors, our credibility as a community and our commitment to the rightful safety of our children for all the future is at stake. No man in my valley will ever be punished for putting the safe care and well being of a child first."

Torrin stood with his mouth firmly clenched. The tankard he had been holding lay in the grass next to him. His eyes were wide. He could not believe what he was hearing.

Bartoly glared down at the judge. "It is not the fault of Ohzcar the judge that this decision has been made. We came up with the rules many winters ago, and we as a people can change them."

A cheer arose from the crowd.

"All in favor of allowing a competitor to re-throw if a child runs in their path, say aye!"

And as a people, they created thunder.

So it was decided. Torrin would have another chance to throw the hammer after breakfast on the morrow. It was getting on in the day and there were just too many things to attend to if they were to do it right. A number of folks headed down to the waterfall to clean off the mud. Fires were stoked for cooking, libations were pulled up from their cooling places and the stories of the day needed to be told, retold and embellished.

And so the valley spent another wonderful evening in celebration and freedom.

41.
The Teacher – The Taught

Dessa sat quietly on a flat sided log and retied her bow string. The sun was high in the sky, warm and inviting on her neck and arms. She had removed the big coat. She figured Tallon would not move to kill her, yet, and anyway, it was warm.

He arrived, carrying the long, black, vile looking bullwhip in one hand and a bowl in the other. Green jewels adorned the grip of the whip. Long strands of thin rawhide dangled gently off the well worn handle. It was ironic that such a beastly weapon be gilded so handsomely.

She looked up at him, her hand on the black dagger in her boot.

"Now that was predictable and stupid," he said with a large smile on his face.

"Why?" snarled the girl who looked at him with blazing eyes.

"Because in your hand, you have a bow," he said "bow" slowly, emphasizing each part of the word. "A good dagger is useful at a range of just a few paces. A good arrow will travel a hundred paces. That is, if you can shoot straight. I am carrying a long bullwhip. Yes, it's nasty." He looked lovingly at the long wound leather. Its oily surface glistened black in the morning sun. "If I was going to whip you, it would take me longer to unwind this and get it on you than it would take for you to slide a long lethal arrow through my patient and loving heart."

His grin told her he was right. She needed to approach things differently.

"You are right," she sighed in a quiet voice.

"Of course I am," he bellowed and gave her a hearty laugh. "If ye want to live, ye got to think. Not just react. You are so hot headed, you are going to get whupped because ye don't think. Take a few moments to take stock, think and then move. Unless someone is comin' at ye, ye'll most often have time to think. Tomorrow we'll work on what to do when someone is coming at ye."

Continuing on he said, "Now, here in this bowl, I have some nice cooked chicken." Tipping the bowl forward, he showed her a number of well-cooked, evenly golden brown chicken pieces.

Dessa's mouth instantly watered. She had been surviving on mutton and deer jerky for over a week now. Fresh meat seemed almost foreign. She looked up at him with wanting eyes.

"You can have all the chicken you like; just put six arrows in one of them targets there. Six in a row, mind ya. Stand behind that row of stones." Tallon pointed to a rough line of stones that marked the range.

Without speaking, Dessa smiled, got up and took her position behind the range marker. This she knew would be easy. It was a stationery target, shaped coarsely like the shape of a man. She was on her feet, there was a low wind, broken clouds, plenty of light. It would be like stealing cookies from the kitchen when she was little girl. I must be hungry she thought. All I am thinking about is food right now.

Taking an arrow from the quiver on her back she nocked it and aimed. Without really trying, she put the arrow into the narrow part of the neck of the target.

Not daring to look at Tallon, she set up for the second shot. Deep inside she wanted to glare at him. Spite his fornicated wisdom and let him know she was already an expert at this. Hell, she could ride by on Uta and hit these targets at a trot on a windy day in the rain.

The arrows were still in good shape. Straight, clean and solid. Some were discolored, and she had lost two of them to wildly gnashing wolf teeth and the one who had escaped at the shepherd's place. Fortunately, the arrows that were left did the job.

The second, third and fourth arrows found their targets with true accuracy. The arrows came to rest with a soft thunk and then a silence, that evidenced their deadliness.

Arrow five was in the bow string. Dessa decided to go for a head shot. She had the range, the wind was steady and this was almost boring. Just as her fingers began her practiced, steady, slow and level release of the thick leather string, her ear exploded in a high pitched thunder clap. The sound was so loud and piercing that not only did she blink, but her nose started to run, her eyes watered and it felt like her heart stopped beating. For a moment she was entirely disoriented.

The arrow went wild.

Dessa turned to face Tallon. Her eyes wild. Her hand over her ear, expecting to feel a hole or at least blood. But there was no blood. Just a stern looking Tallon, bullwhip uncoiled and ready in his hand. And Dessa, breathing heavily.

"No chicken yet," he said.

"You miserable knullare bastard," she said through clenched teeth.

"No. You were getting cocky. You were not paying attention to what was going on around you, and you let a little bullwhip snap distract you." Tallon sighed heavily and sat down. "Any little cach can shoot arrows at a stationery target and hit it. I must admit, you are relatively good. But you think you are good. You have to know you are good and never get distracted. Don't let your surroundings surprise you. Ever!"

Tallon picked up a large golden chicken breast from the bowl, the scent of the food was almost sexual for Dessa. "I do hope you get six in a row soon. I don't know if I would be feeling rather well if I had to eat all this myself. Now go get yer arrows and start over."

This time Dessa shot six arrows in quick succession. She kept an eye on Tallon as well as the rest of the landscape. For all she knew he might have some loathsome slave or servant kicking around who might pop up out of nowhere. She was sure she would kill him, or her if they did appear.

Fortunately for any humans in the area, they did not show up at that time and Dessa enjoyed her fill of the chicken. For a young girl who had survived so much, she was beginning to understand how little she really knew. Was it teaching she needed or experience? She guessed the teaching was needed now, so she could live long enough to gain experience.

After the chicken feast, Tallon showed her a deadly quick shoot trick. He showed her how to hold four arrows next to the bow and after a shot she scooted the next arrow toward her waiting right hand. With some practice, that right hand in one smooth motion, nocked the new arrow, pulled back the bow and she let it fly with her normal deadly accuracy in the space of two heartbeats.

Tallon explained that this technique was rather handy when you were being charged by multiple enemies.

She agreed and thought him somewhat clever for a while. Deadly, but clever.

Later, he had her ride by on Uta and shoot arrows. He was actually impressed with her abilities. And, he played no mean spirited games or tricks. Later he would tell her that he never plays tricks around the horses. It's just not fair; the horse might get hurt or spooked.

Dessa thought that he might have his priorities mixed up.

She was wrong.

*   *   *

That night, Dessa slept in the outbuilding. She mucked a stall out, laid down fresh hay and slept like a baby. Tallon had told her to be up at daylight.

"And is that really daylight or are you still screwing with my head?" she asked him as they had sat around a small fire outside the cabin, enjoying the stars and cooling air before she had gone to bed.

"Yes, I am screwing with your head, but not 'til later. Yes, come daylight, tomorrow we will study the best ways to fight, defend yourself and kill a man, or," he sneered, "in your case I would bet a jealous wife." His eyes seemed to feed on her anger. The sneer on his face told her he was looking forward to it. "Also, you will pay me thirty gold pieces, which is my fee, in the morning."

"You never cease to amaze me," she said with a calm that she had practiced while riding, preparing for this conversation as well as she could. "Gale told me you get five gold pieces. And, if you ever really begin to know what you are doing, he is willing to pay more. Anyway, that is all I have for you."

A long slow smile spread across Tallon's dirty, moist face. It was still warm out, even if it was becoming bearable. Flies buzzed around him in a happy delirious frolic.

"I know Gale is a tight-ass bastard, but I did not think he would put his granddaughter in a position of paying me in my alternative method. Why, some of the castle guards leave here more a man than they figured since they want to keep some of that gold for themselves. Or, maybe Gale shorts them? Whichever it is, they walk away from here, not riding a horse, which is a sure thing! As far as me learning my trade, he knows there is none better." Tallon looked at Dessa with a steady gaze. "If there was someone better, would he have sent ye here?"

Dessa decided he had a point.

Tallon stretched out on the long grass. He closed his eyes in what looked like a gentle relaxed slumber. His old tired body lay heavily on the ground.

Dessa wondered how long he had been doing this. What got him into training people to kill others? Why did he like it? Maybe that would be a good discussion for tomorrow.

Without warning, Tallon's feet flew up, backward, over his head and he stood up. He had done a backward somersault, from a laying down position and stood straight up, in one fluid motion. He did it so fast, and without seeming effort that Dessa was caught completely off guard and surprised.

He stood over her. His stern face returning, his black eyes glaring. "Tomorrow, we start with reviewing what you have learned so far. You are telling me. You better be right. Then, you pay me. It will be the right amount, or your arse will think it has found a new reason to live. Then, if you are still a customer, you learn how to live. If you are not, you fight to live. Sleep well."

With that, he turned and stomped off to the cabin. Dessa thought of packing up and going. Then, she decided, no. It was time to play the ace card. That would be in the morning.

She longed for the peace that she had found in the genuine company and heartfelt warmth of Phlial's. Even that though, was out of her reach for the long term. She liked it there, but she could not fit in as anything other than a guest. She was destined to continue on.

Making sure their little fire was almost out, she walked toward her bed. Suddenly bone tired. Hugging both Uta and Calandra made her feel better. Not so lonely, not so very much by herself.

Her mind went back to the days, not so very long ago, when she was convinced that her life would be full, happy and content when she found her prince. She had longed for a man to fill her days and nights with ardor, peace and security. She had dreamt of the languid hours they would spend riding in the woods, making love in all the right and wrong places. How her life would settle and she would begin the role of training to be the queen of her father's kingdom. It seemed like a lifetime ago. Multiple lifetimes ago. The fantasy was gone. Like a wonderful dream that had shattered on awakening.

How she so wanted to blame Darius. It would be easy to decide that it was his fault. It would be easy to say she had been duped. It would be easy to let responsibility go to someone else. But it occurred to her, that if she did, she would lose not only herself to that abhorring and deceitful louse, but she would be giving up. Giving up on herself. And at this young age, that might be foolhardy.

Her father had risked not only his life, but his very kingdom for her survival. Sanura had risked everything. Gale believed in her. Thank goodness, they were there, not only in her mind, but also still part of her survival, to help her move on and make the most of today and whatever challenge awaited.

Before she went into the shed to join the dead tired, she looked up into the sky. It was a heady black.

Sometimes a dark black looks almost blue. It's a trick the mind plays on the eyes, because true black means there is nothing to see. So we put some color in it; it's more peaceful that way. We like it.

But the sky was deep inky black. It took the breath out of her mind and laid it aside. It cleansed the wretched thoughts she had. It told her the path she was on was not lit with a brightness that she could understand, at least not for now.

The tears in her eyes blurred the stars. Her heart beat with a heavy rhythm. The sadness she had was all about her. She felt weak. She just wanted someone else to take over for a while and tell her everything would be all right.

Tonight, that was not going to happen.

But, what haunted her mind was the question—would it ever?

* * *

Morning swept across Tallon's little kingdom the way the shadow of smoke from a forest fire smothers clear blue sky. Dessa had been up getting ready since light had begun to wash the stars away for another day.

With a speed borne of desperation, she took care of the horses, ate some jerky, got water and packed. She had vowed to spend tonight in peace—somewhere else!

Just as yesterday, Tallon arrived with his bowl of chicken. Dessa realized he must keep them in the house too. Maybe that was all he ate. It didn't matter anyway—unless of course he choked on a chicken bone. That would be true genuine fun she decided.

He sat down, picked up a large leg and started to eat. "OK little girl," he spewed forth, bits of shredded chicken flying from his mouth. "What have you learned?"

Dessa slowly sat down. She kept a few extra paces between them. She looked up warily at the big man, not rushing, but firmly ready to say

Catlan Samuels

something. After a few moments when he had consumed a few more mouthfuls, she began. "First off, I don't think you care, nor will you care. I rubbed wet chicken cach all over the hens you had hanging in your kitchen last night. So in just a few minutes, you are going to start throwing up and running your insides out in wet cach. If I am lucky, you will die. If I am really lucky, your brain will bleed from the poison and I will watch you die an agonizing death."

Tallon's eyes were wide. His mouth hung open. Chunks of un-chewed chicken sloshed around amid black crooked teeth.

She stood up, as tall as she could, "So long asshole. Next time you decide to knull with someone, you better not make it someone smart!"

With that, Dessa turned and walked toward her horses. "Don't try to chase me, every extra moment you keep that cach in your stomach means more poison in your old and wretched body. And, anyway, if you live, Gale told me to tell you this little fact: If I don't report in, he will tell your mother where you are." She noticed he was quite red in the face, and figured she had scored the points she needed to score.

She leapt up on Uta, put her hat squarely on her head and said, "Isn't the first lesson to be a little unpredictable and become enough of a threat that the other guy stops thinking and starts reacting?"

Tallon's shoulders relaxed. He just smiled and went back to his chicken.

Dessa climbed off Uta, (who had not been happy with all the standing around; he thought it was time to get moving anyway) and came back to Tallon's breakfast area.

"OK, I became unpredictable, I became a threat, I exercised options by faking a poison and being ready to leave. I figure you were either more pissed off by being had by a girl, or that your breakfast had been ruined. I'm sure you've gotten sick on food before and in a few moments would have figured out dying was not a high probability. But, either way, I was winning." Dessa stopped and waited.

"Good," he said and offered her the bowl.

"No thank you," she declared.

He looked at her with a sort of condescending gaze that teachers give to cocky students and then raised his eyebrows, indicating he was ready to hear more.

Taking a deep breath Dessa continued, "You came out this morning for two reasons. First, to see if you are a good teacher. Second, you want to get paid. The teaching thing is all ego. You know I'm smart and you wanted to see if you could teach a smart girl vs. a trench hole palace guard." She steadied a look at him and asked, "How am I doing?"

"Go on," was all she got.

"Finally, the money. You more wanted to see if I would come forth with the proper sum than cave to your ridiculous price from last night. That is more about true honor than anything."

He nodded.

She handed him ten gold coins. He looked at them and slid them into a small bag that was attached to one leg.

"So, you never killed a man?" he asked in a nonchalant manner.

"No. Many animals, all for eating, but no men, or women for that matter."

"Well, killing a person is different. And this is important to remember. Never kill out of fear or anger," he said.

"That just doesn't make sense," Dessa said slowly. "Why else would you do it? If you fear for your life, you have to defend yourself. If you are fearful, you get angry. They go hand in hand."

"Quite the opposite my dear. Quite the opposite." Setting the empty bowl down, he began, "Both fear and anger are crippling. They suck the strength out of you. When you are fearful, you react and most likely react poorly. When you are angry, you lash out. Again, depleting your strength. You also then minimize options, and don't even see options. Ever hear of blind rage?"

Damn, he had her again. He was right. Her mind went back to that fateful evening, what seemed many nights ago, when Valdemar arrived in her bedchambers. At first, she was fearful. But then, she became determined. She exercised options. She was unpredictable. She had become a threat. Dessa grinned and then set her attention back on the dark man. "So when do you kill?"

"That is easy. First you decide if he needs killing or just punishment. If he needs punishment, you wear him down, get him tired, then do it. Tired men don't fight well. If they need killing, you do it fast and you only do it for one reason," Tallon looked stern.

"And that is?"

Dessa was on the edge of her seat.

"When it is the right thing to do and the right time. It's as simple as that," declared Tallon, somewhat quietly. He had a far off look in his eyes.

Dessa was confused. "There has to be more to it than that?"

"No." Tallon was prepared for this too. "You see, once you kill someone, they can never come back. You cannot make it better. If you try to kill out of anger, you probably will get killed anyway since you will not have your wits about you. If you try to kill out of fear, you are not exercising your best options and you will most likely screw up. When you wait for the right time and you do it because it was the right thing to do you will not suffer so much from it."

"Suffer?" asked Dessa

"Yes, suffer. I have killed dozens of men. All but one deserved to be killed for what they did. All but one. I killed that man out of anger. His face still haunts me. I wake up at night in a cold sweat. I would give my arm to take it back. If ye want to live with the ghost of a man in yer head, just kill him wrong. They never go away."

Dessa suddenly had respect for this dark man, and she saw some tiredness amongst the darkness. She was still wary, but she had respect.

"There is another thing too," Tallon said after thinking for a few moments. "If ye need to extract information from someone, wear them down and then put high paced, intense fear into their very soul. Tired men don't fight well; they also don't handle fear well."

"That sounds like a good plan," said Dessa. "But I have met men that seem to fear nothing. They have been cut, broken, bruised and altogether bashed about, but they seem impervious to pain. How do you deal with someone like that?"

Tallon looked at her with that evil smile, like he was dealing with a small child. She really loathed that smirk of his, but then he said, "Everyone is afraid of something. I don't care how beastly, nasty or tough they seem to be. Everyone is afraid of something."

Dessa decided that she had to take this knowledge on faith, since it was all she had for now.

"Come on, it's time ye learned how to use all those daggers ye carry on yourself," said Tallon.

They climbed the hill to the area that was all torn and matted.

For the better part of the morning, Tallon showed Dessa how to parry and thrust with her daggers and sword. She was an accomplished swordsman, ere swordswoman. But she had thought the dagger work to be all brute power and slashing—she found otherwise, the power of the weapon is in using the energy of the enemy.

Tallon showed her how to bait the enemy. "Make them come to you in a close fight," he admonished. "And when you are fighting to the death, fight dirty, nasty and viciously. Never stop until they or you are dead. Never slow down. You lose momentum and focus. It is not a game. Use every tool you have."

She learned to sidestep and use her attacker's momentum to her advantage. He told her time and again to let the enemy keep coming, keep charging; it saps their strength and muddles their focus.

She also learned patience. Tallon said, "When you are killing, take your time to do it right. If ye don't ye might be the one killed."

"Then there is the hard part," said Tallon after a quiet thought.

"Hard part?" asked Dessa.

"Yes, the part that comes mostly with experience and it gets more people into trouble than not," he said furtively.

After a few more lapses of quiet, Dessa finally asked, "Are you going to tell me or do I just die someday guessing?"

Tallon's shaggy head turned slowly in her direction. He had a very serious look on his face, and then started to slowly talk to her in low tones.

"When ye decide to go after a man, or a woman I suppose, you get a rush in ye that is hard to explain, but even harder to control. A drive will grip yer innards that just makes ye want to run helter-skelter to the enemy and crush them. It's a fantastic feeling of power and purpose."

"Yes?" She knew of what he spoke. She figured her patience with the mountain lion had probably saved her.

"So when you are gripped with purpose and find yerself runnin hard, strong and hell-bent on destiny to crush the enemy," he paused and looked to make sure she was listening, "just stop and think or you'll wind up running yourself right to dead."

Dessa looked at him. He was so intense it was scary.

A quiet silence ensued for a short time.

After a time of contemplation, they covered how to crush a man's throat so he could not breathe. He showed her the big artery in the leg where a person could bleed to death within twenty paces.

Tallon took a fair amount of time to explain the differences and techniques for quick and slow killing. "To make a man suffer, run your knife or sword through his stomach. The acids eat him alive, but it is painful and takes most of a day. It is a wretched way to go and I don't condone it unless you are trying to make an example of the dying one to others—it gets the point across you are serious."

"Now, a person's heart is the best place for the quick kill," Tallon said in a steady but serious voice. "To get to the heart, go in just below the ribs at a hard upward angle. Don't try to go between the ribs, you will probably catch one and just make the person who needs killing very mad and they will crush your face."

After a long thought he continued, "Push up, push in and push very, very hard! Don't stop, don't back off, just push until they fall dead. That can take a few moments; it can seem like an eternity. You'll know when it's working, because really, it only takes a few moments. But it's faster than having a very angry man running after you with a stomach wound. Most men know a stomach wound is fatal. So when they get one, they get very pissed off and know they have nothing to lose except the joy of making you very dead before they get there. Never underestimate the strength, determination and fury of a man who knows he is going to die a slow and agonizingly painful death."

For Dessa, it was all very interesting, very scary and it made her wish she were back at the castle even more. Darius' wretched soul was damned to hell many times that morning.

Sitting down for lunch, they were a very different pair of people. Mutual respect had replaced most of the loathing.

As they ate, Tallon looked at Dessa and asked, "What did Gale tell you about my mother?" He was trying to be calm, light and easy going about the question. Dessa sensed a strong cauldron of boiling emotions that only heavy strength kept in check.

"He told me nothing, other than to tell you that if Gale did not receive word from me within two summers that I was OK, he would tell your mother where you were, what you did and why you never came back." She looked at him in a quizzical way.

Tallon sighed. "Well, that tells me she is still alive, and must be in good health for Gale to use her for at least two summers as a ransom. Blackmailing bastard!" Tallon smiled.

"I'm sorry," said a slightly embarrassed Dessa. "But you had me pretty scared."

Tallon put up a big, hairy calloused hand. "Don't fret. It's a long story, one that bothers me sometimes, but I had no choice. I guess, just by you being here, you had no choice either. So we are soul mates of sort."

Dessa would never have figured that one out, unless he had said it. But of course, he was right, if this place and vocation was not all of his own choosing.

Tallon said, "It all happened before you were born. Not too long, but it did. Anyway, we can't change it. And so here we are."

The silence between them that followed was warm and satisfying. Presently Tallon stood, held out his hand and wished her well. With that, he disappeared into the cabin. It was all very strange.

Dessa went to Uta and Calandra, untied their reigns and climbed aboard. It felt good. It felt right. She set off in a steady trot to the edge of his clearing and stopped.

Jumping down, she made her way to the cabin door and knocked. After a few moments, Tallon appeared, as tall and menacing as ever, but his eyes were bloodshot. She would not speculate aloud, but it looked as if he had been crying.

"I'm sorry, but I need to ask. How do I get to the Journey Inn? Gale said I should go there," said Dessa.

"Ah yes, Journey," Tallon closed his eyes and blinked. "Go south along the coast until you get to a creek too wide to cross. Follow the creek inland until you reach Journey. You can't miss it. Say 'Hi' to your brother for me." And he slammed the door.

It felt surreal as she rode. This was happening too fast. How come the guards of the kingdom spent a whole summer at Tallon's learning to defend the castle? She had done it in just a few short days.

Then it dawned on her. Besides a few tricks, she had already known everything he told her. Deep inside, she was a little afraid of herself.

Little did she know just how useful it would all become.

And did he say "brother?"

*   *   *

Uta stopped short and snorted. Not a warning kind of snort, but a "pay attention you rider you," kind of snort. Dessa had been riding along, not really paying much heed at all. The sun on her back felt warm. The bird song was a musical feast for her ears. The air was fresh and clean. It had been a good time to think.

A good time to think deep thoughts.

First, she looked around. Wondering if something or someone was approaching. She saw nothing.

Then, she heard it. Water. A dashing sound of fresh water. The cleansing rhythms of frothy cleanliness that come from the rapid movement of water speeding over rocks. She hurried the horses toward the noise. The thought of washing her face, her hair, her arms, maybe everything, was invigorating.

As she came upon the sound she was mesmerized. It was not a big creek, it was not a large waterfall. But it ran steady and cool. A large rock in the center sent small geysers of water up into the air. Frothy waves of refreshingly jumbled coolness spattered about.

After all had drunk their fill and enjoyed the corresponding

coolness, Dessa looked for a place to make camp. Although no rocks gave much shelter, a large oak tree stood nearby. Calandra lost her pack, without protest to Dessa. It sat nicely next to the tree. She tied up the horses in a grassy area, and then started a small fire. The red flames danced and settled her mind. She began to heat water in her pot and to methodically peel her clothes off. She had been too long without a bath or washing her clothes. Everything felt sticky, oily, clammy.

Stripping down to her shirt she looked around. "What an idiot I am," she thought. "There is no one here." Peeling the shirt off, she stood naked in the open forest air, letting the natural cleanliness of the timberland breeze sooth her. The small fine hairs that covered her body stood erect with the goosebumps on her skin. She shuddered a sigh of relaxation and loss of stress.

Unpacking her bedroll and oilskin from the pack, she made ready her bed. Finding the soap, she took the pot, her clothes and her very naked self to the rushing water and began to clean.

After wetting her hair, she then washed it; the lather and freshness was exhilarating. As she pulled it back, cool water ran down her backside. It tickled. It calmed her.

With the rest of the clothes washed and hung, Dessa finished with a good scrubbing of all her body parts. She felt not only clean, but new, fresh and ready to go.

Walking over to the bed roll, she lay down in the shade and closed her eyes. She dreamt of Tallon sitting on a woman's lap. Must be his mother, she mused. The woman in the dream had no face. She saw candles and plates with food on them. It was all around her, but she could not touch the food. It was very frustrating. Then, Darius was on top of her, she was immobile, helpless, trapped. He was inside her and he smelled horrible of stale whiskey and sweat. It was a repeat of the few nights they had been together. She tried to push him off, but he was quite dead. He was too heavy to move. She felt suffocated, doggedly trapped.

In a spark of reality, she awoke. Both her hands were caught behind her head. Her arms had fallen dead asleep and were quite unresponsive. It was somewhat of a helpless feeling, but one she knew would recover soon. Her long legs were pulled up and she was very spread eagle upon her bedroll. A tingle of desire moved through her loins and made the fact that her hands were not working properly somewhat frustrating, for the moment.

The sun had shifted. She looked up and saw glittering rays speckle through the lower branches as the leaves danced in what seemed to be an

omnipresent low breeze. Lifting her head in an effort to let some blood begin to flow to her hands, she saw him.

He had returned from the dead!

Standing quietly beside a large black horse, he was as he had always been. Wonderfully tall, dark curly hair falling in exotic tangles to his shoulders. Appropriately well dressed for a man of too much ego. Rings, chains and charms! He carried himself in an air of royalty, deserved or not.

He had followed her from the grave?

Dessa screamed.

42.
One Good Deed

Torrin had spent the night before conversing with Larenzque about "flow" and the deeper meaning of life. Unfortunately, as they consumed the mead, the conversation got deeper, as did the headache plaguing Torrin the next morning.

Karina appeared with a large platter of eggs, meats and breads that they all ate with gusto. Except for Torrin. He sat quietly picking at the top of a warm brown roll. Eyes gazing off in the distance.

Quillan sat down next to the idly contemplating young man and started to shovel all sorts of breakfast food into his mouth. He did not talk until his belly was satisfied and he had taken a time to think. He figured he knew what was bothering Torrin. And, he was right.

"So, ye arn sure ifn ye should try and beat Bartoly, Davis and Fornel? Am I right?" said Quillan.

Torrin moved his gaze around to his friend and said, "Huh?"

Quillan grunted. He was not used to not being listened to, so he was obviously annoyed. "I said, ye arn sure ifn ye should try and beat Bartoly, Davis and Fornel? Am I right or have ye got bubbles on yer brain?"

Torrin nodded, and shaking his head said, "It just seems wrong to try and take away their honor by trying to beat them when they were so honorable. I am at a loss."

"Well now boy," Quillan's steady gaze told Torrin to listen and not argue about his maturity level. "That is where ye gots it backwards. Let me try an explain it so even you understands it."

Torrin raised a dark curly eyebrow and waited.

Quillan began, "These men belong to no one but themselves. Here in the valley, we have no king or queen. Have ye noticed what's missn from the playn field?"

Torrin thought for a minute and then concluded that Quillan was right. There was something different. At home, all the jousting and competitions were focused on winning the approval and honor of the king. Here, there was no reviewing stand where the royalty sat. There simply is no royalty to sit there.

"There is no king," Torrin simply stated.

"Right," said Quillan, who by now had refilled his mouth with eggs. "So these men decided to let you have a fair go at your ammer attempt. They fully want ye ta do good. Ifn ye screw it up and don try, ye'll ave dishonored them. Bein' beat fair and square is what honor is all about. So ye better try an beat 'em or they'll think ye a twit and they'll be right."

Torrin looked at Quillan, the fear plain in his eyes. He felt like he had to beat them or it would look bad.

"Now don worry yer lil ead off if ye don't go and whup ther butts. But ye better get damn close." Quillan stopped talking, smiled and forced the rest of Torrin's lacerated roll into his mouth.

"OK," Torrin said with a shrug of his shoulders and a long exhale of air that he just noticed he was holding.

"Now jus go out there and do wha ye did yesterday. "I'll hol Shimkus by the neck. Now go warm up and get yer ead into the game." With that, Quillan slapped Torrin on the shoulder, gave him a big smile and walked out.

Torrin wondered to himself why men smacked each other when they were trying to be supportive. Oh well, it didn't matter. All he needed to do now was focus on that little white rock.

It was time.

* * *

Everyone was at the field. Big blankets, furs and skins had been spread on the already well trampled grasses. Breakfast had been a bit of a hurried affair so no one would miss this grand and completely unprecedented event.

Large, white fluffy clouds floated slowly over the warm blue sky. Birds sailed over the field in playful flight, darting to and fro. Three small sparrows flew over a large crow, pecking the crow's head, shrieking angry expletives at the big bird. That is what you get when you try to rob someone's nest.

All in all, it was a normal summer day, just very exciting and different.

The location of the white marker for the best throw yesterday had been agreed upon by all the parties and now sat quietly in the morning sun. Shimmering as it had yesterday, performing its duties fearlessly.

Davis and Fornel wished Torrin well adding all the regular words men say when they aren't really sure what to say. Bartoly however, was a different story.

Bartoly was a big man. He stood one and a half heads taller than Torrin. Sporting a happy face with strong white teeth that shone brightly when he smiled made him pleasant to look at. He was strong too. A smithy by trade, he swung hammers all year long. Word was, he had won the hammer event as far back as memory allowed.

As Torrin was stretching and trying to concentrate, Bartoly came up to him, folded his long muscular arms across his expansive chest and said, "Torrin, I hear from Harold that ye have quite the road ahead of you. It won't be easy, and sometimes you won't want to take the path for which you have been chosen. But one thing is for damn sure; you have to take control of your destiny as much as you can."

Torrin looked up while stretching and said, "Well, I guess you're right, I just don't know what that path is. No one wants to tell me."

"Did ye ever think that none of us really understands it enough to explain it to ye clearly?" said a firm and confident Bartoly. "We just know, it was time for you to arrive, and ye did. More has to take place. Just be patient. In the meantime, do your best. If ye get used to doing that, you'll be better off for a long time." With that, he turned to walk away. But stopping after just a couple of steps he turned back around and said, "You win, drinks are on me; I win, you do the serving."

Torrin nodded his approval.

*   *   *

So, as the story would be retold repeatedly, time and again for a long while, it really was what they all expected. Everyone in the valley knew that Torrin was destined for something different. Something special, and they all expected him to win. And of course, he did, but how he did it was what was unexpected.

When Torrin entered the circle and picked up the hammer, he looked around. A wide arc of people filled his vision. A wide arc of smiles, families and friends. No two alike, no two perfect or wrong in any way that mattered. For the first time, he began to understand what it felt to really belong. To be part of something that was bigger than yourself, but without you there, it did not exist. It was really hard to imagine until you stand there. Part of something where you fit in. Where your heart melded with the hearts of many; where your thoughts and actions mattered not so much for you, but for the greater good. And when you think about where he had come from, this was so very different. So very foreign to him.

As he stood there, he was all alone and on his own. But at the same time, he wasn't alone or on his own at all. The paradox and the irony were startling. A small chill went through him.

He gazed at the target. And directly, he fixed his gaze on a spot just a few hand widths beyond.

Now it was really time.

Closing his eyes, he focused on the task. When he opened them, all was gone but the goal at hand. It was an amazing thing to be able to do this on command. He sensed the crowd, but did not hear or see them. They were there and gone all at the same time.

Torrin's three swings trailed in neat and graceful spirals. The damp end of the soft and pliable wood bent almost to a point where it seemed surely it would break.

As he released the big hammer, you could see the wetness snap off from the handle in a blast of tiny water particles that looked like steam, the pressure was so great. The hammer sailed as though it was a bird riding a warm thermal high above the hills on a sunny day. The flight lasted all of one breath. But, as a valley, all the people held their breath while this weighted flight took place.

Then, with what seemed to be a very fast ending, the heavy metal head thunked into the soft earth. You could see, from every point of view, that the hammer was right next to the stone. In front, behind, next to or just where was impossible to see though, from any distance.

The judge walked out to inspect the results. The twittering and muttering among the crowd were muted, but omnipresent. Some were sure it was a winner, some bet it came up short—just a hand, but short for sure!

One thing they all agreed upon; the judge walked very slowly. Torrin decided that the man was either really angry from being overturned or he was just having a wonderful time. It didn't really matter, it would only be a few moments, he could wait. And anyway, Torrin was sweating from every pore; long beads of perspiration clung to his hair and rolled in trailed lines down his back.

Bending down, the judge looked sternly at the pair of objects in front of him. He stood up and walked around to the other side. Bending over again, he put his hand down and seemed to be feeling something. After a few moments, he stood and proclaimed, "The winner of the hammer throw is Torrin."

The crowd went crazy.

They had their champion, and they had done it right.

43.
Terror

"That is a lovely scream. Can you do it again?" said the ghost of Darius, in a hauntingly soft and dangerously mellow tone. He sauntered over to where Dessa lay, all bound up in nothing but her numb and useless arms. The worst part was, he was actually serious—he wanted her to scream.

"No for god's sake! You miserable beast" cried the very naked woman. "Can't you see I'm stuck? Help me!"

"Of course dear lady," said the ghost. The tone of his voice was soft and deep. At any other time, it would have been like the gentle articulation of a kind and gentle grandfather, soothing the harried worries of a little child. Fleeting away her cares and making the world a better place. The soothing tones just added to the nastiness, since he obviously had no intention of helping her. Maybe just helping himself.

He knelt down next to Dessa, wrapped a large leather gloved hand around each side of her heaving middle and flipped her over on her face as easily as one flips a slice of bread over on a plate.

He then moved her arms to her sides. Instantly the blood rushed in. Thousands of sharp needles began to assault her skin and muscles. She felt as if she were on fire.

Dessa began to flex her hands. Her fingers felt like risen bread dough. No substance, just there. All airy and now cooking in her own blood, as her body raced to renourish the energy and oxygen starved appendages.

It felt so foreign. So unreal. Almost like her hands and arms were moving without her willing it to happen. Then she decided her arms were moving. As the feeling returned, it dawned on her that this miserable bastard was tying her up!

"What are you doing you low life cach?" she screamed with her mouth still buried in the bedroll. It came out as a muffled gurgle.

"Well you seem so feisty; I figured tying you up now would be far less dangerous than having to do it later. You see, I have been lost in these woods for a few days now, and I mean to make the most of your wonderful and tasty surprise," crooned the ghost in a strangely calm yet ostensibly excited voice. With that, he brought his large leather covered hand down on her soft pink bum, with a loud crack.

Again and again he beat her bottom. As she tried to rise or turn over he sharply kicked her feet out or savagely grabbed her hair and crammed her back down. The more she struggled, the harder he slapped. And, she could hear the illegitimate, lame and half baked excuse for a man laughing.

Then, without warning, a gag ran around her face. She tried to bite at his fingers. He just laughed louder.

Pain tore through Dessa. Her eyes watered, her hands burned. She felt abused and violated. She was angrier than when Tallon had jumped her just two short nights before.

Tallon!

She squeezed her eyes tight and thought, "What does he want? What does this miserable scum sucking scurvy pig want?"

He wants pain. He wants suffering! He wants me to struggle!

As he beat her, she willed herself to relax. Turning her head to one side she took a deep breath and let all the stress out.

He smacked her again, the loud crack reverberating through the forest, falling deaf on unseen ears. There was no one about to save her but herself.

She smiled.

He stopped.

He flipped her over and looked at her with the quizzical stare of a hunter who just discovered he had shot the wrong prey.

Dessa decided he had no idea what to say, do or think. All of a sudden, things were not as they should be for his little mind.

So he slapped her across the face. The sting from the leather was hot. She could taste blood inside her cheek where her teeth had cut the tender membranes.

He hit her again, just above the eye.

She smiled at him through the gag.

He tore the gag from her head. A look of either panic or madness crossing his face. Dessa hoped the shudder of fear that shot through her did not show.

"What is wrong with you, you little whore?" he grumbled. All the pretend softness in his voice now gone, replaced by an abhorring snarl. "Why are you smiling? You should be begging for your knullare life!" He was almost screaming. His eyes grew maddeningly wide.

He grabbed one of her breasts and twisted savagely. The pain brought the tears back to Dessa's eyes, but she persevered.

"The other," she gasped. "Twist my other tit! Make me hurt. Make me feel pain. Make me love you!" She screamed this last part as a command. Lifting her middle high off the blanket, soggy with her sweat, she ground her hips in a lustful gyration of desire.

He stood. Perplexed and dazed. His fun was ruined. His mind was shattered. He was not sure what to do. He just walked away, head down, muttering.

Dessa lay in what should have been a splintered daze. Her body was wracked in pain. Her hands were tied behind her. Her bottom stung and burned. She tasted blood. Her own blood.

Her mind swirled in thought. She couldn't wait for this to continue; she was on the offensive and she was going to win, if it killed her.

Little did she know.

He turned and walked back from his black horse. His dark eyes burning with hate and loathing.

Dessa shuddered throughout her insides. She had seen these eyes before. She had experienced the deep hatred of women. The lack of trust in the wonder of life itself that comes from a person who not only hates others, but truly themselves. She wondered what had happened to him through all his time to cause this much anger and detest for others to erupt so violently.

Again, as before, he knelt beside her. His face in a deep funk. She sensed he was a lost soul, searching for meaning he now had lost. Whatever sick and twisted meaning he thought he had been so close to finding.

She continued her attack.

"Cut me," she proclaimed. "Take your knife and cut me across my tits and belly. Leave long scars so I can remember you. Make me bleed."

Taking a long dagger from his waistband, he smiled for a moment and slowly slid the point up Dessa's leg. The metal left a scratch, but nothing permanent.

She almost forgot to stay in her act, as scared as she was. But it did dawn on her that he was beginning to follow orders. She still had hope.

Then he cut her.

A long fissure ran suddenly, and without warning, from her throat to her knee. He had broken deep enough through the surface of her skin that she could see the end of the knife disappear; she hoped it was not fatal.

What she did know was, she was bleeding from the long gash. Long lines of hot red blood mixed with the ponderous sweat running off her skin and ran in little streams in all directions. Her heavy sweat stung the cut in a searing stream of pain.

Abruptly, her mind delivered to her a very important and critical piece of information. Yes, it hurt, it stung, it was overly annoying.

However, it did not hurt that much. It was all healable at this point. Most importantly, he was shallow, he was beatable. He was a coward at heart.

"Suck the blood from my skin. Share my pain," she extolled to him.

He turned white with fear and she knew she had him.

"What is your name?" she asked in a kind and gentle way that was a complete turn from the nasty events taking place.

He turned to look at her. She was actually smiling at him. No woman ever smiled at him. This was not to be. He was a bad boy! He was more feared than respected. Fear—that solemn word that for him, held all the power there was. He had been taught that by his father. He had seen it was the only way to control the mad raving lunatic that had been his mother, and the cheap attendants that hovered around when he was young. All they wanted were things, all the time. All their whining and begging and nastiness had to be controlled. Fear was the great controller. Fear was all that worked. And after they were afraid, you took their bodies and made them your own. That way, you had all the control.

So now, he wondered, she wants to know my name? Maybe she would fear him more? Maybe she knew who he was?

"Haphethus," he said in a somewhat stiff and quiet voice.

"It is all my pleasure to meet you," Dessa replied in what she hoped was a sultry and provocative tone. She knew she had to stay focused. "Most men shy from the best part, and we have only begun. You are quite the man. I cannot wait for you to violate me in the worst of ways. I am wet just with the thought of it!"

He looked at her in a strange way. He seemed stuck. Unwilling or unable to move.

"Keep me tied up; it makes me quiver with desire, but remove your clothes so I can taste the hardness and sweet saltiness of your crann. Do it now; you will not be disappointed. I will be the best you have ever had. When you are done with me, you must beat me again. Beat me so I bleed from my ass."

He stood and began to disrobe. He was a sturdy man, but of no great proportions. He carefully laid his clothes and belongings in a neat and orderly pile. Dessa felt like one of her maids was in front of her undressing and taking care of all the little things. All neat and prissy.

As he worked his way out of his clothes she asked him, "To where are you traveling, or are you from around here?"

"I am on my way to see my twin brother up north," he replied with a grin. "He married some wench princess and I hope he will share her and her chambermaids with me. You see, I lent him my girl before he left to be married and he owes me." Haphethus let out a gnarly laugh. "I bet his little princess is a happy woman!"

Dessa was not only aghast; she was beside herself with wonder that she was not surprised at this. That son of a bitch Darius was so evil he could not just die, he had to haunt her. She looked forward to stuffing this ghost into forever gone.

"You are a lucky man to have such a generous brother," she said.

"Oh, he is not only generous, he is fun. We have quite the time with the ladies." He looked at her, trying to decide if he should say more; he finally did. "Yes, you are lucky you did not come across our little brother Chadus. He would as soon skin you as screw you."

"Hurry, lay down," she said in a tone that portrayed a deep need. She wondered if all men were so easily duped by this acting "While I use my mouth on you, pull my hair, pinch me. The pain makes the sex better."

He performed as instructed. While he did his best to manipulate her, he was quite distracted. There was no cause for concern on her part of not being in control of what happened to her mouth. He was barely there; bottom line he was hung like a rabbit. An issue she hoped was a trait of the family and not of all men. When the right man came along, she wanted something to work with. Sanura had told her of all shapes and sizes and of what to do.

As he tried to deliver his hate, she could feel the strength in his arms start to abate as he grew in his excitement (although it did not seem to do much for his crann). She in the meantime had come to loosen the bonds around her wrists. Not only had the feeling returned to her hands and arms, her blood was boiling with a rage that coursed through her.

It was somewhat difficult to act the part of the willing temptress. As she ran her nose down the dark, thick curly hairs of his not so wonderful chest, she wondered—almost aloud, "if these boys had grown up as real men, they could have been accomplished lovers. Just some training and caring." But they would both have to pay for the path they chose.

We all pay for the path we choose, eventually.

Many a night, during her courtship, before actually marrying Darius, she had lain in her warm soft bed, using her fingers to keep up with the intense fantasy her mind played out; long deep wistful romance and lust. She figured Darius would carry her up from the dance floor, to that very room and make the fantasies real.

Both of them would be hot from the physical exercise of the long tumbling dances, and both in an intense heat of desire and willingness to share each other. His dark features would radiate a confidence that comes from a man who understands that fulfillment is from a mutual quenching of desire. And, that quenching only comes from burning through the mutual heat of the flares of passion. Romance, true romance in the deepest sense, has an inscrutable longing for hot sex, emanating from the pairing of souls in rampant unwashed and unfettered energy. The joining of each other at a level that is difficult to describe. Easy to imagine, but fleeting.

He would start by gently kissing her warm moist lips. Eager exploration of each other's mouth, lips, ears and neck would be joined by the sweet caress of their exploring hands. He would hold her hair back in a firm, yet loving grip as his tongue would dance across her silky warm skin.

Then, when the time was right, he would begin to loosen her skirts. Very slowly. The soft feeling of release as each layer slid to a soft fluttering pile on the cold wooden floor would raise goosebumps on her skin. As he worked through the layers, she would revel in the freedom each loosening created.

He would explore her freshly naked skin gently with his mouth and hands. His calloused palms mildly abrading her hot flesh, leaving warm fluttering sensations as he inquired to all of her, from head to toe. All parts, but ending where he needed to be, at just the right time.

She would desire him most fully when he invested that time and energy to make her ready. Her long legs not only willing, but also needing to hold him tight as he filled her. It would be rapture.

The best component would be afterward. Warm bodies, close and sensitive. Filled with the love and peace of two people who know the power of mutual, respectful love. That wonderful time when all cares and worries vanish, where hearts beat as one. She would revel in the feel of his long warm body nestled against her, warming her, keeping her safe and secure.

Haphethus groaned and brought Dessa back to the issue of her reality. Her little daydream had calmed her. But more importantly, it helped her to understand why she must win. Why she must survive. The adventures that awaited her must be had. She knew, rightfully so, the evil beneath her was not planning on letting her live when he was done here. He was too much of a coward to even remotely let the chance occur that he might have to pay for, or be responsible for, his sins. Therefore, he would kill her here, and leave her for the animals of the forest to devour.

As he squirmed she knew he was getting close. He had become very hard. His breathing was fast and shallow, his moans were deep. The grip he had on her hair was tight and beyond his conscious control. His hips pushed with ferocious need. He was at just the very edge. He let out a little cry as his insides began to contract and lunge his seed out to what he thought would be a magical and wonderful moment. A moment where he was violating her beyond his wildest dreams and fantasies.

Drawing in a great lungful of air, she bit him as hard as she could. At the same time, she had freed one of her hands from the rope and hoping it would work, she crushed his scrotum in a savage smack, followed by a strong twist of rage and fury. Blood and fluids coursed wildly in a completely unnatural shattering as his little world left him.

As he raised his head with a startled "Huh?" she smashed her fist across his nose. Just as Tallon had taught her. "It causes a huge amount of startling pain, makes the eyes water and stuns your victim so you can do real damage," he had told her.

He was right again!

With the speed of summer lightning, she viciously and with every ounce of hate-induced savagery she could muster, brought her forearm down on his windpipe.

With that, she stood as fast as her suffering legs could move and she ran. Glancing back, she saw him groping at his very colorful and wet middle, holding his neck, and she could hear him gasping for air.

Damn she thought. He's still breathing.

She ran to her clothes.

Grabbing the coat she tried to put it on, but her hands and arms were sticky with sweat and yuck. She was stuck. Looking up, she saw him running at her. He was holding his bleeding self, but nevertheless, he was running at full gait with a look of killer rage on his sweat covered face.

Dessa reached into the arm of her coat as he sprang upon her.

"You miserable whore bitch," he snarled in a strangled hateful way.

She let him come.

As he leapt upon her, she rolled to the right. He ran right into the arm of the coat and Dessa's father's knife ran smoothly through the thick leather and deep into Haphethus' stomach.

Damn she thought as he tumbled over, I missed.

She rolled him as he fell, so now she sat on top. Pulling the knife back out she looked him straight in the eye and yelled, "I am the princess your knullare of a brother married. He is dead; he killed himself with his own knife in a drunken stupor. The asshole didn't even have the decency to let me kill him. Thank you for making that up to me!"

His eyes were wild, he grabbed her throat with a massive assaulting strength that terrified her. She could not breathe. He was pushing her back.

She stopped struggling. Tallon had told her, if you think, you will create options. And, the option was right there.

Dessa moved her hips forward, sat up straight to destroy his angle of attack and strength. In one fluid motion, she crammed the knife upward, just as she had been taught, into Haphethus' heaving chest in a deep fatal plunge.

It was a very strange sensation. She could feel his heart beating against the blade of the knife. She twisted in a savage wrenching motion and felt his blood rush over her hand, like warm water in a bath.

He went slack. The evil that had been, left this earth for an eternity in hell.

44.
Breaking Camp

The evening of that special and glorious day Torrin became the new champion would go down in history as one of the best parties the valley had seen in many summers. For all, it turned into a long day of celebration. The pipers piped. The lutes strummed, the horns blared and the drinks flowed.

The people of the valley danced in bone rattling festivity and cheer. It is truly amazing and wonderful how the collective energy of a group compounds itself. Just as when two people work together and achieve something for the same ideal or vision, or when a group reaches a goal in accomplishment, the vigor and internal stoking of the positive mental fires is both a stress reliever and just plain fun.

The older folks knew it was good to celebrate, for there had been harsh times and there would be harsh times ahead. The winter nights would start in only one hundred days, give or take a few. When the snow was piled high around your home and the wind blows for days and nights on end, these festivals and good times make for great conversation, but more importantly, great thoughts. The memories the group as a whole created, celebrated and held dear formed the hope they collectively shared for whatever future lay ahead.

For the younger folk, it was a grand and glorious party. They got to see old friends, make new friends, try new things and work on their future. Some would marry at the fall festival. Some would bring examples of art and creations from the summer. Some would start shaving, and some would die.

Life in the valley had its wonderful moments, and its hard realities. But most of all, it was "their" life, and no other person or entity laid claim upon their heads, hearts or hearths.

Bartoly was genuinely grateful and a regular sportsman about the whole thing. He told Torrin he was actually happy someone else had won. "It gets old after many times winning. I was getting tired of listening to hammer stories. Now it's your turn."

He smiled heartily and raised his big tankard up in a salute to Torrin's honor. His wife of many winters was at his side. She was tall with that wonderful contrasting blond/dark hair that blesses many northern women. The ends were a bright clear shade of yellow white, but near her head, her straight tresses were a soft, gentle darker hue. She was smiling a deep wide grin, and after drinking and dancing most of the day, was sagging a little on his arm.

Quillan staggered over and pounded Torrin on the back for the umpteenth time that day. "Yer so blasted proud of myself, ye cannot shtand it!" He was making less and less sense as the day wore on. Torrin just smiled.

"Bartoly, can I ask you something?" quizzed the lightly, but happily drunk Torrin.

"Certainly," he said. "But let's lay Rebecca down. I fear she will fall down soon and I would not want to get her mad right now. She can turn into quite the bull if she gets bumped wrong in this state of happiness." He kissed her on the forehead and Rebecca sighed dreamily, adding to her wide smile of gentle delight. Her eyes were softly closed, and she had a tight grip on his arm until he tucked her in, snug and warm in their tent.

Sitting by the low fire in the afternoon shade they both refilled their tankards from Bartoly's own keg of evil whiskey.

"What seems to be on your mind?" asked the big man.

"Well," Torrin looked up, not quite sure how to begin. "It's a question about the games. About throwing that blasted hammer. It's a bit strange, but just hear me out. Have ye ever had the world sort of disappear when you get up to throw the hammer?" He continued, looking intently at Bartoly as he tried to carefully choose words that would not easily come. "Well not disappear completely, but sort of fade away. All the people and the noise, the cheering. It is just as almost, well almost, you are there all by yourself?"

Bartoly took a long shallow drink of the fire that was in his tankard. He was an experienced man. Not very old, but he had been around the valley for a while. He knew this answer mattered to the boy. This was not a time to rush. So he pondered as well as he could, being a little on the tipsy side.

Presently, he simply said in a calm, steady voice, "Yes, when the times are right."

"How do you mean?" asked Torrin.

Letting out a long steamy sigh, Bartoly looked at the new champion. He could almost feel the questions painted on Torrin's face. He knew what it was like to grow up some, and not realize it yet. He was glad Torrin took all this in stride, instead of strutting around like a rooster who just conquered his first hen. "It's simply, when you are of pure heart and soul. That's when the magic can be brought up, tamed and incorporated into your very being. The magic is not obvious to us all the time, but is always there."

Torrin looked like a man experiencing stupendous art for the first time. That moment, when you look up at something, expecting to see just another piece of art. However without warning or predisposition, for whatever reason, what you see takes your breath away. The wizard in the artist touches your soul. Sees into your very being and puts you in touch with a depth of humanity you always had, but until now, had not experienced. You begin to hear your own "whisper."

Many people ignore their own precious whisper; many reject its magic. The whisper is your inner soul speaking to you. Those that hear it, embrace it, and then listen and then learn to become truly free.

Bartoly continued, "When you entered that circle, you decided to try and win for yourself. It was not to beat me or the other men. It was not prove anything to all the folk standing around. Hell. Half of them secretly figured you would foul or bang yourself in the head, what with all the stress you must have been feeling. And if ye did not, then they hoped you would win. For all the right reasons."

Torrin asked, "So trying to beat you, I would not have? It would not have worked?"

"I'm not saying yes or no for sure. Dealing from purity of soul is a tricky thing to predict. But, I do know this, when it's right, it is right. When it's wrong, things tend not to work out."

"Did it ever not work out for you?" inquired the somewhat starry-eyed ex-prince.

"Oh yes. I remember my second time at the games. I had come back as a favorite to beat old Harold."

"Harold?" Torrin perked up.

"Yes, Harold has aged quite a bit in the last few years, almost seems like he is aging fast. He was always so young looking and vibrant, both he and Karina. It almost seems strange. Maybe they work too hard?" Bartoly shook his head and continued.

"Well anyway, I come into that circle, and Harold had thrown a wonderful hammer. I set my sights on beating him. I was going to prove to him I was better. Those were the heaviest and hardest swings I've ever done." Bartoly looked off into space.

"Almost tore my arms from my shoulders I did, swinging so hard. I can still feel the heat that burst in my hands from me holding that god almighty handle so tight!"

"What happened?" Torrin was beginning to feel like a child interviewing an old man.

"I learned a valuable lesson," came the soft, distant and sincere reply. "Harold came up, shook my hand and thanked me for being such a wonderful and mighty competitor. Rebecca let me rant and rave for a week, nary a word did she utter, letting me get it out of my system."

"Yes?"

"I had come up almost a stone short, damn it. So when we went home, I banged so hard on so much steel for a time that my arms almost burst. Then without warning, I sat down in the shop and started crying my face off." Bartoly suddenly stopped, looked at Torrin and said, "If you tell anybody about this, I will slit your throat."

The reply was a quiet and definite "Don't worry."

"As I sat there, Rebecca came out, put her arms around me and said "Are ye back to me now? Can you just stand being you and not someone else? I just want you." And, we made warm passionate love right there in the shop, in front of two horses and the goat while the forge melted the bridle I was making. I had never been so happy."

The two men sat and watched the blue sky. The day was getting on. The drinks, the energy, the games had sapped them of all their strength. But, it had taken the used up strength, the old strength, and replaced it with the new fresh vitality they needed. The vitality they could only really get from being together.

"Thank you," said Torrin as he slowly and somewhat unsteadily rose to leave. "You have given me much to think about."

*   *   *

That next day, from early morning 'til dusk, the sun would shine warmly upon the people of the valley as it was now time to take to their respective trails, roads and paths, back to their homes, deep in the wood.

Torrin had arisen with the break of light and stood at the front door of Journey, enjoying the serene view in front of him. He was aware that he had much to do this day; clearing the stables, storing the tools of the games and attending to the various needs of the visitors. It would be a day of many and mighty tasks. At this particular moment though, he was searching for a few bits of peace, before the crazy day began in earnest.

Little did he know just how right he was.

The time was early, and for those who may have drunk just a wee too much that bawdy night before, it was exasperatingly too early to be up. But up they got. They worked hard, played hard and partied hard, but none of them shirked their responsibilities.

The clear sweet dew that eases you into the beauty of a warm summer's day clung with reverence to the leaves and flowers. It was a light wetness that covers your boots when you walk, but is not bothersome. Because you know, those boots will dry with gentle grace as the day warms.

Even the bugs were still asleep, adding to the peace that had enveloped the whole of Journey. Goodness knows they deserved a rest too; they had been buzzing with vigor through each of the days! Only a few birds were aloft, attending to the sunny skies, doing whatever it is birds do.

Today was departure.

After these many days, with all the arriving, setting up, partying, tearing down and sport, it seemed everyone was ready and due for some well deserved quiet. As sad as it was to leave, it certainly was time to go. There was work to be done. Crops attended to. Wood to cut and split. Homes to make ready for the onslaught of winter, games to be played and children to be raised.

As Torrin made his way to the stables to set about making the horses ready for travel, people started to emerge, as if on cue, from everywhere. Torrin saddled and bridled and attended to the horses that had been his stabled, willing and wonderful guests.

The rest of the people of the valley packed up their belongings in a neat, orderly and mostly quiet fashion. Certainly, in distinct contrast from the days they had just enjoyed.

Their spirits were full, their outward energy mostly spent. The inner spiritual cleaning and filling they so desperately treasured from this annual gathering firmly imbedded in their souls.

Of course, the young children danced and sang and had their mostly wonderful time. The older children learned the art of breaking camp, learning from their parents, as their parents has taught them. The day was a blessing, since it was dry. No moldy tenting to deal with at the homestead.

With every steed Torrin brought out for its owner, the mass of tents and camps slowly disappeared. The fire pits were stirred 'til they were cool and the stone circles disbanded. Their blackened and charred borders put back into the woods to wait quietly and without complaint until the harvest celebration in the fall.

And, as is the natural order of events, where people's souls have risen to a new level of attachment, wonder and understanding, it is the time of departure where relationships and hearts are cemented for the future. There is a clear and distinct moment, when people part, that clearly defines that future and relationship. For when you turn away and that other person is gone from your sight, you feel one of three things:

The first being the hope that you are never required to lay eyes or ears upon them and their like again (this first being of rare occurrence with the valley people since they shared such a kinship in their heritage).

The second being a state of neutral unamazement and quizzical numbness. They nor touched each other in soul, spirit or sense of belonging. Most likely, when you meet again, you will remember each other, but the place, surroundings or events from before will be a blank slate. There was no positive or negative impact from before. It is almost as if you are looking, searching or striving for something to share. Now, this is not a bad state. Consider this: you might end up with a cousin or close friend who marries one of their cousins or close friends. Since you are in a state of neutral emotions, you can pick up and maybe find some fun. It's a relationship where the door stands open to the future.

Then there is the third. This last kind of parting is both the most wonderful and the absolute worst. When two souls find a connectedness in their hearts, when there is an association that defies most words, there is both wonder and fear. The wonder is from the depth, the caring and the wholeness the new relationship brings. Where the pairing of two people fills a void that is greater than the two by themselves. That void may not have even fully existed in either's conscious mind before, but when it is filled, it makes you both new people.

It is the most absolute worst kind of parting because you don't want those new feelings to end. And, deep down, you wonder if it will be there next time you meet. It is not a worrisome wonder; it is more a spirit of hope, that the uplifting you are experiencing is real for both of you, and it will last for the time you are apart.

Torrin had experienced the last two in spades during these wonderful few days, and now had to endure the parting. It left him in a higher state of exhilaration. For never before, in his days as the prince, had he connected with people at such a level.

Larenzque had packed and was on his way. Clasping Torrin's hand and arm, he thanked him.

"Ye proved to me, how powerful faith in myself could be. I saw ye do it. I felt ye do it. When I told you about being focused, I believed it; but not until I saw you go, did I have such a complete faith in those thoughts. So thank you."

Torrin looked puzzled and was not quite sure what to say. He had not planned on this at all. He felt he should be the one thanking anybody on this parting. These were thoughts he would ponder at a later date, and at a much more dire time. But anyway, without warning, a tear fell down his cheek; its presence puzzled him.

Bartoly looked a little ragged. Actually, he looked like hell. Both he and Rebecca had bags under their eyes and looked considerably scruffy. But in a mutual way. As tired and worn as they looked, they were both smiling. Torrin suspected some serious connections from the night before, especially from the warm smile that Rebecca applied to all her surroundings. Her long golden locks were mussed to a mass of knots. Knots that would take some work to remove. Torrin figured that when you are that much in love, the knots in your hair somehow did not matter.

He longed to feel that way.

His reverie was interrupted by Bartoly's strong voice. "Don't forget what I told you," said Bartoly. "I was serious. You come by anytime and we can talk some more; its only two day's ride on a good horse to get there. Anyway, Quillan will be coming up for horseshoes, nails and pot fixin in some days anyway. You come too!"

After a hearty handshake, they turned and disappeared up the trail to the north, hand in hand, seemingly unburdened by the big packs on their backs.

Torrin's hands seemed to burn from the grateful parting. He felt strange. In need of rest? Something was nagging at him. He felt like he was forgetting something.

The last of the valley people to leave were the Panoleneys. With the "help" of the children, it had been quite the feat to get the whole mass together. Mr. Panoleney pulled his cart with the children running about, carefree and happy. The new baby at Mrs. Panoleney's breast was quite content. As they vanished, a peace descended.

Therefore, in the short space of a bright early morning, all the people who needed to go, left. Journey and the valley were better than before, all the people a stronger community, just as they had hoped.

Maybe as they planned, maybe as nature intended?

Attending to the chores at hand, Torrin chopped the heads of the throwing hammers off, storing them on sturdy pegs in the woodshed. The handles must be cut fresh each year since only springy new wood was acceptable.

While he worked, he was tormented some with a shrewish headache. He figured it was time to quit drinking for a few days. It must be getting to him. He worked steadily, the headache growing. He decided to see if Quillan wanted a late breakfast, hoping that eating would help— he was craving something fried.

As he walked out into the warming sun, the brightness hurt his eyes and added to the pain in his head. He and Quillan had been working steadily, picking up and putting away the elements of the festivus, and were almost finished in the striking of the games. But, as he looked around, it seemed someone had forgotten something.

From across the clearing, one of the valley folk were riding back into Journey's area, heading straight for Quillan, all their gear packed neatly on their trailing horse.

Quillan was carrying two of the large round stones that had created the boundaries of the throwing circles. These well worn rocks were stored at one end of the big building, safely protected until the next spring. You see, the fall festival would be more about food than sport. And anyway, when everyone arrived in the fall, they would be generally tired, what with the harvesting and all.

Hefting stones all morning had put Quillan's hands and arms into a serious state of tired. So without really looking up, he said, "Did ye forget somethn?"

The horse and rider stopped right aside the big man. As Quillan became alert (courtesy of a loud shout of alarm from Torrin), he quite suddenly and rightly, ascertained that the rider was either falling at him or attacking him.

When instinct takes over, a man like Quillan can move fast. And, fortunately, his experience helped him move quickly and rightly.

Dropping the stones so they did not crush his feet, Quillan's large arms caught the falling figure. He was still not sure if he had a fight on his hands. But then he noticed that the other person was not moving. It was as if death lay in his big tired arms.

A large black hat covered the face of the surprisingly light body laying quite prone and still in his almost quivering arms.

Torrin started running toward the very strange and mysterious scene. His head was pounding savagely.

Quillan set the mystery rider down. His arms were cramping from carrying the heavy stones. When he looked up, he saw the horse that had carried this ghostly person was in terrible shape. Frothy at the mouth, burs and cuts on his legs, the saddle askew, blanket dragging in the dirt. Glancing at the other horse, the one with the big pack, he noticed she too was in a spiteful and hideous state.

Kneeling down next to Quillan, Torrin carefully removed the big black hat.

He and Quillan looked quite surprisingly, at the most beautiful, bloody, black and blue redhead they had ever seen.

Her lips were puffy. One eye was swollen shut. A deep wet gash oozed a nasty pus from her neck that ran in a sticky plastered line all along the length of her shirt. Her hands were swollen, raw and bleeding. One cheek showed the clear imprint of fingers. But most of all, the dry hot shallow breaths that gurgled from her mouth scared them completely. It was as if death had arrived, but not yet settled in.

With that, a third horse sauntered upon the scene. Its polished saddle empty. Since it had no rider or load, he was not in as such a sorry state as the others, but he too looked spooked, tired and in need of attention.

"That's that asshole Haphethus' horse!" proclaimed a slightly breathless Torrin. "Who is this? He pointed at the pale and all together too colorful form of the girl who seemed almost dead at their respective knees.

With a flash, Torrin started to shake; his heart was hammering. He was sweating. The pain in his head burst into wild lights that danced before his startled eyes.

After a moment, shaking his head to clear it, he looked at Quillan. The big man had a strange and powerful look on his face. It was neither anger, love nor questioning.

He muttered a one word question, that that left Torrin wondering, "maybe?"

"What?" For Torrin it was as if his mind had lost all control and a passion within him was to explode. He sprang, turned and ran as lightning. He felt like his feet were stuck in harsh sucking mud. He could not seem to move fast enough. Yet, if you saw him, he was running as fast as the eagle dives toward fresh game.

"Karina, Harold, come quick!" he screamed so as all the world might hear.

      *   *   *

As you can imagine, Karina's kitchen was in quite the shambles. She and her help had dispensed massive quantities of food, beverage and of course, advice over the last few days.

Today, a light breakfast had been set for those who desired, in the great hall. So far, there had been only a few takers. All had been very busy! It was quite a morning. A morning to put things away, clean up, get organized.

Well, at least it was.

Karina had heard the shouting and was walking from the kitchen to the big room when Torrin came stampeding through the front door. She just sighed and thought "he is so much like Harold."

"Come quick, a girl, she is almost dead, bruised, cut…" blubbered a clearly distraught and worried Torrin.

"Have Quillan bring her upstairs to the third room," replied a non-pulsed Karina. "I'll take care of her and give her what she needs, for now. You attend to the horses, give 'em a good washing and brushing. And mind you, take good care of all of them. None of them is guilty for any of this."

With that, Torrin turned on his heel and ran. Quillan was already carrying the girl toward Journey. His features still set. He looked pained.

"Now I guess we go and find that evil bastard and slit his throat," came the thick comment from Quillan's stiff lips as Torrin held the door.

The "I told you so" was a wise thing for Torrin to keep to himself. Instead he said, "Karina wants her in the third room."

Quillan took the steps gracefully two at a time.

* * *

Torrin worked until lunch on the horses. Buckets of cool water and vigorous brushing helped some, but did not bring their gleaming coats back, just yet. They needed to eat, rest and de-stress before they would return to normal.

He had developed a way with the animals that came to visit in the stables. He was kind and gentle with them. They appreciated him back and rarely kicked. Even Haphethus' horse seemed to settle in and relax. Of course, this was familiar territory for him. He enjoyed the familiarity of the place since he hardly stayed in the same place twice.

As Torrin worked, he wondered who she was. She had a familiar look about her. But oh, was she a mess. He hoped she had not died while he cared for her horses! They certainly were large, well kept (mostly) steeds. Strong, tall and smart, they were wonderful beasts.

Suddenly, straightening up, Torrin became acutely aware of something he had missed. How? It was impossible. It did not make sense!

How did Karina know the girl had horses? She even knew there had been more than one?

45.
Meeting

It was three of the longest days Torrin and Quillan had ever endured.

They waited.

They waited for permission to see the girl.

They waited to ask questions about Haphethus.

They waited to gather information they needed to satiate the enormously powerful feelings each of them had churning on their insides. Feelings that percolated to their inner most selves. Strong notions they could not, or actually chose not, to discuss with each other.

Torrin held that he felt an odd familiarity with this red haired, mysterious visitor. Quillan, normally a happy-go-lucky, entirely casual sort of man suddenly started shaving and bathing. It was all quite unusual.

Normadia, the head girl in Karina's kitchen, was quite clear in understanding her orders. Karina firmly stated to keep "those two at bay" and let this orphic girl rest.

Chasing Haphethus, they decided, with input from a calm and sensible Harold, was pointless. The miserable scumbag was without a horse; at least that was the assumption. He could be anywhere. No one knew which direction he ultimately traveled in, how fast or whether or not he was still alone. And, they did not know from which direction the girl upstairs had come from. Did she come from the south, the north, the west or from the seas to the east?

They did decide to inform any of the traveling peddlers about Haphethus. It would be a warning as well as spreading information about a dangerous and violent man. Somewhere along the line, fate or some armed warrior would catch up with him and deliver justice. They all spent a lot of time and energy arguing the merits of every approach, as well as the demerits of such a frightful and useless creature.

Oh the waste of it all!

Anyway, the crops needed tending, wood needed cutting, and neither Quillan nor Torrin seemed remotely interested in venturing very far from Journey, just yet.

During these days of waiting, Harold was smart enough to keep both boys busy. He regarded them carefully, and watched them with a steely eye. He did not know the outcome of the next few days, and he hoped they would all survive in good stead. There was much ground to cover here, and some very important futures depended on key things going right.

He wished he knew the answers that plagued him and Karina. There was, as they had been told, only one outcome possible. They felt relieved that the day now seemed close at hand, but troubled and with heavy heart just the same.

You see, only one of the two boys would be chosen. Assuming the red haired girl was the right one. For now, all signs pointed to the happy fact that she was.

The end though, could be painful.

However, in the grand scheme of nature and the power she holds over all who dwell here, it was the right way to go.

At the field, the crops bloomed. As it was the usual summer weather; it had been very dry for many days and nights. Harold was intent on carrying water from the creek up to the parched ground. Wagonload after wagonload of water-filled barrels came tumbling up the trail. It was hard dusty work, but it seemed to help the parched plants. It also kept the men busy focusing their energy on things besides an imagined halcyon future mussed in those enticingly red locks of hair.

The third evening, after a wonderful supper of roast pork, Quillan and Torrin were busy at one of the tables discussing ways to get water to the field from a nearby spring. They had been stymied in their attempts so far, and were quite annoyed. They had tried ditching a path for the water, but the terrain was too rolling and just after a few paces, the water had melted into the dry earth.

Many options were now the source of very opinionated discussion and consideration. Of course, the two of them were getting plenty of advice and free wisdom from travelers staying at the inn. A large mass of creative humanity crowded at the table, sharing their expertise and ideas. Some real, most of it imagined. The reality of which, though, was obvious to any outside observer, enhanced to the point of legend by Dunwidy's carefully crafted brews.

One man suggested cutting tall trees and hollowing out the trunks to create huge pipes for the water. Another described a large windmill with long straps that moved barrels across the rolling hill from spring to field. Back and forth, like a magic hand. Torrin and Quillan decided he was either drunk or crazy.

He may have been both.

They had just decided to find, dig or cut large flat stones and create a manmade canal of sorts when Karina arrived holding a platter of sweets for dessert. Long rivers of honey swam warmly around tall mounds of golden shortbread. It was a fitting end to a wonderful meal and grand discussion.

Harold was lighting the big hearth. As hot as the days continued to be, the evenings were starting to cool; an annoying chill and dampness crept in during the night. Harold's fires cured that problem though.

Karina said, "Well, I have here some sweets for you if you like," as the entire table of aspiring engineers salivated as one. "Of course, Quillan and Torrin, you can eat, or go upstairs. Seems some young lady has been asking about the nice men who 'saved' her when she arrived."

It is said that when a man has worked all day, eaten a large hearty meal and taken on heavy discussion that he is somewhat slow to move— being relaxed and full and all.

This proved to be a very wrong theory.

As the two of them as one and in a flash arrived at the bottom of the stairs, they were stopped short by a bold command from the smiling, almost giggling Karina. "Whoa you two! She is still mending. Get yourselves gentle, settled down and kind right now, or you are going to sit down here fidget'en for another three days."

Our two heroes climbed the stairs as gently as a baby dove ascends toward the morning sun on the first warm day of spring.

*   *   *

She lay propped up by a pile of soft pillows on a sturdy bed; white sheets under golden red hair outlined an angelic luminescence that took their breath away.

Her face was pale; a thin scar which was mostly healed ran across her upper cheek. The new bruises were still visible, but the normal purple puffy discoloration had abated some. The long cut that started at her throat was covered with a thin strip of cloth, colored yellow by Karina's special ointment. The strip disappeared under a thick, dark blue, but soft looking silk nightshirt. Golden threads outlined the front ties. Karina's handmade quilt covered the girl almost to her slender, yet sturdy looking shoulders. Her arms rested on top of the quilt. Arms that were long and strong looking. Her nails were short, but unmarred, and lay as a delicate cover on long, gracefully slender fingers.

The window was just slightly open; a gentle breeze brought in enough cool evening air to keep the room fresh. A low brass lantern sat quietly in the corner casting its light and dispensing gilded shadows that added to the stillness of the calm that surrounded her.

Normadia sat on a low chair next to the bed. A basin of water next to her, as well as a soft towel. The small cloth she held in her hand was wet and she was gracefully dabbing the girl's forehead. A look of worn peace and solitude was on her patient's face. She was lying peacefully with golden lashes laying softly upon the tops of her cheeks. Her lips were pink, and at rest.

The two young men stood just inside the doorway. Both in a silent state. Both chewing the inside of their lower lip. Both waiting for the other to speak.

Normadia smiled and took the lead. "Gail," she said. "You have visitors. They seem to be the boys whom you fell onto when you arrived. You might have done better you know. Shall I send them away?"

Both men looked panic stricken. What if she said yes?

The bedridden girl slowly turned her face up toward the new sound of staggered and labored breathing at the door. Her eyes opened and the most beautiful opal blue orbs ever to grace the earth gazed upon two men, who in all their lives had never expected to be in this position.

A slow, low smile crept across her face as she sluggishly sat up straight. Some color inching up into her cheeks. As she spoke, the dulcet tones of her elegant voice shook both men to their boots. To them it was the music of a mountain lark.

"Normadia," she said. "You should be more kind to the men who came to my aide. Please, sit down." She gestured to low stools against the wall.

They sat. If they'd had hats, they would have been clutching them. But since no tool was available to occupy their seemingly useless hands, they just folded them.

Normadia eyed the two of them with an amused curiosity, her eyebrows scrunched together. Never before had she seen them quite this tamed. She sighed a little, thinking to herself, "So all I have to do to get noticed is come in all bloody and fall off my horse into his arms?"

She allowed the strained silence that covered the room to continue for a few moments. Normadia and the girl traded some interesting and quick glances; furtive smiles helped trade the knowing secrets that only women understood. She decided the agony for the boys had gone on quite long enough.

"Mr. Torrin and Mr. Quillan, this is Miss Gail. Have both of you lost your voice or did Karina rip it out so you wouldn't say something unmannered?"

Quillan spoke in a slow voice; it seemed as though he was laboring over his choice of words. "Miss Gail, it is a pleasure to meet you." Then he hastily added "Again, I mean awake, I mean OK," he stammered. Quillan's usually pink complexion was now crimson and the room suddenly felt stiflingly warm.

All the eyes in the room turned to Torrin. He felt like his face was caught in a hot frying pan. Flames must surely be ready to erupt at any moment from his burning ears. His mouth was dry; the room swam in front of his eyes.

"I is likewise too," he sputtered.

The girl settled back onto the bed with what the boys would have called an elegant smile and sigh. "I owe you both a debt," she said. "What with being cut and having lost a lot of blood, and being sick, falling off Uta might have done me in."

"Uta?" Sputtered Torrin. "I mean, that is your horse's name? Uta?"

"Yes, how is the old brute?" inquired the girl, her eyes wide with the question.

"He is fine. As are the other two. They have been sleeping a lot, eating well and they have begun running around, playing like colts in the field over by the other side 'o the creek."

"Two?" she sat up quickly, with the question forgetting her injuries. A look of alarm on her face.

"Yes. When you arrived, you had two other horses with you. We are actually familiar with the last horse to arrive. He stayed here at Journey for a night not long ago." Torrin glanced at Quillan. A look of worry on his face. The embarrassed silences and wonder gone.

Quillan added, "His owner was non too fond of people or women. And actually, we figure he attacked Karina here at Journey. Did he do you harm? Torrin and I were figurin to go off and unt him down so he can pay for his misdeeds."

"Gail" lay back down. Her eyes closed, a tear appeared at one corner and she breathed in and out, deep, long and slow. Her jaw was clenched, her nostrils flared as she fought to control the rush of emotions flooding her brain.

"So this is Journey. I made it! Thank God," said a now relieved looking girl. Her hands had been clenched in a white fury on the cover:

they opened slowly now, the tenseness that had rushed upon her drained away in an almost visible form.

Her eyes opened and she looked at the two young faces who were scrutinizing her. She wondered if one of them was "him." But Gale's words came back to her...

"When you arrive there, you must find him, but you cannot ask for him outright. There are things he can tell you, which I cannot. He is in danger and will not reveal himself easily. I am sure you will find each other. But take care, be cautious and move slowly."

Gaining some composure and control, "Gail" said "Thank you for taking care of Uta. The other is Calandra. I do not know the name of the third horse. You may have him. I don't want anything to do associated with that dark bastard."

"What direction did he go?" asked Quillan, eager to make things even. "We could go and hunt him down. Actually we want to, but did not know which way he went. Did he hurt you?"

"As far as I know, he went straight to hell. There is no bother or reason to go after him." She closed her eyes; sweat had burst upon her forehead. She looked absolutely drained.

Normadia sensed that this visit was over and ordered the two young mavericks to go. Tomorrow, "Gail" would come downstairs and get some walking in. "She needs to start moving about. I am sure she will need assistance," came the final remark; this was accompanied by a sly smile.

The discussion that followed downstairs was rather boisterous. Was Haphethus dead? Hurt? In prison? Had he hurt Gail?

The conjecture of that scummy beast in chains and at the mercy of guards made for wild speculation until the wee hours of the morning.

After much discussion and talk, both Quillan and Torrin bedded down.

Each looking somewhat odd at the other.

46.
Harold

The next morning, Dessa rose from her bed in that small upstairs room where she had spent far too much time. Systematically, she began the slow, laborious, but wonderful act of putting on clothing.

Just the very thought of putting on regular garments had been invigorating. Thinking about the rest of the day ahead, going downstairs, eating with people and being a free human again was intoxicating. For evermore, she would have the highest level of empathy for anyone bedridden for more than just a few days.

She was thankful not only to be alive, but also to be mobile. The trauma of her experience with Haphethus and the long unending ride to Journey had drained every ounce of vitality her body held. Trauma does that to a person. You feel recovered, healed, well; but, as she was discovering, you start to move around, and every little movement brings you to a level of weariness you did not even know existed. That happened to Dessa as she dressed, even though she moved slowly.

For three days, Dessa had been rising from the bed to use the chamber pot and walk unsteadily around the room. The first attempt was somewhat telling. She made it to the pot and then back to bed with Normadia's gracious help. The whole business exhausted her completely. Lying there, she wondered how long this state of "having no energy" would last. Fortunately, the body is a wonderful machine. Plus, she was young and she was strong, not to mention she was a fighter.

The weariness, it would not last long. The fourth morning found her ready to go. Quickly she had healed. As is the custom of most active people, once she started feeling better, lying in bed became painfully boring. So by the fourth day, the room felt like a comfortable, but very small prison.

It was time to get up, get going and explore this place.

The dressing took a very long time and severely sapped every bit of her energy. Normadia had brought up a dress of heavy cotton. Plain and well worn, it fit her well. The dark green of its origin had faded to a gentle forest shade. The shade you see on a humid day, half way through a parched summer, where the greens of the plants look somewhat tired.

Taking Normadia's hand, after resting for a moment, the two of them slowly made their way down the narrow stairs to the great room. On the way, she marveled at the heavy wooden planking, well worn steps and the warm comfy feeling the building held. Not unlike Torrin's experience not too long ago on that late afternoon when winter's last gasp was leading to spring.

Although she was somewhat exhausted by the final step of the stairs, it was a relief to be in her freedom. The great room of Journey stretched before her. The tables, benches and hearth all set in their normal situation. A wonderful, welcoming place.

Near the hearth stood a long table with a large platter of food, neatly prepared, light in nature, well presented. The smells brought Dessa's stomach to a flip-flop state of anticipation and glee.

At the table were two older, friendly looking people. The woman she recognized as Karina. The man was new, but seemed a comfortable addition to the faces she had met here. As she entered the room, he slowly stood and approached her. His smile genuine, his gait gentle, his demeanor that of a kind and wise man. Dessa felt comfortably at home.

"My name is Harold," he simply said. "It is my pleasure to welcome you to Journey. We have been waiting for ye. Please take a seat."

A very puzzled, but hungry Dessa sat down slowly at the table. She felt like she had run endlessly for days. It was good to be out, but it was tiring. She rightly figured, after some food and fresh air, she would begin to feel more like herself again.

"Please my dear, eat something before you fade away to nothing," said a most accommodating and gracious Karina. "You have had nothing but broth for two days now, and nothing before that, while you slept."

Dessa did not need a second urging. Taking a bowl, she helped herself to what looked like barbequed pork, mixed greens and some boiled roots. She avoided the chicken. It reminded her of Tallon and she needed a clear head right now. He had done her well in the training, and the teacher of the deadly skills had turned out to be a regular sort after all. He had some real fears he was hiding from; it was just that every time she smelled chicken, she heard the crack of that damn bullwhip and her ears rang.

Although she was ravishingly hungry, it did not take much food to fill her up. It was delicious, satisfying and the feast was the best she had encountered in her memory.

The two people across the table sat quietly, ate with her and watched her eat with a level of attention that reminded her of Gale and her father. It was as if she were at home, eating dinner.

After some time, it became evident that this great large room, enormous in its dimensions, was oddly empty, except for the three of them. Normadia had disappeared. It seemed rather strange.

In the castle, the common room always had some kind of commotion going on. A peddler might be selling wares, games of chance hardly ever stopped. Eating and most of all drinking were an all day affair for many, depending on the time of the year. Hunters would take many days off between their jaunts and trade stories. Farmers had quiet days between planting and harvesting. Mothers and children would come in to play games. Fortunes were told.

It was very still here in this room. Dessa gave a slight shiver. A quizzical look crossed her face as she thought of a way to start the conversation. Harold beat her to it.

"Yes, it is never this quiet," said Harold calmly. "I told all of them that the room was off limits this afternoon. We wanted the place peaceful for ye. Figured ye might have some questions and such, or maybe ye jus didn want a bunch of people watching ye eat for the firs time in a whil."

Dessa smiled. She felt somewhat relieved, more welcomed, and she simply said, "Thank you."

"Have you had enough my dear?" asked Karina. "There is plenty more."

"Really, I am fine, and I feel much better. Almost human again," replied Dessa. She was beginning to feel a little awkward. Questions were piling up in her head. She was not sure where to start.

Karina began, "OK, let's see. Here is what happened, as far as we can tell. You arrived four days ago on your horse. His name is Uta as I am told."

As Karina spoke, Dessa was wide eyed with wonder. This woman was answering the very question she was going to ask, "What happened?" so how did she know!

Karina continued, unabated, "You fainted off the horse you were riding and fell into the arms of our very own Quillan. He is such a wonderful man. Been here for a time now. We don't know much about him, but he is part of the situation. Do you remember meeting him?" It really was not a question; Karina did not seem to be ready to stop talking.

But then Karina did stop, looked at Dessa and asked, "Did you want to say something?"

Dessa just nodded "No."

Karina continued, "Quillan took you upstairs. Torrin, you have met that dear boy too, has taken very good care of your horses. He has even cleaned up that poor steed ridden by that devil man Haphethus. You dispatched him in the woods, did you not?"

Now you must remember where Dessa came from, and why she was even in this somewhat wonderful but foreign and confusing situation. Any sort of killing in her father's kingdom was punishable by death itself. And, in this particular place she had no obvious or unobvious saviors ready to whisk her away to a different location of safety.

So, she sat, immovable and flushed. At once, she felt almost sick to her stomach. What had been a wonderful change from the prison upstairs looked like it might end in a terrible way downstairs. The look of panic was palatable on her face.

"My dear," Karina said in a startled and worried tone. "You suddenly look like you are going to be sick. Don't worry about defending yourself against that bad man. He quite beat me up, cut my arm and knocked a tooth out. People here will understand if you sent him to forever. Around here, you may defend yourself."

Dessa looked at the two people seated on the bench across the big table. They seemed honest, they seemed normal. But there was something strange about them. She could not put her finger on it. Anyway, they seemed trustworthy and that was the most important thing for right now. So after a few deep breaths, she told her story:

"I was resting in the woods by a creek. It had been days since I had washed, so I had cleaned up and I layed down in the sun. The warmth and peace of the moment lulled me to sleep. When I awoke, he was there." She wondered if she should tell all. She decided to leave the naked part out. "My arms had fallen asleep and I asked him for help; he then proceeded to tie me up and began beating me." Dessa paused to gain her strength.

"Yes, even though you were stark naked, he should have been more of a gentleman," added Karina, nibbling on a chunk of pork.

"How did you? I never said...?" sputtered Dessa.

"Oh, you'll get used to it," sighed Harold. "She just has a way of knowing. Don't fret, we won't tell anyone." He smiled. "Go on."

It took Dessa a minute to collect herself. It was obvious, she could not lie. Not that she needed to. "I was able to coax him into a compromising position. When I ran away, he chased me, certainly intent on my destruction. I was able to pierce his heart with my dagger. I must tell you, he died quite quickly and with little suffering." She sighed, remembering what Tallon had said, "I guess in the long run, it's better that way."

Harold looked up at her in a stern way. He asked, "When you remember how his face looked when you took him, does it haunt you?"

Dessa closed her eyes. The picture was still very clear. Haphethus' look of rage and terror mixed with that final blank stare of death seemed burned upon her memory.

"No."

"Then ye did fine," said Harold in a quiet tone. "Killn is no fun, but when ye hav ta do it, the test is that last image. It's right bothersome that look of death, but if it haunts ye, then ye gets a problem, ifn' its just bothersm, it's part of the cycle. No, it's not fun." He shook his shaggy head.

Karina put a warm hand on his shoulder and squeezed a gentle bit of support into the man.

"Well, we have taken much of your time for now my dear," said Karina. "I will fetch Normadia and the two of you can go outside and walk some. The fresh air will do ye good. Just don't over do it now. Ye may be strong and young, but ye have been through a lot."

"May I ask you something?" asked the quizzical lady sitting on the other side of the table.

"Why of course."

"Can I stay?" Dessa was stumbling on her words, not sure what to say next. "I mean, can I stay here for a while? I really have no place to go. (pause) I mean for now, and I really appreciate your generosity, and I will work for my room, but I…"

"Hush!" commanded Karina. "Of course you can stay. You certainly can't go home. Yes, you will work and help out, we all do that. Your place is here, for now. Anyway, things have been set in motion and it is nigh for you to choose your prince."

Dessa was staring at Karina with wide doe eyes. She felt somewhat exposed to this woman who seemed to know all about her. This was new. As comfortable as it was here, this turn of events was somewhat frightening. Very intriguing, but frightening.

All she said, and at this time, all she could think of was "Thank you." It almost sounded like a question.

"You are most welcome, Gail. Journey is a welcoming place, as are the people from all around here. You will learn to appreciate much about this valley," Karina smiled. "Oh, and please tell us your name soon. It is rather cumbersome calling you by something which you do not own yourself." With that she turned to the kitchen to get Normadia.

47.
Meeting Friends

Dessa blinked as she and Normadia walked slowly into the warm sunshine. A variety of people were milling about. Many soon disappeared into Journey. Some were muttering something about fairness or thirst. She paid them no heed.

The heat of the day seemed to melt into her skin. She turned her face to the sunshine and soaked up its energy. The strong glare shone through her eyelids, the heat warmed the green dress. The air was warm, not too muggy. It was a fine summer afternoon.

Walking over to a log bench, she sat down and took in her surroundings. To the west, high mountains dominated the land. They were far off, steep and commanding. Their rocky tops showed large ragged windswept rocks, parts covered in snow. The blue hue that surrounded them betold of their height and distance.

To the north, east and south, only the deep forest that lined the big clearing around Journey could be seen. A few paths and trails opened up to the clearing, but a few paces into that forest and you were in a deep dark forest. She pondered the fact that she was here. As hard as she tried, she could not remember following a path or attending to that long ride after leaving the creek. That creek with the beautiful rushing water and quiet solitude should have been a charming place. Instead, evil had crawled in and made it a place of anger, hurt and now death. However, since Haphethus had attacked Karina too, that creek was now a place where justice had been served.

Certainly, it was a place of cleansing. She had been able to clean herself in that wonderful water; her clothes too. She had cleansed her senses of the stress of the training at Tallon's. She had relaxed. And maybe, she had cleansed some of the anger from her soul. Courtesy of Haphethus. She supposed that being able to dispatch Darius' brother was almost as much an evening of the score as she could ever hope for. At least the world was rid of two evil scums.

It was time to look forward and make the most of the situation. She guessed, it was time to start over.

Normadia asked if she would be comfortable by herself. And of course, Dessa was entirely comfortable. Therefore, Normadia scurried back to her duties in the kitchen; she had said Karina needed help attending to dinner, there were many folk about.

Her eyes closed. She listened. She listened very carefully to the sounds about her. A wagon wheel creaked somewhere. Feet trod on grass, stone and dirt. A baby was crying for its mother. Conversations were taking place, unheated, some passionate though. She sensed water running, she could hear the wind in the leaves high above. A squirrel scattered about behind her and the birds called to each other.

It was a peaceful place.

A loud whinny gave her a start.

Uta! Where are you, she almost said aloud.

Fully awake now, Dessa stood up and slowly made her way toward what looked like a stable door. It was high, wide and had accessories for horses all about its entrance.

Entering the dim room, she marveled again at the size of the place. High strong beams supported a well-canted roof. The thick walls were sturdy and well preserved. Open windows let in fresh air, and even though it was a warm day, it was a wonderful place for horses and all sorts of animals of labor.

The whinny came flying to her ears again. Almost forgetting her reduced state of strength, Dessa ran to the stalls where Uta and Calandra stood. They were on clean straw. A well-filled, deep bowl of clear water stood near each of their heads, as well as fresh hay for chewing.

Both horses pranced in their excitement as she got closer.

Wrapping her arms around Uta's big head she buried her face in his. Tears welled up in her eyes as she hugged the only living thing she was familiar with for hundreds of miles around. She felt so lost, but this felt so good, especially right now. Here with her Uta.

Turning to Calandra, she hugged her too. Talking her usual soothing talk to both horses calmed them and assured them of her presence, her love and her caring. For the big animals, it settled them down and they knew she was still committed to them and they would continue serving her as they had, as they had chosen to. It was comforting.

She told them how much she appreciated them bringing her here, unharmed. How proud she was of them finding their way. How they gave her hope, because she knew she could count on them.

Now Dessa did not know if these companions of hers could understand even one word of this. But she could feel their demeanor. She sensed their ideas. They seemed closer to her than ever before.

Stepping back, she looked at Uta and asked, "What? You look like you want tell me something?" The two stared at each other for a few moments. As Dessa turned around, a thought struck her. These two have been here before.

Focused now on the unknown, she walked with measured cadence to Haphethus' horse. He stood a full two hands smaller than Uta and Calandra. He was sturdy though, well bred. His eyes darted about with nervous energy. He was lost. Dessa heard his distress, she felt his suffering.

"Hello," she said to the yet unnamed beast. He settled a bit, turned one big brown eye her way and watched. It was a wary look, one learned from many moons of learning mistrust and fear.

"You decided to join us did you?" Dessa began. "I must apologize. When we left, I really did not pay any attention to you. I don't remember anything I was thinking anyway. But you are welcome to stay and be part of whatever it is we are part of here." Dessa carefully stroked the nervous horse. His distress abated. He settled, she settled. She could tell he was taking careful stock of her. That was the way it was done.

In her heart, she felt a hot tear form for this horse. As bad as his life may have been for him, she took from him the only thing he knew. "I guess we have something in common. You are as alone here as I am."

Picking up a brush, she gave Calandra a quick few strokes. She then turned her attention to Uta. Her strength waning, but she knew what she must do. She needed to pay attention to her beloved horse. It was in her heart.

The brush slid effortlessly through his thick coat. He was silky smooth. Uta had been well taken care of. She felt his deep regular breathing. He was warm and strong, he was of her home, he was of her house.

As the brush wound through his coat, she leaned her now tired head against his big side. The warmth of his body melted her. The welling up inside could be contained no more. She leaned against him and the tears began to flow.

She cried for the mother she lost so long ago. She wept for her father and the sacrifice he made, the sacrifice he must feel. She sobbed for Sanura, the love she had brought her. And she poured forth her loss of the grandfather she had just only met, yet had known all her life.

It was the crying of her losses that tore from her in great heaving sobs.

*   *   *

Torrin entered the stable from the connecting door from Journey's big room. He noted that the door swung hard. It did not get much use in the summer. She was there, stroking her horse with a love that could only be true. He did not move, he did not want to interrupt this special time she was spending with Uta.

Then she started to cry. Great throbbing sobs came ripping from her heaving body.

He instinctively moved toward her. He was afraid she would fall and hurt herself. He felt a need to try to protect her. He did not understand it, it was just there.

She was pressed against the side of the big horse. Her head buried in his fine coat. Her arms were draped over his broad back. She was gasping for air as the tears flowed from what must be a broken heart.

He longed to make things right for her.

Then, as he stood there, the sobbing subsided and this beautiful woman started to slide toward the floor.

Torrin did what any man would do; he caught her in both arms, lifting her up. She was light as a feather to him.

Tears streaked her porcelain face, her breathing shallow.

She had fainted dead away.

He walked carefully and as on air to the big room. Karina was there with Normadia. Quietly she said, "Take her upstairs."

As Torrin climbed the stairs, he marveled at the lady in his arms. She was so very much like everyone else. Yet, she was so very different. He felt a kinship with her.

As he laid her on the bed, he gently swept his hand over her warm, moist forehead. She let out a little sigh and he swore he could hear her say, "They talked to me, they did, really."

Normadia took over, shooing him out and closing the door.

Torrin would never be the same.

Ever.

48.
Ride

The next day, Dessa inquired with Karina as to whether or not she and Uta could venture out for a ride.

The reply was an interesting one. Not exactly what she expected. As capable as Dessa felt she was of taking care of herself, she acquiesced though, with just a moment's consideration.

Karina had said, "Of course, Gail, you may take your friend for a ride, with one small condition. I do rather suspect he has decided you are either crippled or have lost interest in him. Horses are like children, and men. They need attention to be happy." After a thoughtful pause, she added, "Of course I have known women who are the same way."

Dessa waited before she asked, "And that condition that you are entertaining?"

"Oh, I am sorry, forgot my head," chuckled Karina. "Take Torrin with you. He is a fine rider, and knows his way around the area. He is strong and will protect you too."

Dessa's face clouded, "I rather don't think I need protection, but the guide will be handy."

"Now dear, you are certainly a strong capable woman. You have experienced things most people don't experience, let alone imagine in a lifetime. You have developed a savvy about you that is cautious, maybe to the point of stand-offish. However, there is one thing in your heart that you need both to mend and to start to experience, since you most desperately desire it."

Dessa cocked her head to one side. She noticed that her hair moved gracefully across her shoulders. It was a familiar feel and she was pleased it was growing back. These golden, curly red locks were a part of her identify, part of who the real "Dessa" was. All the people in her family had forever marveled at those deep raven waves. For her, it was like carrying memories of the people she loved with her, everywhere she went.

Focusing back on Karina she asked, "And that might be?"

"Deep in your heart, you long for a man to be at your side, and you by his. Not so much a friend, but a partner. Someone with whom you share an equality with. Someone who may be very different from you, yet adds to your sense of self, by being a true collaborator in every sense of the word. A person you can trust, one who trusts you."

Dessa was watching this lady, listening intently. She felt a little like she was hearing her grandfather, Gale.

Karina continued, "To find a person that we trust, to find a partner, we must be willing to faithfully accept and see what parts of us are not so much as empty, but understand and be calm with the parts where we are willing to have another be that for us. This is where two people become more than just two. There is more to it than that, oh so much more. Especially for you." She paused, catching her breath. "Did that make any sense at all?"

"Yes, I hear you and this all makes perfect sense, but I don't think that fantasy of a man or partner will work for me." Dessa was not so much mad as firm in her stance. "I had looked for a prince; I was ready to lay my soul into the arms of the man I loved and let him take me away. I was completely and totally prepared to let him be part of me. Nevertheless, so far, that does not seem to be possible. I don't want to say I have given up, it's just that I am pretty sure it won't happen, and now, I really don't need it. Maybe don't want it."

Karina pushed a heavy lock of partially grey hair back behind her ear and smiled. "I don't mean to be vague dear, but what you said is perfectly correct and also completely and totally wrong. Give your time at Journey a wee bit of a chance, a wee bit of faith and a lot of open mind. I hope you will be enchantingly enthralled."

"So is Torrin that man?" asked Dessa. "Is that why you want me to ride with him?"

"Oh my dear, that is like asking me what the weather will be like in a fortnight. No. I am not saying Torrin is that man. I am saying that Torrin is a man, and part of this valley. He is a good man. Somewhat young in some ways. But trustworthy. He is a good person for you to get to know. That is all."

Dessa was not only confused, she was a little muffled. Karina seemed to be talking in circles. Circles she did not see, nor was she part of them. She decided to make the most of the ride with Torrin and let her mind unclutter.

*   *   *

She felt like she was getting a child ready for a picnic. Uta was so excited about going out riding with Dessa astride his big back that he could not contain his excitement. And, when an animal that big gets excited, it can not only be dangerous, but a pain-in-the-ass to saddle him. Dessa had long ago learned to operate safely around the big childish brute, but the mechanics were wearing her out.

Torrin had carefully and deliberately saddled the more calm Calandra. After that, he had taken Happy out to the field so he could run on his own today. They had decided on "Happy" since it was such a divergence from Haphethus, yet was part of his name. You might consider it mocking the dead man, or you might consider it due justice. More refined folk would say it was fitting for the horse to be given such a fine and positive name. Regular folks said it served the dead bastard right that his name should live on in a positive way; it was part of his perpetual penance.

Torrin walked over to where Dessa was struggling with Uta and asked if he could help.

"I can manage," replied the flushed and somewhat sweaty girl.

Torrin stepped back for a moment, watching. She certainly knew her way around horses, but her way with people seemed a little bent toward stubborn. His ears turned bright red and hot when his thoughts turned toward memories of himself and he thought of a cocky lad he knew who might have been, or may be still, a little that way.

As he watched, he became aware of something rather odd. She was wearing her breeches and heavy shirt. What was odd was that it did not strike him as odd. No other woman he had ever met wore breeches. Yet with Gail, it seemed perfectly normal. She was normal in the dress from yesterday, yet this seemed right too. He decided this might be a good topic of conversation to share with Quillan later. Now was not the time. The time now was to get going.

"Gail?" Torrin declared, somewhat sternly, but with what he hoped she bemused as friendly.

"What?" came a bit of a frustrated reply.

Carefully Torrin remarked, "I bet Uta would appreciate it if you went to his face and talked to him while I did the saddling. He is so excited about going; he is just getting in his own way. He doesn't know that; he needs you to do the right thing so we can be underway before dark."

Dessa dropped the saddle at Torrin's feet with a look that was not so much nasty, as it was "fine, prove it." She walked to Uta's big nose, put her hand on it and started to talk to him.

Torrin waited a few heartbeats for her to connect with Uta, and then said, as he hoisted the saddle, "OK Uta, here comes the saddle. You relax while we get ready."

Dessa flashed a look at Torrin, which he either did not notice or chose to ignore. He went on calmly preparing the horse for a fun ride through the countryside.

Soon, all was ready. The four of them headed out to the hazy warm sun.

Before the time at the creek with Haphethus, Dessa was able to almost spring up on Uta without a thought. As was her habit, she put one foot in the stirrup and prepared to spring into the saddle. About half way up, she ran out of spring. Putting her foot back down on the ground she would have stomped it in frustration if she could. But that would have put her on the ground.

Dark clouds formed on her face. She was not used to this. She had been looking forward to a nice ride. A ride to reconnect with the world, her horse and herself. All this work and sweat were fine, but nothing seemed to be going right, nor as expected.

With a purposeful and not un-loud grunt of effort, she hoisted herself up upon Uta. Instantly the world righted. She was tall upon her horse. She could see far, she was in control. She was reconnected with an animal she not only loved, trusted and respected, but one who gave all that and more back to her.

She could have sworn she heard a muted "finally" come from the horse. She glanced at Torrin who just smiled back and then at Uta's twitching ears and wondered.

Torrin had sat quietly by, watching in silence. His urge was to jump down and help the struggling girl. It was in his nature. That was the way he was built.

That natural "helping" tendency had caused many lectures from his father. Torrin had been told many times that real men don't do that. That was for women.

But especially after talking with Harold the night before, Torrin had held his tongue and his wits at bay.

Harold had told him in low tones by the little fire that chased away the night chill, "Now lad. Yer goin on this ride with yon Gail on the morrow. She is a lovely lass an all. But she has a streak of stubborn in er that will break rocks, includn yer head if yer not careful. Now mind ye, don' be lettn er get hurt. But don't try to elp her too fast. She'll bite yer head off. Let her find her lead. Sort of like lettn a horse that is too spirited finally get calm. Ye let em go for a while."

It may have been the best advice Torrin had gotten since Larenzque had pulled him from his funk before the hammer throw. He was glad he had listened.

* * *

They stopped after a short distance at the field to look at the crops and the new irrigation canal Torrin and Quillan had managed to piece together. A few people milled about, weeding and thinning the plants. They were tending to this big garden of sorts.

Actually, with all the care, and now water from the irrigation, it was a glorious collection of thick foliage. There would be a good harvest this fall.

Dessa seemed genuinely interested in the canal. She marveled at the way the rocks were overlapped to keep the water flowing. She was impressed with the added abundance of the plants where the water kept the earth moist.

Soon they headed off up the valley. Torrin had decided to show Dessa a very special place. At least it was special to him. He hoped she would find it intriguing for a variety of reasons.

As the horses carefully and expertly picked their way along the path as they headed up, they both began to relax. The heavy scent of humid pine permeated the rich forest air with the smell of turpentine. The sun leached the sap from the trees and the turpentine smell was elating in a heavy scent that cleared one's air passages. All around them, the wonder and power of nature unfolded in a cascading stream of endless beauty.

When they stopped to gaze about, all seemed silent. But then, after just a short while, their senses became aware of a bounteous and wild pace that fairly flew about them. Birds twittered. Squirrels chased. Bees buzzed. Butterflies flew in their uncontrolled way, feverishly painting the morning sky with their colors. A large reindeer walked calmly across the path. He stopped and looked at them, head cocked to one side, as if they were the most interesting things he had ever seen.

As Torrin slowly raised his bow and moved his hand toward his quiver, Dessa told him to stand down. She explained that hunting must take place soon. But it was time for the animals to fatten up. And anyway, cleaning and carrying back a large carcass was not her idea of an idyllic ride in the forest.

Furthermore, this buck had a family to guard for the rest of the summer.

Torrin agreed. The buck walked steadily on, his antlers growing at a tremendous pace.

It dawned on Dessa that she had no idea how she knew the buck had a family. She just shrugged her shoulders and they continued on.

Around mid-day Torrin did find a wild hare for their lunch. A low fire soon sizzled while they sat under a large oak and began to share something about each other.

"How long have you been at Journey?" Dessa asked.

"I seemed to have arrived this spring, before it was warm at night," said Torrin, looking off.

"Seemed to have arrived? That is an odd statement. How do you mean that?"

Torrin was not sure how to continue. The whole adventure of showing up had somewhat blurred in his mind. He had thought about it from time to time. Often, he had pondered the whole thing very deeply, but many holes remained in the story. The entire fast paced and harrowing sequence of events perplexed him, and he longed for answers.

"You might say, I was delivered here. Although not of my own choosing." He was not sure how to continue. She would probably laugh at him or think him mad if he told the raw truth. "Of course, when I got here, I had a nasty gash on my leg. Karina fixed it up, but a pretty deep scar remains. I guess the scar is my reminder of the journey to get to Journey."

He smiled at his own joke. Dessa groaned a sly groan. But she smiled at him in a friendly way.

"So we both have scars, maybe of different kinds, but deep scars," she said.

He felt a magnificent sorrow coming from her. A sorrow of some wrenching loss, yet the fortitude of the wonder of discovery that follows such a terrible loss. Her eyes were a deep clear blue, almost translucent. He marveled at how they changed color and intensity. If he had not trusted her somehow, he might have been frightened by that piercing stare. Yet in that stare's depth, he found solace. He found comfort in his soul, like being home, while he was with her.

"Where do you come from?" she continued.

"I am the second heir to my father's throne," replied Torrin. He had not talked about his family much for what seemed like a long time. The games had occupied his time for a while.

"Actually my older sister Gretatia is heir to the throne. My mother always said she would explain why, when I grew up."

Dessa pondered this news. The first son was always heir. Something strange must have happened. Something strange enough to alter the natural order of events—as they were. "Do you plan to go back?"

Torrin looked at this woman. He looked around at the forest that contained them here. He looked around in his mind. What he saw swirled. It was unclear, but it was comfortable.

"My plan was to leave soon, around mid-summer. Harold told me I could have Quillan as a guide. It is said to be a thirty day hard ride to get there."

They sat quietly. At first looking at each other, then slowly turning away. They experienced the type of silence that comes between two people when something important, deep and meaningful is communicated, yet neither is quite sure how to address it. It's an awkward silence, but not brutal like an angry silence.

Torrin broke the spell that had ascended, "But that is why I brought you here. I wanted to show you something." He turned to her, waiting to make sure he had her full attention.

"Will you come and let me show you?"

Dessa had a small chill run through her. She did trust this man, yet after all she had been through, she was somewhat wary. Although, Karina had put her faith in Torrin and he seemed to be a fine fellow, her guard had gone up for a moment. But as she looked at the purity of his face, the gleam in his eye and that wonderful boyish state he was in, she decided that he meant something wonderful. Something to truly share.

This moment reminded her of meeting Phlial. How her antenna had gone up. How she initially mistrusted the man for his loping walk and carefree demeanor. It was not something he was doing; it was all in her mind. He had been a wonderful man. She vowed to work on her predisposition with people.

It was funny; she was better at understanding and knowing animals than people.

"Certainly," she replied. "Where is it?"

"Just beyond these trees." Torrin stirred the fire out. They stood and he turned toward what looked like a solid wall of pine. It reminded her of the wall she met before entering the shepherd's valley.

"Come on," he said.

She almost grasped his hand. It was an instinctive motion. An almost unconscious act. Her hand had gone towards his. But she stopped in time, before she touched him. Her mind racing with millions of tiny personal thoughts that were congruent and conflicting all at once.

Torrin looked down at that hand that was partially open and had almost touched him. He had felt a tug. A tug in the air of something.

Something he had felt before, something that was familiar, yet foreign. It was not of a physical nature, yet was a force to be reckoned with. It was more powerful. Yet completely non-understandable. His memory shook as a small bit of distant memory of the overwhelming feelings he had had for Gwendolyn surfaced. Instantly he felt a sheen of sweat emerge. It seemed to egress over his entire body.

So the two of them shared another awkward moment. This one powerful.

Dessa took control, simply smiled and said, "Lead on."

He did.

For a short while, they traveled on foot around large well-spaced pines. Heather and assorted wildflowers colored their path where the sun was able to break through to the ground. They walked in a silence that felt odd, but necessary for both their brains and emotions to catch up and recover. For Torrin, he felt peculiar, yet happy. Anyway, coming to this spot was always exciting for him.

Presently, he stopped and then did turn and with purpose, took her hand saying, "Now, be very careful where you walk, pay attention to where you put your feet."

Hand in hand, they stepped around a tree and faced a large boulder. He slowly led her to the right and out into the sunshine. The heat from the sun, compared to the cool damp shade of the forest, was a welcome and exciting contrast.

Dessa was watching the trail and carefully stepping on the clean granite. Torrin had stopped walking. His hand was holding hers tight. It was not a romantic grip. It was for guiding. It was for holding on.

"Look up," he said quietly, a small choke in his voice.

Dessa raised her face to the warm sun. A light fresh breeze blew her hair to the back.

She gasped a deep intake of the air that swirled about her. For it was truly magical.

Some might call it a vista. Others might refer to it as an incredible view. People with little regard for their world might simply say, "no big deal."

Dessa however was, in the greatest sense of the term, completely and absolutely speechless.

Delivered before her astonished eyes was the most magnificent and thoroughly spectacular sight she had ever encountered. Of all the magical moments blessing her life, and of all that were to come, this very intense assault upon her view of the world would stay happily engraved in her mind as one of the most genuinely glorious ever.

From almost every direction, a huge and seemingly endless valley stretched before them. It did not end; it simply faded off into the distance, farther than she could see or imagine. A large stream fed by a waterfall higher than her imagination could ever have considered emptied into a lake near the center and shimmered sunshine from its rippled and moving surface.

Herds of reindeer ran across the bottom plains. They seemed as if they were giant waving blankets moving with rhythmical precision through a dream. The few stragglers appeared as threads floating as if on air at the ragged sides and then reconnecting as they moved.

Great birds prowled the air, lending an occasional horrid screech that echoed with stark wildness. Their very presence giving light to the fact that a myriad of small wild beasts scampered about on the valley's broad surface, their lives in peril.

A gentle wind blew steadily, raising up the sounds of the valley to their prying ears. A warm low hum throbbed deeply more as a vibration than a sound as the winds sailed through the trees and rocks, playing nature's melody.

When a person first encounters such a view, the details are at best sketchy, the brain being so completely overwhelmed. Dessa began a systematic look, starting with her feet.

It was at this point, she was very glad Torrin was holding her hand. As she looked down, a second gasp emerged, this time with a small squeal of fright. Just the width of a finger, from her toes, was the sharp edge of a cliff that seemed to fall squarely straight down to forever.

Torrin had one hand firmly planted on the boulder to his side. The other had a vice like grip on her hand. She could feel his natural backward pressure, keeping her on balance.

Slowly leaning forward, she looked over the edge. A straight downward fall that took her breath away met her gaze. Large boulders, rocks and gravel lay strewn about. Some rugged plants and trees struggled for life in cracks and crevasses that littered the sheer rock face.

However, it was clearly obvious, one more step and she would have gone back to the earth from whence she came.

Dessa looked up at the happy face of the young man at her side. His pleasure in sharing this view was genuine. His intent pure. He looked at her face and smiled. His eyes arched up as he said, "So what do you think?"

"It is the most wonderful thing I have ever seen. It is by far..." she stopped. Tears welling in her eyes. Her emotions had caught up with her. Her heart was in her throat. Although she did not understand why—it would be many more summers before she could understand.

A mountaintop experience can change a person, if they are ready. Sometimes even if they are not—and not always right then. It's not the view. It's not the scenery. It's the very nature of seeing yourself as you are in the grand picture of the world. And it's one a person cannot, and will not ever forget. To experience the exhilaration of something so wonderful, large and expansive is a jolt to the soul. In the experience is a cleansing sort of birth. One of the revelations is how very small you are in the expansive scheme of things. The other is to know you are a part of it. Only people who have climbed their mountain can appreciate the beauty of the summit. And you carry the experience with you until it is ready to explode upon your mind.

Dessa was still climbing to her summit so to speak. For that matter, so was Torrin. They now shared the path to a degree. Maybe more than they realized. Maybe less. To either of them, it was not apparent yet nor cast in stone, for what both of them did not know, fate had yet another turn to take before they could fully appreciate the view.

Torrin stepped them both back a few paces and pointed with his free hand to a mountain, hardly visible through thin haze, infinitely far off in the distance. "That is where I come from. Over that mountain. The first time Quillan brought me here to look, I vowed to go back there as soon as I could."

"That was before." He looked at Dessa with the solid look of someone who had ascertained something new about themselves and then words gushed out that he did not know were there. "I guess I have discovered that here, I have more of a home than I had there. I'm not sure I want to go back. I know I must. It might be a while before I do." He finished with a sigh and she could feel his mind leap into the distance. Dessa felt his soul take flight and shimmer around in the vast depths of the perfect splendor that lay before them.

"At least you can go home," she said. She had muttered the words almost by accident. When she would think about it later, it was no accident. She needed to talk. She knew she needed to, just not right now; the story though was burning inside her.

"What do you mean?" he asked.

Her eyes cast down and she went silent. He could feel her thinking. He felt some great force keeping her tongue frozen. It was as if she had turned to ice.

She simply said, "I cannot talk about it now, maybe never. Just let it be. Please!" The last part was more a plea than a command, but with a tone that belied discussion.

Torrin was quiet for a time. He let the view before them pull whatever deep pain she held from her. He said then, "Gail, we all have our stories."

With that, he slowly and carefully turned around, her hand still firmly clenched in his, and he led her back to the horses.

When they arrived to the grazing animals, they both seemed to look down at their entangled fingers at the same time. Neither drew their hand away. Both stared for a moment and then their eyes met.

"I'm," sputtering, Torrin was trying to speak, "I'm sorry, I did not realize…"

Dessa looked at his face. She realized how far from home she was. She understood how she would have to trust her instincts and learn to trust others. At least when the time was right. And she had liked walking with his hand in hers. It fit, in many ways.

"No need to apologize, Torrin. I rather liked it. It was nice," she said in a quiet voice that held a smile of sorts, although a somewhat embarrassed one.

The ends of his ears went bright red as he stammered out, "Me too."

＊　＊　＊

The ride back was calm and serene. They arrived rested and relaxed in time for one of Karina's full dinners at Journey after having taken special care of what seemed now happier horses.

It was a quiet evening. The air had cooled, the food was good and for all at Journey it was a restful leveling from the typical busy day.

Except of course, if you had someone on your mind and you were not quite sure what to make of him/her.

*   *   *

Quillan had been hunting for the day. He now sat with his back against the wall, his legs propped up on a stool.

Unless you knew him well, you might think he was frowning.

49.
Water

It was not Torrin's choice, nor was it Quillan's.

It was Karina's.

It was best for all for her to decide since Harold would have nothing of it and no one else was brave enough to make the decision.

Karina asked Quillan to accompany the two ladies, as their guard and chaperone. Gail and Normadia were to venture out to the waterfall. Gail had been up and about for a few days now and Karina decided it was time for a good brisk bath, especially after riding through mountains and valleys all afternoon with Torrin the day before.

As the little entourage trekked off into the sunshine, Dessa decided to learn a little more about the big red man. He was rather cute, and from what she had heard, he was quite smart and gentle, even if he was strong as a bear. As much as she liked Torrin, there was something about Quillan that held a mystery for her and made her curious, or maybe an enchantment. He had a way about himself that was comforting, yet uncivilized. Her feelings were open and looking. She of course always wanted excitement in life, but she needed trust. And anyway, after lying around for a few days and then with the exhilaration of the trip with Torrin, she was getting back to her old self again.

She wanted to see if she could have some fun while getting to know him. He seemed a pleasant sort and all; she figured she could find out if he was amusing or serious. Maybe both?

"Karina tells me you are a well practiced and successful hunter", she began, casting a furtive glace at Normadia who just smiled knowingly.

Quillan, not used to such open and positive comments from a woman, was not quite sure how to answer. "Uh-hu," came his muffled reply below red scrunched eyebrows.

The dust from their boots rose in the warm air as they walked along the well worn path. Squirrels jumped back into the woods from the toasty warm places where they had been soaking up the sun. Birds exited trees in massive numbers all around them, squawking at the interruption to their day.

"Where did you learn to be such a hunter?" she continued.

"Well, I don rightly remember. Jus been doin it all mh life I guess," said Quillan in straightforward tones.

He is nervous, chuckled Dessa. Does this big guy like me? I wonder if he is my kind of prince material. Or is he just nervous around women?

She sighed. Choosing and looking was much more fun than having your father drop the "man of your dreams" at your feet. She decided to continue on. "Well maybe you can take me out and show me how to shoot a bow and arrow sometime," suggested Dessa with a cherub smile.

"I'll be ri glad too," said the still slightly embarrassed man.

As they arrived at the waterfall, Dessa turned to Quillan while she was loosening the ties to her dress and said with a clear smile, "Guard us well."

Then with a serious tone and look, she said to him, "I have not had the best of luck bathing in creeks."

Quillan, who was beet red guaranteed a safe and wonderful time. With that he turned around, walked behind a hill that made the spot private and planted his feet firmly on the ground. Wild boars would have died trying to get past.

Something told Dessa she had nothing to fear.

* * *

Normadia and Dessa swam, washed and played in the cool water. The summer had heated the hills, warmed the fields and removed the normal bone chilling iciness from the mountain creeks. It was finally that short window of time in the year when the waters were not their usual nasty chilly self. They lacked that bite that stole your breath away when you plunged in. It was a marvelous swim, refreshing and cool. The flow of water over the falls had slowed to a soft trickle. The docile splashing at the bottom where the water splattered onto the surface of the pool produced graceful undulating ripples across the water.

After a while, they were finished— drenched, washed, clean and happy, they dried while sitting on a large warm rock. Dessa marveled at Normadia. The young girl had the strength of a blacksmith but the grace of a morning dove. She was tall and solidly built with a full head of long curly chestnut hair that matched her large brown cheerful eyes.

As she dressed, Dessa felt different. It was as if she had washed away the wretchedness of the past days. The pain was subsiding, both mental and physical. She felt welcome, safe and as much as possible, at home here.

The meltdown with Uta a couple of days ago before the ride must have been good for her. Although she was embarrassed that Torrin had been forced to carry her upstairs in a dead faint. It had purged some of the mental poisons. The trip to the mountain with Torrin had done her good.

The two women got along well. Dessa was beginning to like the unpretentiousness of the people she now found surrounding her.

Normadia announced it was time to return to Journey.

With some effort, Dessa was able to convince Normadia to let her stay here with Quillan for a while longer. She promised that supper would not be missed.

Grudgingly, Normadia allowed the detour and change of plans. She warned Quillan that should anything happen, he should just set out on his own. Coming back would be hazardous to his health.

Quillan assured her that nothing, short of a freak snowstorm, would make them late for supper.

They sat on the big rock, enjoying the warm sun of late afternoon, watching the deep blue sky. The peace of the woods around them was enchanting.

And then quite unexpectedly nature treated them to a spectacular show.

On a hot day, when you watch the sky, sometimes you are allowed to see a magical event take place. High above you in the heated sky, when cold air falls down into warmer air, the moisture in that warm air turns to vapor as they mix. What you are regaled with is the violent formation of a cloud. And it is not a calm event. There is a problem though. The rolling violence is silent, and your mind says with all that commotion above, there should be sound. It is an eerie feeling.

As they lay there, Quillan noted to himself that the blue sky looked, literally, as if it were falling.

Quillan quickly said, a slight tremor invading his voice, "Maybe we shou be findin shelter?"

"No," said Gail. "Just watch!"

As they watched, the vaporous air fell at an amazing speed toward them, roiling and boiling with the ferocity of a large pot of boiling clothes under a roaring fire. All of this upside down mind you, which added more to the natural excitement.

As the air warmed, it began to rise. All around the center of what had just been a small wee cloud, nature's power and fury could be seen, almost felt. Although the power and fury were doing no harm and there was no sound (although, again, it seemed like there should be much sound with all that movement), you could feel it. Feel the might. It made you feel small, and it made you feel good to be part of something so wonderful.

It seemed all at once to Quillan's untrained eye, that a new large cloud appeared. Thick and fluffy at the core, wispy and graceful at the edges. It reminded him of his mother's spinning. She would take large combed piles of soft wool and carefully twist the fibers onto her large wheel. As a boy he would lay on the floor with his head quite buried in the soft woolen piles pretending to be flying in the clouds. The sounds of her spinning wheel in his ear was the sound of the air under his wings and with his private "clouds" around his head he was a mighty bird in the air. Soaring ever higher he owned the great peaks and valleys over which he flew. It was fond entertainment and his mother would sometimes add a hard stomp or two for him that echoed through the floor boards of their shack, and that would be the thunder of the clouds that he now commanded—and of course he would giggle uncontrollably.

This was different though. This was real. The movement above scared and excited him all at once. But he was not disappointed. He was enthralled.

So often the musings and theatrics that consume our minds as a child play out in disappointing reality as an adult. As he grew older and gained wisdom, the child in Quillan soon enough learned he would never take to the skies. The great bird within him was grounded forever.

But here, right now, he was thrown back to those happy moments he shared with his mother. For a few instants of time, his brain played back the happy reality of his boyhood.

Soon, with all the mixing, where there had only been a few wisps of cloud, there now was a large mound of heavy vapor above their heads! The boiling went on, and then, in silent wonder, this new cloud dissipated and disappeared with the speed one blows out a candle. The blue sky returned. Just a few graceful wisps of the marvel they had witnessed were left behind.

It took their breath away.

They sat silently, neither wanting to be the first to break the moment. Quillan did feel wetness at the corners of his eyes and hoped she did not see that. He did not want to appear weak. So he lay there blinking, feeling enthralled, lonely and happy all at once.

He did not want the feeling to leave. He was trying to grasp it, to hold it, to keep it as fresh as it was. It was a moment to treasure.

Nature has a way of taking you off to the edges of your mind with seeming ease. It had certainly happened just now. But if nature can take you there, she can bring you back.

Nature sent a mosquito to do it for them.

Smack went Gail's hand, followed by a firm, "Damn."

"Nasty buggers arn they?" queried Quillan.

Sitting up, she looked at the blood splotch on her arm. "Yuck, guess she got me. Let's go clean this off."

Quillan helped her off the rock. The sun was beginning to set low behind their backs.

As she knelt at the water's edge, she looked up at the smooth pond. Suddenly, and without warning, she pointed and exclaimed, 'Look, the secret..."

Abruptly she stopped and looked quickly at Quillan. She wondered if this had made any sense and now she was suddenly embarrassed. Her childhood memory of the time looking at her reflection with her father certainly would make no sense to him.

She felt his arm on her elbow and he seemed to lift her to a standing position in a firm sort of effort, but at the same time with no effort at all. Her arm was quite clean, but dripping down on the firm rocks at their feet, little spatters spraying cool mist at their ankles. He looked at her in a strange way.

Staring straight at her face, he seemed like a child who had just discovered that fire was hot.

He simply asked, in a careful, and somewhat trembling voice, "Ar ye Dessa?"

* * *

She looked up into his kind and shocked face in utter disbelief.

"Who are you?" she asked carefully, stepping backward. Wishing, even though it might be futile, that she had her coat and knife with her.

"Never mind that for a moment. What I need to know is, are you Dessa, daughter of Tarmon, granddaughter of Gale, sister of Kale? May he rest in peace."

Dessa stepped back a few more paces. Her face was white. Her mouth would not move. She just stared. You could hear the water dripping off her arm on the rocks below. The day seemed to have come to a complete halt. Even the ever twittering birds had fallen silent, for when there is stress about, their singing stops.

A mystical serenity fell over her with the thought that she maybe was with kin. It was a serenity she was not yet willing or ready to trust. Even though she needed and wanted to.

"Well? If you are, say so. If not, say so. Don't just stand there like a blooming idiot," Quillan said a little strongly.

"Who are you?" she asked again. This time, with more verve. It was not an optional question, and he knew it.

"Sanura is my mother."

Dessa looked at him. The eyes were a dead giveaway. Why had she not seen it before? Turning away, she looked hard at the surface of the water. The question she needed to ask caught in her throat. It hurt.

"And?" She began, but her chest would not force the air from her lungs to finish the question.

"King Tarmon," he said slowly.

*   *   *

Dessa was running. Running away, running toward Journey. Running to save not her life but her mind. There was only so much she could bear. How could her father do such a thing? He had loved her mother. He had told her that. Sanura was her friend! Sanura had saved her.

Why? Why! Why?

*   *   *

He let her run for a ways. He knew stopping her would not solve anything. She just did not understand.

She ran until her strength was depleted. He kept pace, a short distance behind, waiting for the right time.

Near a large oak, thick with age, tall and imposing, she collapsed. She fell in a tight fetal position; he could more feel than hear the frantic sobbing. It occurred to him, that whatever evil had sent her on the way to this deliverance must have been close to the devil himself. Although he had been waiting for many a winter, he was not so sure how to go on. It did not matter anyway; it was out of his hands.

Gently, as a mother attends to her fallen child, Quillan knelt beside the sister he had only heard about. The girl who was for him, the only link to parents and family he hardly knew. The tears on his cheeks were for the long and seemingly endless loss he'd endured on this mission. And yet, it occurred to him it would be some time before she would come to look at him as a kin that mattered. If she ever did.

At least now, the wretched and complete loneliness might finally be short lived. Until Torrin had arrived, he had almost given up.

"Dessa," he began. "Tarmon loved Gersemi with his whole and complete heart. That is why I am here. You see…"

She cut him off with a brutal backhanded slap. "How dare you even utter my mother's name, you miserable scum rutting bastard!" She was screaming.

Springing to her feet, she more marched than ran toward the big building. Her hands on her hips, her nose slicing the air in what was really a terrified and indignant defiance.

Quillan just sat on the ground, the massive shade of the stately oak gracing his large frame. He smiled that gentle smile he was so famous for, and slowly shook his head.

Thank goodness, Karina was here to tame her and make sense of things.

50.

Unfolding

The sobs coming from the room echoed off the sturdy walls. Low deep gasping of a broken and downtrodden heart rasped jaggedly in the cool night.

As Karina climbed the stairs, she wondered how she was going to do this. It was not the story that was so hard, it was getting Gail to listen that was to be a challenge.

Opening the heavy door, she was greeted with Gail's long form, half on the floor and half on the bed. Her head buried in an arm. Her red hair was a frightful teased mess with the lower part near her neck wet from the furious sweat that accompanied the heartbreak.

Setting a pitcher of wine down with the large mug she carried, Karina went to sit next to the girl on the bed. She slowly lay a warm and caring hand upon her steaming head. Gail turned away with a loud grunt of despair.

Karina just smiled. She remembered being young and so full of energy and vigor. The righteousness had slowly weaned from her over the winters as she learned what was really important. Right now, by the end of the summer, this girl was vitally important. In addition, they were running out of time.

"Gail my dear," she began.

"My name is Jshessa," Karina heard through clenched teeth that seemed to scream into the bed.

"Jessa?"

"No. Dessa," she said firmly, looking up at the older woman. She peered through red-hot eyes. Eyes full of loss and despair. Eyes that remembered a loving and kind father. A father who was brutally destroyed now in her mind. Not only was her family gone, but also the memory crushed. Her shame of marrying the wrong man and being wrongly accused of his murder she could live with. The shame that her father now bestowed upon her, she could not disclaim. She could not leave it and move on. It was a shame felt she would have to carry as a dreadful burden.

Her world was not only hateful; it was frightful, deadly and full of long, low, miserable, deep loneliness. The loneliness that only comes from within. The worst kind, because you cannot work it out. It lingers in the soul and burns a smoky smothering fire that cooks you alive from the inside out.

"Ah, Dessa!" exclaimed Karina. "Well now, it is good to have a real name for you."

"It doesn't matter anymore," sighed the seemingly broken girl, sitting on the floor.

"Self-pity is a good meal, but usually eaten alone," said Karina. "And alone is never much fun for very long."

"What would you know about that? You are happy with a nice man in a nice place. I am alone and barred from my home and now I find my father is a cheating whoreman."

In what she hoped was a stern enough voice to get the point across without losing the girl, Karina said, "How dare you judge me, or anyone here!"

Dessa looked up, a quizzical frown crossing her flushed wet face.

"You don't know anyone's story. You don't know what path any person down there, or me for that matter, has had to take to get here. Don't think for one minute that any one of them had a route any lighter than yours. I'll bet if you took the time to listen, some of their stories might just surprise you."

Dessa looked somewhat sheepish. Her brain began to set the rampantly hot emotions aside. A heavy sigh seemed to escape from her whole body.

"Get yourself cleaned up, have some wine and come down to the great room. There is a story you need to hear, and I expect you to listen."

With that, Karina rose, opened the window to let the breeze in, filled the mug and left the room carrying the pitcher.

Dessa stood. The cool evening air burned away some of the heat of the passion that had engulfed her. Maybe she was not alone. Maybe Gale had sent her here for a reason? It was not fair, but she supposed burning at the stake would have been worse.

She shuddered for a moment; thinking of the horror Valdemar must have felt, completely helpless. Even if it was justice, it was horrible.

She stripped off the dress she was wearing and let the air wash over her sweat soaked, naked body. The hairs of her arms stood at attention, little chills moved along the skin as the sweat evaporated and brought her back in touch with herself.

The wine was a strong honey mead with cinnamon. The mug was much too small for what she wanted. It seemed to go down in one gulp. There is more I suppose; rather, "I hope," she thought.

Sitting down on the low stool, the wood felt cold and harsh against her naked bottom. The shock of the cold caused a sharp intake of breath and she became aware of her lungs and the sweet happiness of a deep breath.

As she brushed her hair, the memories of her mother flooded over her and she choked down the need to cry some more.

The dress was cool as it covered her. The sweat had dried some and made the outfit passable again.

Standing straight, she grasped the mug and marched herself down the heavy wooden stairs.

It was time.

If she only knew.

* * *

A low fire burned in the hearth. The smoky orange flames danced slowly around large well-dried logs. Candles on the tables broke the darkness and shadows graced the walls.

It was not a busy night at Journey, nor was the great room empty. The low murmur of voices washed smoothly along the walls and swirled lazily amongst the rafters and beams.

Dessa made her way to the table that held Torrin, Quillan and Harold. As if on queue, Karina appeared with a large platter of her famous sweet rolls. Just as it had a few nights before, the honey swirled around the golden mounds. The friendly pungent sweetness of baking filled the room and nary a soul failed to apply for their fair share of this treat.

As they sat eating, Karina settled her frame at the table and looked coldly at Quillan. He seemed to blush some and looked pained.

"Well young man. Is there something you would like to share with us?"

Quillan was generally a man of few words unless something was pressing firmly on his mind. Tonight something was pressing.

"I have been holding this to myself for many a summer and winter. Mostly night is the hardest when my mind goes back to my mum. The quiet and the longing will certainly slay me if I am forced to keep it a secret much longer."

Torrin scrunched his eyes. His dark bushy eyebrows almost touched. Harold and Karina were holding hands. Their backs leaned against the big wall of the great stone hearth. Both had a look of contentment on weary looking faces.

"You see," the big man slowly said, carefully choosing his words, "My mother is a wonderful lady named Sanura."

Dessa gave a great sigh, it was almost a groan.

"Sanura came to the kingdom of Tarmon from the south. When I was just a wee child, she would tell me of her journey. She traveled across large stormy seas. Spent night after night in a huge boat until she was finally delivered upon a rocky shore."

"Wait a moment," declared Torrin. "Your voice, your accent, your words. It's all different?"

Quillan smiled, happy to free of his bonds. "I built that as a cover. My accent was a hoax so no one I might meet would be able figure where I came from. For my very existence could have torn not only a kingdom apart, but also true love as it can only exist, pure in the heart. I have wrecked words and spent the last ten winters falling all over my tongue, hiding. You are the first to know the real story."

"Sanura had been in bondage to warriors. Their boat had wrecked when they lost control of it. She had fed them bad fish to poison them as they approached land. My mother was…err, is, a strong woman. I daresay, Dessa here will testify to that."

"Dessa?" Torrin looked at the lady he knew by another name. "I thought your name was Gail?"

Dessa replied, "I did not know who would be here when I arrived. I did not know if any of you were friend or foe. You will understand with time. I was terrified when I woke up. That is for later. Just for now; yes, my name is Dessa."

Torrin looked confused.

Quillan continued, "Sanura was weak when she pulled herself onto the shore. The cold water had almost killed her. She was picked up by a wool peddler and she worked with him until she arrived at the kingdom of King Keegan."

"As a young, strong woman, she was hired to work in the kitchens and over time, the king came to trust her and had her work closely with the royal family. As you can guess, the elder son was a handsome, charming and feverishly kind prince. His name was Tarmon."

Dessa was sitting very still, very straight and with jaws clenched so tight, they trembled.

Karina looked at her and said, "Dessa dear, please have another take of wine. It is so very good for you on a cool evening."

Dessa was almost startled by the advice. She looked down at her hands. Small red creases had formed where she had been clutching them together. As she reached for the mug of wine, she looked around. What she saw fell upon her heavily, but at the same time began to lift some of the weight she carried.

The men and women who were as much a part of the room as the tables, talked gently and serenely in low voices. None of them paid any heed to the discussion at her table. It dawned on her that she fit in. She was simply another person here.

It was time for her to relax.

Quillan continued, "As I am told, Sanura and Tarmon did not just fall for each other. They fell head over heels madly in love. Mother would tell me stories of their rides in the country, their dancing and their long evenings sitting by the fire. It was a love affair of the heart; they truly enjoyed each other's company."

Quillan stopped to take advantage of the wine in the large tankard that guarded his front. After taking a long healthy and therapeutic swallow, he noticed that not a word had been shared by his most attentive audience when he stopped talking. It was eerie, having all this quiet at his table.

"Sadly, they had to carry on their romance in secret from King Keegan. Sanura was of royal blood from her native land, yet not of this land. So she was clearly, in the eyes of the king, a commoner. When the time came for Tarmon to court, he was miserable. He managed to discard many a wonderful princess who came to hold for him. Eventually, Sanura could see that their love could destroy not only Tarmon's eventual ascension to the throne, but it would destroy them and the love they shared."

"How?" asked Torrin. He was entranced by the story, but he was missing something.

"Mother was very smart. She could see that if their love went public, Keegan would put Tarmon out. Then, many bad things would happen. Mother felt that Tarmon would eventually turn to blame Sanura for his plight. For he would be seen as but a commoner in Keegan's kingdom. Even though their love was true, reality can take hold and make life horrible, especially if your younger brother gets to be king, and your younger brother is a raging asshole."

Harold turned his bushy head toward Quillan and said, "Eh?"

"Yes. You see, Gillespie, Tarmon's younger brother, was none too smart, good looking or kind. He is insanely jealous of Tarmon, and would have liked nothing better than to be king and put Tarmon to shame forever. Gillespie, in mother's opinion, would have ruined the kingdom."

Dessa shuddered. She had heard very little of Gillespie, although what she had heard made her skin crawl.

"Mother told Tarmon of her concerns. She had decided he needed to leave her and marry his rightful and lawful princess. She said it broke her heart, but it must be done for the greater good. Tarmon would hear nothing of it. He was firm in his decision to step aside and let Gillespie rule. Then came the dog."

"Dog," Torrin said, almost unconsciously. He then repeated himself, but this time as a question, "Dog?"

"Most certainly, a dog. Actually a small black puppy that was the favorite pet of the young daughter of the chambermaid. This puppy was loved by all, and one day, as he was playing outside the great room door with the young girl, Gillespie rode up and trampled the poor thing with his horse. Paying no heed to the wailing of the girl, other than to slap her aside, he strode in as if nothing had happened."

"That night, great arguing and debating ensued throughout the kingdom. Keegan was not very old, but he was not young. The people were suddenly in fear of having a ruler who was more interested in hate than fair rule, for many knew of Tarmon and mother's love. Great fights broke out; fear does that to people. Many men and woman were injured or killed, and the infections took a great many more. It almost ruined the kingdom."

"Because," Dessa said, in a hushed voice, "so many were dead, we could hardly plant enough to carry on."

"Right," Quillan agreed. "Tarmon was almost broken. His heart was torn, his hatred for his brother acute and his home in shambles. Therefore, mother did the only thing she could think of to help Tarmon's decision. She knew, if she simply left, he would leave no stone unturned finding her. So she lay with him at the right time, and got pregnant."

"Oh my," said Dessa, now getting red in the cheeks.

"Mother would tell me, when I was older, that she had been in love only once, been close to a man only once, and had been blessed with the most wonderful thing on earth." He stopped, his voice choking. "I was made to save the true love of my parents and to keep the people of the kingdom safe. Guess that is not too bad." He almost ended that sentence as a question, looking around the table, wondering if they took him for himself, just as he was. Accepting him? The faces that surrounded him told him he had nothing to fret about.

"What happened?" Karina asked.

"Since mother would have been stoned, Tarmon was forced to send her quietly away. To Keegan's credit, he must have known, but all went smoothly. I grew up until about ten winters old with my mother and another man, not far from here."

Dessa's eyes closed. She knew. She knew very well. "Tallon."

"He raised me as the son he never had. Tallon was for some reason banished from the kingdom long ago, a story he would not tell. But, he was kind and wonderful to us. He trains the kingdom's guards in all manners of brutality. For such a kind man, his ways are a bit crazy. He never brought that inside his small black cabin though."

"You act as if you know him or know of him?" Quillan asked Dessa.

"I spent a few long and fretful days with him," she replied. "He taught me much, but it was not fun."

"And," Dessa suddenly blurted, "It is starting to make sense. Oh my, yes! When I was leaving, the last thing he said to me was 'say hi to your brother.' He knew."

Quillan smiled. Clean memories from long ago passing his eyes. For a long moment, he just grinned and took a foresightfully deep breath. "At ten winters, my mother and I returned to the kingdom of Tarmon. Through the guards, we had kept up on the news. We knew of Keegan's passing and Tarmon's marriage to Queen Gersemi."

Dessa stiffened.

"I remember the arrival. It was a glorious spring after a brutally cold and snowy winter. We lived in the stables for a time." Quillan looked at Dessa and said, "I should have known who you were when you told us your name was Gail," and he grinned some more.

Dessa smiled; she was roiling a bit inside. So much was coming out, so much settling in.

Quillan continued, "Gale was the stable hand."

"Still is," Dessa interrupted. "He is a wonderful man, please continue." She decided that telling the story of Gale could wait.

"Good, I am glad he is healthy. Tarmon came to the stables often. I was young then, but what mother told me was that Tarmon would not betray his vows to Gersemi, even though he would forever love my mother. She understood, and did not ask for anything but just that. As far as I can tell, they were good friends."

"So," Dessa haltingly began, he did not cheat? He was..?"

"True," Quillan finished for her. "We cannot tell what was going through his mind. Although I would love to ask him; he was a man of his word, honor and true to his kingdom. He loved two women, and loved them as purely as he could. It was his way. My thought has always been, that as hard as it was, my mother made the right choice."

Tears flowed down Dessa's starry red cheeks. "I am so sorry for the mean and cruel things I said. Please accept..."

"No need, but thank you," Quillan intervened. "I understand. You did not know, and only a daughter who loved a father with a virtuous heart could be so angry at such a thing. You have brought Tarmon great honor."

Torrin turned to Dessa. His head was tilted to one side, as if it helped him think, he simply said, "Why are you here? And actually, for that matter, why are we both here?" He had put a distinct and clear emphasis on "you" and "both."

Dessa's eyes met his. Her teeth bit sharply on her lower lip. As she seemed ready to talk, Harold interrupted.

"Weel, that's a fine question for another morrow seein' as ow you and Quillan and Dessa ere are eahed up to pay a visit to Bartoly and Rebecca in a couple of days. We need some ironwork finished. Let's all get ta bed; there is much to do before ye'all leave."

Torrin looked around the big room. So engrossed had he been in Quillan's story, he did not realize everyone else was fast asleep. As he let his attention "see" the room, he heard snoring and the sounds of deep sleep.

As he and Quillan put out their sleeping things, he asked a question, "Quillan?"

"Yes?"

"Why are you here?"

There was a pause; Torrin wondered if Quillan had dropped off to sleep, until he heard that big bushy head turn toward him and release as long, slow great sigh.

In a quiet voice, somewhat deep, barely above a whisper, Quillan slowly said, "I am the guide."

51.
Heat

It seemed an odd sound. Really, the oddity was the noiseless and incessant lack of sound. He decided four heavy horses should make more noise. A thick bed of pine needles softly blanketed the ground and silenced the big heavy hooves. And, to make matters even more boring, as the day wore on, all you had to do was watch for the occasional branch that might sweep across your face and the rest was monotonous to the point of pained boredom. Torrin sighed deeply for the hundredth time that afternoon. He had spent a lot of the day thinking in great silence and he needed to talk.

Quillan led the way. As quiet and serene as it was, there was little room for conversation since they had to travel single file on the narrow trail.

Torrin brought up the rear. Dessa behind Quillan and Calandra with her big pack bounded along gracefully in third place.

As they rode on, their little party plodding along, Torrin watched Dessa from the back and wondered. He was somewhat transfixed by the thick red hair swooshing in long graceful arcs across her back. It bounced in rhythmical fascination off the quiver packed full of lethally straight arrows that seemed to be her constant companion when traveling.

The more he watched, the more questions emerged. She was an enigma for him. Where did she come from? Why was she here? Why did he feel weak in the knees when she looked at him? But most of all, where did she fit in to what seemed to him to be mostly a predestined life?

When he had met Gwendolyn, he knew exactly what he wanted. His desire had been instant and strong. Their mutual wanting had been a powerful elixir. And once you have tasted such an elixir, it is one you crave—forever.

The chemistry here was different though. He was sure there was some sort of attraction, but he really could not pin it down. That bothered him. He knew it was there? He was not sure it was there? All at the same time. His head shook as he tried to clear the confusion.

Samoot, his mount, just snorted and wondered what all this squalling was about from this rider. This boy was squirming around in the saddle like a child. It was a nice day for a trip, just relax.

A little voice blew cautions through deep places in Torrin's mind. The memory of Gwendolyn, lying on the forest floor haunted him. The violence, the sadness, the shock of that event was seared into his head. Somehow, at all costs, he needed to avoid repeating that sort of catastrophe.

This had to be safe. Something told him, it was important.

Presently the afternoon had worn on and they came out of the hills and into a shallow valley of sorts. Trees still abounded, but they were not so squeezed on the trail. Conversation was still hampered as they moved along since they were still dodging branches and stones. They managed with things like "It's a beautiful day, isn't it?" and "The horses seem to be enjoying the ride." Substance in the conversation was lacking.

Torrin decided saying nothing might be more palatable.

The breeze was in their faces and the sun low in the sky when they spotted the deer. A mid size buck, feeding on tender summer grasses. Dessa looked at Quillan, the silent question clear on her face. He nodded a slow "Go ahead and try."

With a silky smooth grace borne of practice and natural talent, Dessa nocked an arrow, and let it fly. She felt secure with the bow string tight in her hand. It was something she could control.

The buck never heard or felt a thing.

Both Quillan and Torrin sat with their mouths agape, with awe at her marksmanship.

While they were cleaning the kill, Torrin asked Dessa where she had learned to shoot like that. Was it from Tallon?

"No," she replied with a smile.

"Well?"

"As a little girl, I rode with the hunters of my father's kingdom. They taught me how to shoot. They were patient with me. I guess they were pretty good teachers."

"Or, you have a natural ability," he replied.

She threw him a light smile.

"Come on you two, we can get a fair distance further before settling down to a nice fire, dinner and roasting session," quipped Quillan.

They rode on with renewed purpose, knowing a great meal awaited. The sky was blue, the air warm and the great stateliness of nature surrounded them.

And surround them it would.

Later in life, when Torrin was more in tune with the special forces at work within him, he would recognize these signs much sooner and be more prepared. As it was though, the pressure in his head and the fact that he felt funny all over did not quite meet with his conscious mind.

As they rounded a turn near a low swampy area, a thick swarm of black flies attacked Dessa. Torrin watched in horrific astonishment as the

black buzzing mass thickly surrounded her entire body. He was
transfixed. Frozen in his saddle. His brain was firing blanks as he
watched her flail her arms about, burbling out muffled screams that
sounded as though she were underwater.

Later he would remember screaming, "No, not again!"

So he did what any man who was clueless as to what to actually
do. He jumped in with both feet.

Spurring Samoot forward, he bounded up to the suffering girl. His
mind still ablaze with no clue as to what to do. Reaching Dessa, he thrust
his hand into the teeming mass to grab her arm. The thought of pulling
her down to the ground and rolling her around was forming in his mind.

However, as soon as he touched her, the most unusual thing
happened. Every single black, nasty, biting fly died and fell to the ground
as one large lifeless mass. They basically slid to the earth. Not one buzz
left in their small wretched bodies.

"Oh, yuck," cried a quite distraught Dessa. A loud "Cach!"
emerged from her as she spat dead flies out.

With that Quillan came bounding back on his horse at a wild trot.

"Where have you two been?" He sputtered like a gruff uncle. "I
relax for one minute, enjoying the beauty of nature and you two..."

Torrin pointed at the large black mass beneath Uta.

"What the hell is all that?" Quillan asked as he slid off his mount
to get a closer look. Bending down close, he reached out with one hand.

"I wouldn't do that," Torrin said.

Since Quillan had yet to listen to Torrin, he was not about to start
now.

Maybe he should have.

Reaching in, he removed his hand. It was covered in a black
spotted and red massy slime.

"Damn, this is burning me," yelled a surprised and now somewhat
scared big redheaded man. He started to dance around and shake his
hand, trying to remove the hot burning ooze.

"When are you going to learn to listen to me?" laughed a bemused,
but somewhat concerned Torrin. With one smooth motion he opened his
water skein, jumped off and poured the cool liquid over the big man's
hand. As the goo washed off, Torrin could see angry red blisters forming
on Quillan's hand.

Quillan thrust his hand in Torrin's direction, "More water," he shouted. Torrin slowly emptied both his and Dessa's skeins before Quillan was finally settling down to his more normal self.

"Blast it. What happened?" asked a wide eyed Quillan. He was blowing on his hand. A few of the blisters had torn.

Dessa moved Uta up and tied him to a branch. After making sure he was calm, she wandered over to Quillan who by now had sat on a large rock, staring at his wounded paw.

"Those damn flies just arrived and covered me," said Dessa. She inspected Quillan's hand. "Those look just like burns."

Torrin tied up the rest of the horses as Dessa went over to inspect the now smoldering pile of dead flies. Bending low, she put her hand close to the ugly pile.

"It's hot," she said. "Like the coals of a good campfire."

Torrin knelt low too.

"Don't you be touchn' that mess," said Dessa. "I'm not babysitting both of you."

"It is hot. Scary hot," said a bewildered Torrin. "What did you do to them?"

"What did I do?" Dessa peered at him. "I was being attacked. I was getting bit all over and could hardly breathe. The question is really, what did you do?"

They looked at each other for a moment. Dessa cocked her head and waited for an answer.

"Me?" Torrin said, his voice rising. "I was going to pull you off the horse and roll you on the ground to try and get them off."

He was gaining his composure. "All I did was ride up and grab your arm and then…"

He stopped in mid sentence. They looked at each other, eyes wide, mouths agape.

They both took a step back, making sure there was plenty of space between them.

"And when I grabbed your arm the whole lot of these buggers just slid off and hit the ground. It was like a pile of warm dough sliding off a pan. Really, all I did was grab your arm."

"Then what do you make of the heat? This tremendous heat?" She was incredulous. "This makes no sense!"

"I don't know. Really, I have no idea. All I remember was wanting so bad to help you, to save you. I was instantly furious that you were in trouble."

Quillan gave a low chuckle. "Do ye see it? You don't, do you? You're both blind as a horses ass at night. There is something between you and you just don't know it yet. Or, you are denyin' it. Whatever it is though, it's powerful. Very powerful."

He continued, "Go ahead, and touch each other. See if ye melt like butter on a fire."

Torrin looked at Dessa.

Dessa looked at Torrin.

As one, they lifted a hand toward each other. Palms out. Sweating in the late afternoon light.

Slowly they came together. Just touching at first. Tentative. Wondering if they would spontaneously combust. Torrin's rough and larger hand did not dwarf Dessa's long slender fingers, but his looked more powerful.

Once they figured out it was safe, Torrin slid his fingers between Dessa's and firmly grasped her hand.

He looked at her through eyes that were not much more than slits, and if you knew him well, there was more moisture at the edges than usual. His voice was raspy, his tone low as he said, "I was scared. We are just getting to know each other. I didn't want anything to happen to ye. I …" and he stopped. His lip was quivering.

Dessa stared at the young man in front of her. She felt tipsy, like she might fall down. Her vision blurred some. "I…," and paused. She breathed slowly and deeply through her nose. Long even breaths that helped her think. "I appreciate it. Really I do." Then words were at a loss for her.

They separated their intertwined fingers. Torrin held his hand to his face. "Well, 'tis warm, but not fire."

"Mine too," she said.

"Come on now you two, you'll have plenty of time for discovering lots of things. We have meat to roast and then a long ride tomorrow, since we seem to be stopped now."

Torrin looked around, "Let's get to some higher ground. There's more wood and," he paused, looking at the now mottled mass of dead flies, "hopefully fewer bugs."

"I'm with you," declared Dessa.

They gathered the horses and found that Quillan was not at all game for any special attention. After a few minutes' walk they came to a sturdy old oak and set up camp.

With a good fire going and numerous cuts of meat cooking on various and sundry sticks and spits, Torrin sat looking up into the tree.

"What you lookn' for?" asked Dessa.

"Loose sticks and logs," said Torrin as he methodically scanned the upper branches. "They can be deadly coming down on ya."

"That is the silliest thing I ever heard," declared Dessa.

Torrin looked up at the girl and sighed.

Quillan stood up, licking a finger and said, "Maybe it's time we both listened to him."

        *   *   *

A generous meal of fresh roasted venison after a long ride and unplanned excitement makes for a good sleep. Nature added her part to the effect of ambiance by delivering a glorious full moon playing brilliantly soft white light down on our little entourage as they slumbered.

Thin tendrils of smoke whiskered slowly up into the moonlight, casting an almost ghost-like moving thin shadow across the cool moonlit earth.

Summer was heading toward its sad but undeniable close and it was one of those magical nights of change. Change that comes as slowly as the seasons can merge into one another and as swift and deep as nature itself. Some change comes with us hardly knowing. Some is fast and furious. The best and most important sneaks up on you. You know it is happening, you don't understand it; it teases you. Yet it ties you in small knots, keeps you running and disturbs the balance of your very soul. And your mind runs on overdrive trying to sort out the feelings, the mysterious thoughts and musings that crowd your head.

Some of it we long for. Some of it we dread. No matter what it is though, when change comes, and it is dramatic change, it is furiously hard for the unconscious to sort out the meanings for a time.

And that leads to some very entertaining dreams.

*   *   *

Torrin's mind was in full stride. Fast, furious, in grave need of balance. He was lying straight and rigid as one of Dessa's deadly arrows in his warm comfortable blanket, holding on tightly to the heavy material as if he would fall off the very earth if he loosed his feverish grip.

He was fast asleep. A deeper sleep than he had experienced for a long time. We shall never know if it was the fresh air, the long ride, the scare of the black flies or the slow creeping of a relationship that took him to this deep and mysterious place. Whatever was the cause, it was as real as all the jumbled thoughts in his racing mind—and he was about to pay the price.

Gwendolyn's warm flushed cheek lay upon his chest. Her naked body dense with the sweet sweat of their intense and almost magical lovemaking. Her normally light soft hair was damp, matted and splayed across his flushed skin. The forest air moved slowly and effortlessly around them, gently cooling the fire of their fervor. The wonderful memory of this shared time cooled undiminished with the breeze as the moisture evaporated and chilled the heat they had shared in a mutual passion.

As he looked around, he remembered that this had started in his special place at the top of the mountain at the cleft in the rocks. Torrin had been standing in the cleft, staring across the valley at the very place he and Dessa had visited only a few days earlier. The warm sun had left the stones radiating heat in all directions. He sensed her presence before she appeared. As her long arms wrapped around his chest he moaned with deep desire. She embraced him almost like a snake would wrap itself around an unsuspecting victim. Slowly, hardly touching at first and then firmer, deeper and with intense purpose. Her hands ran under his shirt and then teased along the edge of his pants, almost tickling him in that sensual area of his stomach. Untying the laces that secured him, she ran a hand down, ever so slowly into his breeches. Her long fingers kept to the edge of his pubis and then stretched long onto a warm and almost trembling leg, pestering him, letting him rise with his desire. That toying hand then smoothly cupped him ever so gently. Her soft fingers felt all at once icy and steamy hot at the same time. The wanting moans that left his lips were thick and nearly sounded like someone in pain.

It was the pain of desire.

Her mouth was toying with him and parted the hair that lay along his ear and began to tease the firm edges of that oh-so-tender place. Moist warm lips caressed hot passion into his being. Her breath was raggedly spicy, almost feverish. He could feel her firm breasts pushing against his back, and as he reached behind to caress her, he found her completely naked.

Turning around, their lips met in a wet cadence, first caressing and then almost a mad coupling. He had to hold to the rock's face lest the force of her desire push them both to a certain crushing death on jagged rocks far below.

Pressing her back, so they were both a safe distance from the edge, he picked her up. Their lips never once leaving each other. Their mutual rapid breathing increasing. Her skin felt hot against his as the perspiration cooled in the air off his skin; one hand cupped a smooth breast, and the other firmly held her soft bottom. The estrus between them galvanized the actions about to occur.

For both of them, their desire had turned to a need that would not be denied.

Laying her upon soft green grass in a sunny open area, he stood and finished removing his clothes—which did not take long.

At first, he was hurrying. But then he saw the hunger in her face and watched in primal satisfaction as she craved him, running her hands firmly across her own skin, pulling him close with urgency.

He was fascinated, and took his time.

When he was done with her, (or she done with him?) he opened his eyes to a new day.

Bright sun streamed through the trees.

And a new day it was. He realized he had himself firmly by his crann under the blanket and Dessa was sitting next to him on the ground. Her back was straight as an oak tree, and the look on her face middling stern, oddly quizzical, but entirely unpleasant.

Then, her lightly red eyebrows scrunched as her teeth seemed to move slowly within a stern jaw. Her lips moved around her face some as she seemed to ponder a question or a thought that was a mighty weight on her mind. She tilted her head, lifted those colorful eyebrows and softly, but with no mistake as to severity of the question asked, "And who might Gwendolyn be?"

* * *

"She was a lass of the valley who had befriended Torrin not long after he arrived," quipped Quillan from across the clearing.

"Was?" said Dessa, looking at him now rather sternly.

"Yes, a terrible accident took her life," he muddled out quietly as he slowly saddled his horse, favoring his damaged hand.

"What happened?"

"She was in the wrong place at the wrong time. A log fell out of a tree and quite did her in." answered Quillan.

Dessa looked at Torrin; the bright red in his face had faded to a warm crimson. "It seems you had an interest in this lass?"

"Well, not what you might think..." he looked at her face and decided she already knew the answer. Trying to explain it all away might do more harm than good. He bit his lip.

"Well? How do you know what I think?" she asked, a bit of fire seemed to be leaping in her deep blue eyes.

All of a sudden, not answering did not seem to be a viable option. Torrin groaned. All the excitement that just moments before was so wonderful, real and hot in both his hand and mind was now entirely gone. The smoky hotness of the dream, so painfully wonderful, was fast fading to what seemed to become a nightmare.

Torrin started to talk; and, unfortunately he had not decided to think before talking. "You see, Gwendolyn was a lass that loved to dance. Quillan introduced us. No actually she and I met first, before the formal introductions when I was taking a bath after butchering a deer and..."

"What? The formality of knowing her name going to slow you down?"

Torrin stopped short. His mouth quite open in surprise and shock.

"Since you have nothing to say, my guess is the truth bothers you." Dessa stood. "To think I was dull enough to conceive that you and I had something to explore just makes me want to spit."

She turned and strode off, quite purposefully, toward her horse. Her back was ramrod straight.

Torrin lay down, his eyes closed. His breathing was fast, his mind racing. But he was racing to no answers that worked. If you could measure frustration, he was at the summit.

Untangling himself from the blanket and setting himself aright, he went to pack his horse. Not a word was spoken. He sensed tenseness in Dessa. He was baffled as to what to do, or what to say. Even what to think.

The roasts had been securely tied in a bundle and he helped Quillan retrieve them from the tree where they had hung out of reach from scavengers during the night. Having cooled nicely they would make a great treat for their hosts that evening.

Torrin was looking forward to Bartoly's evil whiskey. The clean feel with the harsh bite was what he needed now. He also felt that he could talk to Bartoly in ways that Quillan and certainly Dessa would not understand.

Heaving a great sigh, he hoisted himself up onto Samoot. Glancing over at Quillan, he noticed the big man smirking. He seemed to be almost laughing out loud.

            *   *   *

The clomping of the hooves had finally lulled Torrin into a trance where he could no longer wait to ask.

"Quillan?

"Yes"

"A few nights ago, just before we went to sleep, I had asked you why you were here. You told me you were the Guide." Torrin was actually talking to the back of Quillan's right ear, since the trail had gotten somewhat narrow. "What did you mean by that? Guide to what? Who? Where?"

Quillan's shoulders seemed to rise up as he breathed in a deep cleansing breath. But Torrin was not done with his question.

"And, for that matter, how come whenever I broach the subject of why I am here, Harold shuts down the conversation? He told me he would tell me what is going on and so far has avoided the subject completely."

"It's kinda a long story, and we are livin' it as we go. At least some of it. But let's talk tonight after dinner. I think Bartoly can help me make some sense of this, since I don't rightly understand it all. Harold did not tell me everything. Or of course, maybe he has and I don't rightly know what he means by it all. Some things confuse me too."

They had been riding pretty hard most of the day. A short break for lunch had been tense and quiet. At least for Torrin and Dessa. Quillan seemed to be in high spirits.

"At least tell me what you know, or understand," piped Torrin.

"What I understand is that we go right at that big oak, climb to the top of the hill and we are almost there," Quillan informed Torrin and he took off in a gallop.

Torrin was almost knocked off his saddle when Dessa came flying by him, following Quillan up the hill.

Torrin decided to let them go. He needed a little time by himself.

52.
Smithy

Sometimes when we speak of places nestled in the forest we refer to them as "quaint"—for Bartoly and Rebecca's homestead, that would prove to be an understatement. So for this part of the journey for our road-weary travelers, the trip would turn out to be worth it, and then some.

But, you had to get there first.

Finding the Bartoly homestead was no easy feat.

Assuming you knew where to go, once you moved through the thick forest, around some narrow crevasses and over a couple of ridges, you would be close. But you might never know. Bartoly had set up his security by being hopelessly hard to find.

As the threesome continued their trek, they came upon one fork in the well worn trail with three distinct options.

The first option led to the right. A well worn path that disappeared around a long bend into a green set of thick tall pine trees.

The second option was to continue on straight ahead. The path let upward over a rocky trail.

The third turned to the left. Its sandy bottom seemed well used in its shallow descent down the hill. No footprints were clearly evident, but you could tell, even without a lot of tracking experience, it was a well used trail.

None of these options were good, according to Quillan, unless you knew the trick.

"Trick?" inquired a curious Torrin.

"Yes," said Quillan with his now seemingly everlasting smirk.

"Well, it's pretty clear, one of these trails has to lead to their place. You said we were almost there." Torrin was somewhat incredulous. There seemed to be no end to the strangeness of this land.

"Or so you think my friend." Quillan sat on his horse, looking at the trail for a few minutes. Turning his gaze to Torrin, he said, "Which way would you go?"

"I have never been here before. I have no idea! Just get on with it."

"Oh, let me prove a point my friend. Let me prove a point." Quillan shot a glance at Dessa. She had been quietly sitting by. A quizzical smile on her face.

"Fine, we go straight," said an exasperated Torrin. The left is too obvious. Straight ahead or right, either is a crapshoot so I'll just pick one and we'll be on with it."

"Just no sense of adventure in ye?" Quillan glinted smirkily.

"Maybe I'm just a little tired and hungry and not into playing games right now," answered back an almost angry Torrin.

"What about you Miss Quiet?" Torrin looked at Dessa.

She cocked her head to one side. This was good. Very good. Quillan was doing her an immense favor. She wondered if he knew it. Was he that smart? Who knows? Most men weren't, she had discovered. But some men, just by nature did the right things at the right time.

Deep down, her heart had a burn for Torrin. It was a small glow, and one that was, shall we say, fragile. But nonetheless a glow. She knew he was a good man. Well, actually more boy than man, but he was

trainable. Maybe? She had known Darius certainly wasn't trainable—
hell, no one would have ever been able to domesticate him.

So watching Quillan put Torrin through his paces was not only
entertaining, it was educational for her. If she stuck this out, she would
need to know more about him. So she did what any woman would do at a
time like this.

She let him bury himself.

"Torrin. You decide. I'm sure it will be fine," she said with a
casual smile that belied her inner feelings.

With that Torrin spurred Samoot into a walk that was just fast
enough for the horse to deal with. Samoot was getting tired too and was
looking forward to some quiet grazing. He was hoping this trip would
soon be over.

He was close to right. But he would not get much time to graze.

* * *

The trail led up a steep slope and wound tightly through the trees.
The party moved steadily on, a fast pace being set by a tired and
somewhat frustrated "I am not in the mood for games" Torrin.

Quillan rode on with that everlasting smile painted on. Softly
humming to himself.

Dessa was beside herself, waiting for a surprise that she knew must
be coming. She did not have long to wait.

Presently, they came to another crossroads. This time, the path to
the left went up a steep rocky slope, the path straight ahead led to the
pines and the other sloped downhill.

Quillan sauntered up to Torrin.

"Well, where now?"

Torrin looked around. Heaving a large sigh, he said, "The left
takes us up higher. The right seems to go in the wrong direction and so I
vote for continuing straight ahead."

Smiling, broadly, Quillan said, "Look around. Anything familiar?"

"Forest. It all looks the same to …" Torrin came up short.

Stepping forward a few paces and bringing Samoot around, he looked carefully up, and then down the trail. Back and forth he swung his head.

"OK, cute trick. We're back to the same fork in the road. So left or right it must be. The trail we were just on loops around. Big deal."

So off they went. Left this time, ready to be done.

Again, Torrin was wrong. Or, shall we say, 'fooled by crafty maze?'

A short time later, they were back at the same spot, having descended down the rocky slope.

And they were back with a very tired, hungry, thirsty and now mad Torrin.

"How did this happen? Those trails did not separate before!" Torrin was shouting.

Quillan was smiling.

Dessa sat on Uta, her red eyebrows scrunched in mild confusion.

"When ye stop yer bellyaching and whining, I'll tell ya," said Quillan. He was amused at how easy this was.

"What?"

"Turn around and head up the trail. You lead," instructed Quillan.

"But we just went that way. Are you saying Bartoly has moved the trail since we went by?"

"Yer gettn' ta be impossible ye know. Ye must be gettn' tired," laughed Quillan.

Torrin turned his horse around gruffly, and maneuvered up the trail, Samoot's hooves making loud clunking sounds as they fairly sailed along on the rocks.

The trees brushed harshly back into Quillan's face as he tried to keep up with Torrin and Samoot's rapid ascent. He knew he could not carry this on much longer without losing Torrin.

"OK, stop!" yelled Quillan. "Ye missed it."

"Huh? What? Where?" Torrin was twisting in his saddle throwing himself about, looking for something he could not see.

"Ye just passed it."

"Passed what?" Torrin's red face did not hide his frustration. He was not used to, nor desirous, of being made fun of.

"Look to your right, behind ye."

Torrin looked.

"All I see is a big boulder and lots of long branches."

The afternoon sun was casting long dark shadows around them. The breeze moved the light and the dark in long lazy patterns of black, evergreen and sun that tricked the eye.

Quillan was done fooling around. Being a big man, he periodically listened to his stomach, at about now, his stomach had taken control of the situation. Both water, food and strong drink were high on the list of items that needed attention. It was time to move on.

"There is a cut in the rock, just wide enough for you and the steed to go through. Look closely."

Torrin looked, and sure enough, a rounded cleft in the rock, hardly lit, hard to see and hidden by long green pine branches was there.

"I'll be damned," he said quietly and steered Samoot through the cut.

Samoot was not impressed. The space was much too close, the light wrong and the trail wound through the rough rock in a raggedy fashion.

Torrin sensed his mount's uneasiness and gently urged him on with soft talk and gentle manipulations of the reins. This was not a good place to let a horse get spooked and get thrown or even thrashed about. There was no good place to land, and thrashing would just jumble him up against the rocks. He would probably get crushed along the sides or at best trampled underneath.

So the two of them moved on. Both settling down and knowing that they really needed each other right now and that the end of the trip was close at hand.

Torrin's toes scraped along the rock. Samoot snorted as Torrin kept squirreling in the saddle, trying to keep from scraping the rock.

"Oh don't give me your mouth, horse. I am just trying to keep from getting squashed here. Next time I'll walk through, or maybe I'll find a smaller horse."

"Sure," thought Samoot. "And I'll find a smarter rider," as he pressed Torrin's right side against the rock.

"Stop that ye damn horse. Behave or I'll make a tent out of ye."

Samoot just snorted and carried on. Glad he was older and wiser now. A few summers back, he might have hurt himself training Torrin in manners.

Soon the tight trail opened up. Both Samoot and Torrin relaxed. Their breathing trimmed down and as they turned a corner, they found themselves back in a thick dark wood. Tall trees all around. As they emerged from the rocks, the forest floor seemed to move as dozens of small animals dove for shelter, their quiet foraging interrupted.

Torrin pulled up to wait for Quillan, Dessa and Calandra to emerge.

It took a while. He was about ready to head back in when he heard them.

This time, Quillan was red in the face, Dessa was laughing.

"Just shut your mouth and keep quiet woman," snorted Quillan.

"Well certainly sir. I mean, I am supposed to listen to you, you are my big brother." The emphasis of the sentence was on the word "big." "Anyway, do you think I would make fun of a man who almost got squished on the rocks? No not me. I was fearful for your life. Goodness knows," Dessa clutched mockingly at her heart, "the horse could have been hurt."

Quillan glared at Dessa and then turned to Torrin. "Come, on, follow me."

They kept up a quick pace along a trail that had many options. First left, then right, then left, around large trees, boulders and along narrow ridges until they came to a steep slope.

Fresh dirt, loose and dusty, mixed with round stones covering the hill.

"What is this?" asked Torrin.

"Loose dirt and stones make it impossible to climb quickly," answered Quillan. "Get off and follow me. Plant your feet firmly as ye walk or ye'll go slidin' down.

Both Torrin and Dessa did as they were told. A few times, Torrin felt like he was about ready to hurl down the hill. But after a short while, they all stood at the top.

*   *   *

And as we had said, it was worth the trip.

If ever there was an idyllic setting, Bartoly and Rebecca had built it. And now lived in it. The story of their quiet hideaway would unfold slowly in the stories over the days, but in short, this is what our trio faced:

Of the main cabin, thick logs, piled high and long, protected the loving couple from the harshness of nature. When you walked out of the front door of the stalwart and cozy structure, you turned right and just a few paces away lay a majestic view. The long slope down a shallow hill to the valley floor was a serene winding walk on a well worn path. Wild flowers stood guard along the avenue. The buzzing of bees was occasionally disturbed by the clatter of birds going about their business. High mountain hills stood as sentinels of the scene. You would need to be able to fly to come in this way, through the valley. There were no natural entrances or exits that could be found. Bartoly had looked for a way in many a summer and winter. In fact, both he and Rebecca had. They hiked together in the slow careful exploration of the warm nature that surrounded them, and their stories would get wound up later for all to laugh at.

Often deer and other large game roamed in quiet solitude at the valley floor. Their relaxed movements were a testament to Bartoly's claim that he never hunted here nor found a reason for any to feel threatened in his valley. "All were welcome and safe here" would be his everlasting invitation to all who came, for whatever reason. In the evenings, that philosophy caused a steady stream of nature's travelers past the cabin. It was quite the parade of deer, fox, wolves, squirrels and even skunks (who seemed to know this was no place to get mad).

To the left stood the various outbuildings. A small barn for the horse, goat, noisy fowl and whatever other animal or animals were staying on (the threesome would discover a new horse; they called him Mattie). Rebecca was known for bringing home damaged creatures from the woods and nursing them back to health whenever possible.

A small smokehouse was dug into the ground near the barn. Its peaked and thatched roof was thick and mostly covered in dark brown, cracked thick mud for keeping the heat in. A large flat rock covered a wide, almost square hole about half way up the side. This allowed for venting the smoke if you needed to climb in the small door to retrieve a roast.

Just off the side of the cabin was the fruit cellar. Its deep cool interior was accessible from the inside of the cabin through the floor, or from the outside via the thick door of sturdy logs that lay flat on the ground.

The sun never shown on that fruit cellar door, helping to keep the inside cold. The depth of the cellar itself contributed to its effectiveness. Later, Torrin would remark as to Bartoly's genius in building so smart.

The smithy was attached to the back of the cabin. The forge of the smithy and the kitchen of the cabin shared the same flue and main stones in a large double sided fireplace. From a fuel standpoint, Torrin would become intimate with the art of creating pine charcoal. He would find it to be a very sticky sweet art, at best.

As they would discover at a much later time, the heat from the smithy added to a gentle warmth in the cabin that fought off the winter winds in an effective and homey way.

On the kitchen side, the cooking area was actually a small room. Benches along two sides of the big fireplace supplied enough space for up to eight to sit and eat, talk, drink or visit in warmth during the brutal winter.

However, straight ahead of the door, just outside, in this warm summer sunshine was the coup de grâce of the domain. Rebecca had planted not only an abundance of edible plants, but had managed to grow, quite on purpose, a wide teeming array of brightly colored flowers.

It was as if nature had smiled on the land and she supplied the brightness in the smile.

Bright red poppies waved a genuine welcome at the sunshine. Tall sunflowers opened their bright faces in welcoming splendor.

Dandelions grew in abundance. Their tough roots, according to Rebecca, were boiled or ground up and used for all sorts of ailments (although she did admit, even thought they were effective, they tasted like a horse's ass and you had to be pretty sick to use the stuff).

Cowslips in colors Dessa had never seen stood nodding in the breeze. Their vibrant long flowers bunched together and almost looked like a herd of flowing color.

Thick crowds of gentians stood in wild blue, pink, reds and yellows among large flat rock gardens climbing a small hill. It seemed that Rebecca not only loved the colors of the plants, but she planted for their practical use too. It seems that gentian tea was the only thing to help her stomach which gave her fits from time to time.

Against a large rocky outcrop, probably to shield them from the weather, a large husky village of Rhododendrons grew. They grew not only in thick abundance, but in voracious splendor. Bright whites, deep pinks and a mix of large blue and purple flowers gave an almost intoxicating palate of color to the eye. Their thick leaves and flowers stood tall and commanding, as if on alert. If anyone did not appreciate the beauty of nature, they would certainly do their best to change their mind.

Nature's last colors of the summer before winter set in were certainly beautiful and breathtakingly wonderful.

"She is an artist and commander of nature," breathed Quillan quietly. His head was cocked to one side. You almost expected a tear to run down his face at any time. He looked old for an instant.

After another moment, he said, "Come on, I'm hungry and more importantly thirsty."

They tied the horses up to a strong tree off to the side and ventured in.

* * *

Inside the cabin, warmness greeted the trio. Boiling soup in a large cauldron on the edge of a fire filled the air with appreciative kindness. Baking bread added an embrace to the warmness of the room and a heavy cluster of fresh cut flowers on the big oak table cast bright colors over the well made, yet sparse furnishings.

Near the back, almost up against the fireplace room, a woman with thick golden hair, loosed against her back, worked a potter's wheel. Her long thin shift was wet with sweat and clung tightly to her sinewy shoulders. Her left foot moved strongly upon a large wooden kick wheel. Its smooth motion told of its many, many turns over the years. Multi-colored layers of dry and cracked clay lay spread everywhere upon the surfaces telling their story too of the multiple pieces that birthed their way to the world upon the well used surfaces.

Soft humming came from the woman, its melody and rhythm somehow matched with the round about workings of the wheel. A relaxed and joyous air emerged from her soul as she worked the heavy piece at her very center.

Rich yellow sunlight streamed into the scene through high windows that had their thick shutters open and inviting to the fresh air. The strands of sun highlighted and matched her hair. Long crisp shadows brought depth to the picture, a setting that was as beautiful as it was overpowering to the senses.

A tall brown jug stretched up from the wheel head, as her hands moved in magical motion; long slender fingers moving with practiced precision along the tall piece, etching lines and filigree into just the right places.

As the trio approached, it became apparent that none of them wished to speak lest they disturb her almost magical time with the clay.

Stopping a few paces away, they all stood, quietly entranced by her deep oneness with the natural beauty of the work that made her sweat and turn so beautifully.

As if almost by fate, she held her hands at the bottom of the large piece and then slowly moved them up, providing a finish to work that only a master could accomplish. The thin wet rivulets of clay moved in solemn procession from her long strong fingers to the back of her hand then pulsed down her strong forearm, leaving her body in a steady stream of heavy drips to form thick brown puddles on the floor beneath her elbows.

As her hands left the piece, she sat back heavily on a smooth stool, her head tipped to one side, watching the work spin slowly on the wheel head. Her arms seemed tired as they lay at her side. Their natural pinkness masked by the warm brown of the clay.

"Quillan, it never ceases to amaze and delight me what nature gives us and what we are blessed to do with it," she said. "Are ye just gonna stand there and stare or are ye gonna help me move this over to the drying area?"

Her golden face turned toward the trio. With the sight of the three she gasped a mild "Oh goodness," and a wide smile lit her happy face.

In a show of unbridled glee she said, "You all came, this is just so wonderful!" She clapped her hands together, with only a dull brown thud emerging, since they were covered with a thick layer of now dry clay.

Torrin looked at Quillan with a deep puzzling frown. "What does she mean? You all came? She has never met Dessa." Dessa had arrived after Bartoly and Rebecca had hiked out of Journey's encampment.

Without so much as missing a heartbeat, Quillan's response was firm, yet kind. "She knows, just like a lot of the people of the valley know."

With that, Quillan ran to Rebecca and gave her a large hug and brotherly kiss on the cheek.

"You look radiant you evil terrible woman!" he exclaimed loudly and they both shared a hearty laugh.

Rebecca explained she had heard of Dessa's arrival at Journey through customers who had happened by the smithy and ceramics studio. At once the uneasy tenseness in the room seemed to vanish. Torrin, who had felt like the whole world was watching his life unfold before he knew it was unfolding, slowed his breathing.

Quillan just cocked his head and smiled a wide grin, as if he knew something.

"Well, where is that lazy husband of yours?" inquired Quillan after the formal introductions had been made.

"Oh, I would guess he is in with the cow and the horse," said a now radiantly happy Rebecca.

"Cow? Horse?" asked Quillan.

"Yes, one of our better customers had Bartoly slaving all summer on an entire barrel of nails, hooks and farm equipment. Someone from up the valley whose son decided to stay and work the farm with him. They are building a cabin and needed all sorts of goods," Rebecca gave a great sigh. "The milk is wonderful and sweet and this fall we don't have to carry everything to the festival. Mattie is a wonderful steed."

"Mattie? What kind of a horse is named Mattie?" sneered Quillan good naturedly.

"The kind that I get to name, and anyway, she is a mare!" Rebecca stuck her tongue out at Quillan who made quite a show of grabbing for it, but almost lost a finger in the process.

"Well, then let's go and find the old man," exclaimed Quillan. "I'm hungry and thirsty, but not so much so as to drink without him. I hate it when he whimpers."

The smile never left Rebecca as they first transferred the tall damp jug to the drying area from her well worn wheel and then ventured out to the serenity of the out of doors. Of course, they all left the house with full mugs of cool ale from the cellar. But Rebecca admonished them to keep it from their lips until after trying the milk. It would spoil the treat.

As they walked, Rebecca's hair dried as well as the shift. You could see the goose bumps rise on her arms as she cooled from the hard wet work at the wheel. As she dried she seemed to almost glide along in a serene kind of way; at peace with the place.

Quillan looked unabashedly at the strong lithe woman who led them on and thought Bartoly a lucky man. He wondered if he was jealous. Maybe it was envy? Anyway, since his task was close to complete, he thought it time to start looking around for a woman himself.

The thought had just never crossed his mind since his mother had sent him out those many springs before. He was clearly duty bound.

Torrin looked at Rebecca as she dried and thought she might catch cold. It dawned on him that he was seeing things differently now. Just not quite sure what.

Dessa wondered if she could be so unembarrassed with all her body parts in full understanding of those around, the shift was thin and cut loosely, revealing. As she watched Rebecca walk, free and happy, it dawned on her that maybe Rebecca had it right. Dessa felt suddenly somewhat trapped by her clothes.

They found Bartoly in the barn carefully finishing up tending the animals for the day. There were quite a few more than what Quillan had remembered from two summers ago when he had last ventured here. Most glorious though was the cow and the magnificent Mattie the horse. The cow, as Bartoly exclaimed, was named Jacqualde.

Carefully stowing the pints of ale so the goat would not steal them, the little crew made their way over to the barn's newest residents.

"Rather tall and fat," Torrin wondered aloud, "How had she made it through the stones? It would be a terrible place to get stuck."

"Well, I think she was not so very pregnant when she arrived," said Bartoly. "We were wondering how we would get her on, seeing as the only bull around here comes from Rebecca (she punched him in the arm). But lo and behold, she has grown fatter each day."

"So she came to you in this blessed state?" inquired Torrin.

"Yes, and it is fitting for all the work I did to get her. I hope she has a bull so we can keep breeding. I don't want to try and get a bull in here any other way," Bartoly said with a grin.

Rebecca put her arms around Jacqualde's huge neck and gave her a big loving hug. A long, thick and wonderfully pink tongue streamed out of the happy cow and gave Rebecca a glorious slwap.

"Oh, she thinks she's a puppy!" said a slightly bemused Dessa.

Mattie the horse was brown and black. She almost smiled when she looked your way. She was a genuine gem of a horse. You got the sense though, that Mattie did not only like Rebecca, she adored her. Dessa felt as though she was in the presence of a guard wolf when Rebecca got close to Mattie.

Quite the relationship, thought Dessa.

"And who my dear, are you?" inquired Bartoly looking squarely at Dessa. Then, taking on the false airs of snobbery and stuck up royalty, he said, with his nose quite in the air, "It seems I have a new guest I have not met and my insolent wife fails to remember her manners by ignoring both of us and hugging the cow!"

This comment commanded another punch in the arm before Rebecca bowed low with a great swirling of the thin shift that she wore, and introduced Dessa as, "May I introduce to you, my great mighty and most powerfully firm lord, the great crusader of all that walks upright and beseeches the glory of nature; the great and wonderfully mysterious Dessa, late of Journey and hence from parts untold."

Dessa, taking her cue, bowed low in the most feminine curtsy she could muster, considering she was wearing breeches and a quiver of arrows as well as her favorite knife. She felt all of a sudden very overdressed, too terribly male and somewhat out of place for who she was (but more for whom she desired to be). It had been a long time since she had spent any time with a woman near her own age and one who was of the same temperament, so to speak. She hoped she and Rebecca would get some time together.

It would happen, but not what she thought.

          *   *   *

Jacqualde's milk was wonderful. Just as advertised. The warm streams that filled the bucket were thick and sweet. Since she was now again with child, she would soon be bursting.

After sharing the milk experience, they retrieved their ale, and made a mighty toast to a wonderful future. The group shared a good laugh at the ale mustaches they all shared. It was a good start to what would be a most wonderful evening. An evening of new friends, reunions and revelation.

The men set off to take care of the horses. Quillan figured they deserved a good graze in the meadow after a firm brushing and water.

The ladies retired to the house to ready dinner and to stuff the smokehouse with the venison roasts that needed further curing.

However, Rebecca announced to Dessa that it was time for her to "look like a woman and relax some." What with all these men here, you didn't want to get them confused with too many people running around in breeches.

53.
An Evening to Remember

After Dessa and Rebecca had finished hanging the roasts in the smokehouse, Rebecca set the bread out to cool, checked the soup and announced it was time for the two of them to get rightfully clean before eating.

Dessa had retrieved her clothes from the big pack Calandra carried and found a light gown for the evening. It was one Karina had given her and she looked forward to the freedom the skirts offered (to say nothing of the wonderfully erotic touch of the smooth fabric gliding along her thighs as she walked).

Rebecca led the way to a relatively private and humble stream that gurgled lightly over smooth stones and dropped gracefully into a medium size pool. The edges of the pool had been built up with rocks and dirt giving its natural shallowness more depth for bathing and clothes washing.

Before they began their rite of washing, two large earthenware jugs were carefully filled with cool clear water. Rebecca declared she had been thirsty very often lately and wanted a good supply of water around.

Both women washed with luxurious slowness in the cool water. Rebecca commented that it had been days since she had felt clean. Gardening, taking care of the animals and trying to get all the pottery done before the last firing of the summer had kept her busy.

Dessa empathized with Rebecca. Her last good bathing had been at the pool the day she had found out that Quillan was her half brother. As she undressed, she felt as though she were peeling her clothes off. Two long days on the trail had not helped. And most of all, she was glad to be out of the breeches!

As the soap melted the dirt, dust and smoky smell from her hair she could feel her spirits lift. To add more grace, Rebecca had pressed petals from her many flowers into the soap. It made for a heavenly scent. Dessa washed her hair twice, knowing it would flow like sunshine down her back once dry. It was growing back, a little at a time. She looked forward to its length returning. She missed the feeling of its movement behind her head breezing softly across her shoulders.

The two sat on thick buckskin mats upon a large flat rock in the late sun, letting what they hoped was not one of the last warm breezes of summer dry them.

"You are a good looking woman Dessa. I daresay that Torrin is a lucky man. I hope he treats you well." Rebecca said these words with no malice or any hint of hidden agenda.

Dessa was sure she was not fishing for answers. The woman sounded sincere. And all Dessa did for a few moments was look at Rebecca with what looked like a glaze of puzzlement.

"What makes you think Torrin and I are a pair?" she asked.

"Well, the way he looks at you for starters," said Rebecca, face aglow in the reddish sun. Then she added, "And not to mention there seems to be an energy of sorts between the two of you that one quite cannot miss."

Dessa sighed, "Yes, I suppose there is. I'm just not sure if I want to explore it. Something isn't quite right and I can't put my finger on it. Something in my head is sounding off warning bells. But there is almost nothing to confirm that low unearned concern."

"Almost nothing?" asked Rebecca.

"This morning, he was dreaming of some girl named Gwendolyn. He had himself quite worked up into a passion. If I didn't care for him, it might have been somewhat funny." Pausing for a moment, she then finished with, "But I didn't see it funny at all."

"Gwen always wanted what she did not deserve and what she could not have. Also she was not interested in investing the time and energy it took to do things right. She wanted things right now. Her way!" Rebecca bit her lip. "May she rest in peace; goodness knows she was not at peace when she walked the earth. She was a terror. A right terror!"

"You seem almost angry at what happened," said Dessa.

"Well, you see, she was my younger sister," Rebecca's eyes suddenly turned very dark. "She had been warned that Torrin was off limits. She knew the rules. But she never played by the rules."

An evil lurking silence ensued for a moment. Both women watching the water, letting their emotions dissipate. After a while, Dessa turned to Rebecca, laid her hand on her shoulder and said, "I'm very sorry."

Rebecca turned to face her new friend, took a deep breath and just nodded.

Rebecca's hand was gripping tight into the rough fur of the skin where they sat. Her knuckles showed white. "I'm just glad Torrin was not hurt. That would have been worse for all of us."

"What do you mean?"

"I'll let Bartoly explain. He has spent much more time with Harold and Karina. Let's get dressed and wow those evil weak men with our wily women ways."

Rebecca said that last bit with a forced smile. A smile that said there was much more to tell, but one that also meant she was not ready to tell it.

    *   *   *

That evening the four of them ate a feast fit for king, queen, court and jester. The soup was thick and filling, the bread hearty and warm with a chewy golden crust. The ale gave way to Bartoly's special brew after dinner and the lot of them relaxed in the main part of the cabin since it was not cold enough to require sitting near the fireplace.

Laugher and joy filled the air. The hammer throw stories were repeated for Dessa's sake, at least three times. When Torrin told of the incident with the flies, Bartoly was buzzing around the cabin quite happily flying with his arms outstretched. Then when he ran between Torrin and Dessa, he dropped to the ground, feinting that he was burning.

Rebecca did remind him that he only wished he were that "hot," so to speak.

Even with all the drink and fun, both Dessa and Torrin seemed to stay sober. An unsaid agreement between them seemed to say that they should be alert should Bartoly be forthcoming about their story.

Finally Torrin could stand it no longer. After an outburst of ribald laughter stemming from a story of a time when Quillan had thrown the hammer and split his breeches up the back for all to see, he stood up with a tense look on his face.

"Bartoly," he said with a voice as firm as he could muster.

"Whashh!?" came the somewhat sloshy reply.

"Can you please tell us what that devil the story is with Dessa and me?"

Bartoly put down his mug in a slow, sort of careful and deliberate way. He folded his large, strong callused hands in his lap and then looked down, as in a trance.

"Bar…," Torrin started.

Instantly Bartoly's hand went up to silence the young man, "Just hold yer 'orses."

Presently he said, "Sit down, please."

He started slowly. He started in an uneven rhythm. But, he started…

"Harold and Karina have, for as many summers as I have known them, talked of their time coming. The talked of it with a passion I still do not understand."

Bartoly held out his mug and Rebecca took it to fill.

"I am the luckiest man alive. She is beautiful, she takes care of me and…"

"Bartoly, the story. What about Karina and Harold?" said a perplexed Torrin.

"It seems that Harold and Karina showed up on the same day at Journey, from completely separate places, and being altogether consummate strangers. The way Harold tells it, it was love at first sight. At least for him." Bartoly smiled.

"I guess he was not just smitten, he was in a state of absolute frenzied love." Bartoly had found his stride now. He loved to tell a good story and so he was going to make the most of it. He drank a good swig from his mug, stretched his arms and then looked around. Satisfied he had everyone's attention, he went on.

"Karina did not know he existed, when you listen to Harold. Something tells me she knew just how to manage him way back then too. This I have conjectured," said Bartoly with his hand raised high, "since when her troupe left, she stayed behind. Guess she faked a sprained foot or something."

"Well, the two spent the summer helping out at Journey and getting to know each other. Mind you, Journey was just a bit of its present size. I bet Harold has built it over five times and doubled it every time. You ask him to show you the old parts and he'll tell you what he's done. Pretty impressive!"

"Not to sound ungrateful for the background information," piped up Torrin. "But what does that have to do with Dessa and me?"

"Oh, thas shimple." The alcohol was beginning to take effect and Torrin was afraid Bartoly would pass out before getting to the meat of the story.

Dessa shot Torrin a look that said, 'This better get solved soon or I'm heading out.'

"You shee," Bartoly plowed on, "As the story goes, once Harold and Karina were solidly in love, the proprietor of Journey said to them, as Harold tells it…," at this point Bartoly stood up, put his hand out like an orator might, and spoke in a tone like an old man delivering news to children.

"Kids, me and the misses been wantn' you here for the last few summers, goodness knows it's time. You are the ones. Journey is yours." Bartoly shot his audience a thin lipped smile with his teeth gripped tight. "And at that, he and his wife walked; yes I say walked, into the woods and were never heard from again."

"That happened many, many, many, summers ago," Bartoly sat down.

"So if Torrin and I decide we are in love, they hand us Journey?" Dessa asked in a blunt sort of way.

"Do'n be ashking me, I just was telln ye waush happened baafore." Bartoly stood back up and with definite drunken purpose in his step, he strode to the high bed he and Rebecca shared and collapsed heavily on the top.

Dessa and Torrin looked at each other, looked at Rebecca and then looked at Quillan as if searching for answers. None came.

Quillan hastily said "Don't be giving me the evil eye, I was told to bring ye here. I did my job."

Their eyes landed on Rebecca. She just shrugged her shoulders and said, "First I've time I have heard that story."

Torrin stood up and walked to the door, opened it and left the cabin. In just two heartbeats he was back at the door, looked in and said in a forced but kindhearted tone that belied his frustrations, "Dessa, would you care to join me for a walk?"

This Dessa knew was a turning point. If what she felt was true, this would definitely test those feelings. "I would be happy to join you." With that, she rose and walked out the door with an all of a sudden, somewhat tenuous Torrin.

They walked in silence. But they walked together. They stopped at the tree line just at the top of the valley and sat down on the soft pine needles.

The moon was full and bright. The steady warm breeze had cooled and gently washed through the air. Dessa could feel the perspiration dry on the back of her neck as it blew across. Wisps of her now dry hair blew in her face. She felt not so much powerless, but out of control. It was one thing to have to leave home. Quite another to know you are in line for a job that you knew nothing about, let alone didn't know if you wanted anyway. And then so much more for others to tell you that you had met the man you must love and there seemed few choices (and, with a man she hardly knew?).

Torrin felt as if he was coming unglued. Being taken from his home by unknown forces that he did not understand; this he could handle, because he could eventually let his mother and father know he was all right. But being told that his destination in life was to become an innkeeper? This was not what royalty was made for. Also, being told who was for him was not in the cards he had planned to deal for himself. He had planned to be the king of his father's castle at the right time, even if his sister was in line for the throne. This thought had bothered him on and off for many summers, but now he wondered, was this predestined?

Torrin decided he was rather pissed off. But at the same time, this girl next to him made him feel somewhat secure and tenuous.. It was not the kind of attraction he was expecting. Although, he was not sure what he was expecting, since he really had not thought about it much. Talking it out would help.

Dessa's mind was running as a fury too. It occurred to her that in the space of one summer, she had gone from princess to killer. From the favorite daughter of her father's kingdom to the possible future wife of an unsuspecting proprietor of the Journey Inn that held some sort of mystery. To say nothing of communicating with and commanding animals?

Dessa decided she needed some time to sort it all out and put things in perspective. She needed time to think.

Too bad neither knew quite one third of the story. Harold had told Bartoly much more, but Bartoly had put himself into a condition as to forget to tell those parts.

* * *

"Torrin?"

"Yes?"

"How did you come to be at Journey? I mean…," Dessa was chopping up her words. She was not sure what she was saying, "what events caused you to come here?"

Torrin let out a low whistle. "If I tell you the truth, you'll just laugh at me."

"You think so! You have no idea why I am here or the events I had to endure to get here," Dessa said exasperated.

"Well, it certainly can't be any worse than my story."

"What would you like to bet?"

Torrin looked at the young lady sitting next to him. He thought of all the women who had surreptitiously solicited him at the kingdom. How false they all seemed. How shallow. Maybe that was the difference here. This was not a Gwendolyn who was after him; this was an independent, free thinking woman who was free of the bonds of needing a man to fulfill her. This thought all of a sudden terrified him and enthralled him all at once. He would have to progress on his own merits, not on her needs.

She asked what he was thinking.

He truthfully told her, "There is no way I can put the thoughts running through my head into words that make sense right now. It just somehow does not make sense enough to say, but it is important."

She believed him.

"You first. Tell me your story," Dessa said quietly.

And so he began. He started slowly, trying to remember all the important events. It seemed so long ago. Yet, it seemed like so little had really happened this long warm and very different summer.

Then, he started talking fast. He left no detail out that mattered. Even Gwendolyn and the bath. He decided to tell her everything. Including his desire to go home. When he was done, he felt drained, he felt vulnerable and he felt alive.

Dessa sat still and quiet for a short while. Torrin looked at her and said, "Well?"

And then it was her turn. It gushed out, it spilled out. The people, the feelings, the nastiness of Darius, the wonder of Phlial and his sons.

Her killing the wolf, her killing Haphethus. When she was done, she was spent. She was drained. She was sobbing, but she was now even more free.

Torrin's arm wrapped around her shoulder. They leaned close and partook in the intimacy of two people who share a past that locks them together in some mysterious way. Such different pasts but so much the same. Both of royalty who had everything they ever wanted and then lost it all.

No one knows how long they sat that way, but in time, their eyes met. There was nothing but the shallow moonlit night to illuminate their faces.

Torrin's eyes felt humid and he could feel the flush of Dessa's check against his.

Dessa felt the way she imagined it should feel. She finally felt like she could trust the arm and its owner around her shoulder. He was not here under false pretenses. It felt safe.

So, as is often the case, nature took its due course. The sharing, the need, the warmth of the embrace, the caring and the feelings all bubbled up to a head. Nature moved their lips toward each other in that unknown, unexplained but necessary need to kiss a person you care deeply about.

Dessa's head slid back down onto Torrin's chest, her face looked up at his. He saw in the moonlight the most beautiful, fragile and strongest woman he had ever encountered. The passion that they now felt for each other was overwhelming. He needed to kiss her, to hold her, to feel safe with her. Yet, after Gwendolyn, he was not only afraid, he was terrified, lest something awful happen.

But the true deep need of his desire and feelings overwhelmed him. He lifted her head toward his and lowered his lips toward hers.

Flashes of lightning started to spurt around the edges of his eyes. A deep flush of heat began to well up from between them.

The arm that held Dessa's back suddenly felt hot; she swore she felt the earth tremble.

As their faces came close, the intense heat in their shared breathing became like a fire. A fire that nature needed. They had a mutual need to close the gap between them.

"Come quick, Rebecca is throwing up bad; I'm afraid she is gonna die!" came the sudden and terrified shouting from a running and breathless Quillan.

The bare space of a blade of new spring grass had separated their lips. The toxic blast of the interruption was immediate and final for the night. The moment was lost, but only for now.

Both knew that they would find the time to recapture this moment and move on without interruption.

They stood quickly and ran.

*   *   *

"What do you think? Have we made the right choice?"

"You have asked me that over and over and over. Of course we have you dolt." Karina kissed Harold on the forehead. "After all these long summers and winters, aren't you tired? Do you really want to go on forever?"

"I will miss this so much. I will miss you," he said as he entered her slowly with a low moan.

Karina's legs convulsed and then she squeezed him in her oh so special way.

Harold held her close as they made love more than had sex. It was a coupling that they had shared for such a long and glorious time. It was a part of their gift. He hoped Torrin and Dessa would be so lucky as to share the same deep level of never ending passion. To be with someone so closely, to know no bounds and to give yourself completely to them was something hard to express, but forever to cherish.

Afterward, as they lay there in each other's arms, the heat of their bodies wrapping them in a warm memory of this time together, Karina said, "Yes, I will miss this too. Just as I will miss it all. But, it is time Harold. It is time."

"Yes, I know. And I don't have the energy to face the changes I sense are coming. I feel as though we lived through the easy times." Harold heaved a large sigh and held her close, their deep love and devotion melding them as one.

He did not see the large tears running down her face, nor did he notice how much older she looked. He just loved her more than the world itself.

* * *

Torrin, Dessa and Quillan ran as fast as they could. When they got close to the cabin, they could hear a terrible retching coming from inside.

Rebecca was on her knees in front of a bucket. Her hair was covered in thick wet sweat; her hands were clutched tightly to the sides of the bucket. It was almost like she needed to hold on for fear of falling off.

Torrin stood in shock, not sure what to do. Dessa knelt beside her new friend and started whispering that everything would be fine.

Dessa stood, turned to the two frozen men and started giving orders.

"Torrin, boil water and find some herb tea. Don't make it too hot, but get it now."

Torrin made for the kitchen.

"Quillan, open a couple of windows and get some air in here, then build up the fire so she can keep warm; I don't want her getting cold."

Quillan, knowing when it was time to be responsible, moved fast.

Dessa knelt back down next to the now quieter Rebecca. She had either gotten up whatever was bothering her or the fact that help was here was calming her.

Maybe it was a combination of both. Whichever it was, she felt, looked and seemed somewhat better.

After a while, Dessa stood Rebecca up and wrapped a soft blanket of lightly spun wool around her shoulders. Walking her over to the table, she sat her down. Rebecca's face went white looking at the leftover food and dishes scattered about. Dessa quickly made them disappear and put Quillan and Bartoly to work cleaning up.

By now the tea was ready and seemed to help. Rebecca shivered slightly under the blanket but then let out a slow smile. She tried to wave off the crew of attendants, saying she was fine.

None of them believed it, but were relieved to see she was coming back.

Dessa ordered Bartoly to be wrapped in a blanket and to sleep somewhere else.

Rebecca put up a show of resistance, weakly saying that the two of them had not been separated for ten summers.

It was no use. Dessa knew they both needed uninterrupted sleep. One night would not hurt them. Goodness knows she was getting by and it was doing her no harm for now.

* * *

The younger brother of Gaerwn's twin sons Darius and Haphethus, who went by the name Chadus watched the dying fire with a scowling hatred on his scarred face. A scarred face that could only come from many winters and summers of living a wretched, deceitful and viscous life.

The cool night breeze blew the smoke in small round tornados that periodically surrounded him and his rapacious gang. He paid it no heed. He did not see or ponder at the wonder of the stars overhead twinkling through the whisper of smoke. He felt his eyes burning hotter than the embers that glowed at the bottom of the pit. Every time he witnessed the glory of this kind of evening, it reminded him of his first time when that snot Kael had finally gotten his due.

No one forgets their first time.

Nearby, the withering moans of the young man scrawled painfully on the ground seeped into the night air. His broken bones made it impossible to move, and he could only watch helplessly as his new place and his parent's old cabin collapsed bit by bit in such a short time in a shower of sparks. Two full lifetimes had been spent building it all and now in just an evening, it was gone.

All gone.

The animals, his parents, his life, his plans, his future. His dreams.

Eventually the injuries took their toll and he succumbed to a blessed and painless death. His last thought though was that he had failed. Failed all who had come before him and all those that might not come because of his actions. He deserved to rot in hell for what he had done. He deserved torment for eternity.

Because he had told.

He had told a secret.

54.
Convergence

"Just eat a few mouthfuls of bread; you'll feel better," Dessa promised Rebecca.

Rebecca sat at the table, slowly nibbling on the bread in front of her.

The cabin was quiet. After a good breakfast the men had set out to gather firewood and make a batch of charcoal. Bartoly had used most of his stock this summer heating the steel to make the nails and farm equipment.

"What do you think happened to me?" asked Rebecca.

"Something you ate? Drink too much?" came the reply from the kitchen were Dessa was punching down bread dough.

"Well, we all ate the same thing and none of you got sick. And, I only had one mug of ale. I had changed to water after that. I was not drinking that scary stuff my husband brews." Sitting up a little straighter, "Although, I usually like it." She gave Dessa a smile.

"Bad water? I don't know. You're OK now though." It was more of a question than a statement.

"Yes, a little weak, but I will survive. I do say though, I am jealous of that man I sleep with. He can drink like a fish and then work the next day like nothing had happened. He is made of iron, he is!"

Dessa put a steaming mug of gentian tea in front of Rebecca. It seemed to do the trick, judging from the smile she got in return.

*   *   *

For the next couple of days, there was much to do, much to explore and good times to be had.

Unfortunately for Torrin and Dessa, they did not have a chance for any time together alone. It was not on purpose or by any forethought of malice on anyone's part. It just turned out that way.

The forced separation, so to speak, gave them a chance though to collect their thoughts.

As Dessa watched Torrin work, she was not only impressed, but felt more and more comfortable. Even when he came back sticky with pine pitch from making the pine charcoal (it burns hotter and cleaner according to Bartoly) he was affable and friendly.

Torrin quite admired Dessa's warmth and sociability. She fit right into the group, working away, chatting well with Rebecca and not holding back whatsoever, saying she was a princess or something and the labors were above her. For royalty, she did not seem to take on airs.

When he asked Quillan his thoughts about her, Quillan said, "Be careful boy, she is my sister. I am more worried about her happiness than yours."

Torrin's fierce look caught Quillan by surprise and so he added, "Of course, I want you both to be happy. If it is to be, the both of you of course. Well, you see…" Quillan stopped, thought for a moment and then said, "Hell, you decide. Just be nice to her or I'll beat ye senseless."

Torrin, who by now figured saying anything might not be wise, just nodded and walked away.

Quillan decided the boy was well worth keeping around. He seemed trainable.

*   *   *

They planned a hunt early on the morning of the sixth day. By now the ironwork for Harold and Journey were complete, a host of firewood had been put up and the end-of-the-season gardening had been attended to by Dessa and Rebecca, who now sported dirt brown hands (and numerous scratches).

Quillan announced that they would be heading back to Journey the next day since the cold winter storms would be brewing up anytime and they needed to get back to help prepare for the fall festival to celebrate the harvest. There was lots of work to be done for the festival as well as preparing for the oncoming cold and snow.

As the morning sky broke just enough light to see, the party rode hard down the valley trail toward the hunting grounds toward the mountains, sans Rebecca.

She had decided to stay behind and put up a few more pots. Anyway, she was a little tired and wanted to have a quiet day.

As they rode, the dawning sun blistered in powerful reds over the edges of the mountain's flaming color down on the changing trees. The crackling of dry leaves in the breeze had replaced the soft filtering of the wind as it brushed those same leaves that were such a part of summer.

It was a test of talent, mostly with Dessa and Bartoly showing off to each other. Since they were the better sharpshooters, Quillan and Torrin drove game toward them. It was a bountiful morning.

After gathering a couple of large fat turkeys that had almost gotten away by taking flight, the three of them sat down to take a break. The warm sun, they knew, would not last, and they sat with their faces turned toward it.

Dessa felt a tug at her arm and a finger on her lips. She opened her eyes, blinking from the bright sunshine and saw Torrin's face. He had a finger to his lips too and then slowly pointed toward a large and impressive buck, grazing just a hundred paces away. In all its magnificence, the meat there would feed Rebecca and Bartoly for the winter.

Dessa slowly turned, pulled an arrow from the quiver and nocked it. As if she were a breath of warm air upon a down feather, she rose silently, gracefully and smoothly to a deadly and efficient shooting position. Quillan and Bartoly were in awe at her grace, strength and focused determination.

Pulling back the bowstring, you could see the tension in her arm, yet she did not shake, she was as steady as a rock.

"No!" wailed Torrin painfully. "No!"

The arrow went wild, the buck was startled, and instantly took flight.

Dessa's furious look descended upon Torrin until she saw him.

He was on his knees, his hair clutched in his hands, his head almost on the ground and he was wailing hard.

"No! No! No!"

"What is it?" asked Quillan kneeling next to the tormented young man.

"It feels just like when Haphethus showed up, like when the flies were coming!" Torrin was screaming through clenched teeth. His eyes were watering, his nose running; he was tearing at his hair. "But this time it hurts. This time it's stronger. It's evil coming this way. Bad evil! We have to stop it!"

He looked wild eyed at the other three. Sweat poured off his face.

"Rebecca!" Bartoly shouted.

Quillan turned toward Torrin to ask, "Can you ride?" But Torrin was already halfway up his horse and heading up the trail after Bartoly and Dessa.

"Cach," muttered Quillan as he lumbered toward his horse.

* * *

Bartoly felt like he was riding in muck. He knew Mattie was flying as fast as her frenzied state could muster, but it was not fast enough. Fear clutched his heart.

He practically fell jumping from the teeming mount as he came upon the cabin.

Something was wrong, he could feel it. Something told him, as unbelievable as it might seem, Torrin was right. He hoped deep in his heart that he would find his love sitting at her wheel. Racing in through the door, he found the cabin empty.

But not untouched.

The place was a wreck. Pots smashed, furniture crushed, blankets torn.

And then what he saw made his heart sink. A pile of still wet clay sat on her wheel, the remnants of a soup bowl lay in torn chaos upon the gray brown surface. And a handprint was on one side with the distinct look that the hand had been dragged through the clay.

He recognized the impression the hand had left behind. There was no doubt about it, it was Rebecca's.

Dessa came running in, looked around and shouted, "Where is she?"

Bartoly said, "I don't see her, she's not here." He pointed to the clay.

Dessa ran out, calling for Rebecca. As she ran toward the barn, Torrin and Quillan showed up and followed.

The barn doors were open. It was too quiet. Dessa all of a sudden noticed that the chickens and goat were gone. She rushed in and what she saw made her gag.

Rebecca was hung upside down, tied at the ankles with her face toward the door. Her fingertips were just touching the floor. She was naked and pale white. A stark contrast to the large grotesque pool of blood that had started to soak into the dirt below. The blood came from a long slash that started at both knees, met at the center of her stomach and ended at her chin.

Dessa reached her and lifted her up. Just behind she heard Quillan bellow, "Up!"

Torrin knew immediately what to do. He leapt up onto Quillan's broad shoulders, covering a height he could only accomplish in an adrenaline induced state, extracted his knife and cut Rebecca down.

Dessa carefully and gently laid the girl on the floor. A fierce rage building in her, at the same time her heart was breaking.

Bartoly ran in shouting, "She is not in the garden or anywhere..." he stopped in his tracks. The scene before him was not registering in his brain. His love was cut from head to knee. Blood was everywhere; her ankles were tied with rope.

He just stood stock still, afraid to breathe lest it all became real.

Torrin jumped off Quillan's back and the big red man said sharply to Dessa, "Is she breathing?"

Dessa put her ear down to Rebecca's blood caked mouth and listened.

"Barely."

Quillan's gaze fell on Dessa. He then peered at Torrin. Finally, he simply said, in a voice that could not be mistaken as a question or a statement, but as a direct order, "Go outside, kiss each other now. And mean it."

With that he ran toward the back of the barn.

Dessa put Rebecca down as gently as she dared and stood up. Both Torrin and Dessa looked at each other in deep puzzlement.

"Now, dammit! Now! If ye want te save her, do it!" yelled a ferociously mad yet frightened red man who was running back from rummaging through the pack Calandra had carried, with the jar that Torrin recognized at Karina's salve for wounds. It was the stuff she had put on his leg after the bout with the blasted dragon.

Torrin and Dessa ran away from their fallen friend past a gaping Bartoly and out into the barnyard.

"I don't understand this," said Torrin, "But somehow it's real. I don't know what's going on…"

With that Dessa grabbed his head, threw her other arm around him and kissed him fiercely.

*   *   *

Harold clutched at his chest.

"What is it?" came the question from an alarmed Karina.

"I don't know, but evil is around. It's far away, but I can feel it."

"Sound the horn?"

"No, not yet. Not just yet."

*   *   *

Sparks flew before his eyes.

Her muscles felt torn apart.

They both felt like they were burning. The fire was inside. Outside. All around them. Thunder, deafening thunder, pounded inside their heads.

As their tongues met, it was as if a bolt of lightning had struck them both. They clung tighter to each other, the madness of it was exhilarating, intoxicating, overwhelming. Blue sparks of energy radiated from their feet onto the dirt, small sticks burst into flames and then just as quickly died out. Sweat poured off their bodies, soaking them.

They both trembled, not in fear but with an enormous energy that had either been used or created, you could not tell. Neither was quite certain what they were feeling, but for sure, whatever it was, it was powerful and not to be reckoned with.

The melding was not complete by any means, but it had started, and it was potent.

As they pulled back, eyes wide with questions, they felt different. It was a difference that would take some time getting use to and a longer time to truly understand. They did not know the power they had yet, but would soon begin to find out.

Quillan and Bartoly came from the barn.

"Well?" said Quillan.

"I don't know, it was…" began Torrin.

"Never mind, more about that later. I will tend to Rebecca. You both go with Bartoly and hunt these bastards down. They can't be far."

                    *   *   *

As they ran to the cabin, Torrin was wondering why.

Dessa's mind was focused on winning. How many were there? Where would be a good place to attack? Suddenly wary, she looked around lest there be an ambush waiting. Then it occurred to her that if they were around, Torrin would be in whatever painful state he got around evil. That early warning system could prove to be valuable.

They entered the mess of the cabin and heard grunting and muttering coming from over by the bed.

Bartoly had moved the bed and torn up a couple of floorboards. He was bent over pulling up a great assortment of weapons.

In a terrible line of prospective destruction, he had laid out four long broadswords, a couple of light multi-ball flails, two long war hammers and four leather belts filled with closely attached, long silver daggers .

"Put on a belt, each of ye," said the panting, sweaty man. "Take a broadsword too."

After they had all attached the belts and hefted a broadsword Bartoly handed a flail and hammer to Torrin. He looked at Dessa, then knelt down and pulled a large oilskin bundle from the hole in the floor. Setting it on the bed, he tore the skin away, revealing a layer of whitish linen. This he carefully peeled away from the most impeccably tooled leather quiver Dessa had ever laid eyes on. But most importantly, for now, the quiver was full of long straight arrows with perfectly inset feathers. The symmetry of the bundle was almost overwhelming. It was beautiful.

As if they were fragile glass, Bartoly picked up the arrows and handed them to Dessa. "Rebecca made these, I cannot think of anything more fitting right now than you using them on the assholes that attacked her."

Dessa looked up from the arrows to Bartoly's raging face. She looked at the fire in his eyes and the evident fear that seeped forth at the thought of losing the woman he loved so dearly.

She did not smile. She simply gave a throaty, "You know I will put them to more than good use."

The three of them ran to the barn, Bartoly carrying the extra broadsword for Quillan.

Looking in on Rebecca, she was lying on a blanket, all the long gashes now tied tight. She was still blessedly asleep or passed out. It did not matter; she was not in evident pain.

"How is she?" choked Bartoly.

"I really have no idea. I've put Karina's salve on all the wounds and bound them best I could." Quillan was in tears.

Dessa turned her gaze from Rebecca to Quillan. "If she lives, I just hope she does not lose the baby."

"Baby?" said Bartoly slowly.

"Yes, she was going to tell you tonight. She had missed two of her courses as of yesterday. That was why she got sick."

"I?" Bartoly stammered.

"I know you didn't know. But I wanted you to know now." Dessa just looked at Bartoly and let the news sink in.

Suddenly, the man seemed to grow bigger. The red drained away from his face, and his breathing calmed. He had turned. Turned from an angry man to a calculating, cold blooded hunter of evil.

Inwardly, Dessa sighed. She knew she was taking a chance telling him. Knew he might go off into a raging fit and then would be both intolerable and ineffective in hunting down the scum that did this. But deep inside, she also knew that the news of Rebecca's pregnancy might strike him so hard as to calm him. Tallon's words of wisdom not to kill in anger had come back. She knew she needed a team of clear thinking people if they were to have any chance of survival. She felt she had it now.

Quillan stood and said sternly, "Now go. You know what must be done."

*   *   *

Torrin was headed toward the horses until he heard Bartoly say, "No, we are on foot, it's closer than you think."

The three ran as if possessed. Maybe, to an extent, they were.

Bartoly ran thinking of nothing but revenge. And it was not sweet revenge; it was to avenge a so unnecessary and venomous crime. And, as he thought about it, if they got away, all the people in the valley were in danger. For all he knew, they were all dead anyway. But if they weren't, he needed to make the place safe again. Whatever the cost.

Dessa ran wondering even more what the strategy for the attack would be. They had to have a plan or they would run into what would certainly prove a horrible death by callous, uncaring and vicious raiders.

Torrin ran wondering if he could carry all the weapons and most of all how to use the flail (it seemed unsteady in his hand).

Up they climbed, over a shallow ridge and down again. Then up some more, where Torrin began to make out landmarks from their entrance days before. It was evident that Bartoly had hidden them well.

Just not quite well enough.

Suddenly Bartoly lay down on his belly and shimmied up a rock slope. His hand movements could not be mistaken as to telling Torrin and Dessa to stay where they were.

Presently, he came back down. "There are a number of men on horseback, a few walking in the rear. They are a hearty bunch, well armed, rather tough looking and look like they are used to this sort of thing. My guess is they are a bunch from Gaerwn's kingdom. There is never any good when they are around." Looking at his two companions, he took a deep breath, "If either of you are not up to this, just say so, I will not hold it against you; it's not your fight."

Dessa's brain was screaming for more time to think, but on the outside she looked steady and secure. She said, "We're up for it and more, it's as much our fight as it is yours. These people leave here and…" she looked around, not quite sure of the words. Then continued, "you have no idea and I don't think we quite know either, but we are in, lock, stock and barrel."

Torrin nodded his agreement. He was sure the others would be able to hear his heart pounding.

"OK, here is the plan," said Bartoly.

*   *   *

Gaerwn was picking small slimy chunks of roasted pheasant left over from lunch that were stuck between his teeth, with his dirty, split fingernails.

"Squire!" he bellowed.

Most all those around him in the great room winced in fear, knowing a heavy boot could come their way if the squire did not show up quickly.

A young, frail, yet good looking boy, not yet of shaving age came running in to the immense and over-decorated throne room. His first thought was that it was warm. Much warmer here than any other part of the castle. He hoped he could stay for a few moments and let the cold dampness of his clothes dissipate.

Kneeling low in front of the fat man in the throne, he said in a meek voice, "Yes sire, you called?"

The king released a heavy sigh. He wondered why he had to put up with such timid and wormy little boys as squires. He much more enjoyed intimidating the big burly boys. They wept like little girls after he tore into them. This creature would probably wet himself if he said "boo." So he tried it.

"Boo!" erupted king Gaerwn.

The boy fell backward, shrieking as if he had been stuck with a sword.

"Please sir, don't beat me, I will do whatever you desire! Please, please don't beat me." He held his hands over his head in protection, sobbing in terror.

Gaerwn was instantly furious, and standing as fast as his fat belly would allow, he grabbed a sword and seemed to prepare to dismember the frightened boy.

"Sire," came a stern voice from a dark robed man sitting next to the wall eating a turkey leg. He had a short black beard, eagle clear eyes and long black hair. He was tall when standing and when sitting he took up much floor space in a gangly sort of way.

"I know you are not fond of the weenie boy we have right now, but he is here since the truer men are on the hunt, in the scouting party or training in the finer art of killing, torture and mayhem with your growing army."

He stopped talking, making sure this stupid lout of a king was listening. Since news of Darius' death had reached the old bastard, Scraddius, the king's chief advisor, had wondered if the king was ever listening or just plotting more revenge.

Scraddius continued, "I am sure you would find cutting this little pecker up rather amusing," the boy on the floor clutched himself tighter and let out a shrill wail. "But then we will be squire-less, and that could prove to be quite miserable." Because then I will have to do your running and that is not going to happen, thought Scraddius to himself.

"Cach," said Gaerwn, "I suppose you are right Scraddius." He looked down at the trembling boy.

"Get up!" Gaerwn bellowed. "Get up before I crush you with my boot let alone a sword."

The boy sprang to his feet, clutching his hat, eyes low.

"Any word from the scouting party? Have they come back yet?"

"No sire," the boy winced back, thinking that the bad news might cause a few wallops to be placed his way, but seeing none coming, he relaxed some and let the warmth of the room engulf him again. "We have all the hilltops manned with our best men watching for the party. As soon as we see them you will know as fast as we can get word back to the castle." The boy took a long breath and then hastily added, "Sire."

Gaerwn was not listening though. He was thinking. Had the party run into trouble? Were they dead? He was sure no one was ruthless enough to kill Chadus! And, he had given strict orders that this was a scouting expedition. They were to come back with the whereabouts of that brat Torrin so he could mount an army next spring and finally bring him to his rightful home to teach him some manners. He had heard he was in the valley. What he was doing so far from his wench mother Ethelda?

He sat down heavily upon his throne and sighed. That had been a glorious conquest. She had been such a pretty girl—until he was done with her. A deeply sour smile crossed his face.

As Gaerwn was lost in his thoughts, figuring Chadus was probably happily running amok among the peasants and having a wonderful time, Dessa was smiling too.

But for a very different reason.

*   *   *

Dessa jumped down onto a large outcrop of rock just ahead and above the helmeted face of the heavily armed and very vile looking lead horseman slowly making his way through the narrow trail.

"Hello boys," she said throatily, deftly hiding what was left of her apprehension. An apprehension that had diminished almost entirely, after the completely unexpected and surprising events of the last few moments.

She portrayed purpose. She showed confidence; she was a strong woman. An air about her was both exciting and mysterious.

The vile looking horseman looked up, startled not so much by the fact that someone was there, but by the fact that it was a woman. Not like any of the women he was used to seeing. They all wore caps and were either very fat or too skinny. This woman had flaming red hair, loose to the shoulder that was offset by a sheer white blouse that did not hide much of a well built frame. And, besides being tall, she was wearing breeches. The material was tight around her long legs. The look he gave her told her he was only used to seeing this much of a woman's shape when he had paid for an evening of enjoyment.

Then, the scraggly man's eyes grew wide in amazement as this tall redhead reached down and deftly removed her blouse in one graceful motion. Slowly, she let it fall from one long slender and pale arm to the ground next to her. In the sunshine she revealed to him the most beautiful picture his mind had ever seen, let alone imagined. The glint of sunlight from the belt of bright silver knives that encircled her slender waist added to the sheer mystery and wonder of this amazing sight. But he wasn't looking at the knives.

So, this tall redhead, wearing tight breeches with nothing covering her top made his senses slam together, and basically his brain stopped working. He just halted his horse and stared, as did those behind him who were watching with mouths agape.

Just as Bartoly figured would happen and she had hoped.

At this point, none of them even sensed the movement she made to bend down and pick up a bow. Neither did they realize she had four arrows tucked in her left hand next to the bow, as Tallon had taught her. In fact, until the arrows pierced their throats and they fell over choking on their own blood did it occur to them that they had been ambushed. But for the lead warrior and four of the toughest and most ruthless men of Gaerwn's kingdom, it was too late.

The cool breeze made her skin jump with goose bumps. She felt that her nipples were painfully hard as part of the adrenaline rush, and she remembered Tallon's words of wisdom about staying cool when you are so focused on taking another person's life. The thrill of it almost scared her, but she was relishing the headiness of it just the same. Dessa was also glad that Torrin and Bartoly were at the back of the group doing their job there. After she was out of arrows, she stopped and replaced the blouse. There were no witnesses left alive to tell this story.

At that, she gave a loud and commanding whistle. A wicked thunder ensued as the large pack of heavy, hungry snarling and vicious wolves came over the rocks and flung themselves on the unsuspecting and now terribly frightened warriors below. They being trapped from ahead by the dead leaders, trapped on the sides by the sheer rock walls and no room to back up were screaming mad curses in every direction.

The noise was deafening. The shrieking and the barking along with the frightened whinnying of the horses made for a fearful sound.

It was pure bedlam.

Dessa retrieved her quiver and composed it carefully upon its rightful place on her back. Walking along the rocks she came to the place where the obvious leader was fighting the wolves as best as he was able. He did not look afraid. He just looked mean and venomous.

She whistled, and pointed back along the trail and the wolves left him. Dessa carefully nocked an arrow (it was one of Rebecca's) and let it fly. She was almost afraid at the calmness she had. She wondered if it was the training or experience. Whichever, it was proving to be very helpful for her. Not so for her victims.

Her arrow found its mark right through his shoulder. Just as she had planned. Soon, the other shoulder was rendered helpless. He just sat there on his terrified horse, glaring at her. Not one speck of fear on his face. Just mean hatred.

It took all her strength to not put an arrow through his heart. But that was not the plan and she stuck to the strategy they had agreed upon. It seemed like half a day ago when they had had that quick and furious discussion about what to do for the attack, even though it had been just a few minutes ago along the slope of the rocks.

The discovery of her fascinating new and almost frightening power left her wondering. Even though she had felt it before, she didn't really know she could communicate with the animals like this.

It really made no sense at all.

*   *   *

"What?" Dessa had exclaimed as they had planned the attack. She was incredulous, bordering on severe anger. "You want me to do what?"

"Just jump out on the rocks, take off your shirt and then kill the lead horsemen. They will stop and stare, not be able to move at the sight of you and you just put arrows through their hateful necks," said Bartoly.

He was calmer than she thought he should have been, but at the same time she thought him out of his ever-loving mind.

"And," he continued, "look at this logically. The bastards who will be staring at your chest will be dead. Who's to know?" he said now somewhat forlornly. "It's all I can think of. If you've got a better way to stop them and have them freeze in place so you can kill them, tell me."

Dessa felt as though a million jumbled thoughts raced through her head all at once, but she had to agree. None of them really seemed to work any better.

"OK," she said quietly. "It just better work!"

He gave her a quick smirk and said, "I do understand the limits of a man's mind. It will work. Trust me now, believe me later."

"What do we do?" asked Torrin.

"You and I attack from the rear, and once all hell breaks loose ahead, we disable the last couple of riders or foot troops—whatever is there and then systematically dice them up. They will be caught between the rocks with nowhere to go."

The look on Torrin's face was incredulous, until he remembered the sight of Rebecca hanging upside down, almost butchered alive. Dessa noticed he gripped the broadsword so tight his knuckles shown white.

A rustling in the trees behind them caused the three to look at each other, thinking they might have been ambushed by their own prey. Turning slowly around, they were startled to see a large pack of wolves quietly standing at the tree line.

Both Bartoly and Torrin slowly brought their broadswords up, ready to take on the attack that they knew would come.

It was an eerie sight. The wolves' translucent gray-blue eyes were bright with purpose. Yet, the entire lot of them stood quietly waiting, almost at attention, as if expecting orders. One large dark male walked tentatively forward. He was as muscular as his thick fur was glossy. He was clearly the alpha wolf. He was in charge.

As if in a trance, Dessa walked toward the leader.

Torrin started to call out, but she shushed him with a wave.

Dessa knelt in front of the alpha. Torrin and Bartoly could hear what sounded like low whispers. But there were no words. It was just low grumblings and snarflings. After a few moments, Dessa stood. The trance like look slowly melted off her face as she walked back to the utterly stunned and amazed men.

"What was…?" stammered Torrin.

"They are with us. They are part of me now, according to Praritor. They will wait for my signal. They will not hurt the horses or the leader. But they want to eat. I told them that would be fine."

"I…" Torrin began.

"Never mind," said an equally stunned but more believing Bartoly. "It is what we must accept. Something tells me there will be more we must learn to accept. Let's get on with it."

The three went where they needed to go. The wolves had melted into the trees. It scared the jeepers out of Torrin, thinking that so many fierce and usually wildly noisy animals could be so quiet and disappear so suddenly. Heck, how had they suddenly appeared with the three of them never seeing or hearing them coming. And there were so many!

He shivered in spite of being hot.

*   *   *

When the unholy hell started up ahead, Bartoly popped up from behind Jacqualde (yes, they had stolen the cow too), and brought the flail's spiked steel ball around on the trailing warrior's head. It thunked in a hollow way, like hitting a stout stick roundly on a pumpkin.

The man went down without a sound, dropping the hold he had on poor Jacqualde's rein. His companion, who had been walking a few paces ahead turned at the sound of the strange noise and caught a silver dagger through the mouth. Clutching the dagger, eyes wide with terror, he looked as though he wanted to pull it out, but was not sure. He never finished the thought as Torrin's broadsword removed his head from his body.

As if in a trance, in one smooth move, Torrin retrieved the dagger and deposited it back in the belt with the others. If you asked later why he did that, he would not remember doing it. That is often the way in battle.

The walking troops were clustered up around the last horse trying to get a look at what the bedlam up ahead was all about. They had completely missed their companions being killed systematically by two madmen.

They should have been paying attention.

In just a few moments both Torrin and Bartoly were covered in blood and gore. They somehow worked together in a killing synergy that brought a fast and brutal death to all who stood before them.

Given the instruments of destruction they were both equipped with, dispatching the soldiers was mostly by crushing or dismemberment. The two of them were in somewhat of an adrenaline powered, spellbound state. Every move was a killing move. There was no wasted effort or movement.

Once the foot soldiers were gone, Torrin went after the last horseman. He knew that taking control of the last horse and blocking escape for the others was critical to success. He simply sprang up on the back of the horse and slit the rider's throat. Torrin's hand covered the dying man's mouth until he made no more sounds or struggle. The warm blood ran quickly over the front of the soldier's breastplate. The coppery smell and thick redness made Torrin shudder for a moment. It distracted him.

And, that distraction almost got him his fool self run through.

The next horseman, being of quicker response than most of the others was turning in his saddle, trying to back up. When he looked at the rider who was supposed to be following him, he was at first surprised to see all the blood. Then instinctively he knew he needed to protect himself. He drew his sword and proceeded to charge backward toward Torrin.

As it was, it was too late for Torrin to move. He had nowhere to go even if he could. But as it was, the dead weight of the soldier he had just dispatched was holding him tight on the horse. The fear that slammed through his head and heart was acute. Just as the sword looked like it was going to run him through, a large black wolf flew through air and clamped down on the attacker's arm. The sword went wild but cut Torrin from shoulder to belly in a long fast slice. And just as quickly another wolf clamped his mighty jaws on the man's throat and it was over for him.

Torrin sat for a moment. He was breathing hard and finding it even harder to move, until Bartoly smacked him on the back and broke the trance.

Torrin's wound was not deep, but it was pestering. He knew he needed attention from Quillan and Karina's salve, but they had work to do.

Before long, the biggest challenge the three of them faced was getting the horses backed out of the narrow pathway. The wolves on the other hand were savagely efficient in removing their spoils.

It took the three of them the better part of the morning before they were done.

55.
Friends

"Why were you here Chadus? What purpose could you have by terrorizing the people of this valley?" Quillan asked for the hundredth time.

Chadus just looked at the big red man and wished he could choke him slowly to death and watch the color drain from his face as he died. Just the idea of it made him feel better and he smiled. His black teeth dark against angry lips.

Quillan walked stubbornly from the barn where he and Bartoly had been trying to get the prisoner to talk. He met Dessa near the cabin and sighed deeply.

"It's no use. The man cannot be frightened, beaten or tortured into saying anything. We have tried everything we know."

"Do you know who he is?" she asked.

"He is Chadus, the youngest son of King Gaerwn," said Quillan.

Dessa froze. Haunted again! She faced not a terribly cruel man; she faced another brother of pure evil. She breathed deeply and slowly through her nose. She decided she had to think. It was time to get this over. She was filthy dirty, tired and she wanted some time with Torrin. No, she decided, she very much needed some time with him.

"Quillan, is he tied tightly?"

"Yes," he responded. "At least we have him under control. Even with an arrow through each shoulder he was a struggle. I don't think the man feels pain."

"You sure he is secure?"

"Yes! He is staked to the floor. He is laying spread eagle with his arms out above his head." Quillan held both arms high to prove his point. "Bartoly bound him with irons and chain. He is not going anywhere."

"Ok. I'll be back in a moment. When I go in there, you stay out here unless you hear me call for you. But no matter what you hear, you stay outside unless you hear me use your name."

"No," replied Quillan tersely. He is too dangerous. If he got loose he would tear you apart in an instant."

"But I thought he was secure?"

"Yes, he is secure! Damn it!" Quillan's frustrations were rising up. "I just don't like my sister going near some cold blooded half insane killer without some protection."

Dessa looked up at his concerned face. She calmly told him, "Who said I would have no protection?"

With that she walked away, towards the rhododendrons.

Quillan thought he heard a rustling, but he was intent on paying attention to Chadus and not letting him get away, so he paid the sound no heed.

              *   *   *

As she walked into the barn, the bile rose in her throat. Beads of perspiration cooled her forehead and neck. When she wiped it away, blood and mud streaked her and made her feel even more miserable.

The man lying on the floor reeked of evil. He was bound hand and foot. The shackles were obviously tight and uncomfortable, but he did not squirm or try to escape. He just lay there and looked at her with black eyes.

"Chadus," she said. "I don't know why you are here, but I have come to find out."

He spat in her direction.

Walking up behind him, she grasped his shirt and gave a might pull. She pulled so hard it ripped into a number of small parts and left his body.

Underneath the shirt, he had hidden a well developed set of hard and sinewy muscles beneath a thick mat of black hair.

Dessa thought that he looked nothing like either of his brothers. This one was not the life of the party like Darius or the evil schemer Haphethus. This one was just pure bad.

Two holes in his shoulders were all the evidence that was left from the arrows. She wondered if he had taken them out himself.

"You don't scare me, even if you are lucky with a bow," he said in a low voice that she figured was supposed to be scary.

"I know," she said slowly. "I know, and really, I don't care."

Dessa sat down on a barrel where he could see her. With all the calmness she could muster, she crossed her legs, folded her arms and looked at him.

She let the tempo of the room fall into the rhythm she wanted before speaking. It did not take long, but it was important because she was only going to have one chance for this to work. Once it started, there was no turning back.

"Neither of your scheming brothers was afraid of me either," she paused to let his brain catch up and sort through the meaning of the words.

"You see, I am Dessa."

He had been looking away. She figured he thought he could intimidate her by being nasty. It just made this all the more interesting. But now, he slowly looked back, scrunching his eyes.

"You're Dessa? Kael's brother?" He knew he should not have said it the moment he did, so he tried to buffalo his way out. "Sure," he said incredulously. "Dessa was burned at the stake. Nice try. The whole kingdom turned out to see that nasty murdering bitch burn. It's just too bad I got there a day too late to see the fun myself. Although I did get to see some of her partially burned hair. It had flown across the courtyard when her head exploded from the heat. The peasants were weeping over it."

Dessa shuddered.

"How do you know Kael?" she asked. The calm in her voice did not tell of the sudden churning in her stomach or her desire to slowly remove his eyes with her fingernails.

As he answered, the look in his eyes did not match his words. She knew he was lying.

"I had heard of Kael and some tragic event, that's all."

"You had something to do with his death, didn't you?" Dessa found herself screaming at him.

"No, what makes you think that?"

"Just a hunch," she snarled.

Chadus took the upper hand, or so he thought, "So we are both liars? Is that what you are saying? Eh?"

"What do you mean?" Dessa asked, now calmer. She knew he could get her to lose all control if she let him.

She breathed deep and slow.

"You say you are Dessa. Cannot be true. Too many people saw her burn that night. I say you are some scheming whore who heard of the poor woman's plight and took on her name," he snorted a wet chuckle. "Just because you have red hair. It's a shame what some people will do to get attention."

"Well, you see, I had a stand-in for the night. I was busy escaping."

"Whether I believe you or not, does not matter. You are obviously a whore and only good for one thing. Why don't you untie me and let me do to you what I know you want."

Dessa smiled as she said, "OK. That sounds like fun. But first, let me tell you a couple of things." She paused for dramatic effect. "Darius had a mole above his left nipple and gray hairs grew from it." She waited some more for that bit of news to sink in.

"And you're oh so sweet brother Haphethus could only get excited with a woman if he was abusing her. He got some sort of sick glee from it." There was no use in rushing this, but it was getting old and she was tired. And anyway, his quick glance at her shoulder told her all she needed to know.

She continued, "He is dead too. At least I got to run a knife into his heart and feel it pump dry. Not like that slob Darius who got drunk and fell down on his own knife. How stupid can a man be?" That last part was delivered in a high, mocking tone. She knew this would work better if he was a little riled up.

And then almost for fun she added, "Does stupidity as well as a smallish cran run in your family too?"

Dessa stood up and walked casually over to a table where his weapons lay. She picked them up and examined them. They were crude, brutish and not well taken care of. Finally she settled on a small lightweight hatchet.

Turning around, she found him staring at her. He swallowed hard, trying to not let the fear that was seeping in show. She knew he would not last long.

"I am not afraid of you," he said. She could tell he was mustering his last bit of bravado. She wondered where it came from—this fear that she was now exploiting. A fear that seemed deep and might drive him to do what she needed him to do.

"So what if you knew my brothers. The only thing they did wrong was not teach you your place in this world."

"And that place would be?" she asked, walking toward him with a measured and sluggish pace. She slowly wet her lips with her tongue, smiling a big sultry smile.

"Either on the floor washing it or on your back servicing me," he spat out, almost trembling.

"Well, now. Maybe you're right." Dessa stopped. She held the hatchet in one hand. Reaching down with the other, she removed the pins from the ankle shackles. After that, she tossed the hatchet onto his stomach.

His legs were free, but his arms were still secure. She figured he would squirm a little more this way.

She was right.

For a moment she just looked at him, trying to decide if she should do this. Was it the right thing to do? Was there a better way?

Finally, she let out one low whistle.

With that, they started to arrive. Mostly on his chest. At first there were just a few of them, but they were active. Some in bright vibrant colors. Some thin and spindly, some thick dark and hairy. A variety had evil black eyes that looked at you with an odd twist. Others, you could hardly tell which was the front or the back.

Anyway, they came as a fierce little horde. Some jumped down, some flew and some hitched a ride. However they got to him, did not matter. But they did get to his bare chest and seemed to have purpose.

Spiders.

The spiders that lived in the rhododendrons.

"Stop them. Get them off me! What are you doing you fiendish bitch?" he was screaming.

Dessa found she was rather enjoying the tempo this little meeting had taken on. She felt very much in control. Ever since he had nervously glanced at her shoulder, she had been relaxing. Tallon's words had come back to her, "Everyone is afraid of something." She picked up the gray and black wolf spider that had been quietly and gently exploring her shoulder and set him down so he could play with his friends.

"Will you tell me what you were doing in the valley?" she asked.

"Scouting party," he was panting hard now. His neck muscles strained as he looked to see what was happening on his chest. "We're going to raid this miserable valley next spring and we needed to know more about it." He was squirming hard trying to shake her little friends off his very sweaty belly.

"Get them off me!" Fast ragged breathing kept his chest heaving. He laid his head back, eyes clenched tight and then he looked up at her and said in a most gentle tone, "Please?"

Dessa muttered a simple, "Muh." The little horde scurried off his chest and sat next to him on the floor. They twictcherd with each other and jumped about. They were excited and hoping to have a great feast. If you listened, they might have been talking. But for now, they left him alone and waited.

"Why Rebecca? Why did you do that to her?" she asked quietly.

"Nothing bleeds the soul like terror. We wanted all of you to know there was danger coming." His steely tone had returned. He was sure he had the upper hand; after all, she was just a girl. "Now untie me and I will go. I will tell my father the valley is not worth sacking. I will tell him that Torrin is not here. We will leave you alone."

She may have jerked her head a little when he said Torrin. It did not matter.

"What do you want with Torrin?"

"Gaerwn wants to talk with him. I don't know what it's about."

"You are a close family?" she said, "communicate well together?"

"Are you going to let me go or what? I have told you what you want," he was getting snarly again.

"One last thing before I untie you," Dessa said with a tone that said, don't try to lie. "Tell me what happened to Kael."

"We were hunting," he said, now relaxing, thinking this almost over. "We came to a cabin where a bunch of boys were playing. They seemed rather rude, so we decided to teach them some manners. Challenged them to a little cudgeling."

"You. Full grown soldiers challenged boys to cudgeling?" she winced at the thought.

"They seemed to like it. It was a grand time, until I broke one boy's hand. Then that little cach Kael started beating me with his cudgel."

She had heard enough. Her skin crawled with disgust. As she threw the bolts in the hand shackles, she could feel the heat rising in her face. She told herself to hold on. Stay in control. Lose control and you die. It is the way of the warrior.

Trembling, she stood up. He slowly brought his hands up, wincing at the pain in his shoulders where the arrows had left clean holes and rubbed his dirty palms together. The color started to come back. He grinned.

She grinned.

But then she whistled again, just like before.

When she whistled, he looked up, and saw her firm, set face. There was no glee. There was no happiness. Only purpose. He had not noticed that the little group of spiders had grown to an uncountable number. When she whistled, they did what they were commanded to do.

They ate.

The terror was instantaneous. He felt completely powerless and overwhelmed. They came at him from all sides. And now they had purpose.

The way a spider eats is that it sprays digestive juice on its victim. The flesh starts to melt, and the spider basically drinks its meal. The victim has to be alive though. Spiders are very picky about their food. They will not eat dead meat. So the thrashing Chadus was displaying actually got the little horde more excited. His display of strength told them he was a wonderfully good meal.

And eat they did.

Some of them paid a dear price for this meal. But many would eat their fill.

He tore at them and tried to brush them off. But their cheliceral teeth held on. They held on tight, waiting for just the right time to partake of their generous morsel set before them as the acid from their little mouths softened his skin into tasty meals.

The wolf spider that had enjoyed the warmth and softness of Dessa's shoulder decided to go for the tenderest of meat. He clamped himself firmly on Chadus' lip and sprayed a mighty spray of acid.

The thought of this spider clamped to his lip was more than Chadus could stand. He was used to being the torturer. He was not used to the other side.

It was like the drowning man who kills his potential lifesaver by trying to climb out of the water on the lifesaver themselves, drowning them. It makes no sense. If you drown the lifesaver, you die. But the brain in panic does not have much reason left. Just a scary burst of white energy looking for survival.

Chadus' brain was in such a state. He picked up the hatchet and cleanly split that poor wolf spider in two.

Of course, he also buried the hatchet deep within his face. However, he did achieve his goal.

As he fell over dead, the spiders after a few moments left. They were not interested in dead meat.

Dessa had been watching captivated. She was fascinated by the level of fear this fierce warrior had displayed. Tallon had been right again. And this time, who knows how many lives he had saved.

She walked over to the now mostly still body. A couple of spiders were crawling around, maybe hoping he would wake up. She just shook her head and walked outside.

"What the devil has been going on in there?" shouted a very nervous looking Quillan.

Dessa looked at him in what he thought a queer sort of way, and then she said, "It pays to have friends in high places."

"What?"

"Never mind, I'll explain later. He said his job was to take information back to Gaerwn," said Dessa. "He wants him to know how frightened we are."

"Oh?"

"I think we should let him complete his task."

*   *   *

"She is scaring me I tell you," said Bartoly as he tightened the rope around Chadus' body. The horse whinnied some, but it was not from the rope. He had been doing it ever since Dessa seemed to have had a talk with him.

"Yes, it's a little strange, but I think she is under control," said Quillan as he tied a cover over the dead man's face. This would add to the surprise when he got back to Gaerwn's castle. They would have to take off the mask to see who it was. This did not bother him. What bothered him was that Dessa seemed to think the horse would find its way back. Granted, it was a fine horse, and given even a large area, it might find its way home if it wandered off. He had seen it many times. But this was many days' ride. No horse knew that path.

He did not have to wait long for an answer.

Dessa rounded the cabin with the largest mountain lion in tow he had ever seen. It felt like his heart stood still. Slowly he reached for his knife.

"Stow it Quillan," came the terse voice of his sister. "He will not hurt you."

The knife went back into its sheath, but Quillan did not tie it down.

The horse pranced about, somewhat excited, but not as excited as it should have been. Lions and horses are generally not friends, since lions tend to feast on horses.

Dessa walked up to the worried pony and put her hand on his long wet nose. He snorted and looked at her, all business. She talked for a while with him, his head moving periodically. Quillan and Bartoly just stared.

"What's going on…" Torrin stopped in his tracks. The long bandages around his chest dark red from dried blood. His eyes big as saucers.

"There…is…a…lion right behind you. Don't move," whispered Torrin.

Dessa walked over to Torrin, put her long arms around his neck and gave him a quick gentle kiss on the lips. "I know. I called him; we know each other. He is going to lead Chadus' horse back to Gaerwn's castle. They will get along fine, and anyway, he is a cougar, not a lion and the horse agreed not to pound him to death if the cougar agreed not to try and eat him."

"You will get along, won't you?" she said sternly at the cougar. He was calmly licking one large paw, the nails of which were sticking out long enough it seemed to carve even the biggest of legs into thin edible slices. They looked very sharp. He looked up at her and blinked.

"Oh, he is just showing off", she giggled. She turned to Quillan and Bartoly, "Is he ready?"

"As ready as he'll ever be," said Quillan. "I just hope it doesn't get too warm out."

"That will be Gaerwn's problem in a few days," commented Dessa.

She walked with the most unlikely pair, a large horse and extremely large cougar, to the edge of the valley. At that point she hugged them both and they set off down the trail.

When she returned, Bartoly said, "There is no way out of that valley. Why are they going that way?"

She looked at him and smiled, "Maybe you don't know as much as you think about this countryside. Come on Torrin, it's time for us to get cleaned up."

56.
Consilience

The water was cool and foamed lazily around the rocks as it slid by on its way toward the valley floor. The warmth from the golden embers lying in a low mound from the small fire they had built chased away the coolness of the evening. The smoke moved with lazy purpose up in a straight path toward the heavens. Its slow ascent by no means frantic, but nonetheless, on its own journey.

The stars overhead beamed down as brightly as they could. They seemed to strain at their work just now. But strain as they might, they were no match for the moon's white brilliance.

It had been an amazing experience. Not just the rapid, deadly events of the day, but now, this. Torrin just shook his head and relished the feeling of Dessa lying here with her head on his now dry thigh. She had wanted to lay her cheek on his chest, but the long gash from the sword kept that from being a reality. That did not matter one bit. What amazed him was that the gash was almost healed. What amazed him more was how he felt.

Torrin felt absolutely calm, utterly terrified and excited all at once. It was a feeling he would cherish forever. He had never felt anything like it, yet he would find that over time, the feeling would not only be wonderful every time, but would get better. This was the start of a new journey for him, a depth of meaning he had not known existed.

Dessa reached up between his legs with her hand and cupped him in the most tenderest of places. "So tell me, what you are thinking?" she whispered slowly and softly.

He hesitated. It was difficult to think when his body was flaming in glorious wonder. The words were caught somewhere between his brain and mouth. His deepest feelings were there, but explanation was beyond him. The wires were crossed and on fire. So he settled for, "I want to do that again with ye." It was not a lame answer; it was the only answer that worked at the moment. He hoped dearly it did not disappoint her. He was not sure what to say just right now.

With time he would come to understand that the right thing to say was the truth.

"Good, so do I," she seemed to testify to him. A satisfied smile crossed her face.

Turning to her, he asked, "So. What are you thinking?"

"Well, I had always imagined it one way, but this was unlike anything I had imagined."

"Oh?" he sounded worried all of a sudden.

"It was better. Relax will you?" It was more an order or a request than a question.

"How do you mean?"

After a long sigh, some obvious organizing of tender thoughts, and more teasing (which he would never tire of), she said, "I think I feel safe, wanted and respected. There is probably more, but that comes to the top of my mind."

He agreed, and they just lay there for a while, both replaying the searing and happy events of this evening in their minds. The meaning of it all slowly beginning to seep in.

* * *

The evening had started after the horse, cougar and body of Chadus had disappeared into the valley. The three of them had returned to the cabin. Rebecca was lying in bed, quite awake now.

"You are going to have quite the scar," said Dessa, kissing Rebecca on the forehead.

"Yeah, if I heal," came the quiet and pained reply.

"Bartoly, get some of that evil whiskey in her. Not much, but at least enough to take the edge off," ordered Dessa.

Once she was satisfied Rebecca was being cared for, she put Bartoly and Quillan to work getting the cabin back into some semblance of order. Then, Dessa and Torrin left the cabin. They carried the mats Dessa and Rebecca had used days before, two large thick soft wraps and a good supply of the perfumed soap.

After they had arrived at the stream and little pond, they spent a little time gathering wood. By now it was getting later in the day and cooler. Somehow they both knew they would not be going back to the cabin for a while.

Torrin got the fire going and then stood and faced Dessa. She had been silently watching him work. She looked horrible. From head to toe she was covered with blood and gore from the events of the day, as well as having the look upon her face as someone who was thoroughly stressed. Mixed under that face of stress though was a longing and need for release. He sensed she too had traveled a long way to be here now. Her journey had been far, and in the course of time, he wanted to hear about it.

But, for the moment, he had other things on his mind as did she.

Of course, he then looked down and noticed he was an absolute mess too. At that point, he finally figured out that how he was dressed or whether either of them was dirty did not matter. This moment, this evening, this time—was their time now. It had been a long while coming and the fact that they were there together, without interruption, was more important than anything else. He hoped that neither Quillan nor Bartoly would come running with some evil emergency to disturb them. This concern he relayed to Dessa.

"Don't worry. I told Quillan to leave us be, even if the place burns down and the forest catches fire."

"Oh," was his smiling reply.

Dessa winked at him and he melted a bit more.

He reached out and gently slid his callused palm around the back of her neck and pulled her close.

And she came to him without resistance or hesitation. He felt her long arms encircle his back and hold on. He felt the heat of their bodies merge and come close to his heart. He felt right.

After a long while, a while that seemed much too short for the both of them, they pulled back and without so much as one word, systematically undressed each other.

There was no hurry, no fussing or mad desire to be naked. They both knew they were traveling down a path that they hoped led to a whole new life. Rushing would get them nothing.

The buttons on her shirt were crusty and grimy. Yet as he worked she would sigh as the pressure behind each filthy crescent released, exposing more and more of her radiant and slightly blushed skin.

When the buttons were all conquered, he grasped the carefully sewn frills of her shirt, moved the fabric down her torso, and with a gentle push released it to fall to the ground. As he had moved the dirty material, his nails trailed long white paths as he gently scratched her skin. Her warmth radiated to his fingertips.

He marveled at how smooth her skin felt. He decided she was like warm clean porcelain. Smooth to the touch, yet with a richness that was hard to describe.

Dessa's face got serious as she let out a great heavy sigh when she ran her hands across the hairs of his chest. For the longest of time she had thought a big strong man was all she wanted. She figured he would be as wise and caring as was right for a strong smart man to be. She decided she had been a fool.

For a while now, she wondered often in her musings, if most men were stupid pigs. But she all at once thought this a crass judgment. Her father was nice. Gale was certainly a gentleman, and Phlial had been mysterious, yet sweet and kindly. Bartoly was wonderful with Rebecca and Quillan was surely a man of honor. So there were really only a few men who had tainted her mental images. It was the intensity of the badness she decided, that left such a nasty impression. Yet, she did not want to experience that badness again.

She wanted compassion. She wanted partnership. She thought that maybe she had found it. At least this time, it seemed to be worth a try. And that was what she aimed to do!

As of now, they were both hot with a burning desire that needed quenching.

Next he undid the breeches that clung to her hips. The soft hammered leather was tight against her skin from the sweating and movement of the day. He had to shift and push the heavy material to get it off. He worked methodically and carefully.

Finally she stood tall and naked before him. Warm skin, flushed lips, hard nipples and soft hair met the smooth touch of his hands as he now embraced her by exploring all of her, part by wondrous part. Her moans and mutterings mixed with her wetness now gently caught upon his fingers made him almost succumb to his need to be with her now. And, she would not have protested. Deep down, she wanted to have him at this very moment; she did not want to wait. A clenching need was gripping her and she wanted it fulfilled. Needed it fulfilled.

But at an even deeper level, they both knew that waiting and paying attention to each other would only make the experience better. It was an understanding that they would find very useful later. One of the many ways their relationship would remain different, fresh and exciting through all they had yet to conquer and experience.

And that was more than either could imagine.

So before they crossed that threshold of becoming as one, they slowly explored each other for a last time in their old world. For their new world would be different. They both knew when they went over that edge they would be different forever. It scared them really. It scared them as it should. For in a truly rich relationship, when you care about someone, you want to leave the lovemaking as a closer and deeper couple. Not wondering if it is right.

So they forced themselves to take their time—but not too much for the current reality was very hot for both of them.

Dessa removed his clothing as slowly as she could (although the desire to rip it off in the space of two heartbeats was strong). She explored him as she went, finding nothing of surprise except one thing. Finally she thought, a man built like I want. She had a feeling that all the proportions were going to work well and it made her tingle.

Dessa took both her hands and cupped him behind his knees which made him groan and she thought he might collapse. She was looking at his face, watching his eyes with an interrogating intensity. Slowly she moved her hands up the backs of his thighs, and the desired result was evident. Bringing both hands to his front, she just brushed the tender sides of his raging hard crann and then continued moving up his body. She finally reached his shoulders and then slid what now were her very warm hands down his arms to his own warm hands.

Grabbing tight, and then giving him a deep smile she led him into the water and they washed not only themselves but their clothes. After some work, it was evident that they would have to boil the clothes in the morning. They would not come clean. And at this point, they were not going to waste any more time on laundry!

They decided their skin would come clean and they made sure of it—together.

It was a long slow scrub. He explored her with his slippery soapy hands. She let the tension of the day melt away as his strong fingers kneaded her skin with a wonderful pressure.

He had thought her soft before, but now wet and slippery, his mind was overwhelmed with the depth of her as not just a woman, but a woman who wanted to be with him.

They washed each other's hair.

They washed each other's legs, arms and backs.

At this point, Dessa started scrubbing his chest—as well as she could, considering the long cut. And as she worked down, she eventually got to her knees.

Tilting her head to one side, she admired his crann for a moment. And then, without another thought, she engulfed him. Her soapy hands held onto his slippery butt as she worked him over. He felt good inside her, warm, moist and delicate. It was the closest, most intimate feeling he had ever experienced.

For Torrin, he had never imagined anything like this before. Actually, he had never ever come close to experiencing an evening like this before. The closest he had come was with Gwendolyn. Sure, he had done his fair share of petting and exploring with the girls of the kingdom. But this was just so very different; this shuddered deep within his very soul.

He stood with the fingers of both his hands deeply intertwined in her hair. He did not push or pull, he was with her movements.

As much as he never wanted her to stop, he finally said, "Come, to me."

She slowly released the hold her mouth had on him, looked up and smiled. When she stood up, they kissed each other.

The water around them went instantly warm. Small jagged blue sparks tore from their pairing and struck the rocks around the pool. Their kiss was not just deep; it was the entrance to their passion. It seemed to ignite them both. It ignited the world around them.

The large rocks hissed steam and their tops dried. You could see the wetness leave the rough surface as the heat built. Torrin could feel the rocks under his feet begin to move. It was a frightening reality. There was a power in this growing bond that moved beyond the two of them.

Pulling back, they explored each other's lips, ears, face; the intimacy of their touches growing.

Quickly as if on cue together, they made sure they were rinsed of the soap. Torrin then picked her up and carried her to the thick mat where he lay her down as gently as a goose feather floats to earth on a warm summer afternoon.

Lying next to her, he cradled her head in the nook of his arm. The heat from their kissing dried them both and it occurred to them that starting fires could be a problem.

"We shall have to kiss in the rain," Dessa whispered to him.

"We shall kiss whenever we want," he breathed into her ear. "We shall just have to warn everyone around us."

Dessa giggled.

Rolling over on top of her he put one hand behind her head and the other encircled her shoulders. The strength of her muscles brought a feeling of security to him. He worked to keep from crushing her. In his mind she was as fragile as a newborn kitten.

"You won't hurt me you know," she smiled up at him. With that, he relaxed and she relished his warm weight on her chest. It was a pressure of caring.

Bringing her knees up, she reached down and grasped him firmly. And with a sure deftness of desire and need, guided him inside her.

He slowly pushed and the ensuing moan from her made him know that what he was doing was right.

He felt a peace descend upon him.

They did not sleep for a long while. They both enjoyed a long night of discovery.

       *   *   *

She was cold. Moving up next to him she laid herself alongside his warm long frame and the heat returned some. In the dark, she noticed something. She could not see it, but she could feel it.

It seemed impossible. It seemed out of order, but the long cut on his chest was all but gone. There was no oozing, no crusted blood. With her lips, she could feel the light scar. Inwardly she trembled some. It was too much to think about. Had their lovemaking endowed him with some healing energy? Maybe it was the salve? Still, that took some time to work. Sighing, she laid her head back on his chest.

"Are ye OK?" he said in a caring whisper.

"Uh-huh," she said, somewhat eerily. "It's just weird, your cut is all healed. It seems unnatural."

"It still feels strange inside though, and it itches."

"Shall I move my head? Am I hurting you?"

"No, never. I want to lie like this forever."

"Well, we can, but I fear we shall freeze to death."

And then he reached down, held her head snug in his hand and kissed her. Immediately, they both got warm, the mat sizzled with heat. They tenderly explored each other's lips as the rocks warmed and they could feel the chill air leave.

When they had parted their lips, she said, "We are going to have to be careful where we do that, we are going to start fires."

Chuckling softly, he said, "That might come in handy someday."

"Let's go to the cabin or the barn."

As they walked, hands intertwined, Dessa seemed a little too quiet.

"OK, what's on your mind? I can tell something is troubling you," he said.

She hesitated, then decided that not saying something was worse than saying it. "You said you had never been with a woman before?"

He replied, "That is right."

"Now mind you, I am not complaining, but...," she took a deep breath, "How did you know," she paused, "how to do what you did to me with your mouth? I mean if you..." her words were somewhat jumbled. She knew she wanted an answer, to erase the little doubt that has crept in. Too much had happened before for her not to worry some. But she trembled inwardly.

He put one finger on her almost quivering lips and quietly said "shhhhhh."

He had stopped walking and had turned to face her, "Last summer, my father caught me in the barn with one of the milkmaids. We were kissing up a storm. It was right pathetic. I was trying so hard to be sexy and get turned on but it was no use. Thank goodness he strolled in."

"What happened?" she asked.

"I thought I was a goner. Really figured I would get a whippin'. But he shooed the scared girl away and then looked at me. The thing is, he didn't just look. He looked and smiled. Said to me, 'I guess my little guy is growing up.' And then he held me by both shoulders, looked me square in the eye and said; 'Son, loving a woman, loving her unconditionally and with all your heart, and having her love you back is the greatest gift a man could ever wish for. You'll know when you find her. You'll know it not by what you feel between your legs, but in your heart. Because when you kiss her, when you hold her, something inside will guide you to treat her the way she needs to be treated. Just remember to listen to that voice and do what it says. And, if you don't hear that voice crying out to make you both happy, then it is selfish and not love. Stay away from that.'

"With that, he walked away. I just stood there shaking all over." Torrin's arms held her tight; as though she would fall if he loosened up.

"So with me? With us just now, I mean…"

"Yes," he turned and kissed the top of her damp head. He relished the way she smelled, the touch of her hair on his lips. "The way you moved, it spoke to me. The way you moaned told me what to do. The way your hands held tight or pushed and pulled. It all came together for me in a constant flow. I have never experienced anything close to that before. And to be honest, it was a little scary because I felt quite vulnerable and somewhat out of control, but wonderful all at the same time. Does that make sense?"

"Yes," she said. And she knew exactly what he meant.

They stood in silence, the space between them warm.

"So?" he asked. "I guess I shall ask the same."

The moon reflected the tears in her eyes. When she swallowed, it was hard, for the knot in her throat was massive.

It took a while before she started to talk; and when she started, it was almost a whisper.

"Since as early as I can remember, I had looked to the stars and asked for my prince to come and take me away. To hold me tight, to keep me safe and warm. To love me so I could be whole."

"And?" he asked.

"I told you about Darius. I told you how awful it was."

He nodded in agreement.

"Well, he shattered my dreams. I figured I would never love anyone, nor could anyone do for me what I wanted. No one could make me feel the way I had imagined feeling. Until I met Phlial. There was something pure about the man. At first he scared me, then I quite came to admire him. For he was happy and secure in his own right, even though the love of his life was dead. It seemed so unfair. He loved her so." Dessa wiped her nose and had settled down now. She was getting comfortable with the truth.

"I did not see it then," she continued. "But I see it now. He learned to trust himself; therefore, much of the rest of his world works. Certainly, yes, there is the struggle of life. But, he is content with, most of all, himself. And that is what is important."

"How does that work for us or me, or you and me? You know what I mean," said Torrin.

"It's just what your father said. Listen to your own heart, and when it's right, the rest will fall into place."

One of the odd moments between lovers ensued. One where no words needed to be spoken. Their bond was beginning to form.

That was a good thing, for over time, it would be tested.

* * *

For another couple of days, they stayed; helping Bartoly put everything back together. Even Jacqualde had settled back into her normal routine and was giving sweet milk again.

They decided to take two of the "new" horses with them to Journey to sell and trade. Bartoly used his blacksmith skill to quickly make a brand that turned Gaerwn's hateful X into two opposing diamonds. They figured by next spring the old and new brand would be merged, and that was as early as anyone would see it for trading and would minimize questions.

Rebecca healed well, although it was bothersome with all the itching. She was a strong woman and well intent on living to the fullest. Dessa could not decide if it was her fortitude or attitude that was her best friend. Either way, it worked.

As the five of them settled into a long dinner and some good wine before setting out for Journey, Quillan asked Dessa about the wolves. "Tell me dear sister," he said somewhat teasing, but not so much that it was joke; you could tell he was serious, dead serious. "You seem to have a way with them. Eh?"

Dessa pondered for a moment before slowly telling the story that had been brewing in her head.

"I really don't know much about the wolves, but I expect they will return again. When I escaped from the castle there was a lone gray wolf that seemed to haunt me. He appeared and disappeared so fast I kept second guessing myself. Was he really there or was it my mind playing tricks on me?"

She paused, took a long drink and without thinking wiped the back of her wrist across her mouth. Torrin smiled. So much of a lady he thought to himself, but so unpredictable and down to earth. When she was lost in her head, she really did not know what was going on around her or what she was doing.

Dessa continued, "That old gray wolf is the one who attacked me at Phlial's cottage that night." Her hand rubbed along the scar. "Just like other evils, I think he was trying to stop me from getting to Journey. But he failed and here we are." She smiled and toasted with her mug, and the others happily followed.

"So are there packs of good and evil wolves traversing the countryside?" inquired Bartoly. A look of concern drawn on his face.

"My guess is there always have been, always will be," said Dessa. "It's good to know they are not all bad though."

Quillan piped in, "So just how do you know how to speak in their language? How did you learn to speak wolf?"

She looked at him, some fire showing in her eyes as she said, "I don't really know, it's just there."

*   *   *

For the past two nights Dessa and Torrin had slept in the barn. Quillan had told Torrin that as much as he had approved of their being together, he could not stand the sounds of it at night. They had both smiled and happily set up a nice place in the hay to keep the noise down for their final evening's rest.

As the party set to leave early in the morning, they bid their goodbyes.

Rebecca gave Dessa a neat bundle of petal perfumed soap. Dessa tearily told Rebecca she had nothing for her.

"My dear, you have given me my health, my life and my husband. Go in peace and take care of Torrin. He is a good man, but he is still in need of training. If you know what I mean." Rebecca smiled a coy smile.

Dessa smiled and wiped away a tear. It felt good to be loved and cared for.

Bartoly led them his private way through the woods and showed them the way to the main trail. It saved almost half a day.

As they started down the main trail, Torrin looked back and saw the smithy brushing the pine needles back to their original position. Torrin thought it very wise, and hoped that people like Bartoly would be able to keep their places like this and not have to live near a castle for safety.

He was beginning to get the picture.

But the picture was about to blur.

57.
Plans Befuddled

It had never looked so good. The tall walls and heavy logs of Journey reached out—inviting. Torrin swore he could smell Karina's cooking when they were half a day away.

Not much had changed, except that Harold and Karina had aged terribly. Harold blamed it on the wood cutting and hunting.

When they walked inside, Torrin was surprised to see firewood piled high from floor to ceiling on most of the walls. But he did not have much time for daydreaming or questions.

They had arrived near the middle of the day. After a hearty lunch and some quick storytelling, everyone who was around, except for Dessa and Quillan, were dispatched to the great garden to harvest all that was edible. It seems the irrigation had done a good job in fattening up the plants. Given the fact there were two more mouths to feed for the winter, this blessing was not only considered wonderful, but necessary.

Dessa and Quillan were sent out to hunt. Even though Harold and company had put up some large game over the past days, Harold was not comfortable with the larder. He sensed a gruesome winter and wanted to be ready. He was taking no chances.

Torrin missed Dessa terribly that afternoon. It was the first time they had been apart since their time by the stream. As he worked in the cool sunshine though, he thought it might be good for Dessa and Quillan to talk.

It was a fruitful afternoon for all. The vegetables were mostly all harvested from the big garden and the two hunters had come upon a large flock of fat summer pheasants.

According to Quillan, Dessa scared him quite right with her shooting ability. As soon as they spied the fat dark buggers, she started picking them off before they knew what hit them. Got six before the rest flew off. Made quite the racket too, all their screeching and hollering.

So the result of their labors caused everyone to work well into the evening, cleaning and gutting and stripping and washing. It was not until very late that Harold sat down next to Quillan by the fire.

"Hown' did it go?" he asked, somewhat tentatively.

Quillan's green eyes reflected the low fire that chased the evening chill away. His long eyelashes were relaxed. He was butt tired, he was sore, but he was happy. He has done his job.

For now.

"They did fine. I figure that one of them will be askn' for a room," he smiled.

Harold sighed. It was good news, but part of him had hoped the news would be different. "OK, I'll tell Karina."

They just sat there for a while, watching the fire. Breathing slowly. Quillan noticed that Harold blinked in a steady pace—were his eyes tearing?

*   *   *

"Karina?" asked Torrin.

"Second room on the right," she said smiling.

"Is there a room that…what did you say?" inquired Torrin.

"I said second room on the right. I got it all made up for ya. Nice fresh bed spread and a pitcher of ale. You know that room. You had just jumped the gun a little my boy," she said smiling at him.

Walking up to her, he gave her a big hug. How did she know? She always seemed to know!

*   *   *

That night Torrin and Dessa made love at a quiet slow pace. The newness had not abated, the fervor had not abated, but the need tonight was for a slow deep coupling. They were experiencing each other in new ways (as they would for a long while).

As they lay there, her hair tickling his nose and their bodies spooned close together, she said something that made his heart stop. "Tomorrow we need to talk to Harold and Karina."

"Yes, but I don't want Journey yet. More importantly, I don't want to lose them."

Dessa turned over to face him. As she did, one of her nipples gazed his chest, and he swore he had never felt anything ever so wonderful in his life. He had noticed that feeling at the stream, and had not paid it much heed, but in the barn and tonight he had paid careful attention. He did not know what it was, but when it happened, it left a line of fire on his skin.

"You're not paying attention to me," she quipped, biting him playfully on the nose.

"Well, I was paying attention. Just not to your words," said Torrin

"What are you saying? Never mind. Just listen now," and she ran the sharp nail of her index finger down his arm.

"Well?"

"Well is, Gaerwn is going to be furious. He cannot come here until next spring; there is no way to put an army on the field in the winter, but why don't we go to him before he can mount his hateful army? We get to him, kill him and set his people free. Simple as that."

Torrin looked at her and smiled, "I thought you were practical?"

"I am. This way we get to keep Karina and Harold; they can't leave if we are off to save the valley, and we beat Gaerwn at his own game," she snuggled close to him.

Her bottom was warm and wet from their coupling, another feeling he relished. It was all too contrary. Talking about conquering the most brutal king on the earth and feeling his love's warm bottom snuggled up against his drained and happy crann. Some conversations are best kept 'til morning he decided.

* * *

In a back room of Journey in a very strange and large bed a different kind of conversation was taking place.

"What do you think?" Karina asked Harold.

"It seems right. I get no sense of hesitation or issue," he remarked somewhat matter of factly.

"So we go?"

He was not sure if it was a question or a statement, but anyway, he replied, "Tomorrow after breakfast."

* * *

After all the travel and the hunting and the woodcutting, Karina announced that breakfast this morning would be special and that no work would be done until after the midday. Normadia had conjured up a few helpers for the kitchen and true to her word, Karina outdid herself.

Roasts, eggs, sweetbreads and more filled the table. And considering the adventures and work of the past days, everyone ate heartily.

After eating, Quillan and Torrin were sitting outside enjoying the filtered sun in the great open space that surrounded Journey. Quillan asked Torrin if he had talked to Harold.

"No, I figured he would bring things up in his own time, it's his place. Maybe he changed his mind. It's all so different now. I came here a prince. Now the story goes that…"

A large hand fell on Torrin's shoulder. Harold looked down at him with a broad smile. He looked old. But he looked more relaxed than he had been in a long time.

"Karina and I need to talk to you and Dessa."

"How is after dinner?"

"Now," and with that, he walked away.

Torrin looked at Quillan; he was searching for answers. All he got was a raised eyebrow and after a few moments a simple, "Go. Ye know what happened last time you did not listen to them."

Torrin got to his feet and started walking toward the big building. It loomed large. It seemed massive and foreboding. He felt completely out of control until he walked in.

Dessa sat at the big table with Karina and Harold. She had a smile on her face that lit Torrin up. As it usually did. And all at once, it occurred to him that even though he had not chosen this path, he did want to travel upon it.

Torrin's mind ran quickly through the events of the summer. It all seemed to happen so slowly, but now it seemed like it was just a flash. He came to this place seeking shelter. He was wounded, wet, tired and hungry. Yet, he had not known how wounded and hungry he really had been until now.

He had come to this place a lonely boy. Full of himself and even more full of his own centered ideas. His false bravado had not shaken the residents of Journey one bit. They saw through it, discarded the garbage and by in large, believed in him. They helped him to grow.

And now too, there was Dessa. He looked at her radiance and sighed. Predestined or not, he was falling in love with this young woman. And it felt right.

Taking a seat at the table next to Dessa, Karina offered him a mug of ale, which he gratefully accepted. It flooded his head with the memory of that cold wintry afternoon when he had dragged his body into the big room, soaking wet, bleeding and scared. Harold had given him that wonderful hot wine.

He felt like he was dreaming.

Harold broke his trance by saying, "Well, it is time."

Both Dessa and Torrin gripped each other's hands.

"Remember the story of the dragon I tell the children?" began Harold.

"Yes," said Torrin. Dessa looked puzzled. "I'll tell you later," he told her.

Harold said, "Valterra was da first person and founder of the Journey Inn. He built this place," Harold was talking low and steady. "He 'ad such crude tools, he worked hard, and he made a wonderful start. What now with steel and iron and bronze, we have such tools, and so, Karina and I were able to add quite a bit to the building and make it a much nicer place, especially for da winters."

Karina interjected, "But Kaitlyn and Valterra made this place what it is in name, lore and tradition."

"Kaitlyn?" asked Torrin.

"Yes, Kaitlyn was Valterra's love," sighed Karina. "They were so very much in love. For the longest time, they worked to build a place of dreams and safety where people would be of their own, and of their best." Karina could sense Harold itching to talk, so she just looked at him, smiled lightly and let him kick in; she loved it when he got excited about something.

And Harold did just that, he excitedly picked up the story, "When Karina and I arrived at Journey, we, like you two, were verra much strangers. But Kaitlyn and Valterra treated us well, and when we got to know each other, something happened and we fell madly and deeply in love. I canna really explain it. It wasn't anything either of us planned. It happened and we embraced it," Harold smiled at Karina, who returned the favor, giving his bushy cheek a nip.

"Valterra and Kaitlyn told us they had been waiting for the right couple to come along. They told us the couple had to have the gift to take Journey, and we just assumed we would run it with them if they liked. Goodness knows, it always needs work, and willing helping hands are forever welcome," said Karina, now holding Harold's big hand in hers.

"But in the end, and it only took a few days, they gave us the place and walked off into the woods, hand in hand and happy as can be," said Harold. "And we had the whole lot of the Journey Inn. Not only did we have it, we had the gawful responsibility to keep up the promise, which when they told us what that was, all made sense."

"So what is this gift and promise?" asked Torrin, getting a sense that all this talk of change was not foreboding well for them.

"Well, you sense danger and evil, when you are paying attention. Right?" inquired Karina of Torrin. "It comes from deep inside you, very deep."

"Yes," he said rubbing his neck. That harsh burning sensation when he sensed Rebecca being attacked returned to haunt him for a moment.

"And does anyone else do that?" she asked him quietly.

"No, not that I know of," he replied, "except for Harold. I seem to be unique, in more ways than one I guess." He had a twinkle in his eye as he looked a bit longingly at Dessa.

"And you my dear, there is a bit of the wild thing in you; you have something special going on with the animals; right?"

"Yes, but how did you know?"

"You see," continued Karina, "I can see the future and see someone's past. Like yours, our gifts are different, but they are connected in some magical way. And when we connect," she winked at Harold, "something completely new happens."

Harold blushed.

"Just like you Torrin, Harold senses danger, when it's around. Sometimes it can be far away and he feels it. He sensed Chadus the other day," Karina finished.

"Oh?" uttered Quillan from the far end of the table.

Somewhat formally, Torrin began. He sensed also, he needed to take control. Something was smirching at his sense of danger, different, but there. "You have done a great service for Dessa and me to let us discover each other, and we have never been happier. And yes, we will take over Journey; we have much to learn," Torrin bowed his head, "You have taught me so much, let me learn so much about myself. I don't know how I can repay you."

Karina patted his hand and smiled at him. Harold just arched a bushy eyebrow and grinned.

"I lost everything, only to find it all again, twofold," said Dessa. "I always wanted a prince; I didn't think I would find the real thing in a prince turned commoner." Torrin felt a warm squeeze on his hand under the table, which stirred him in all the right places.

"And the promise, this is new? What is this promise? I can understand the animals and you will have to explain to us the fire when we kiss, but what is the promise?" asked Torrin, speeding up his words, the energy in him growing.

"My, you are so much like Harold," said Karina. "Well, you see, the four of us have our own special gifts, but we all share one gift along with having to guard the promise. It all started back in Valterra's boyhood…"

Karina had begun in earnest, talking steadily as one would talk to a close friend when delivering important news. But a commotion at the big front door stopped her short.

"Help! They're all dead. Burned to the ground. I have run this many days to warn you!" the little boy cried holding up three fingers as mud stained tears dripped down his sad pitiful face before he fainted dead away on the broad wooden floor of the Journey Inn.

The End

Coming soon…

Now available (as of July 2014)

Journey
Part II of III

The news had left them all startled. All the Haradins dead? It seemed so unfair. They had just announced at the games the building of the second cabin and their boy had decided to stay and work the farm.

It only took a few moments for Dessa to figure out that the responsible ones must have been Chadus and his raiding party. The little boy, once he had settled down some, had told them the fire was cold and the bodies had been all torn up by wolves. It was a gruesome tale that his young high voice wove in quivering tones of terror and anguish.

"He must have tortured them to get the directions to Bartoly and Rebecca's place," said Quillan.

Quillan was quite green. He did not do well with tormented children. The fact that they had decimated the scouting party and sent Chadus back on his horse with his face split open did not calm him. He had a steely look on his face. His crimson jaw was set as if in stone. His generally warm and caring eyes were almost on fire. You could sense not so much the rage as the helplessness and underlying hopelessness.

"I have come so far, brought ye to the doorstep of the future only to have this befall on us," he said. "It breaks my heart, but it also inflames me soul!" Quillan sat down hard on a bench and groaned.

Dessa watched him and made a note to talk with him later. His fury was evident.

She was right, but she had no idea how deep it went.

"Chadus told me they were on a scouting mission to get information about the valley so they could raid it next summer," said Dessa.

"Why here?" asked Torrin.

"I don't know, but one of the reasons was you," she said looking at Torrin.

"Me? Why?"

"I am sure that when we find out, we will find we already know, but for now we need to think clearly," said Dessa, looking fierce.

Torrin looked at the large timbers; all of a sudden they looked very fragile. To an advancing army of marauding murderers, Journey would last not even a morning. He walked over to Karina and Harold. The two were standing at the door, a small package of food in one hand. They were leaving. Leaving for forever.

"If you want us to take this," he said gesturing to the big room, "and the promise, I need to ask you one thing." Torrin gulped hard and said. "Will you stay until next fall? We'll, um, need your help."

Afterword...

So very often readers, friends and family (who are very supportive - for which I am grateful) ask me about the origins of the Journey trilogy. And after having told the tale below a number of times many told me (and they were quite frank about it), that the origin of this trilogy should be told to you, the faithful reader. They have implored to me that this little background adds something because the underpinnings of Journey come from real life, a little anguish, but none-the-less, real.

Since they have been so adamant about me adding this tidbit, it is here for you if you are interested in a bit of real life romantic drama.

Here goes...

At a very difficult, yet very telling time in my life, I was in a new and intensely dynamic relationship with an extremely energetic and extraordinarily beautiful lady. Things were quite exciting as they often are early in such relationships, but there was something nagging at me. The nag was deep in my head, and it was not a good one. It was, I would find much later, a tiny yet very accurate little voice that was giving me a warning – and it was quite some time before I really learned to listen to that voice (foolish me).

Anyway, back to the beginning – as I had said, things were very exciting and I had sat down to compose a 'love letter' to this lady. This letter would tell her from the bottom of my happily pattering heart how I felt about her and our relationship. It was important for her to know how she made me sparkle, how special she was and how meaningful her friendship. Please understand, it was a very personal letter, and my plan was to write it as a short adventure/romance story – it was to be something different. In my head the plan was to read it aloud over candles and wine with all sorts of flourish and panache to truly express the depth of the feelings I had at the time.

Alas, it did not work out. The letter (a.k.a story) was about half written when she told me, and quite nicely too, that our relationship was over. It was not working for her and she needed to move on. At least she had the strength of character to do it in person and with real tears; for which I am grateful, and do honor her forthrightness and honesty to this day.

To be honest with you though, at the time I was devastated.

So, that night, after getting dumped, while it rained outside and grief poured from my heart, I was but one small step away from turning that half finished love letter into a forever gone shredded pile of mostly worthless trash, destined as insulation for some cold northern attic with nothing left but the memory.

Instead, I decided to bid her and our now lost relationship a final farewell. This small act was to re-read what I had written, and see if after the 'fall' I still felt the same way about her, and us, as I had when I started the letter.

The rest, as they say, 'is history.'

That night, after I read the story I did not sleep. Instead, I sat and wrote. I wrote with my head, my heart and through my tears. That night Dessa, Quillan, Torrin and all the characters were born of love and loss, of fear and courage; of anger and justice - of all what we face in life. The whole thing just poured out, and continues to do so.

You see, Journey is not just a story - it's real… And, so with a little research, a long grasp back to my ancestors (thanks to some thoughtful digging on the part of my cousin in Paris) from the old northland and a dash of faith, I let the characters go; and go they do.

So if you have, or are reading Journey, and there is a tug at your heart strings. Well, now you know the real truth.

Are you wondering…

- If Karina and Harold stay, will they break the chain of the gift? Does it end if they don't follow the rule?
- How can they guard the promise? What is the promise?
- If Torrin heads for home, what will he find?
- Gaerwn wants to talk to Torrin. We think we know why, but is it something else?
- Dessa wants to see her father again, but what of the law?
- Will Rebecca be giving birth in the middle of a war?
- And then there is Gillespie. He has been quiet for a long time. What has he been up to?
- If Quillan is the guide, where does he go next?

These questions need answers!

Stay tuned for the high rolling adventures of Dessa, Torrin, Quillan and the rest of the valley as their times change in

Journey - Part II of III, available July 2014. Search Amazon and other fine booksellers worldwide.

For more information about Journey, to order bulk copies, or have comments directed to the author, send an email to:
catlansamuels@gmail.com

For character charts, answers and more, go to our site at:
www.TreborArthurPublishing.com

Never stop

believing

in the magic…

…may you find peace

Catlan

About the Author...

Catlan Samuels was born and lives in the upstate NY Finger Lakes wine region. He is an organizational development expert and trainer for companies, government agencies and executives. His background in psychology helps him to weave the impassioned tales you find in Journey.

His children, to whom Journey, Part I is dedicated, are well on their way to grown (one almost done with high school and the other is a math wiz in college.)

The author experiences life as a journey, found in the many microcosms of the people he meets and works with everyday. "Tie them all together and you see a mosaic of an incredible journey. All of them and none of them at any time make up this amazing story." In his view, all of us travel together, yet each of us travels alone, but the true journey is impossible without the other.

Mountain climbing in the Adirondack's high peaks left a lasting impression on Catlan as a young man ('Thank you Ned,' you made a difference!). His love of the forest is clearly evident in his stories. He is passionate about the power of people working together and the everlasting quest for finding true love and freedom dominates a large part of his somewhat oddly wound brain.

Experience Catalan's musings at his Blog or send him an email. He corresponds often with readers. He has even been known to email a snippet of a book he is working on to a fan to experience their reaction. According to him, the journey is more fun in a group.

Email - catlansamuels@gmail.com